ALONG THE WAY

ALONG THE WAY

TGC Prasad

Rupa . Co

Published in 2011 by
Rupa Publications India Pvt. Ltd.
7/16, Ansari Road, Daryaganj,
New Delhi 110 002

Sales Centres:

Allahabad Bengaluru Chennai
Hyderabad Jaipur Kathmandu
Kolkata Mumbai

Typeset by
Mindways Design
1410 Chiranjiv Tower
43 Nehru Place
New Delhi 110 019

Printed in India by
Rekha Printers Pvt. Ltd.
A-102/1, Okhla Industrial Area, Phase-II,
New Delhi 110 020

To

Rishi and Savi

Contents

Disclaimer

This story is inspired by my work experience in the software industry for the last two decades. Let us first get the usual caveat out of the way, 'This is a work of fiction and all characters in this book are fictional. Any references to any person living or dead are purely coincidental.' I feel better now.

Now, let us cover all the other caveats. As authors, we are left with little choice but to depend on popular icons. In that context, references alluding to the software industry and specifically to TCS, Oracle, Shah Rukh Khan, other celebrities, HR function, Coorg, Andhra cultures and popular brands are purely to aid storytelling. I believe TCS is one of the best software companies to work for, and in my references to TCS, I have aptly changed the titles, procedures, etc., to suit the story and appeal to a wider audience. Shah Rukh Khan is an icon of Indian cinema and I hardly know of any female in the age group of five to seventy-five who doesn't swoon at the thought of his charms. Similarly Ekta Kapoor is the undisputed icon for making 'popular family serials' in India. Digs at the HR function and fraternity are meant to generate humour and nothing else. I view the function and HR fraternity as my own, because I have been a part of HR function and also led it for a few years. I believe Coorgis have an amazing culture. Great food, lots of magic brews (euphemism for booze) and hospitality are part of their everyday life.

I am from Andhra and proud to be part of a culture which has a unique heritage. We love our 'Andhra meals', which are refreshingly spicy (euphemism for, guard your guts!) and movies, movie heroes and obviously movie heroines. The cultural differences and nuances have been highlighted to embellish the story and not to belittle anyone. I have used the names of popular brands in this book and I have not been paid to endorse them, in fact I don't even use some of the products. For example, I don't drink, but have included details on Glenfiddich, Glenlivet, Chateau d'Yquem, etc. Similarly, I have never been to Atlantic City. I had just heard about it. I have written the book based on some basic research and popular perceptions. I have used quotes from Mario Puzo's *The Godfather* as appropriate. I referred to popular Internet sites and quiz books to build some portions and references are provided.

Acknowledgements

I am deeply indebted to Revered Professor P.S. Satsangi Sahab for his constant guidance.

Rishi, is the perfect Calvin and an absolute joy; I imbibe a part of my sense of humour (if any) from him. Thanks to Savi for being there. Mom, Dad and my brother Das have been a great source of love and inspiration. My sincere thanks to our house-keeper Kala for taking care of Rishi, buying vegetables, feeding us and nursing me back to my feet. Mahesh, my diver for running errands and Meena for keeping my den clean.

I would like to express my sincere gratitude to my friend Ramya, because she was the first to hear the story and inspire me to write. Thanks to Shweta for patiently listening to all my stories and for encouraging me to pen them. Bhuvan and Vish, my close buddies, goaded me to write despite knowing about my writing abilities. Special thanks to Surya for being a springboard for many ideas we discussed.

Sudarshan and Kiran have been sincere, friends who stuck with me through thick and thin. Thank you fellas!

I wish to thank Kapish Mehra, managing director of Rupa for personally interacting with me and for agreeing to publish this book.

Prologue

Anjali, my wife screamed in the pre-delivery room, 'Idiot, go call the doctor now.'

I ran out of the room, grabbed the nearest available nurse and said, 'She is calling, urgent.'

The nurse said, 'Ok. I am going in, stay out of the way.'

She pushed me aside and went straight into the delivery room. Women in power can be tough, especially when they know that you are at their mercy.

I sat down on a plastic chair outside the delivery room, meant for expectant fathers. My sister-in-law Ameya, all of twenty-one, paced the corridor. I looked at her and wondered why everyone from my wife's family always paced.

She said, 'Don't worry Venkat, all will be well.' I nodded.

A few years back, when I met my father-in-law Colonel Krishna Cariappa for the first time, on Anjali's birthday, he was pacing too, and asked, 'So, what is the most popular song in the whole world?' I thought: Interesting introduction, another nutcase in my life.

I blurted out, '*Crazy Kiya Re*, from *Dhoom 2*?' I could be quite innovative at times. The movie was the highest grosser in 2006 and I thought atleast 300 million Indians, roughly the population of the US, would have seen it. Besides, that was one of the few Hindi movies, which ran in Sridevi Talkies for more than hundred days and the song was played in every Irani tea and paan shop in the entire state of Andhra Pradesh. Also, Andhra has the unique distinction of tilting the popularity charts for most blockbusters, including the Bollywood ones. The state runs on movies and mass hysteria.

Raj looked at me as if I was some kind of a suicide bomber who was ready to blow up any moment.

Adi added, 'Uncle, I am sure Venkat is kidding. Let me guess the answer—Rasputin, BoneyM?' Probably that was the only English song he had heard in his entire life and his effort bombed.

He laughed aloud and said, 'What did you say? Wrong answer.'

Adi meekly asked, 'What is the right answer sir?' and the colonel jovially replied, 'You cannot question a colonel, only colonels have the right to question you'. Krishna is a retired colonel from the Indian army, medium built, thick mush, sharp eyes and wholesomely gregarious, sometimes bordering on being invasive.

I was meeting Anjali's family for the first time and wanted to make a good impression. I put my best foot forward and respectfully asked, 'Sir, that is a very interesting question, what is the answer?'

He laughed aloud, his whole body shook and he started singing, 'Happy birthday to you, happy birthday dear Anjali, "Happy birthday to you" is the answer to my quiz question.'

He then added, 'Let me remind you, just in case you forgot, today is my Anjali's birthday. She was a pre-Christmas baby, the joy of our lives.'

I looked at Anjali and it was too late, in my anxiety to meet her parents, I forgot that it was her birthday. Even before I could wish her, Anjali hugged her dad and said, 'Papa, you are so sweet'.

Raj, Adi and I were again made aware, that we were morons. Nothing unusual about it, it was just that the timing was not right. I realised that to get married, I might have to go through a buzzer round with negative marks for wrong answers. The things people do to get married! Thank God, the Colonel was not fond of equestrianism, else he would have asked me to learn horse riding, my nuts would have split even before I got married.

Adi said, 'Sir, this time ask a simpler question and we will crack it.'

I looked at Adi in in sheer disbelief. I wanted to choke him. Going to Anjali's house was like entering the lion's den and encouraging the Colonel to ask quiz questions was like putting your head right in the lion's mouth. Adi avoided me; he could have been turned to ashes by the intensity of my third eye. '*Bhasmam*' as they in Telugu.

Krishna said, 'Alright, here goes the next one and an easy one boys. Who said "I'm the President of the United States and I'm not going to eat any more broccoli?"'

I thought, 'The only idiot who could say such a thing could be Bush Junior.' I said, 'Uncle, is it Bush Junior?'

Krishna Cariappa gleamed and said 'Good. Atleast you guys seem to know the idiots.'

Placement Day

DURING THE SECOND HALF OF OUR THIRD YEAR IN CAMPUS, some time in November 2004, NIT Kozhikode (Calicut) opened its door for placements and TCS was one of the first companies to come to campus. Raj, Adi and I applied. We were wing mates, batchmates, classmates and department mates. We met on the orientation day, were ragged together and if you draw a scatter graph, our grades almost merged at the same point in the lower quartile. Inevitably and especially when grades merge, you hang out and become thick pals.

Raj said, 'Don't worry guys TCS makes offers to all. We will make it too.' Raj is a practical guy and has distinct views on almost everything. Raj is about five eight, weighs about 65 kgs and has a near perfect body. He is originally from Punjab and his dad owns a Maruti showroom in Delhi.

Adi replied, 'But we have to get through the quant exam.'

I said, 'Everybody gets through that Adi, TCS is an inclusive company, it doesn't eliminate. Have they eliminated anyone from the senior batch? None, right?'

As expected, we cleared the quant exam. We could answer the questions in our sleep. I think the exam was more of a formality to ensure that we hadn't forgotten the basics.

Then we were called for a quick interview. Each interview lasted less than five minutes. The panel consisted of one HR guy and one technical guy.

I was summoned in and I said, 'Good morning sirs.'

Both the panelists nodded in unison. When you have to interview 200 people in a couple of days, I guess, every motion becomes rhythmic.

Then one of them said, 'My name is Amit, I take care of HR and this is my colleague Jivan, technical manager from our Mumbai office.'

Amit asked, 'So, you are Venkata Subramaniam Adisankara Tanikaburla?'

I said, 'Yes sir'.

Amit said, 'That is a long name. From Andhra?'

Almost everybody from Andhra has long names. After several miscarriages a baby girl was born to our neighbours and she was named 'Manda Venkata Appala Taratarini Bala Satya Surya Mangala Madhuri',—MVATBSSM Madhuri. The Gods felt appeased and the baby had a bright future. Andhraites took good care of all the Gods. Leaving any one out would be tantamount to blasphemy.

I said, 'Yes sir, Kazipet ... I mean Warangal.'

Amit asked, 'What do friends call you?'

I said, 'Venkat sir.' I didn't want to tell him that my friends actually call me 'VSAT', by joining the first alphabets of each of my sub-names. Like you have clauses and sub-clauses.

Amit continued, 'Would you join if TCS made you an offer?' I instantly replied, 'Sure sir ... 100%.' I should have given a five second gap. It would have seemed like a thoughtful answer. But there was hardly anything to think about since I didn't have any other offer anyway.

Amit said, 'How come you are so sure?'

I just said, 'Sir, TCS is a great company. Our entire senior batch says that sir. Also, my parents love Tata companies sir. Life-long employment, they take good care of people, sir.' Raj told me that adding 'sir' before and after every sentence increases interview points, he referred to this concept as '*vinamrata*', courtesy *Munna Bhai MBBS*.

Meanwhile Jivan rubbed his eyes, as if he had just woken up from a deep slumber. 'What did you say? Were you born in Japan? Life-long employment? Only if you perform well!'

I smiled and said, 'No sir, I was born in Jammalamadugu sir. I agree with you sir. Performance determines life-long employment.'

Never contradict the interviewer is another golden rule.

Jivan said, 'Your grades don't say much about your performance.'

I said, 'Sir, grades are not indicative of real-life achievement. Often people with good grades don't do very well in careers sir. People who don't get good grades do well sir. Actually my friends say that doing well in life is inversely proportional to one's education and grades sir.'

On hearing this, Amit and Jivan looked at each other and smiled. Somehow, this statement rang a bell for both of them. Probably they too were like me, scrappers.

Amit grinned from ear to ear and said, 'Congratulations Venkat. You can pick up your offer letter in the evening. I look forward to your joining TCS.' I think Amit and Jivan felt that I was part of their elite scrappers gang and personally, getting the TCS offer was like winning an Olympic gold for me. All my perceived troubles pertaining to livelihood, vanished overnight.

I said, 'Thank you sirs. I will surely join. Where will be my posting sir?'

Amit replied, 'It could be anywhere in India, but do you have a preference?'

I said, 'Sir, I would prefer Bangalore. I have relatives there and I would be thankful if you can get me Bangalore sir.' I continued to add 'sir' at the start and end of each sentence. It just amplifies the intensity of the request.

Amit replied and said, 'I will write down your preference, but I can't assure you. You have to work anywhere you are posted. That is company policy.' That was the first time I had heard the words, 'company policy.' Little did I know that I would keep hearing it again and again for the rest of my life. The two words 'company policy' gives as much euphoria to HR folks as much the word 'Kingfisher' gives to Vijay Mallya.

I said, 'Sure sir. Thank you sir.' Then I walked out of the room.

Adi who was waiting for his turn asked, 'What happened?'

I said, 'They asked me to collect the offer letter in the evening.'

Raj grinned, 'See I told you, every moron gets into TCS.'

I hugged Raj. He said, 'Don't, don't hug me. I hate it when you hug me. You become too senti for me to handle, VSAT.'

I smiled and said, 'Yes, I am sure both of you will also make it.'

Adi asked, 'What did they ask?' Adi wanted me to leak the question paper. In any case, all of us are expected to prepare the question bank after every interview for the next batches to use.

I told them about our conversation. Both were ecstatic.

Adi said, 'No technical questions and no difficult questions. Wow! TCS is truly the best employer to work for.'

I called home and Mom picked up the phone.

She said, 'Tell me Kanna (my pet name), did you get into TCS?'

I said, 'Yes Ma. I did.'

She said, 'Praise Lord Venkateswara. We must go to Tirupati. I prayed that if you get a job with TCS, I will take you to Tirupati and offer your hair to the Lord.'

I said, 'Lakshmi, you can't do that to me. How can you pray on my behalf?' Often, I addressed Mom as Lakshmi.

She said, 'Ok, ok, don't yell at me. I am your mother. I can do what I want. I have raised you, fed you, educated you and you have stopped listening to me ...'

I said, 'Mom, stop ... please don't get into the lecture mode now. Tell Pa I called and inform him about TCS.'

She said, 'Ok, I will tell him to call you. By the way when are they sending you to America?'

That damn question always stumped me. To my mother, all IT companies were travel agencies that sent people to America—29 nights and 30 days covering Statue of Liberty, Niagara Falls, San Francisco, Grand Canyon, Disneyland, Washington Memorial and World Trade Centre—all the known desi icons.

I sarcastically added, 'Mom, along with the offer letter, they are also giving US visa and tickets. We can catch a flight on the day of graduation. What do you expect? Ok, sorry. I mean, it is going to take some time Ma. I think Raj and Adi will make it too.'

Mom nonchalantly said, 'Don't be angry with me. Call me later and tell me if your friends also made it.'

'Sure Mom, will do. Give the phone to grandpa.'

'Venkata, you got the job with TCS?'

I said, 'Yes Grandpa.'

He said, 'Last year in college, especially after you get a job, is the best time of your life. Once you take a job, it becomes stressful and when you get married, everything crumbles. Ha ha ha! So, enjoy as much as you can now with your friends.'

I laughed and said, 'Ok Grandpa, give the phone to Ma.'

My paternal grandfather, Adisankara, was a teacher and is the best. He has the best sense of humour and his timing is perfect. I love him immensely. My second part of the middle name came from him. Confusing, right? But that is how it is. It is a ritual to add your maternal and paternal grandfathers' names in the same order to the grandsons' names. My maternal grandfather has the same name as my father, Subramanyam. It could be in the top ten commonly used names in Andhra after Srinivas, Venkat, Kumar, Reddy, Rao, Naidu, Sharma and Sastry.

I asked, 'How is Swati?'

Mom said, 'Swati is fine, I am teaching her how to cook. Her music lessons are going well.' Swati is my sister and is studying her class tenth and has a deep inability to keep anything private. God gave her two special eyes at the back of her head and a pair of extra ears which could pick up the remotest of sounds from the neighbouring houses from half-a-kilometre away. Besides, Swati's wiring in the head is mixed up. Her vocal chords have a direct channel to the speech centre in her brain. Words tumble out of her mouth; there is no gap between thought and speech.

I said, 'Good, talk to you later Ma.'

Meanwhile Adi came out of the room beaming. I was sure he had also made it.

He said, 'I also made it, asked for Bangalore too.' He too felt like winning the Olympic gold. I think for all of us scrappers, getting into TCS was like winning the Olympic gold.

Adi's father has a small tailoring shop in Begumpet, Hyderabad. Adi loves chewing his nails especially when he is stressed or when he is thinking. Once he is done with his, he might he even chew yours! When he laughs, his whole body shakes and his white teeth gleam. At five feet seven inches and about 75 kilos, he loved food (and drinks too). Last summer his parents had said, 'Adi, you are becoming too fat. You must go on a liquid diet.' He agreed and lived the whole summer on beer.

Meanwhile Raj also went in and joined us within minutes. He said, 'As I told you, all of us are in. I also asked for Bangalore. You know this whole selection process is stupid. They could have taken our roll numbers from the rosters and issued us offer letters.'

I said, 'Listen, we are not studs; we are probably the lowest graders in Mech. You should be happy that you are getting a job atleast.'

Raj said, 'You know how much these guys pay right? ₹1.98 lacs per annum, minus all the cuts, you get to take home about 15K? After struggling for so many years, you get to take home so little. Don't you guys feel bad? We should have checked out a multinational company.'

Adi said, 'MNC? Look at your face and grades. Is there any correlation?'

For me, 15K is a lot of money. My dad made that kind of money after slogging for a couple of decades as a primary school teacher in a government school. For Adi, it was decent money too, but Raj came from an affluent family and the TCS salary sounded too measly for him.

Adi said, 'Guys, forget the pay, let us celebrate, we have jobs in hand. Let us go to Calicut city, have a drink, eat good food, watch a movie and enjoy the rest of the day. What do you say?' The whole campus was planning to do that anyway. There was euphoria in the hostels. Almost everyone was placed and students were rejoicing.

Meanwhile dad called and said, 'Congratulations son, so you made it to TCS. I am happy for you. It is a stable company. They take good care of people. Once you join them, you can retire from there.' Somehow dad always thought of retirement, job security, stability, savings, etc. My dad, Subramanyam Garu, is deeply sentimental, highly religious and eccentrically conservative. He worked as a primary school teacher in a government high school at Hanamkonda and hardly smiled all his life. At times, he could be extremely rational and at others, completely emotional. You had to gauge the situation and work your way through.

I said, 'Thanks Pa.'

He said, 'See, you have one more year to go. Make sure you do well and complete the course. You have to get distinction; almost everyone in our family is a distinction holder. Promise me that you won't break the tradition.'

I said, 'Yes Pa.'

There was a pause and then he asked, 'Do you want money? Are you doing okay?'

I said, 'I am fine Pa, don't need money.'

He said, 'Ok, don't worry, I will send five hundred rupees. Have a nice party with your friends. This is your first job and we all are proud of you.'

I knew he was swinging on the emotional side.

I said, 'Sure Papa, thanks. Talk to you soon.' We stopped talking. Conversations with my dad are limited. It has always been like that since my childhood.

By the next evening, the list of people who made it to TCS was hanging on the main building notice board. It was the best list I had seen in my four years of college life. There were no red remarks, or grades put up next to my name and most importantly, all the names were arranged alphabetically and not rank-wise. I loved TCS instantly. This was the kind of company I wanted to work for, a place that encouraged democracy and gave a fresh start to nitwits like me. Anyone with 75% attendance, reasonable grey matter and who was potentially graduating had got an offer from TCS.

Raj said, 'Ok guys, let us go get our offer letters.' We sauntered to the placement office. About 150 students were standing in queue to get the offer letters.

Adi said, 'Hey VSAT, your babe is standing in the queue. You want to walk quickly and stand behind her?'

My babe meant: I liked her but had never talked to her. Given an opportunity, I would have loved to make friends with her. Her name was Anjali and she was in third year Electronics. She was a beauty. Apparently, she had crushed the advances of many an aspiring stud with just one look. Unidentified sources had revealed in confidence that she hailed from Coorg and that her dad was a high-ranking army officer.

I started noticing Anjali in my third year. Probably a little late in the day, but how could I help it? The first year went in ragging, working for seniors and then studying. For the first three months, seniors crammed us, the next three months professors crammed us and for the last three months we crammed for the exams. The First year is the toughest with most number of credits. In the second year we were introduced to cricket, movies and booze, and the ladies hostel didn't make a dent in our thoughts. Suddenly, by the end of the second year, something happened to our respective libidos and we had a deep awakening, that we were missing something drastic in our lives. With gusto, we sprang to life and I started catching up on all the lost time.Sometime during the end of my second year, I once tried talking to Anjali in the corridor. We were standing outside her classroom. I walked up to her and said, 'Excuse me.'

She said, 'Oops, I am sorry for blocking your way.'

I bent my head and walked straight ahead. That was the high point of our conversation. I reminisced about those few seconds of interaction for weeks. Another incident: She was standing adjacent to me at the fee counter and asked, 'Excuse me, do you have change for ₹500?'

I fumbled and gave her the change, but had such a large lump in my throat that I couldn't speak. She smiled and said, 'Thanks.' She left. That was the second interaction and I almost had an orgasm.

The third was in the college canteen when she spilt coffee on my jeans and said, 'I am so sorry.' Once again, I was so tongue-tied I didn't say anything. Probably, she thought I was born dumb. I let the coffee remain on my jeans for months in remembrance. Raj and Adi refused to go out with me whenever I wore those jeans. They said, 'Idiot, it stinks, don't come near us.' I couldn't smell anything. I thought they were jealous. Only later did I realise that my sinuses were perpetually clogged.

I thought this was a great opportunity for me to stand close to her.

Raj said, '*Jaldi* ... before somebody else beats you to it.'

I increased my pace, joined the queue and stood behind her. She didn't turn to see who was behind her. She was wearing a pair of blue jeans and a white shirt and looked ravishing. I was so close to her and yet so far away. She was fair-complexioned and was about five feet five inches tall. She had fantastic curves. But I didn't have the guts to talk to her. I was tongue-tied as usual.

Raj stood behind me and whispered, 'Moron, talk to her now, you have no guts or what?'

I whispered back, 'Thanks for the encouragement sir. You give me confidence. Now, shut up. Don't make me nervous and spoil this whole thing.'

Adi was standing behind Raj. He said, 'Shall I give one push, so that the whole queue will fall in a sequence?'

I whispered back quickly before he could really do something stupid. 'You guys are friends or enemies? Just shut up and let me think.'

At that precise moment, she turned, looked at me and before I could smile or say anything, said, 'Would you mind holding my place, I will be back in five minutes?'

I said, 'Sure.'

She left.

I was happy that my first conversation had taken off. I had used the first golden words with her ... 'Sure.'

As soon as she went, Raj and Adi pounced on me and said, '*Pagal hai*, you will never get this chance again, talk to her man.'

I nodded and said, 'I will.' I rehearsed what I would say.

She didn't come back for atleast fifteen minutes or so, and meanwhile the queue moved ahead a little. I was wondering whether she would turn up and suddenly she appeared. She came close, smiled and said, 'Thank you.'

I said, 'My name is ...' and before I could complete, Adi said 'VSAT.'

She looked at us and said, 'What?'

I said, 'My name is Venkat. These guys call me VSAT because my full name is Venkata Subramaniam Adisankara Tanikaburla ... you can call me Venkat.'

She giggled and said, 'Phew, what a long name!'

I said, 'Most people from Andhra have long names and I am in Mech, third year.'

She exclaimed, 'Really!'

I said, 'I mean all of us are in third year, I know ... I mean, I am also in third year and so are you ... by the way congratulations for making it to TCS.'

She said 'All these people who are standing in the queue have made it to TCS.'

I said, 'Yes, congratulations to all of them ...' She just laughed at my naivete.

I asked, 'You are Anjali, right?'

With a mischievous smile she said, 'Good guess. How did you know?'

I thought—damn, this babe is tough! I said, 'Well, I face read. You know the guy standing behind me, let me guess, his name is Raj and the guy behind him is, yes, his name is Adi.' And both Raj and Adi exclaimed loudly, 'Absolutely right Guruji. How did you know?'

I smiled back. Anjali started giggling.

She said, 'You must be a Golt.' People from Andhra are called Golts (that's Telugu spelt in reverse order).

This time, it was my turn to say, 'You too are good at guessing. Face reading?'

She was amused. She said 'May be … you are fast.'

I smiled and said, 'Sorry, didn't mean to, yes I am from AP. Heard you are from Coorg.'

She said, 'Yes.' There was a pause.

I wanted to do something different; I turned towards her and said, 'Anjali, would you mind holding my place? I will be back soon?'

She said, 'Ok, but come back soon.'

I said, 'Sure, I am just going to get some water.'

She said, 'Ok.' She hesitated for a moment and said, 'Would you mind getting me some?'

I thought to myself, 'Just a bottle of water? I will fly the whole damn water cooler for you.'

I casually said, 'Yes, if I can get an empty bottle, will do …'

Raj and Adi looked at us, completely stupefied. They never expected me to be cool.

Adi gave a coy smile and said, 'VSAT, *mere liye bhi* … one bottle of water.'

Then Raj said, 'Me too.' Hearing these two idiots, ten others in the queue said, 'Me too … me too.' I just sighed, shook my head and walked away.

From the corner of my eye, I saw that Anjali was amused by this whole conversation.

I went to the water cooler. My heart was pounding. It was too much to take. A TCS offer and I had had my first conversation with Anjali, and she asked me to get her a bottle of water. I bent down, put my hand under the tap and had a few sips of water and ran towards the nearest hostel, picked up an empty bottle from the first room, I could enter and ran to the water cooler, filled it with water and almost dashed back and suddenly stopped. I wanted to slow down a bit and make it appear casual. So, I took some deep breaths and slowly walked back to the queue and stood behind Anjali.

She didn't say anything. I handed the bottle to her, she took it, had a few sips and gave it back to me and said, 'Thanks.'

Raj then took the bottle from me. He had a few gulps and then Adi took it. Once anything gets to Adi, especially if it is a liquid, it doesn't come back and you shouldn't expect it either.

Another long pause. Then I asked, 'Hey Anjali, did you ask for a preference for your posting?'

She said, 'Why do you want to know?'

I said, 'Generally, shouldn't I ask?'

She said, 'Obviously Bangalore. It is closer to home, to Coorg.'

I said, 'Coorg must be a beautiful place, I am from Warangal.'

She said, 'Naxalites?'

I said, 'Yes.'

I asked, 'How long does it take to go from here to Coorg?'

She said, 'About four to six hours and the drive is great. I usually go via Ooty.'

I said, 'Wow, you must be enjoying every ride home.'

She said, 'Kind of.'

Meanwhile the line inched forward and our conversation too inched quite a bit.

Finally, the TCS personnel gave us our letters and asked all of us to read the terms, sign the letters and submit them at the placement office in a few days. We collected the letters and started walking towards the canteen.

Anjali was walking a few paces ahead of me. Adi asked Anjali, 'Hey Anjali, we are going to the canteen, want to join us?'

She turned and looked at the three of us and said, 'Ok, let us go, I am famished anyway.' Raj winked at me and I smiled.

We started with *ghee* roast paper *dosa* and ended up having a full-fledged dinner. I didn't want the dinner to end. Adi and Raj were at their best and I was a bit quiet because it was too much to take in one day.

Anjali laughed and asked, 'VSAT, are you okay? You seem to be a little lost!' I was surprised because she had used the name VSAT. Only close friends call me by that name. But what option did she have anyway; I was sure nobody could ever remember my full name.

I said, 'Yes, everything is fine. It's just that I am very happy about getting the job. My parents are happier than me.'

Raj said, 'Now, our dear VSAT will have to give his hair, I mean get tonsured at Tirupati after he graduates, his mother had vowed to part with VSAT's hair if he got a job with TCS.' Raj was laughing. Anjali couldn't control herself. She too joined in. 'Is that right?' she asked.

I smiled and nodded.

She said, 'You seem to be a sweet son.' We spent a good two hours there and then Anjali said, 'Ok guys, all of you are fun. Happy to meet with you. Congrats to you all as well. Now I have to head back. Good night' and she left.

After she left, Adi turned to me and said, '*Tera toh kaam ban gaya*, sweet son ... ha ha ha. ...'

We went back to the hostels and Raj organised a few beers. We drank till the wee hours.

At 3 am, Raj toasted his last mug of beer, 'To TCS, Anjali and VSAT ... probably Bangalore too.' Raj always becomes philosophical after drowning a few bottles of beer. He said, 'You know guys, this world is bad. Nobody here cares for anybody. The Profs are worse; they are utterly miserly when it comes to giving marks. Marks are the equivalent of pension money, to be saved and not to be spent on students like me. If only Prof. Ramachandran had given five marks more, just five, I would have scraped through Fluid Mech. Now, I have to repeat the whole damn course. Why do these Profs feel so bad when it comes to parting with a few marks?' Adi was fast asleep, his mouth was wide open and his big belly was going up and down rhythmically like a piston. Overall and strangely, he looked like a stationed steam engine. I was feeling 'technical' after so many beers. Everybody seems to have their quirks.

I said, 'Raj, I think I am in love with Anjali yaar.' Raj patronisingly said, 'She is a nice girl, you must pursue her. She seems to be fond of you. I could see it in her eyes.'

I got up and hugged Raj. He said, 'Oh my God. You are hugging me again. My mother wouldn't have hugged me as many times as you have hugged me in the last couple of years. Don't, don't hug me. Get off me now.'

'You think so?'

'Yeah, I am damn sure. You hugged me more times than my mom and I hate it man!'

'Moron I mean—you think I should pursue Anjali seriously?'

Raj said, 'Yes, only if you are interested in a long-term relationship. She doesn't seem to be the fast kind—you know what I mean. If you are looking at screwing and all that, then forget it. Her dad is a colonel or something like that, he will come with his double barrel gun and shoot your ass off. So be careful ...'

I thought for a while and asked Raj, 'How do you think I should take it forward?'

Raj said, 'You should ... zzzz ...'

There was no reply from Raj. Now there were two motionless, alcohol-filled bodies snoring in the room.

I looked out of the window. It was a starry night. I thanked God for such a wonderful day. Job, Anjali, good food, nice friends and a new hope.

I cleaned up the cluttered bed and went to sleep.

Final Year

AFTER GETTING THE JOB, I DIDN'T FEEL LIKE ATTENDING CLASSES any more. Not that I was motivated earlier, but now it became absolute drudgery. The rest of the third year passed very quickly. During the three months preceding the summer vacation, I met Anjali a few times. Our conversations were short. Everybody was busy with lab and semester work. We prepared hard and wrote our sixth semester exams and subsequently summer vacation was declared.

During summer vacation, Anjali went home as did most of the students. Since this was the last summer we would be together, Raj, Adi and me decided to stay back at the institute during the entire summer vacation. We told our parents that we were on a very confidential NASA project. They knew we were up to nothing and and we knew that they knew, but they sent us the monthly cheque and life continued uninterrupted. A time comes in everybody's life, when you develop the uncanny ability of exactly knowing what your parents want to hear and they exactly know what you mean. Both keep each other happy in deception.

Sometime in June 2005, the South West monsoon arrived in Kerala and our fourth year classes started. The rains pour in Kerala for months at a stretch, but the state doesn't have adequate drinking water and there is a shortage of power. My Keralite batchmates blamed it on Communism. I referred the Web to find the meaning and there were too many definitions, but the common theme was abolition of classes and state control over property. I didn't understand how Communism was connected to provision of drinking water and power, but somebody added two new words, 'Karl Marx and union problems' and I decided not to pursue this any further, the words appeared too potent for my pea-sized brain. My grandpa says, 'The deeper you dig, the more the stench, get out when the timing is good.' This philosophy has helped me skim through life happily, atleast so far.

Anyway, I hadn't seen Anjali for almost two months and it was killing me, I was digging deeper here. Seeing my restlessness, Raj said, 'VSAT, if you don't make a move in this semester, you can as well kiss Anjali goodbye. This is the final year on campus man, and is the best time to *patao*.'

I asked, 'You think, I should go to the ladies hostel and meet her?'

Raj said, 'Why not? Give it a shot seriously.' His intellect in matters of this kind was far superior. I wondered if it was a family specialisation. He seemed to know everything about girls, how they think, what they do, etc. He often comes up with theories and to test the hypothesis, he eggs me on till I end up being the guinea pig. If I get screwed, which was often the case, his hypothesis was proved null and void and if I emerged successful, which was remote anyway, he would say, 'I told you so'. Either way, he had a result and was happy. Adi, on the other hand, was a simpleton. He was brought up under a Singer sewing machine (his father owns a tailoring shop). So, his brain functioned in a binary fashion. The trouser zip was, either on or off—there was nothing in between. Either he likes something or dislikes it. It was as simple as that. I was always sandwiched between a pseudo intellectual theoretician and a practical moron. It was not a bad proposition after all for a confused fellow like me. I was happy in my own way, so were they.

The next day, I summoned the guts to go to the ladies hostel and ask for Anjali at the reception desk.

She came downstairs with a stern expression.

I smiled and said, 'Hi Anjali, how are you doing?'

She asked, 'Why have you come?'

I said, 'Just to meet you and say hi!'

She said, 'Look Venkat, I am not the kind of girl you are thinking. I don't like you coming to the ladies hostel to meet me.'

I am always wary of the sentence, 'I am not the kind …'—it hits you hard where it normally shouldn't. Below the belt!

I gulped and didn't know what to say, there was a lump in my throat again, a big one.

I said, 'Well, I am sorry, I don't know what you mean. I didn't come with any preconceived notions.'

She looked me in the eye and said, 'So, you just came to say hi?'

I put my most truthful face forward and nodded.

She said, 'Ok, now that we have met, now what?'

I had read somewhere that female black widow spiders ate male spiders. How true!

I said, 'Is this how you usually are?' Wrong sentence, wrong timing, and right girl.

She twitched her brow and asked, 'What do you mean?'

I said, 'I mean … being mean.' Digging deeper, it starts to stink now. Grandpa was right—I should just beat a hasty retreat, now! My mind said, 'Time to scoot VSAT, move your butt NOW!'

She said, 'Oh … so you have come to tell me that I am 'mean'? Girls have an uncanny knack of making you the say the wrong things, making you apologise and putting you under their thumb. Kind of their birthright. I don't blame them; it is in their genes.

I just looked at her, shook my head, and walked back to my hostel. Obviously, our conversation wasn't going anywhere.

Adi and Raj were playing TT in the recreation room.

Adi saw me and said, 'So, what did your babe say?'

I said, 'My babe? My foot, stop calling her my babe.'

Raj said, 'Oh, so Mr Venkat had a fight with her. That is a good start. Now both of you will feel guilty and will try to get back together, *aisa hi hota hai pyaare.*' Another theory and I was in no mood to test this out right away.

I just left. I was in a bad mood. I couldn't understand why Anjali was so mean.

A week of classes happened. Get up in the morning, attend classes, go to the mess, play TT, go to the mini-canteen, drink chai, smoke Gold Flake and sleep. I had the worst moods—I was irritable to the core and sulked too. I badly wanted to get back on good terms with Anjali. Several times I almost walked to her class but my ego didn't permit me to meet her. I wondered why girls are so temperamental.

Adi came to my room and said, '*Saale*, you have a problem if you meet her and you have a problem if you don't. Why are you screwing us with your moods?' Binary thinking, that is okay, acceptable from a guy like Adi.

'Get lost Adi. I am not discussing Anjali.'

'Chal chal ... I bumped into her yesterday and told her that you are sulking.'

I said, 'Are you mad? Why did you do that?'

Adi said, '*Aur kya karta*? Keep seeing you brood all the time? Anyway, I said what I wanted to say ...'

'What did she say?'

Adi replied, 'Said she will talk to you.'

'By the way, who asked you to do that?'

Adi said, '*Tu paagal hai.*'

I wondered whether he had done the right thing. Meanwhile Raj threw a pebble at my window from downstairs. I looked out of the window. He said, 'VSAT, your mom on the hostel line, talk to her.' I wondered why mom had called on the hostel telephone number when she had my cell number. Anyway, I ran downstairs.

I picked up the phone and said, 'Hello Lakshmi ... what's up?'

The voice on the other end said, 'Hi, this is Anjali here. Who is Lakshmi?'

I said, 'My mom.'

Anjali said, 'You address your mom by her name?'

I said, 'Yeah. Sometimes, depends! Today I felt like it.'.

She said, 'Or is Lakshmi your girlfriend?'

Often people say, God created 'Man' and then 'WoMan' but that is not true. After creating 'Man' and before creating 'WoMan' he created a funny little fellow with a spear in his hand, horns on his head and a sharp, pointed tail called 'Doubt'. Between 'Woman' and 'Doubt', they destroyed mankind. Thank you your honour, the defence counsel rests its argument.

I said, 'Ok, shall I put the phone down?' *I had to sound disconcerted, right?*

She said, 'Ok, ok calm down VSAT.'

I said, 'Why did you call, you are not that kind of girl, right?'

She said, 'I just called to say Hi! Long time right? Where have you been? I haven't seen you in the common canteen or in the admin block after classes.'

I said, 'Does it matter?' Of course it matters. But as a general rule, you have to say the opposite. *The games girls make boys play*! That is a separate book by itself, an international bestseller published in more than 33 languages and sold more than fifteen million copies.

She said, 'VSAT, I am sorry that I wasn't very nice to you, the last time we met. I don't like to get visitors at the ladies hostel. It gets recorded in the log book and I am uncomfortable about it.'

I said, 'You could have said so.'

She said, 'Let it go ... I am willing to make it up to you. *Chalo*, my treat for a lime soda at Nair's shop, coming?'

I wanted to jump up and say, 'Of course sweetheart,' but I dragged my voice a little, as if to sound reluctant and said, 'Ok, I will be there in fifteen minutes. Bye.'

I went back to my room. Raj was waiting. He said, 'How is mom?'

I said, 'It was Anjali'.

He started laughing and asked, 'Going to meet her?'

I sarcastically added, 'Yes, do I have your permission sir?'

He said, '*Jao jao*, but remember don't drool all over her and make it too obvious. Keep up a decent flow of conversation.'

I said, 'Yes Professor Raj.'

He grinned.

I said, 'What should I talk about? When do I tell her that I love her?'

Raj said, 'Avoid *luv-shuv* and all that. Keep the status quo going for some more time and things will slowly fall into place. Girls take time VSAT. They are not like boys to say—I love you, can we have sex, I am done, thank you, and can you leave me alone now? It doesn't work like that with girls.'

I said, 'But I never talked about sex.'

Raj replied, 'Eventually everything will boil down to it *puttar*!'

I asked, 'I wonder how you have so much experience!'

Raj said, 'Runs in the Malhotra khandaan and Punjab *da munda hoon* yaar, trust us for our exploits.'

'Ok, catch you later,' I said as I walked out. Raj said, 'Go slow. Keep listening. It will help.'

I reached Nair's place and sat down on a bench. She hadn't arrived yet.

I asked Nair, 'Hi Nair, how are you?'

He was tying a jute rope around a few Kerala reddish brown bananas. Kerala bananas are the size of your forearm. A better simile would be, 'the size of a donkey's …' I am sure you got it this time. If you eat one, you can forgo eating any food for the whole week and you will only crap the following week. Sounds crass, but this is true. They are powerful human stomach immobilisers. In the last three years, I have eaten only one of them, that too in my first year and haven't gone anywhere near them after that.

Nair looked at me from above his half-rimmed spectacles, smiled from behind his thick black mush, and said, 'I didn't exist for you for the first three years, now you are asking, how I am doing? Which girl are you waiting for?'

Nair must have seen atleast twenty batches of students before me. I guess all of us fell into the same behaviour pattern. Boy comes and waits, then girl comes, they both order lime soda, talk for endless hours about nothing, boy pays and both head for their respective hostels. A few lucky ones in the advanced stages might head for the bushes. *Don't know, can't say!*

I smiled and said, 'Anjali.'

Nair said, 'That final year electronics, smart Coorgi girl,' and then he looked at me and quizzically asked, 'She agreed to meet you?'

'Why, what is wrong with me?'

He said, 'No, nothing wrong with you. Venkat from small town Andhra and Anjali from Coorg, sounds … interesting.'

He smiled and said, 'Enjoy, enjoy!' He made it sound like an unlikely and unholy alliance. Atleast he was not discouraging, and that was good enough for me.

I waited for ten more minutes and Anjali joined me.

She said with a smile, 'Hi VSAT, How are you? Good to see you.'

I said, 'Fine, doing good. How are things with you?'

'Adi said, you are sulking? Is that right? Why?'

I said, 'Adi is dumb, don't bother.'

Anjali looked at Nair and said, 'Two lime sodas please.'

Nair nodded.

Anjali coyly said, 'So, what is it with you Venkata?' There was a bit of a drag in the word Venkata. I said, 'Anjali ... I like you.'

She said, 'Really, I didn't know that.' According to Raj Shastra, 'When interested, girls play a lot, if they don't, they are not interested in you.'

I said, 'Stop being funny Anjali, I really like you and want to be good friends with you.'

She said, 'Is that it? Done. We were friends anyway, so what is new?'

There is nothing like 'friendship' between a great looking chic and a decent guy. It is just a ruse! One of our classmates tied a Rakhi on a girl, got close to her, then both of them performed an 'anti-rakhi puja' and entered into a relationship. Also, it doesn't even happen in movies, so the question of friendship doesn't arise. I was pretty sure that she knew my intentions. Anyway, all love stories start like this and I am not about to enter into the *Guinness Book of World Records* for trying any other novel way.

She said, 'So, are you looking forward to joining TCS?'

I said, 'Yes.'

'Why not higher studies, like M.Tech or MBA, etc.?'

I thought, 'Writing GATE is the most painful thing on planet Earth. Who would like to revise atleast fifty credits all over again? And MBA—my grades suck, my communication is barely okay and I have no clue of trivia or general affairs.'

I said, 'Never thought about it and I heard some experience is required before taking up an MBA. I would like to work for sometime and then figure out what to do. And what about you?'

Anjali said, 'I am not the higher studies kind. I think I will join TCS and work for sometime before dad pushes me to get married.'

I said, 'Oh, so you don't have a boyfriend?' I wanted an affirmation.

She smiled and replied, 'Who knows?' Can girls ever give a straight answer especially when you are looking for one? No! But that is a good sign.

I said, 'So, you have a boyfriend?'

She asked, 'Why do you want to know?'

I thought, 'Why do I want to know?

Here, I am thinking of luv-shuv and all that and she is fooling around with stupid questions.'

I said, 'Ok, don't tell, I was generally asking.'

She looked at me from the corner of her eye and giggled.

We talked about family, movies, classes, profs and everything remotely connected with NIT. She told me that she was from Coorg. Her dad was a colonel in the army and after his retirement, spent most of his time reading trivia. Her mom was a housewife and loved to cook and shop. Her sister Ameya was doing her pre-university. Anjali showed me the picture of her family. Her dad had a thick mush and bald head. He was chubby. Her mother Kaveri appeared taller than her dad, but I refrained from asking. What do I ask anyway—your dad is shorter than your mother, please explain? That would be a disaster. Her sister Ameya was a chick in the making. Anjali told me that she liked travelling to new places and was looking forward to joining TCS.

I told her about my family. My grandpa, dad, mom and sister. I told her that I liked NIT, Raj and Adi. I could not tell her that I loved her too. The timing was not right.

She asked, 'Who are you closer to—mom or dad?'

I said, 'Grandpa obviously. He is the best and has a great sense of humour. And you?'

She said, 'Of course dad. He is so sweet and cute.' So far, I have not met a daughter who didn't find her dad 'sweet and cute'. This was to be expected.

We talked for a couple of hours and she insisted on paying. Nair looked at me as if I was committing blasphemy.

I said, 'It is okay, let her pay.' Nair shrugged and took the money.

She went back to her hostel and I went back to mine.

During the next few weeks, I met Anjali quite a number of times. Once in the library, where she said, 'Shhh ... no talking' and I had to leave and she refused to come along. On another occasion, I bumped into her when she was walking with her friends. I said 'Hello' and she said 'Hi' and rest of the girls giggled. I didn't know how to react. One day, I called her and she agreed to meet at Nair's canteen. We drank the stupid lime soda and talked for hours. It is nice to drink lime soda, the problem is with the after-effects—you let out too much gas (euphemism for fart). Once, I met her outside the computer centre and walked her to the canteen, where we had tea and banana *bajji*, called '*pazhampori*' by Keralites. Bananas are mixed with flour and deep-fried in coconut oil. Man, the dish is un-fucking (this word doesn't exist in the dictionary, just coined it to give you a feel of how gruesome it is), imaginable. I mean, it is like having sex with a grasshopper. But guess what, I ate the dish for almost three years, on and off. You don't have a choice when you are at the mercy of the 'mess mashs' (mess workers were popularly called 'mashs' I was told that it was a Kerala short form for 'mahoday'.)

Once I invited Anjali for dinner and to my surprise, her best friend, Srila Iyer also turned up. We ordered *masala dosas* and coke. Srila is a great girl and she regaled us with her family stories.

She said, 'My dad is an Iyer and my mother an Iyengar and I am a pure chicken eater. So, Venkat do you eat non-veg?'

My interview was in progress.

I said, 'No, of course not. We are staunch vegetarians.'

She smiled. 'So you never eat non-veg? But of course you smoke and drink.'

The question on vices. Have to answer carefully. I imagined a scenario in which girls lived in hostels with boys. No one would ever agree to getting married or fall in love. Most guys walked the corridors in their underwear. Most smoked Gold Flake at the start of the month and graduated to beedis by the end. What one smoked was directly proportional to the money in one's pocket. I am sure there is a law to explain this social economics theory and somebody must have got a Nobel Prize for researching and proving the obvious.

I said, 'I don't smoke, may be sometimes. Kind of occasionally, and I have had some beer, but nothing more than that. No, I don't run behind girls, looks like you are interviewing me.'

Srila said, 'No, no, nothing like that, I was asking casually.'

Girls never ask anything 'just casually' during the courtship stage. The detailed evaluation process involves multiple interviews by self and peers. The grand finale usually ends with an interview with the parents. After that it is anyway curtains for the rest of your life.

I said, 'I love watching Telugu movies, listen to Bollywood songs, like Amitabh Bachchan, Shah Rukh Khan, Aamir, Hrithik. I love Katrina; she has such a nice face. Look, I am a regular guy. I love travelling and seeing new places.'

Srila pulled my leg, she said, 'Achcha, so you are a Katrina fan, eh? And you like her face only?'

I grinned and said, 'Everything about her ... Hope it is not a mistake to be a Katrina fan.'

Anjali was just listening to our conversation intently, perhaps awaiting a verdict.

I said, 'Srila, I heard some nice things about you, that you are friendly and help out your lab mates with reports, etc. That is so cool. Not many do that in the Insti.'

Srila beamed. She said, 'Who told you that?'

I said boys in the hostels talk about girls and that is what I heard.

Anjali jumped in and said, 'What do you hear about me?'

I laughed and said, 'I'll keep you guessing.'

Anjali put her hands on my neck and said, 'Tell me, else I am going to kill you.'

That was the first time she had touched me. Any self-respecting male will melt when his potential girlfriend touches him for the first time. I melted faster than ice and became a puddle of water. I just turned my head towards her, looked into her eyes and said, 'They say that you are a beautiful girl and that I am lucky to be friends with you.'

She smiled and didn't say anything.

Srila coyly said, 'Only friends with her?'

Neither Anjali nor I replied to Srila's question. We just looked at each other and the question stuck in the air and the conversation shifted to mid-sem exams. We had dinner and I walked both Anjali and Srila to their hostel gate. This time, there was no, 'I am not that kind of girl ...' sentence. I was not expecting that anyway. The initial days were gone long back, now it was the evaluation stage.

As I was walking back to my hostel, I thought that things were going in the right direction. But the pain of writing seventh semester exams was bothering me and we hadn't done much preparation. I met Adi and Raj at my hostel. They asked me how the dinner had gone.

I said, 'Srila joined us, yaar.'

Adi said, 'And you have a problem if we join you. What kind of a friend are you?'

I said, 'Shut up Adi, I didn't expect Srila to come.'

Raj said, 'That is a "confirmation meeting" my friend. If Srila gives a good reference, you are in.'

I said, 'What do you mean?'

Raj said, 'Girls confide in each other a lot. If Srila is Anjali's best friend, then Anjali must have brought Srila to check you out. If you pass with Srila, then Anjali will move forward, else it will be one more hurdle to cross.'

A couple of weeks passed and I met Anjali almost every other day. We either sat on the main building steps or in front of the CS lab or in the canteen. We talked for hours. But when I got back to the hostel, I could hardly recollect what we talked about and as days went by, we became really close.

Then one day, she said, 'Look, I can't meet you till the exams get over, I need to focus on my studies and you seem to be a big distraction.'

I smiled and said, 'Oh, so I am a distraction. I thought I was your best friend.'

Anjali said, 'You are, but if I spend all my time with you, I can't pass exams and then my dad will shoot me.'

I said, 'Ok, let us meet once a week till exams start.'

By now we had got stamped as a couple on campus. Most seniors and juniors who used to pass wisecracks about us stopped doing that. There was no more novelty left in us.

Even Raj and Adi took it for granted that we were a couple. The only question that flummoxed them was whether we had kissed or not.

I said, 'We didn't come as far as holding hands man. Why are you talking about kissing?'

Raj looked at my groin and asked, 'Everything working fine downstairs?'

I sniggered at him.

But the thought of holding her hand and kissing her was now deeply planted in my head. I thought probably after exams I should take it a step further.

We prepared hard for the stupid end semester exams. There were about seven credits to cram and each subject was a pain. We were just going through the motions and hardly had any interest left. That is what securing a job does to you. Raj, Adi and I sat late almost every night. To beat the boredom, we took chai and smoke breaks, almost every hour.

Mom, dad and Swati continued to call once in ten days and dad kept his reminders on, 'Remember Venkat, get distinction going.' That put additional pressure on me. Somehow dads the world over are the same. Don't know who trains them how to put pressure but they all seem to be masters at it.

Anyway, by November the seventh semester end-term exams were over and I felt totally relieved. I called Anjali a day before the final exam and asked her, 'Hey, let us go to Calicut city tomorrow and have a nice dinner. What do you say?'

She agreed and we met at the bus stop by 5.30 pm. I hadn't seen Anjali for about two weeks and she looked ravishing. She gave me her best smile. The bus arrived and we got into it. It was crowded and I stood right next to her. I could smell her perfume and it was intoxicating. After sometime, we got a seat and both of us sat next to each other. It felt good. I wanted to hug her then and there, but public display of affection is not too common down south, especially in Kerala. We got down in the city and sauntered around a bit for sometime. Then we went to the Taj Hotel and ordered dinner.

I asked Anjali if she was game to go watch a movie. She hesitated for a second and said, 'Won't we be late? What time is the last bus to the Insti?'

I said, 'At 11.50 pm. Let's go Anjali. Please.'

She said, 'Ok. Lets go.'

We went to Crown and watched *Before Sunset*, a romantic flick starring Ethan Hawke and Julie Delpy. Most of the movie, the lead pair walked hand in hand around Paris and talked about themselves and their feelings. While we were going back to the hostel, it started to drizzle. We managed to make it to the bus stand. We got on the last bus. The bus was dimly lit, the drizzle was trickling through the cloth tarpaulin and a cool breeze soothed our faces. The driver and conductor were not to be seen and we were one of the few passengers in the bus. Anjali looked a little tired and was looking out of the window.

I slowly took her hand in mine. She turned and looked at me, but didn't say anything. She held my hand too. I bent forward a bit and slowly whispered, 'Anjali, I ... you know ... actually ...'

She giggled and asked, 'What?'

I said, 'Well ...'

She looked intently into my eyes and said, 'I am waiting, say it.'

I just couldn't.

She then said, 'Venkat, I love you.' I was stunned. I didn't know what to say. I just blinked.

Anjali then said, 'Idiot, do you want to say something now?'

I said, 'Yes, yes ... I was just about to say that myself.'

Anjali said, 'Say what?'

I said, 'What you just said.'

Anjali fondly said, 'What did I say?' I said, 'I love you and wanted to tell you this for a long time.'

She laughed and held my hand tightly. There was silence for a few minutes.

I leaned forward to kiss her. She turned her face away.

I asked, 'Can I kiss you?'

She released my hand and said, 'All you guys are the same, want the same thing.'

I thought I had spoiled the whole damn thing. It was going so well. Anyway, why do girls have a problem when it comes to physical intimacy? What is wrong in kissing anyway?

I stammered a little, 'No, I mean, I am not like that. I mean I am like that to an extent …'

The hell man, why do I have to be tongue-tied every time I am with Anjali?

She smiled at my stupidity and took my hand back in hers and said, 'Not now, may be some other time, I am not the kind of girl who does all that before marriage.'

Again the same sentence, 'I am not the kind …'

I said, 'Yes, ok. I understand. I didn't mean to, but just look at it this way. I am so close to you and I can't even, you know what I mean, kiss you.'

Meanwhile the conductor came and interrupted our conversation. We bought tickets and within a few minutes, the bus started.

It takes an hour to reach the Insti from the city and we continued to hold hands in silence for the first fifteen minutes and then Anjali asked, 'Do you want to marry me? Or does this whole thing stop at kissing'

I asked, 'What do you think?'

She shrugged and said, 'I asked you the question. The answer for a question is not a question.'

'Anjali, I love you and want to marry you. What else do you expect? I am a simple guy yaar, I don't know any other way.'

Anjali's eyes became moist and she held my hand tight. I think she felt a little secure. I wanted to ask again, 'Now can I kiss you?' but refrained. She is the daughter of a colonel, bloody hell she could do anything—maybe throw me out of the running bus. Why risk it? I wanted my best behaviour to continue.

I asked, 'Will your colonel dad allow a small town boy to marry his princess?'

She coyly replied, 'Depends on you honeybunch. Depends on how well you can convince him. He likes people who are smart and who are good in trivia. For him that is the mark of a respectable man.'

Honeybunch! I liked the word; romance started to flow!

She asked, 'Will your parents accept me?'

I said, 'With jeans and tops, it is going to be tough. But with salwars and saris, it can help speed up things, and if you can pick up a little Telugu, it will be the icing on the cake.'

Anjali said, 'Telugu … gosh!'

I said, 'Trivia … gosh!'

Both of us laughed.

After about half an hour, our bus reached the Insti. The drizzle almost was a mild rain now. In any case, it rains for six months in Kerala. There was no power and the streetlights were off, so I decided to walk her to the hostel gate. We walked in silence for about five minutes.

We almost reached the hostel gate and I said, 'Good night Anjali, see you tomorrow.

I turned back. She took a few steps towards her hostel, then turned back and whispered, 'VSAT, come here.'

I said, 'What, go now … it is okay.'

She said, 'Idiot, come here …'

I went back meekly.

She came forward, put her arms around my neck, pulled me down and kissed me passionately. It was dark, raining and both of us were drenched. It was a wonderful experience.

After she finished, she said, 'That was good, any prior experience?'

I said, 'What? I am supposed to say all that. Good girls don't say such things …'

She laughed, leaned forward, pecked me on the cheek and said, 'Who said I am a good girl?' She tickled my ribs and said, 'I could be very naughty. Enjoy the night thinking of me.'

The kiss and the rib-tickle sent an electric shock through my body. I smiled, shook my head and went back to my hostel. What a day—exams over, great evening, nice movie, wonderful dinner, playful girl, and the first kiss. I felt alive and at the top of the world. I felt wanted, loved and cared for. Life couldn't have been any better.

I went back to the hostel and woke up Raj and Adi.

I said, 'Morons, wake up. The stud is back. Yours truly has finally kissed the girl.'

Then I gave them the full dump of the evening's events. Both listened to my story intently.

Adi exclaimed, 'Kiss is done! How was it man?'

I said, 'Wet and can't be described. You feel amazingly alive man!'

Raj said, 'How do you expect it to be?'

Adi said, 'Now only the final act is pending.'

Raj laughed and said, 'She will screw you, but will not allow you to screw. I guarantee, girls of this kind do everything after marriage only. You have come so far, that is good enough.'

I said, 'We are thinking of getting married.'

Raj laughed and said, 'I felt the same way when I kissed the aunty next door for the first time in my life. I proposed to her and she laughed and sent me home ... *hota hai, hota hai*.'

Adi laughed louder.

I said, 'But I am serious, guys.'

Eighth semester is a carefree semester for every engineering student. The course work is not too stringent. We had to do a project and complete three to four credits. Life was peaceful. This was the time to bond, feel emotional and believe everything had a happy ending. I spent most of my time with Anjali, Srila, Raj and Adi and we almost became an inseparable gang. We did innumerable lunches and dinners and watched a ton of movies. At one point in time, I thought Srila showed a soft corner for Adi, but Adi was oblivious to it. Adi loved his food, his independence and his computer architecture. Though a Mech student, he spent a lot of time in the CS Labs and mastered C, C++ and Java very well. He thought Dot Net was frivolous. Raj on the other hand was good at testing whatever Adi did.

Raj said, 'My brain works differently. It tries to identify problems and so I test whatever Adi does and I enjoy it, man.'

I was not good either in architecture or testing. I was a regular programmer. Given a problem, I would write computer programs to get the functionality going.

Anjali and Srila were great at programming and when they compiled programs, they worked. Srila also had an offer with TCS, but her parents would allow her to join TCS only if the posting was Chennai. So she chose the Chennai posting and was eagerly awaiting the outcome.

In the last few months, all of us became a little more senti. During the last few weeks, Anjali and I kissed a few times. Once, I saw her in the library and signalled her to come upstairs. Once we reached a remote corner, I said, 'Please, please, one quick kiss.'

Her eyes darted around and she said, 'Ok, teddy bear, let us do it quickly.'

We ended up kissing passionately. In another instance, she called me and said, 'I want to meet you, come to the Admin building, and stupid listen, come alone.'

Raj and Adi were with me when she called. So I said, 'Come guys, let us go to the Admin building, Anjali wants me to meet her alone. You guys stay downstairs for a few minutes, I will go up and come back in a jiffy.'

Raj laughed and said, 'Quickie?'

I reached the Admin building thinking she had something important to say. She took me to a corner next to the principal's room and started kissing me passionately.

I stopped her and whispered, 'Anjali, Raj and Adi are downstairs.'

She giggled and said, 'No, I am not kissing them.'

I said, 'Stupid ... I got to go.'

She got angry and said, 'Go, and kiss their ass. What ever happened to your priorities Mr Venkata Subramaniam Adisankara Tanikaburla?'

I smiled and gave her a long kiss. After that we went downstairs to meet Raj and Adi. They looked at us quizzically.

I said, 'Come let us go.' End of discussion.

Finally, the end semester exams were due and we performed reasonably well. A dozen farewell parties were thrown and with every farewell party, we got drunk almost every day. Raj, Adi and I had a private party and we talked till the wee hours about the Insti, our future, Anjali, Srila, professors, seniors, juniors—anything remotely connected to the last four years. Within a week of finishing our final year exams, the hostel warden issued notices to the final year students asking them to vacate the hostel. Adi had tears in his eyes. He said, 'Time to go buddies.' Raj felt emotional too.

He said, 'Guys, I am going to spend the next few weeks in Delhi and after that let us meet at the TCS training centre.' I didn't know what to say and I hugged Raj and this time he let me. He asked, 'Ok, are you done now?' I nodded. I liked hugging Raj because he felt uncomfortable and I loved watching him when he was irritated.

Next day, I went to the ladies' hostel to catch up with Anjali before she left. She had told me the previous day that her parents were coming to pick her up.

When I went to the hostel, Srila said, 'VSAT, her parents came early, spent an hour with us and they packed and left. She felt sorry that she couldn't meet you. She gave me this letter to give you.'

I had a sinking feeling in the pit of my stomach. I suddenly felt hopeless and dejected. I quickly tore open the envelope and read the letter.

Dearest Honeybunch,

I am sorry for not calling before I left. Dad, mom and Ameya came to pick me up a little earlier than expected, we packed and now we are leaving for Coorg. Don't call me at home; I will give you a call as soon as I can. Look forward to meeting you at the TCS training centre.
Love you, lots of hugs and kisses. Already missing you VSAT, my teddy bear
Love you a lot ...

Yours ever,
Anjali

I decided to talk to her as early as I could. On the same evening, we had to catch the Kerala Express. Raj, Adi and I packed and left for the railway station.

Training and Posting

THROUGHOUT THE JOURNEY, I FELT QUITE DEPRESSED. THOUGHTS about the Insti, Anjali, Raj, Adi and Srila kept coming back again and again and I had an empty feeling inside me. I vowed to go back to the Insti sometime soon. I was feeling bad that I couldn't meet Anjali one last time before she left. I somehow attributed all my pain to that colonel father of hers. Why did he have to come early and whisk my angel away?

It was early April 2006 and Warangal was burning at 45 degrees and I got down at the railway station. Mom, dad and Swati had come to receive me and it was nice to be back home. Grandpa, mom and dad were pleased that I had finished my engineering. Swati wouldn't let go of me and told me all the local gossip. I went out in the evening to meet some childhood friends. When I came back, Mom said, 'Kanna, let us go to Tirupati. We have to give your hair to Lord Venkateswara.'

I said, 'Mom, do I have to really do it? What happens if we don't?'

Mom said angrily, 'You are playing games with the Lord? You don't have any respect for my wishes?'

Dad added, 'Venkat, you mustn't talk like that!'

Grandpa said, 'Venkata, give your hair, you will look sexy. Most software people nowadays don't keep hair. That is the sign of nerds.'

I understood the gravity of the situation and said, 'In which case, this is the last time I will get it done. Let us go at the earliest. I don't want to join TCS with a tonsured head.'

The next week, we left for Tirupati. I prayed to the Lord and asked for a reunion with all my friends and especially with Anjali. Then I sat down to get my head tonsured. There were a zillion people sitting in rows to offer their hair. The barbers took less than a minute and eight strokes to clean up the head. My barber looked at me and asked warmly, 'What did you get from the Lord, for you to give him your hair? '

I looked up and said, 'Job ... *udyogam* babu.'

He asked, 'What job?'

I said, 'Software.'

His eyebrows shot up and he said, 'Wait a minute.' He opened his small briefcase. There were several envelopes in it. He took one out, handed it over to me and said, 'This is my son's CV. He has done engineering from a government engineering college. Can you refer the CV in your company?' I was stunned. His knife was on my head and his hand was extending his son's CV and I thought it was wise on my part to take it.

I said, 'Sure.'

The barber said, 'Sir, I give the résumé of my son to all the people who are in software. Lord willing someday, my son also will get a software job.'

I nodded silently. Once done, I thanked him and left. I thought, 'Drill a well and a software engineer will emerge. India has changed so much!' I promised myself that I would help the barber's son get a job in TCS, if possible.

I looked into a mirror. Sandalwood paste was smeared on my tonsured head to keep it cool. I ran my fingers across my head. It felt soft and contoured. Looking at me, my mom was ecstatic and asked, 'Shall I put some coconut oil on your head?' I stared at her. My dad didn't say anything and Swati made fun of me.

She said, 'You look like Bruce Willis minus all the muscles and the six pack.' No gap between thought and speech. I stared at her.

Grandpa joked, 'Aha, that looks nice. You can replace Amrish Puri as villain in Hindi movies.'

I said, '*Et tu* Grandpa?'

He waved and grinned, 'Don't bother Venkata, the follicles will re-emerge within days.'

I didn't say anything. I was displaying passive resistance. From Tirupati, all of us went back home. The journey was uneventful, other than my tonsure that felt rough. From day two onwards, small hair follicles started making their presence felt.

I spent the next few weeks aimlessly. I was a little restless because I missed Anjali a lot. We talked to each other a few times a week.

In our last call she said, 'Teddy, I miss you.'

I said, 'Me too babe. Looking forward to seeing you soon.'

She said, 'Same here. Did you talk to your parents about me?'

I said, 'No, not right now. Timing is not right. I will, once I settle down a bit. What about you?'

She said, 'Same here, timing is not right, maybe later. How are Raj and Adi?'

I said, 'Yeah, they are doing good. Raj is having a good time in Delhi and Adi is enjoying Hyderabadi chicken biryani.'

Anjali giggled, 'I miss the gang. Ok listen, I can't talk much now, but will catch up soon, love you Venkata.'

I said, 'Love you too babe, bye.'

With every call, I was missing her more. Probably long distance relationship is very difficult to work.

I was thinking of getting back at the earliest, and finally I got a letter from TCS asking me to report on May 15, 2006 at Bangalore for training. The next few weeks went by in anticipation and finally the D-day arrived.

Mom packed my bags and loaded them with sweets and pickles. She was happy that I was about to start my professional life. Deep inside, she was worried that I was heading on my way out and things would never be the same again. My dad came and sat next to me on the bed and said, 'Son, here is a pen for you. My gift for you. Grandpa gave it to me when I started work and now I am passing it on to you.' It was an old Camlin pen and was wrapped in tape at the bottom. I looked at it intently.

Grandpa laughed and said, 'I gave him a brand new pen, look what he is giving you. A pen that is cello-taped, *kanjoos* ...'

Dad quickly retorted, 'The bottom is broken, so I taped it.'

The senti value attached to it was way too high for me to say anything else.

I said, 'Thank you Pa.'

Swati purchased a tie for me. She said, 'Wear it on the first day to office, you will look nice.' I smiled and hugged her.

Grandpa said, 'Come, come, quickly fall at my feet and I will bless you. That is the best present I can give you.'

I smiled and dutifully touched his feet. Grandpa quickly lifted me up and hugged me. He whispered gently in my ears, 'Venkata, may the Lord be with you. Have a good life. Stay away from wine and women.' He repeated the famous line from *The Godfather*, *'In Sicily, women are more dangerous than shotguns.'* I smiled.

He gave me a black backpack and said, 'Software engineers use backpacks, you will like it, bought it with my pension money.'

I had tears in my eyes and I hugged Grandpa again. I had lost my granny when I was a kid and since then Grandpa and I have been best friends. We went out, played chess and quite often, he protected me from my dad's ire. Besides, both of us loved *The Godfather*. We must have watched the classic a few times, but Grandpa must have read the book to me atleast ten times. I grew up on quotes from the movie. Don Veto Corleone was a family member for us. If Grandpa had a chance, he would have changed our surname from Tanikaburla to Corleone! Mom, dad and Swati came to the station to say goodbye.

Mom and Swati started crying.

Dad said, 'Call us regularly, eat well and keep good health. Remember, you have a quick temper and it doesn't work in the office. Have patience and take it easy. You will have *to work for the* rest of your life, so may as well enjoy the ride.'

Then he came a little closer and whispered, 'Don't smoke too much, it is bad for your health. Best would be to quit.' I looked at my dad and didn't say anything. I wondered how dads knew everything. He took out his wallet and put an additional five hundred rupees in my pocket.

The journey was uneventful and I landed in Bangalore. It was a beautiful place, but for the traffic. We were given accommodation for the first week in the TCS guesthouses and were expected to find a PG accommodation within a week or so. Adi and I reached a couple of days in advance on the pretext of exploring the city for accommodation. Raj was expected the day after and Srila was not sure about her plans until the last minute. She said that she would catch us on the first day of joining. Anjali said that she would meet us at Barista, opposite Barton Centre on MG road the following day. We waited for her and she turned up fifteen minutes late. Those fifteen minutes felt like an eternity. She looked beautiful and as soon as she saw us, she said, 'Hi guys, I missed you all so much.' She hugged both of us. I realised that graduation and city life enhances public display of affection (PDA).

She looked at me and said, 'So, handsome, you have put on some weight, huh? You look like a stud with your haircut.'

Adi said, 'Tirupati style', and all of us laughed and she touched my hair. That was the moment I had been waiting for. I twisted, melted, morphed and was almost on all fours, ready to be taken home, fed and cuddled. We talked for hours as we ate muffins and sipped coffee. Adi obviously had to eat something.

After a while, Anjali said, 'Ok, time for me to go. My dad is in town and I am happy to introduce you all tomorrow when he comes to drop me at the training centre ... as friends ... obviously, you know what I mean.'

We both nodded and she left. We were left to fend the bill, which was about ₹400 for a few muffins and coffees. We realised that Bangalore was a damn expensive place. In our Insti canteen, we could have paid around ₹30 for the same order.

Adi said, 'Bangalore is way too expensive. Chalo let us split. You pay two-thirds.'

I said, 'Why?'

Adi said, 'Won't you pay for your babe?'

I just shook my head and paid up.

We headed to the guesthouse and waited for Raj to arrive. He turned up very late, at about 2 am and we were fast asleep. He said, 'Morons wake up. The great Raj from Delhi has come.'

We woke up, and I hugged Raj.

He said, 'Idiot, your habit of hugging me has still not gone.' Both of us smiled.

Raj then spoke of his Delhi exploits for an hour. He said, 'I have given my virginity all over again, many times in Delhi.' He gloated about his sex-ploits and we both listened to him intensely. Adi and I visualised Delhi as the sex capital of the world, where teenage girls, aunties, neighbours; almost anything remotely human and female, barring grannies, were horny.

We hardly slept that night. We woke up at 7 am and got ready to go to the TCS training centre; we had to report at 9 am sharp.

I looked at myself in the full-length mirror and felt nice—twenty two years old, sixty eight kgs, five feet eight inches tall and decent looking, Venkat the latest software engineer from smalltown Warangal has arrived. I wore my favourite blue coloured shirt and black coloured trousers. They fitted me well, actually the only trousers that fit snugly. I sat down on my bed and tied the laces of my black shoes. The heel was almost worn out. It needed a change. I wore the tie given by Swati, took the backpack given by Grandpa and was ready to go.

Raj said, 'Tie *shie, kya baat hai puttar!*'

Before heading out, I looked at the photo of Lord Ganesha. Mom said, 'Pray daily before going to work, Lord Ganesha is the God of good fortune.' The photo was pitch black with all the incense that was burnt in front of it. I could barely see the trunk to identify Lord Ganesha.

I prayed, 'Lord, I don't know what to ask, just make it all work out—at work and with Anjali's family and mine. Wish me the best.' We grabbed a quick sandwich and went to the training centre.

By which time the colonel had dropped Anjali there and left.

Anjali asked, 'Where were you guys? Dad is already gone.'

We were not used to coming on time anyway. We kept mum and all of us went inside. There were probably a hundred young software engineers at the training centre. We were assembled in the conference room and waited for the show to begin. At 9 am sharp, Amit, the HR guy, Jivan the delivery manager, Arun Gupta, Ashish Srivastav, Manikantan the three project managers and Sankar—the vice president came in.

Amit, the HR guy began:

'... Ok, ladies and gentleman, welcome to TCS, welcome to the Tata Group. Thank you for accepting the job offers and for joining us. I believe you have chosen the right company to start your careers. People build strong careers and stay a lifetime with us.

This is a company that leads change, respects individuals and gives opportunities to grow. We believe in teamwork and people are our assets. Let me now introduce Sankar and the team.'

All of us were intently listening to the speech.

Sankar said, 'Young men and women, I am so happy to see you all. I joined TCS 18 years back as a young campus graduate and today, I head one of the largest programs in the retail segment. TCS gives that opportunity. I implore upon you to have patience, believe in the company, serve your customers well and be a team player. There is no rocket science to growth—just keep your heads down and work hard—you will be rewarded. You come from different colleges, different branches and probably have different grade points, but today all that doesn't matter anymore, all of you get a fresh start to build a new life and a great career.'

I loved what Sankar said. *'All of us start as equals, no grades and no ranking. Teamwork is given credence over individual contribution, excellent!'* I felt thoroughly motivated. Raj and Adi exchanged glances with me and smiled. I looked at Anjali and she winked. We were enjoying ourselves. Then the training coordinator came and explained the schedule for the next sixty days. Half-a-day passed and we split for lunch. The five of us sat together.

Srila said, 'Hi guys, I am glad to see you all'.

Raj said, 'So, your dad allowed you to join?'.

Srila smiled and said, 'I don't think he had much choice.'

Adi said, 'I liked all the sessions today. I hope we get a good project to work on and I would love it if all of us are posted in Bangalore, then we are done.'

Anjali said, 'Let us do dinner together, it will be fun.'

I asked, 'The colonel left?' and Anjali replied, 'Yes.'

Raj said, 'Chalo, now you guys can get back to your romance.'

Everybody laughed.

In the afternoon we were given our ID cards and asked to fill a hundred forms. I filled the application form, security form, declaration form, PF form, gratuity form, datasheet form, library form, system form, email form, security form, etc., etc. I must have written my address a zillion times. We got tired of filling all the forms and cursed the HR. Why can't HR simplify, why can't all these be web-enabled? One of the HR coordinators said, 'It is legal to fill all these forms.' I imagined a devilish looking government servant sitting in a corner of the TCS building, giving instructions and checking all the forms. He had two horns on his head and canines extending from under his lips. Next to his chair was a nicely oiled leather whip.

Anjali said, 'What do you guys know about HR, just wait and see, they are the most powerful guys in any company. It is best to steer clear of them.'

I think there is a universal consistency in the perception about HR departments.

Adi said, 'What does HR do?'

Raj replied, 'What don't they do? They hire you, decide your salary; rating, performance, promotions; and they can fire you too.'

Adi said, 'So, then be on good terms with them.'

Raj replied, 'Good terms with HR? You must be kidding man. As Anjali said, best is to steer clear of them.'

I was taking in all of this. I had no clue how a company worked. This was my first experience and I was sure it was the same with Adi. But Raj and Anjali had got some insights from their parents.

That night all of us went for dinner at Queens. We had North Indian food and it was great. The weather was beautiful.

During dinner, I said, 'Guys, we need to get a PG accommodation. Why don't we take up a two bedroom flat and all of us can share it?' Raj said, 'Flats are expensive VSAT. You have to pay maintenance. Let us look at independent houses where they rent a portion of the house and we can share.'

Anjali said, 'Why don't you guys take a place close to where we stay? My dad has a friend in Koramangala and Srila and I can stay there. You guys can also take a place close by?'

We agreed and in a week, settled a place in Koramangala. The rent was ₹7500/month and we agreed to split it. The advance was ₹75,000 and we borrowed money from our parents. It was a simple, functional place. We bought mattresses, a cooking gas stove and a few utensils and moved there over the weekend. Meanwhile Anjali and Srila also moved to a paying guest accommodation run by an old couple. They had a single room upstairs for themselves. Bangalore doesn't have public transportation and we had to depend on company vehicles to reach the training centre.

Our training was split into essentially soft skills and technical skills. Soft skills covered the protocol of interacting with customers, peers and managers; writing emails, answering calls, basic dos and don'ts, intellectual property protection, etc. In technical skills, we were taught the basics of software methodology, waterfall method, agile method and programming fundamentals. Then we were split into Java and Microsoft streams. Fortunately, Raj, Adi, Anjali, Srila and I were in the Java stream. Apparently, Microsoft stream is also not bad, it is just that the testing happens at customer sites and feed back incorporated into the software is sold as the next big version.

After we shifted to our new place, Anjali and I went for a movie in PVR on the weekend. We chose corner seats and suddenly Anjali pulled me close and started kissing me. She always had the first mover advantage. After sometime, I put my arm around her neck and casually touched her breast. Then the whispered conversation started.

She turned towards me and said, 'What are you doing?'

I said, 'Nothing.'

She said, 'Really? Look, none of that before marriage.'

I acted innocent and said, 'None of what? I didn't do anything ...' and let my hand slide forward a little more.

She said, 'Mr Venkat, not now. I am not ready.'

From her tone, I understood that she was serious and removed my arm from around her neck. Kissing is ok. Hugging is ok. Public Display of Affection is ok. The moment you touch those vital parts, somehow, the alarm bells in every girl's head goes off and the picture of doting parents flashes before her and the poor boyfriend is curtly asked to stay within his limits.

She said, 'Teddy, I am in love with you, but I am scared of all this.'

I said, 'That is ok, it is just that I can't wait. I love you, I will marry you and I don't see any reason why we should wait ...'

Anjali said, 'Let us not discuss that now, please?'

We watched the movie in silence. After the movie, we had dinner at Shanti Sagar, a fast food vegetarian joint. Then I dropped her home and went back to my place.

Raj and Adi had gone for dinner and were not back. I took a shower and watched some TV.

They came in and Raj said, '*Aur* hero, how is it going? Any progress beyond kissing, huh?'

I ignored his question.

He said, 'Achcha, so you guys fought. Good, you will make progress.'

I didn't reply.

The training continued at its pace and things were progressing well. We had about ten days to go before we would be deployed on live projects.

The following weekend, one late evening, I went to pick up Anjali for dinner.

Anjali asked me to come in.

She was wearing a pink nightie and looked sexy. I gaped at her.

She said invitingly, 'There is nobody at home'.

I said, 'Ok. Get dressed and let us go quickly. I am famished.'

She said, 'You are the stupidest guy I have ever seen.'

I started blankly.

She sat next to me and said, 'Honeybunch, do you want to make love?'

'I ...' she started kissing passionately.

Then she quickly got up, bolted the door and came and sat next to me.

She took my hand and put it on her breast. I could feel her softness. Then I tried sliding my hand inside, but it was uncomfortable, so I quickly helped her out of the nightie and stared at her. That was the first time I had looked at a completely nude girl. I let out a gasp. God had made women so beautiful.

She smiled, came closer and said, 'Stupid, will you keep staring at me or do something?'

I fidgeted with my shirt buttons and quickly took off my jeans and shirt.

She was a little anxious and said, 'Go easy Teddy bear, this is my first time.'

I grinned and said, 'Me too, babe.'

She giggled.

We made love for the next one hour and lay back, exhausted.

She asked, 'It was great. How was it honeybunch?'

I just cuddled her and we lay on the bed in silence for another half an hour. I felt complete. It is an inexpressible feeling—the mind drifts. I felt like having a smoke.

She said, 'Honeybunch, we should quickly tell our parents.'

I couldn't understand why having sex and the thought of parents were so deeply inter-related. Nevertheless, you concede to such requests, affirmatively, especially during those delicate moments.

I said, 'Yes, let us get on to our projects, spend a couple of months on them and then break the news.'

She liked what I said and kissed me on my neck and I felt aroused again. I took her in my arms and she said, 'Oh, stud. Enough for today.'

I kissed her and let go.

She asked, 'Do you think your parents will agree?' My erection went for a toss. I knew it was going to be really difficult. I said, 'We will make them agree. What about the colonel and your mom?'

Anjali giggled and said, 'If you are good in general affairs and trivia, you stand a good chance. Don't worry, we will make it happen.'

Both of us were famished and went to Sharmas and had a sumptuous meal. I felt that our relationship was consummated and both of us were at peace with each other. There was contentment on Anjali's face. I think making love changed our lives forever.

A month passed attending classes and we got our first salary. I called my father and said, 'Pa I got my first salary, I have posted the cheque to you.'

My father said, 'That is nice of you, but you didn't have to do it Venkat.' I could feel tears welling up in his eyes.

I waited for a few moments and he said, 'Venkat, I am proud of you. Do well and don't get into trouble. I will talk to you soon. I will write a letter to you.'

'Ok Pa.'

We were almost nearing completion of training and one day Anish, our resource manager, called me for a meeting. Most of us knew that this meeting was meant to give us the details of our posting and the project. Raj told me, 'Stick to Bangalore, don't worry about the project, anything is fine.'

I went for the meeting.

Anish smiled, shook hands and asked, 'So, how was your training?'

I said, 'Great sir. We learnt a lot sir.' I started to add 'sir' at the end of each sentence. It helps, trust me! Even the most obstinate idiot on planet earth melts when you address him by saying 'sir'.

Anish said, 'Good, I called to discuss your posting and project.'

I nodded. Staffing managers are gods in software companies. They pretty much decide your project and eventually your fate.

He cleared his throat and asked, 'We were thinking of posting you to Chennai. What do you say?'

Chennai, my God! The land of lungis and checked shirts. Sambhar sells more than any other commodity in that state. The weather is awesome—unwaveringly sultry. Tamil is the national language. The only silver lining is Rajinikanth, the movie actor. No way, I condemn this dastardly act.

With a quivering tone I said, 'Sir, I would be very unhappy. Most my friends and relatives are here and I would appreciate if you consider Bangalore.'

Anish said, 'So, you wouldn't accept Chennai?'

I replied, 'Sir, it is not about my acceptance. I just have a request for you to consider. At the end of the day, I have to go where you post me, but you will have a very unhappy employee. I am sure you don't want that.'

Anish peered at me and kind of liked what I said.

He looked at some charts that were in front of him and said, 'Ok, we will start with Bangalore then, but you must be open to other locations subsequently.'

I said, 'Sure sir, definitely in the future.' Grandpa always said, 'Agree immediately if you are getting what you wanted. Who has seen the future? Elephants may fly and *jahapanah* might croak.'

Anish added, 'Ok, I will put you with Mani. I mean, Manikantan Doraisamy. You can report to him from Monday.'

I heeded Raj's advice, smiled and said, 'Sure sir, no problem. I will always remember this kind gesture.'

After I stepped out of the meeting, I informed the gang about my conversation with Anish. The question paper was again leaked and they agreed to follow a similar methodology. We Indians are extremely good at replicating success forumulae very effectively.

Srila said, 'Guys, I have no option, I have to choose Chennai. Dad is very particular about that.'

Raj said, 'Delhi would be better for me guys, but since all of you are here. I'll stick to Bangalore for the first few years.'

Adi said, 'I love Bangalore and other than the weather and Naidu, there is no big difference between Hyderabad and Bangalore. I will stick to Bangalore.'

Anjali laughed, looked at me and said, 'Bangalore of course, is there any doubt?'

One by one, each person in the gang met Anish and we were all posted in Bangalore except for Srila. She was posted in Chennai. Raj was also deployed under Manikantan Doraisamy. Adi went into a maintenance project with Ashish Srivastav and Anjali was put in a development project under Arun Gupta.

We were ready to start work.

Letter from Pa

A WEEK LATER, I GOT A LETTER FROM MY PA BY POST. I TORE open the letter and read,

My Dear Son Venkat,

Hope you are well.

I am old-fashioned and hence chose to write a letter. I was very touched when you called and told me that you had sent your first pay cheque home. Today, I feel happy that your mother and I have brought you up with good values. I told grandpa that you sent the cheque. He asked us to give it to the Hanamkonda Government Primary School. The school's library is not in good shape and with the thirteen thousand that you sent—which is a lot of money—we can equip the library well. Please let us know if it is fine with you.

Son, having self-respect and a good reputation is very important in life and you should never compromise on these two. You are fortunate to be making a decent amount of money from your first salary itself. So, make sure you don't squander what you earn. Learn to save and ensure you open a recurring deposit with State Bank of India. I prefer Indian banks to the foreign banks. Your money will be safe. People talk about investments in shares and mutual funds; you may want to be careful about investing in them. I have been a school teacher all my life and I may be conservative in my views, but I guess there is no harm in being like that, atleast we may not make a lot of money, but we won't lose our hard-earned capital.

Venkat, I had to teach children for almost three decades before we could own a house of our own and I am proud of that. Since you are making decent money, you must start thinking of purchasing a house in Bangalore at the earliest. Plan your career in such a way that you go to America to gain experience and become a good manager. Don't worry, the Tatas will take care of that. In a few years, we will get you married and we have already started getting some nice proposals. I am sure you know Srimangala, who lives at the end of our street. Her father has already approached us. We said you were still a kid and he was willing to wait. Grandpa, your mother and I believe that it is a decent match. She is doing her BA, knows how to cook, is a nice girl and can keep you happy. Besides we know their family well.

Please don't smoke too much. I would appreciate it if you can totally give up smoking. I hear that software engineers in Bangalore get into vices. I hope you are not into drinking and other such things. These are all bad habits and will pull you down. Hope your company is providing you with nice breakfast, lunch and dinner. Eat good food and try to avoid eating in hotels. Most hotel fellows mix 'soda' in food. It will spoil your stomach. You won't know now, in a few years when the stomach lining erodes, you will end up with gastric problems. Be careful about your health. Are you eating fruits or not? Banana is good for energy and papaya helps clean bowels. If you have clean bowels, your mind will work well and you will get promotions.

What do you do for commuting? I am sure the Tatas must have provided for your transportation. However, if you buy a bike, ensure that you wear a helmet. Ideally, having a small car helps and it is possible if you go to America and save. We pray for your good health and happiness. Eat Nuxomvica 30 whenever you have tension related headache. Avoid eating allopathic medicines. They are not good for the body in the long run. Homeo medicine is better.

You must go to the temple regularly. Only Lord Venkateswara protects us all.

With lots of blessings,

Yours ever,
Pa

I read the letter a few times and summarised his thoughts: Indian banks are better, recurring deposits help save money, avoid hotel food—it has soda, fruits help good bowel movement and good bowel movement helps get promotions, plan for America, manager position, bike, car, house. Marry Srimangala, eat Homeo medicine for tension headaches, go to temple …

Everything about the letter was ok, except for marrying Srimangala, no way! I decided never to discuss the topic of Srimangala with Anjali. I couldn't visualise the wedding card—Venkata Subramaniam Adisankara Tanikaburla weds Srimangala Srivari Buchi Seemanapalli—both our names would fill the whole damn wedding card. The whole Telugu world will turn up to give us blessings, which subsequently anyway, we would need badly. I would prefer the wedding card to read—Venkat weds Anjali—a six-letter name will wed another six-letter name, that would be simple and neat. Problem solved! There will be no global warming issues.

Fuck, what a choice ma and pa had made!

I carefully folded the letter and put it away. I called my dad that night and told him to give the money to the library. He was ecstatic. My conversation ended there. I didn't want to discuss anything else and disconnected the phone in a hurry.

Starting Work

ON JULY 17, 2006, A BEAUTIFUL MONDAY MORNING, RAJ AND I reported to Manikantan Doraisamy, the esteemed project manager for North Eastern Drinks (NED), a US based company which made fruit juices. He had about twelve years of experience in the software industry. He was short, portly, dark and a straight shooter. He had studied at GCT, Coimbatore and started as a software engineer. In eight to nine years he had been made project manager.

He called us into his cabin and said, 'Sit down guys.' He was going through our files.

We were quiet.

As he went through the files, he kept talking to himself, 'NIT, Calicut, bad grades, classmates, not a great performance in training, Java stream, preferred Bangalore. So, you joined TCS because you didn't have any option?'

Raj quickly retorted, 'TCS offered us a job and we joined sir.'

Mani said, 'Smart boy, you know how to answer questions and you, Mr Venkata Subramaniam Adisankara Tanikaburla, what is your special comment? I am sure you are from AP? What do I call you? You know what the Americans will call you? Mr Burla.' He was laughing.

This was our first meeting and I didn't like him too much. People told us that Mani was a workaholic, a super performer and Sankar—the vice president, was very fond of him.

I said, 'Nothing sir. Don't have anything to say sir. Yes sir, I am from AP sir and you can call me Venkat sir.'

He said, 'Ok guys. I want to tell you a few rules that I have set in my project. Rule # 1—don't ever try to be oversmart and don't fuck with me. Rule # 2—don't do anything stupid on your own. Do, what you are told. Rule # 3—don't ask for vacation, you are expected to work late hours and weekends. Rule # 4—the boss and customers are always right. Rule # 5—the boss comes first, then the team and then finally yourselves. Rule #—6 don't ask for salary increase for the next twelve to eighteen months, it is futile.' If only he had added four more, it would have been the Ten Commandments and we would have proclaimed him as the 'Neo Moses.'

Both of us said in unison, 'Yes sir. Understood.'

Mani called Jayanthi, the project lead for a module and said, 'Explain the project to these two and give them some work.'

Jayanthi had about five years of experience and did what she was told. She had joined about five years back from Mangalore University. If you had to convey anything to Mani, all you had to do was tell Jayanthi and Mani would know about it instantly. They shared a 100-gigabit superfast information line.

Jayanthi introduced us to ten other engineers in the project. Almost all of them had experience ranging from two to five years. Anjan Banerjee was from Kolkata. Anjan had about three-and-a-half years of experience and looked fazed out. He spoke in monosyllables and spent most of time downloading content from the net and perpetually had earphones on. Josy and Joby Mathews were the Kerala twins, and their official language at the workplace was Malayalam. Srinivas from Andhra was obsessed with Telugu cine star Mahesh Babu (his screen saver made it obvious). Harpreet was from Chandigarh and was a budding architect. Joel was from Goa and had spiked hair. He said, 'Hi fellas!' with an American accent. He looked like Remo's fourth cousin. Savitha was from Lucknow and was on the phone, chatting with her friends, which she did anyway most of the time. Nagaraj was from Mysore and Narayana Murthy of Infy was his idol. A small poster of a bespectacled Narayana Murthy adorned his desk. There was a small incense stand in front of the photo. Apparently the security informed him not to light any incense sticks inside of the office. They feared that the fire alarm might go off. Manoj was from Himachal and spoke English with a heavy North Indian accent. Guna came from Assam. He was a bulky guy—imagine packing a twelve-inch sub into a six-inch bread pack. He had big protruding eyes and spoke in Assamese to his friends. Apparently he was the national TT champ. Divya was from Kerala. Her father was a police sub-inspector in Cochin. She was tanned and was a decent-looking chic. She smiled most of the time. Her nickname was 'Bipasha' and some also called her the 'sexy, dusky South siren.' Whenever I saw her, a factory siren went off in my head. I smiled to myself. Manoj was constantly hitting on her, but she was oblivious to his existence. Raj gaped in awe at Divya and I gently kicked him on his toe and he averted the stare. Raj and I shook hands with all of them.

I said, 'Raj, you see a good-looking chick and start staring? Saala, you will never give up, will you?'

Raj said, 'How can I not stare when Bipasha is working in your team yaar? Somebody said a thing of beauty is joy forever. It is so true man.'

A software project is like building a house. Software architecture and design are like laying the foundation, columns and beams. Software programs are akin to masonry, plumbing, and electrical work. Once the programming work is done, you test the software to ensure that the programs are working fine, just like the way you flush water and check the switches once the house is done. However, it is not as simple as that. The real problem crops up when module leads and software engineers decide to do their own thing and the architecture (foundation, columns and beams) doesn't support all the modules. So, it is the job of the project manager to ensure consistency. Every decent-sized software project has a project manager. The project manager divides the project into multiple modules. Each module has a lead and junior level software engineers report to the module leads.

The first task given to me was to document functionality. Subsequently, Jayanthi called Raj and said, 'You will work with Divya on testing.'

Raj didn't know how to respond.

Jayanthi said, 'What? Do you have something to say?'

Raj blurted out, 'Hmm ... yes ... yeah ... good ... happy ... thank you.'

Raj's job appeared simple. He had to take the functional document, write what had to be tested and test software programs or code written by the rest of the software engineers. Then he had to compare results and produce gaps. But if the scope of the project and functionality is not nailed, testing becomes a moving target.

Raj came over to me and said, 'Fuck, look at my luck factor man; I am going to work with Bipasha. Ha ha ha.'

I said, 'Her pop is a police inspector. You do something stupid and he will take his stick and shove it.'

Raj grinned and said, 'For Bipasha, I am willing to take the pain.'

Adi was deployed under Ashish, who people said was a decent guy. Adi's job involved a maintenance application that calculated the number of stock keeping units for Merck, a US based Pharma company. He had to ensure that the application was up to date and was capturing the overall stock at the right intervals. He didn't feel the least challenged. In any case, most software engineers on maintenance projects are under-utilised, under-worked and reasonably over-paid (an oxymoron again!). The irony is—their domain knowledge makes them absolutely retainable and their under-utilisation at times makes them unfathomably painful. My father's third cousin's fourth son Satya Sai Suryanarayana Sarvottama Vijay Bharadwaja Tanikaburla foundly referred to as SSSSVBT, works for a factory in Montana as a maintenance software engineer and out of sheer boredom took up hair cutting, pedicure and manciure as a hobby. He ended up painting red nail polish on all the secretaries' toenails and his claim to fame was that he laid most of them.

Anjali was deployed with Arun Gupta on a retail project. They were developing a dashboard to capture retail analytics for CostCo, a large retail mart in the US. Arun was a true peoples' manager. He personally introduced Anjali to the team, explained the project and assigned her to work with Shikhar. Shikhar had joined from NIT, Warangal and was two years senior to Anjali. Much to my chagrin, he developed an instant liking and soft corner for Anjali. Who wouldn't, anyway? There is something about men. They just can't resist a good-looking woman. First the eye conveys the signal, then some chemical reactions take place in the mind, and all brain circuits get damaged. The knees go weak, the mouth automatically gapes, something stiffens, and an uncontrollable urge to say any gibberish takes over.

Jayanthi said, 'Listen, team work is the most important thing and we help each other out here.'

I nodded and said, 'Yes madam.'

She said, 'Just call me Jayanthi, that will do.'

Raj and I said in unison, 'Ok Jayanthi.'

That evening, Raj imitated Mani. He put a towel around his neck and it looked like a cape. He stood on his mattress and said, 'Rule # 1—don't piss with me. Rule # 2—whenever I enter the room, bend and show me your ass. Rule # 3—I screw you, and you have no right to screw me back. Rule # 4—My subjects, thou shall obey me. Rule # 5—Don't do anything on your own, do what I tell you to do.'

Then he concluded by giving a Nazi salute and said, 'Hail Hitler.'

We started laughing and I hugged Raj. As I said, I loved hugging and irritating him.

He said, 'No, go away. Saala, you are a pain.'

Adi and I burst out laughing.

That day we nicknamed Mani – 'Hitler'. It suited his personality well. Adi downloaded Mani's picture from the Net and added a 'Hitler mush' to his picture, scanned it and circulated among us. The picture was absolutely hilarious. I forwarded it to Anjali and Srila. Srila forwarded it to some of her TCS friends in Chennai.

All of us had a good laugh.

Mid-Term Evals

SINCE MY JOB WAS TO DOCUMENT FUNCTIONALITY, I STARTED spending time with all the module leads and software engineers who reported to them. They had to explain what they were doing. At times, when they were stuck with a software program, which was often the case, I also sat down with them to understand as well as help them with whatever little I could. Interestingly, none were too happy explaining the functionality for me to document, because not everybody understood the holistic picture and most were focused on their respective smaller pieces of work. During my interactions with the team, some dumped a portion of their work on me and I gladly accepted it. After all, we stood for teamwork, right? Soon I made friends with most of the teammates and everybody started calling me VSAT.

Once a week, Hitler called for a stand-up project review meeting to understand what we were doing. Stand-up meetings were really funny; somebody said it was 'agile methodology', each one of us had to speak for a minute or two. People spoke about what they were doing and nobody connected the dots. Mani goaded us to fill timesheets and project trackers. Everybody followed that to a 'T', because nobody dared to cross Hitler.

Four months into the project, one day Savitha called me and said, 'VSAT, I am going home for a few days, can you help code a piece of work and submit it to Jayanthi by next week?'

I said, 'Sure Savitha, will do.' Obviously we were working as a team.

Once I got deep into it, I realised that there was a lot more to do and it was not a small piece of work. So, I stopped doing documentation for a week and focused on completing Savitha's work. I worked over the weekend too. I started by understanding the functionality and then the project architecture. After that I started programming. It took me almost eight days of continuous hard labour to get to some level of completion.

Anjali, Adi and Raj asked me, 'What is wrong? Why are you working so hard?'

I explained the project's functionality, architecture and what I was doing. Adi, whose understanding of architecture was much better than any of us said, 'That architecture is outdated, we can do better. Probably that is the reason it is taking so much time to code.'

I said, 'Exactly, why don't we attempt to re-architect? Why don't we write a concept paper first?'

Everybody agreed to participate and for the next few weeks, Adi, Raj and I worked hard on the new framework and came out with a white paper. Then Raj and I sought a meeting with Jayanthi and explained how we could re-architect the project. Jayanthi liked what we came up with. She discussed our white paper with Savitha and Harpreet, packaged it well and presented it to Hitler. Hitler presented it to Sankar and they pitched it to the client. Cathy Baker, the client from North Eastern Drinks (NED) liked the concept paper and agreed to go ahead with the architecture revamp and that was a big win for the project.

Hitler called a team meeting and announced a spot award for Harpreet, Savitha and Jayanthi for doing such a wonderful job. He said, 'I am thankful to the team for working well on the project. Without their stupendous effort, we would not have got past Cathy.'

In passing he said, 'Thanks to Raj and VSAT—the new members, for their efforts.'

Jayanthi, Savitha and Harpreet felt on top of the word and pinned the spot award certificates to their desks. Each of them got ₹1000 as gift vouchers.

Raj and I felt totally dejected. We had done most of the work and had got absolutely no recognition. That evening, Raj bought some beer and all of us sat down for a long griping session. Griping is a big stress-buster; it motivates you to go to the office next day. I guarantee that if griping were removed from software engineers' lives, absenteeism would soar and shrinks would thrive.

Adi said, 'Hitler *bada kameena nikla yaar.* How could he do that?'

Raj was angry. He said, 'Even Jayanthi, Savitha, Harpreet also didn't support us yaar.'

I said, 'Jayanthi is the lead, she should have atleast acknowledged us. Where is the teamwork out here man?'

Adi said, 'Teamwork ... my foot.'

I asked Raj, 'How is your testing coming up?'

Raj said, 'If functionality and coding keep changing, what do you expect me to test? It is like firing at a moving target. I am just going through the motions and not enjoying at all. How is your documentation coming up?'

I said, 'Hitler called me the other day and told me to do technical documentation as well. It is almost five months now and I have not finished the full functional documentation because it is all so disjointed and besides I hardly get support from anybody.'

Adi enquired with concern, 'Mid-term evaluation is just round the corner. What will you guys do?'

Raj asked, 'Adi, how is it going for you?'

Adi said, 'I have automated my backend, and it throws up an email and an SMS alert every time the stock moves below a threshold, so

I pretty much have nothing to do other than monitor the screens. That is why I could spare the time for the white paper. Ashish, my project manager, feels that I could do more.'

I asked, 'So, what do you think we should do?'

Both of them were quiet for a few minutes.

Then Raj said, 'Can't do much. We have to wait and see.'

Adi changed the topic and asked me, 'So, when are you speaking to Anjali's parents?'

I was so busy for the last few months that I had not thought about it. Poor Anjali had not pushed me at all.

In the past few months Anjali and I had made love a few times at her place. Making love to Anjali was a great stress buster. We looked forward to such occasions. After one such long love-making session, I asked, 'Anju, why don't you and I move in together?'

She mocked at me, 'Yes, why don't we have a few kids too? You have no idea of the amount of risk I am taking by sleeping with you. I am sure no one in my family would have done what I am doing.'

I said, 'How do you know? People don't discuss their sex lives, Anju. It is common for people to have pre-marital sex.' Even Khusboo endorses it.

'Who is that?' asked Anjali.

I said, 'That Tamil film actress yaar.'

Anjali sighed and said, 'But I still believe that I am the first one in my family to have pre-marital sex.' She sounded so confident as if ORG-MARG had done some opinion poll of her family member's sex lives. Imagine asking Anjali's grandmom, 'Ajji, did you have pre-marital sex?' She would probably give her best toothless grin and say, 'Actually that wouldn't have mattered much because I got married on attaining puberty at fourteen and there was no stopping after that!'

I set aside my thoughts and said, 'Are you feeling good about it or not?'

She smiled and hugged me. When you don't get an answer for such questions, it meant things were okay.

She had never asked me to talk to her parents, except for the first time when we had made love.

Anjali asked me, 'Don't Raj and Adi have girlfriends?'

I said, 'Raj is a free-hitter, I mean he likes girls, especially Divya.'

Anjali said, 'Divya? But she is older than him. Did he talk to you about Divya?'

I said, 'So what if she is older? He didn't tell me anything about Divya. But he seems to be fond of her.'

She asked, 'Are they sleeping around?'

I said, 'You women love to gossip, don't you? How do we care yaar? If they are, Raj will tell us one day.' Anjali asked, 'What about Adi? Doesn't he have a girlfriend?'

I said 'Adi and girlfriends! I have never seen him with girls and he doesn't talk about them anyway.'

She giggled and said, 'Probably, Adi is gay.'

I didn't say anything. For a moment, I wondered if it was true. 'No way,' I said. 'Which girl will fall for Adi anyway? He loves his food, drinks his brain out and loves software architecture. Nothing else interests him.'

A few weeks passed. Jayanthi and Hitler called me to discuss my mid-term appraisal. Hitler started the conversation.

'The good news is you are working hard and the bad news is you haven't completed what is assigned to you. Results don't show.'

Jayanthi nodded. I said, 'Mani sir, you know that the functionality is disjointed and I have been pulled into so many things in the last six months, obviously I couldn't complete the full documentation. Also, none of the team members are willing to share the full functional and technical documentation. For example, Anjan is the worst. He never tells me anything, so how do I document? How do you expect me to complete my work, sir?'

I didn't want to say that Anjan was born with earphones. He never removed them. How could one have meaningful conversations with somebody whose ears were always plugged? Similarly, imagine having a conversation with Srinivas. One day, I asked him to explain functionality and he told me the story of one of Mahesh Babu's Telugu films called *Athadu*, a blockbuster. I got to know that Mahesh Babu could knock down concrete poles with his bare fists.

When I sat down with him, Manoj showed me his photo album. Savitha discussed things about her in-laws. Spiky Neil talked about Angelina Jolie's adoptions and her relationship with Brad Pitt. Divya talked about perfumes—her favourite was JLo. She took it from her bag and sprayed it on my wrist. The cold mist tickled my skin. She didn't know that I had bad sinuses and most perfumes smell the same to me and at times I can barely smell them.

It was a freaking circus. How could I document functionality with this kind of team?

Hitler said, 'You seem to be having an issue working with people. Teamwork is an issue? People work hard to complete things and you seem to be stuck on the wrong things.'

I said, 'But I was helping the team, I have been the perfect team worker. Raj, Adi and I also wrote the white paper which Cathy Baker appreciated. She agreed to revamp the project.'

Jayanthi butted in, 'What you did was too rudimentary and we had to change and improvise so much.'

Of course it was a lie, but I couldn't say, 'You guys hardly improvised, you just submitted what we did.' Raj and Anjali had cautioned me to keep my temper in check.

I said, 'Sir, give us a chance to re-architect the solution.'

Mani smirked, 'You will re-architect the solution?'

I said, 'Sir, I understand functionality reasonably well. I could with some help from the team, join the disjointed pieces and we can get a holistic picture. With help from a few team members, we can arrive at a comprehensive platform to address the needs of all the modules.'

Hitler pushed back, 'You seem to have forgotten the rules which I told you when you joined my project? What did I say? The boss is always right and don't do things which you are not assigned. Did I tell that or not?'

I said, 'Yes sir, you did.'

'Then?'

'Nothing sir'

Mani added, 'Look VSAT, at the rate you guys are going, you are heading for a below-expectation rating. So, I suggest you to stick to your deliverables. You have no clue what re-architecting a platform means. Writing a white paper is different from actually doing it.'

Jayanthi quipped, 'First, finish documenting and complete the assigned programming work, then we can discuss re-architecture.'

When the hero flexes his muscles, the sidekick also displays courage. I thought of Salman Khan and Johnny Lever, not a bad combination. There are similarities between software projects and Bollywood movies. The success formulae are the same. One villain, one hero, one sidekick, one heroine-cum-vamp-cum-item girl, one sister who gets raped, mother who is blind, father a government servant, who is implicated falsely and languishing in jail.

I said, 'But nobody in the team has the hang of it. That's why the code redundancy is so high. Give us a chance and we can try.'

Mani shook his head and said, 'Ok. Get going now. I'll see you at the weekly meetings. Focus on your work, be a team worker and don't screw up. You are bordering on PIP (Performance Improvement Plan). One more mistake and you will hit the bottom. Dismissed.'

I wanted to give him a Nazi salute and walk out; instead, I just left.

I had finished my first corporate mid-term appraisal and to say the least, it was a disaster. I went back to my desk and stared at the blank computer screen. I was visibly upset. Savitha asked from the next cubicle, 'All well? You don't look all right.'

I said, 'I am fine Savitha. No problems.'

She caringly said, 'No problem, you can confide in me.'

I melted, 'That idiot Hitler says that I am heading for below expectation rating because my results don't show, but I have been busting my ass for a long time.'

She asked, 'Hitler ... who?'

I said, 'Mani, who else?' She started laughing at the nickname and said, 'That is an interesting name.'

I barely smiled.

She said, 'Don't worry yaar, you still have six months to go and things will be okay.'

Meanwhile, Hitler and Jayanthi had finished Raj's mid-term appraisal and a similar feedback was given to him. Raj came out of Hitler's cabin with a frown. I felt good that I was not alone. It always feels good to have company, especially when the ship is sinking. The movie *Titanic* is a classic example. People felt secure and thought of love, even when they were getting screwed. The ship tanked and the movie grossed USD 1.8 billion in revenues. De Caprio became a superstar, Kate Winslet became a global icon, Celine Dion arrived and we continued to code.

Raj came straight to me and said, 'I want to leave.'

I said, 'Yup, me too. Let us take the 6 pm bus today.'

He said, 'Moron, I mean I want to leave the company. That fellow Hitler is a dictator. He says, I have no clue about testing programs. I have been spending sleepless nights here trying to figure out how to test a moving target. Tell me, can anyone do it?'

I just shrugged and said, 'We can talk about this later Raj. People are looking at us.'

He walked back to his cubicle.

Raj opened his chat line and pinged me.

Raj: So what do you say? Jump ship?

VSAT: Let us talk tonight.

Raj: You won't chicken out, right?

VSAT: You are emotional now.

Raj: Screw emotions man. Hitler treats me like dirt.

Anjali and Adi saw us live on the chat board and jumped in.

Adi: What are you guys talking about?

VSAT: Hitler screwed us in the appraisal, said we are heading for below expectations.

Anjali: BE??? You guys must have really screwed up.

Raj: Anjali, you are saying this? We screwed up? What is wrong with you?

Adi: Take it easy guys, things will settle down.

VSAT: Raj says we should leave TCS and wants to talk about it.

Anjali: You guys are crazy. One feedback and you want to leave? Weirdoes!

VSAT: Guys, can we cool it for the time being. I am getting out of the chat. We can talk later. Bye for now.

Raj: What kind of friends do I have, people who don't support me?

Anjali: We support you Raj, it is just that you are being impulsive. Let's talk later.

Adi: Anjali, how did your appraisal go?

Anjali: Let us talk later guys. Bye.

Adi: Chal Raj ... baad mein ... bye ...

All of us dropped off the chat board and got back to work.

Arun Gupta and Shikhar gave a glowing feedback to Anjali. I expected she would come out with flying colours. She has a way with people and manages their perceptions, besides she is a hard worker. They identified her as a person with great potential and told her so.

Ashish Srivastav, Adi's manager thought that he was a lazy bum and warned him, 'Take initiative or you will continue where you are. Fortunately, the client feels that you are doing well, so you are heading towards the "marginally meeting expectations" rating.'

Adi didn't expect any better anyway.

Bottom line: As of now, all three of us were at the 'almost bottom 10%' of the performance curve. There was consistency in our scatter graph; it converged at the bottom left-hand side quartile once again. We are like homing pegions; leave us anywhere you want to and we eventually end up in the bottom left hand quartile. Feels nice, you know!

Nicknames

A COUPLE OF WEEKS PASSED BY AND JUST WHEN I THOUGHT life had come back to normal, Raj and I got a one-liner email from Mani. It read,

My Dear Able Lieutenants,

Meet me at 11 am. I will buy you both coffee for being so creative.

Yours truly,

Hitler

Below the mail was a photo of Mani with the Hitler mush, the one Adi had created. Some moron must have circulated the photo over the Net and it had finally made its way to Hitler's mailbox. I quickly typed 'Mani and Hitler' in the images section of Google and the image popped up. I knew we were in trouble. Nothing should be put on the Net. Everything gets digitised, stored for posterity and returns to you at the worst time of your life, when you least need it. As per Murphy's law, you never get the file which you desperately seek, instead you will end up getting all the old files which you deleted and don't need at all, *ever!*

As soon as Raj saw the mail, he ran to my desk and I looked up.

He anxiously asked, '*Tu ne bataya*? Moron, tell me you didn't screw up again?'

I said, 'I kind of blurted out his nickname to Savitha, didn't expect it to reach him, Raj.'

Raj smirked, 'You are a fucking genius. Why did you tell her?'

I said, 'One day I was upset and cussed his name out and she caught it.'

Raj smiled and said, 'Now, we can have a nice cup of coffee, pack our bags and go home. Get ready to kiss the company and your babe goodbye.'

I kind of thoughtfully said, 'Let us see. We will apologise.'

Raj rolled his eyeballs in exasperation and said, 'If you apologise, it means you agree to have coined the nickname. Best would be to flatly deny it VSAT. Just say not guilty and get out of the mess man.'

I said, 'You think he will buy that? He is freaking Hitler man. By now, he must have figured out everything.'

Raj said, 'So what? Nobody can prove it.'

I said, 'Ok, let's play it by ear.'

Sharp at 11am, we went to Hitler's cabin. He asked us to come in. As soon as we entered, he laughed. He said, 'My trusted lieutenants, why aren't you saying "Hail Hitler"? Come on, salute me now.'

I said, 'Sorry sir.' Raj completed the sentence for me, 'We don't understand what you are saying.'

Hitler added a huge potion of sarcasm to the medley and said, 'Oh, you pure souls, you have no idea what I am talking about, right?' Mani could really get sarcastic when he wanted to. He could beat anybody on this act. It was a talent he was born with, definitely not acquired. Some people are gifted, what to do!

I continued to stare blankly and I have a unique capability to put on a blank face that I believe, even the best interrogators from the CIA and FBI could get flummoxed at times. I think I can even fib the polygraph comfortably. Again, a hidden talent!

Hitler continued, 'You don't get results, your work stinks, you are almost in the bottom 10% in our performance, you give nicknames to me and you circulate my picture with a Hitler mush on the Net?'

We didn't respond. Obviously, he knew everything.

I said, 'Sorry sir, but we didn't circulate it on the net. We just coined the name "Hitler" sir and nothing else sir. It is for fun, sir.' Hitler smiled and said, 'Ok, atleast you agreed. Now both of you listen carefully, stop all this nonsense and put your heads down and work hard. I am putting you on PIP. You know what PIP means, right? "Performance Improvement Plan." I have asked Amit from HR to talk to you guys.' Raj looked bewildered and I was almost shaking.

I was almost on the verge of tears and said, 'Sir, please sir. Don't put us on PIP. We are doing what we can and we will do better.'

Hitler said, 'Go talk to Amit and justify yourselves. If he agrees to your plea, I will talk to you guys again.'

Raj and I hurriedly walked to Amit's cabin. He was talking on the phone and signalled us to wait. Once he was done, he called us in and asked, 'How are you guys? Mani briefed me about your performance. What is the issue?'

I said, 'Sir, there is no issue. Project functionality, technical docs and design are not in good shape. It is like a moving target and we are finding it difficult to document or test it. In addition, we get pulled into odd jobs and Mani sir says we are not meeting expectations. We don't know what to do sir.'

Adding 'sir' at the end of each sentence started all over again.

Amit asked, 'How well do you know Anjali?'

I was stunned. This had nothing to do with the topic at hand. Raj had told me ahead of time, 'Remember HR guys have a unique ability to mix things up and come out with conspiracy theories. They can connect unrelated things and make it look real. They could even concoct and prove the story that both of us were harassing Anjali in absentia.'

I said, 'She is our batchmate from college.'

Amit said, 'Oh really, I didn't know that.'

I thought, 'Conspiracy theory … play it safe.'

I said, 'Sir, we are friends and we go around.'

Amit sighed, 'Yes, I know. Just keep your "friendship" off-premises and if either of you become pregnant, don't come back running and create a mess for us. Office relationships go only so far.'

Connected unrelated things, forecasted the future and issued a warning. That is the power these guys wield on innocent software engineers like us. I felt crucified, I prayed quickly: Lord, please pardon them, for they know not, what they are doing and secondly please get me out of this hell hole!

I almost grinned but I controlled my laughter and said, 'Yes sir.'

Amit turned to Raj. 'Sir-ji, I heard you are great at giving nicknames to seniors. Here is a chance, what would my nickname be?'

Raj said, '*Aisa kuch nahi hai* sir. Generally sir.'

Amit said, 'It is ok Raj sir. If you had to give me a nickname, what would it be sir?'

Raj smirked. 'Nothing sir. Why would I give a nickname to you? You are such a sweet person.'

Amit laughed uncontrollably. He said, 'I am a sweet person. That is wonderful to know. Nevertheless, come on, give it a try.'

Raj scratched his forehead, grinned and blurted out, 'Pappu sir.'

I almost fell off my chair. Amit looked at me in utter disbelief. Instantly his eyes narrowed and lips twitched.

I knew that Raj had just kissed our jobs goodbye.

Amit relaxed back in his chair and said, 'Pappu? Ha ha ha, what a cute name! But Raj sahab, why Pappu?'

I suddenly thought of Cuba Gooding Jr in the movie *Men of Honor* and with deep aplomb, I said, 'Sir, I know it is over. There is no point in any further discussion. Both of us are willing to tender our resignations peacefully. You can relieve us honourably.'

Raj grinned and dug further. 'Sir, in the North, Pappu and Guddu are standard pet names. I just picked Pappu sir, it sounds cute.' Perhaps he had given up all hopes, so he decided to have fun? Whatever it is, he was on a freaking roll!

Amit laughed aloud. He looked very amused actually. With deep sarcasm and a twitchy grin he said, 'That is great, you boys are very creative, if I hear anybody calling me by that name, it will be my pleasure to fire you guys. Until then you survive.'

I said, 'Thank you sir, I mean okay sir.'

Amit shook his head in complete dismay and said, 'Ok boys, I am preparing the PIP documentation for both of you. Come tomorrow and sign it. You will be on a ninety-day performance improvement plan with specific objectives. If you don't meet them, we will help you get a job with the competition.'

Raj jerked his head sideways and innocently asked, 'How can you get us jobs with the competition sir?'

I was wondering where this conversation was leading. Amit said, 'Simple, we will float your names with external recruitment consultants and tell them that you are our best performers and they will pick you up and we won't resist. They will make an offer which you guys cannot refuse.'

A voice in my head screamed, 'The Godfather! Don Vito Corleone, I am gonna make him an offer he can't refuse.' From that moment onwards, whenever Pappu spoke, I was reminded of the movie The Godfather!

Amit Bagaria was in his mid-thirties. His hair was thinning but he tactfully covered the bald patch. He weighed about ninety kilos and had a squarish jaw and a drooping moustache. His small eyes narrowed when he smiled, one could see only the pupils and they looked pretty piercing. Anyway, to the best of my knowledge, most HR people looked like that, so the difference was not significantly discernable.

Raj and I looked at each other and I said, 'Sir, would you like to reconsider? This is our first job and the first appraisal of our life, please give us a chance sir.'

Amit smiled, 'If you guys do well in thirty to forty-five days, then we can always reconsider. Ok now, get going and come see me tomorrow.'

Raj walked out with me and said, 'How is the name Pappu? Or did you prefer Guddu?'

I was shaking with anger and said, 'Raj, today I whole-heartedly certify you as the "greatest moron on planet earth"; nobody can dare to beat you to that title. Do you realise that you have successfully screwed up whatever little chances we had? Now what do we do?'

Raj smiled. 'Let us do our best. If things work out, TCS will be fortunate to have us. Else we will leave and join the competition.'

I was miserable. I said, 'Do you know that if you leave during or after PIP, nobody gives you a job? I feel very messed up.'

The image of my dad flashed in front of me. I imagined him saying, 'What did I tell you, Tatas always take good care of people. "*You*" must have screwed up.' In the situation we were in, parents would always side with Ratan Tata and not with their wards. Imagine a picture where Ratan Tata and I are standing next to each other. Who would anybody believe? Take a guess!

Raj said, 'Don't be dejected my friend. Look at me—take it easy. There is no point in fighting a losing battle. If things don't really work out, we can join my dad's Maruti car dealership in Delhi and sell "pre-owned" cars.'

I asked, 'Pre-owned?'

'Used cars yaar.'

I imagined myself selling a battered Maruti Esteem, trying to negotiate a deal with a rude Delhi customer and the customer loudly calling me '*chutiya*' and I immediately came back to my senses.

I said, 'Are you freaking crazy?'

I silently walked to my cubicle. Sometimes silence is sobering; obviously I couldn't instantly switch on my headphones and listen to rock-music. I am not Anjan anyway. At that moment, I felt that he too had a unique talent of compartmentalising everything.

Raj said, 'Let's get some beer after work and gripe our hearts out.'

Given the circumstances we were in, it was the best possible idea. Anjali agreed to join us at our place.

After drowning a few beers Raj said, 'My father says, people lose out not because they are not intelligent, but because they are not street-smart. I think he is so goddamn right. If we had sucked up to Jayanthi and Hitler, then we would also have shone like the rest of the crowd.'

Adi said, 'At this rate, we are going to be unsuccessful, just like the way we were at the Insti.'

I said, 'What do you mean Adi? I thought we were fairly okay there.'

Raj said, 'Fairly okay means almost bottom 10% VSAT. All our lives we are only fairly okay.'

Anjali said, 'And you guys gave a nickname to Amit! What is wrong with you? Morons!'

Raj looked at Anjali and said, 'Birds of the same feather flock together madam! If we are morons, ask yourself who you are.'

There was a pause and Anjali turned her third eye on me. I ducked her glare and escaped unhurt, else I would not have been alive today to tell this story.

Raj said, 'Amit is a real Pappu and I was anyway sure that he will screw us, so I had some fun. By the way, he knows you and VSAT are a couple.'

Anjali was shocked. She asked, 'What? How does he know?'

Adi said, 'Come on guys, everybody knows it, what is the big secret here?'

Anjali had tears in her eyes. She asked me, 'So, when do you intend to talk to your parents? Once you lose your job?' Remember, if you see tears in your girlfriend's eyes, just duck, irrespective of whether it is your mistake or not. You will be undoubtedly the object of her deep consternation.

I said, 'Cool down guys. Anju, I love you, please have patience. Everything will work out fine.' Tears can be overcome 'only' by bravado and nothing else.

Anjali said, 'How?'

I said, 'I have a plan.'

Raj said, 'Not again. I am not doing any more white papers. It's a big waste of time. This time around, our Kerala cousins Josy and Joby will get the spot award. In the last six months, the only two words we heard from the Kerala cousins was "yes sir" and "yes madam" and they are presumably in the top 15%.' I had always seen Mani being overtly patronising towards them. I wondered momentariy if Mani was a heterosexual indulging in "group orgies". Anyway, it didn't matter now and I didn't want to start another Internet chain mail—'send this mail to ten more and your libido will increase. True it happened to all the previous people who forwarded the mail.'

Also, what Raj said was true, white papers are written by consultants and they are best read and least implemented. They are like porn for management consulting business. Great to visualise, but not so great when it comes to actually making things happen.

I said, 'At least listen to what I am saying guys.'

Adi said, 'Bol ... bol.What do you want us to do this time?'

I said, 'Let us do a parallel project this time. I mean let us complete what is assigned to us and in parallel, complete the architecture revamp and showcase it. The functionality is anyway disjointed and nobody knows it better than us. So why don't we do it? What do you say?'

Anjali said, 'Why don't we ask Mani to give us a chance to do it?'

I said, 'I asked, he dismissed me unceremoniously.'

Hearing the idea, Adi's eyes lit up. He loved secret projects and anything remotely related to architecture and design. Adi said, 'Sounds good. I don't have anything to do anyway. I can spend most of my time on it.' I think Adi secretly thought he was 'Chet' in Enid Blyton books. Though physically oversized, he had not grown mentally.

Anjali said, 'I can spare some time too and we can pull in Srila if need be.'

Raj looked at the three of us and said, 'Ok, I will work on testing the design, provided VSAT documents the functionality. It has to be really limited in scope. Else we will kill ourselves.'

I said, 'Fine. We have a plan. Remember guys, re-architecting is going to take atleast six months if not more, so brace yourselves.'

Recognition from Steve

We met Amit Bagaria the following day. He gave us letters with detailed terms and conditions. I had four objectives to comply within the ninety-day plan—

- Complete Functional Documentation (Write what has to be coded. You are screwed if you ask questions)
- Complete Technical Documentation (Write what has been coded, please don't try to innovate)
- Be an effective team worker (Smile and say 'yes', don't be a smart ass, don't ask questions)
- Maintain office decorum (Don't assign nicknames, especially to seniors and yeah, don't get pregnant)

I barely read and signed the letter. In any case Pappu wouldn't change a word in the letter. Raj had three objectives: Complete test pack for two modules, be an effective team worker and maintain office decorum. He also signed the papers. We were now the accomplished lot, the only guys from the fresher batch who had the unique distinction of being on PIP within a year of joining.

Dad called on the day I got the PIP letter and he ended the conversation by saying, 'Wasn't I right? TCS is a people-oriented company and guarantees a lifetime career.'

I meekly said, 'Yes Pa, it is a great company.'

He said, 'You don't seem to be convinced.'

I reaffirmed his view, 'I know it is a good company Pa.'

'So, are you enjoying yourself?'

I replied, 'Yes Pa.' Life screws you with wrong questions at the worst times.

Then mom came on the line and excitedly asked, 'So, when are they sending you to the US?' Another screwed up question. I was not sure whether they would keep me in the company after ninety days and my mom was asking about the US! But I didn't want to disappoint her. I said, 'Maybe next year Mom.'

She said, 'Ask them not to delay, Raghuveer, our neighbour, who works for Wipro has already gone to the US. Do you want me to make some laddoos for your manager? I used to make them and give them to your dad. He used to gift them to the DEO (District Education Officer).'

I looked at my office, the carpeted floors, my desk, an air-conditioning vent, my PC, the IP phones. I could not relate to laddoos and DEOs. They were two different and completely disjointed worlds. Me, the modern software engineer, was the only connect between these two worlds. I had to swim in both these oceans of emotions simultaneously. I was turning philosophical. After all, it was not a bad alternative in the given circumstances.

I said, 'Sure Mom.'

Parents in Andhra have only one dream: Sending their sons to the US. Though money is perceived as the prime component, it is not really so. It is the pride associated with saying, 'My son is in Colorado' that ticks parents to push their wards. For all you know he might be filling gas in petrol stations which is totally acceptable there as a noble way of earning and learning. (Not in India, of course!)

Swati came on the line and said, 'So, have you quit smoking?'

I was irritated. I said, 'Swatiiiiii ... can you just shut up?' I smoked only when I had drinks. I drank only when we griped. And we griped a lot. Remember Sholay—Amitabh Bachchan takes Dharam paaji's proposal to the *buddhi* Mousi to seek Hema Malini's (Basanti's) hand in marriage and the ensuing dialogue?

Mom came back. She said, 'Kanna, don't smoke *ra*, it spoils your health. Promise me now. Do you drink too?'

I said, 'Mom, I have to go now.' And I disconnected.

My family still lives in the 1900s. I wondered how they would contend with colonel and family. That was going to be another battle to fight. Ah, why does life offer so many battles? Why can't it be smoother? Maybe I wasn't praying enough. So I prayed at that very instant, 'Lord, I am an average guy, almost at the bottom 10 %, so you should not be putting me through this ordeal. Instead you should test the top 10% folks like Jayanthi, Joby, Josy, etc., because they always get rewarded anyway. Just make life easier for us, please.'

I started working with renewed vigour on functional documentation. My first conversation was with Srinivas.

I asked, 'So, in your module, what are the key parametres that you are programming?

Srinivas said, 'Do you know something? In the film *Pokiri*, Mahesh Babu wore Levis jeans which were ...'

'Do you look at integration of these parametres with other ...'

Srinivas said, 'The jeans were torn at the knee. It was a style ...'

'Do you program at the component level?'

Srinivas said, 'Mahesh Babu is called The Prince.'

'Srinivas, Srinivas—can we talk about functionality please?'

'Ok. Once we finish with the dialogue of ...'

I patiently listened to Srinivas and then he answered my questions on functionality.

I approached Anjan next. He removed one earphone from his left ear and asked, 'Yes?'

I said, 'Functionality.'

He said, 'Yeah.'

I asked, 'Which pieces are you working on and how do they tie at the architecture level?'

He said, 'Analytics.'

'What in analytics?'

He said, 'Reporting.'

'What reporting?'

He said, 'MIS.'

I asked, 'What MIS?'

He said, 'Stocks.'

I asked, 'What stocks?'

He said, 'Soft drinks?'

I got thoroughly frustrated. I said, 'Anjan, if you keep answering in monosyllables like this, how do you expect me to document?'

There was a pause. He said, 'Let us have beer in my room tonight and I will explain.' Now 'functionality' and 'beer' would go hand in hand. Somehow, I remembered that the movie 'Superman' was made in Telugu and NTR, the evergreen super mega star of the Telugu silver screen wore the red underwear outside and the film turned out to be a blockbuster.

I agreed and went to his room with my notepad and pen. We had beer and he opened up. Words tumbled out of his mouth. Not everything he spoke was related to work, but nevertheless he spoke and that was important. I wished they would allow him to drink in the office too.

A couple of weeks later Hitler called me and said, 'Cathy Baker assigned Steve Turner to work on functionality. So, I have no choice but to make you interact with Steve. Remember, if you fuck with Steve, I will roast you alive.'

I thought, 'Nice encouragement, great pep talk, improves my motivation levels. You could make a good coach for Indian Hockey!'

Hitler continued, 'Remember, the customer is God and is always right. Don't ask too many questions. Follow instructions carefully and execute them well. Tell me if Steve gives any feedback. I have asked Jayanthi to join in the first few calls.'

Assigning a secret agent to track me! Madam M in James Bond movies looked like Mother Teresa to me.

I said, 'Yes sir.'

The very next day, I got a mail from Steve Turner. It was a nice, warm mail and he set up a conference call for our first discussion. The call started at the designated date and time. Even if his wife was hanging at the edge of a cliff, an American will call at the designated date and time and inform others about the status. He would dial into the con-call and say something like this, 'Good evening everybody, I have bit of an emergency. My wife is hanging from a cliff out there and I have to run to help her, so I can't take the call today. Any questions?' If a stupid software guy asks, 'How come she's hanging from the cliff?' He would respond, 'I caught her with an another guy, I started to chase them and she tripped, so she is hanging out there, from the cliff. Any more questions?' If there were no more questions, he would continue, 'Great, I am glad all of you understood. Since there are no more questions, I will go back to rescue her. Meanwhile, I will ask my secretary to reschedule our call for tomorrow same time. Thanks everybody, have a nice day and appreciate your kind gesture in letting me go and attend to my wife' and then he would disconnect the call. They are made like that. Centuries of uncertainty have drilled way too much predictable behaviour in them. They call this zany behaviour, 'professionalism'. I have no problem with them as long as it is their wives who are hanging from the edge of their cliffs. On the other hand many of my colleagues drop calls with the weirdest of excuses. The other day somebody wanted to drop off a call saying, 'It is the Snake God festival' and that they had to pour milk into the ant-hill. Most Americans are respectful of religious customs and let him off. Before he was let off the call, he was asked, 'What do you mean by Snake God?' and the software engineer replied, 'Black King Cobra, is the Snake God.' The line went dead on the other side.

Steve started by saying, 'Good evening Jayanthi and Venkat. What time is it for you in Bangalore?'

Jayanthi replied, 'Good morning Steve. It is 7 pm here.'

Steve said, 'Uh, I am sorry for holding you guys late. Let us keep it short and simple. I am Steve Turner assigned by Cathy Baker to review and redraw the functionality document because that is core to defining our architecture. Venkat, since you are my contact person in Bangalore, we will set up calls once a week and review the progress.'

I said, 'Sure sir.'

Steve said, 'Just call me Steve, that is good enough.'

I noticed that Americans are addressed by first names and they take their calls during office hours and expect us to dial from homes at all odd hours. Weird, but I don't have a problem, because they have dollars and one dollar is equal to about forty-five rupees. When one rupee becomes forty-five dollars, probably they will learn Telugu, may be Hindi? Until then, we will continue with odd timings and first name basis and do what they want us to do.

I replied, 'Sure Steve, thank you.' This was my first interaction with an American client and I was quite nervous and nobody had made it easy for me so far anyway.

Steve ended the call by saying, 'Thank you for staying late. Jayanthi, from now on, I will deal with Venkat and you won't have to waste your time attending calls with us.'

The American government had asked the Russian spy to stay away from the Indian interactions. I felt great about Jayanthi not joining our calls anymore. She was a pain of the first order.

The call went smoothly and afterwards the spineless Jayanthi said, 'Take care VSAT, he is a very important client for us.'

I nodded.

In my next call to Steve, he asked me about the status of the documentation. I explained to him what I was doing and sought his advice. He said, 'You are doing great, keep working. Make sure you document all the changes in the new version of the document.'

I liked Steve. He was very supportive. Within the next few calls, we established good rapport. During one of our calls, he asked me my full name and I told him it is 'Venkata Subramaniam Adisankara Tanikaburla.' He struggled to pronounce my full name. He asked, 'What do your friends call you?'

I said, 'They took the first alphabet of each of my names and started calling me VSAT.' He was amused. He told me that he liked playing basketball and was from Boston. He was forty years old and divorced. He had a daughter from his first marriage and a foster son from his second marriage, and both were in college.

Steve asked if I had a girlfriend and I said I did.

He asked me whether it was common in India to have girlfriends. I kidded, 'Not really, it is a luxury item Steve, you have to pay entry and exit tax.' He laughed and our conversation continued. In the next two months, we became very close and he almost became my mentor and I started confiding in him. He helped me with his advice. Besides functional documentation, I spent a lot of time doing technical documentation too and turned it into a reasonable shape. Besides documentation, I had to do small pieces of programming that Jayanthi assigned to me from time to time.

On Monday, February 12, 2007, I had a scheduled a teleconference call with Steve, but I couldn't take it due to 'Bangalore bandh' and I sent him a quick mail on the previous Friday.

Dear Steve,

Hope you are well. Can't take call with you on Feb 12th, because of 'Bangalore bandh', called by some political parties to protest against the Cauvery water tribunal verdict with regard to sharing of water between Karnataka and Tamil Nadu.
Will catch up on Tuesday.

Regards,
VSAT

Steve replied:

Hi VSAT ... I didn't understand what you wrote. If you are taking off on Monday, enjoy the long weekend. Catch you next week ...

Regards,
Steve

I called Steve when I returned on Tuesday.

He asked, 'Did you have a good vacation combined with a nice long weekend. By the way, which "band" did you go for?'

I said, 'No, it was not a "band". It is "bandh", meaning ... hmm ... Bangalore was closed.'

Steve was perplexed. He asked, 'What do you mean?'

'Some political party called a general strike and asked everybody to shut shop.'

'But why?'

'Because they didn't like the verdict given by the court.'

'So, if a political party doesn't like a court verdict, they will ask everybody to shut shop and everybody does?'

I said, 'Not all the time, but yes, most of the time'

'And what if we don't shut shop?'

I said, 'They will break window panes and assault people who are going to work.'

'Wow, don't the government and police do anything?'

I said, 'Police help in peaceful closure of the city.'

'What?' said Steve.

'Yes, they make sure that the bandh is peaceful and typically on bandh days, they paint traffic signals on roads, like lines for Zebra crossing ... because there is no traffic.'

Steve laughed aloud.

'Ok. But what is the issue for closure?'

'There is a river called Cauvery, which flows from our state, that is Karnataka, into the neighbouring state called Tamil Nadu. Our state has built a dam on it and has not released water to the neighbouring state. The neighbouring state complained to the court stating that our state has to release a minimum amount of water and the court agreed with their view. So, the opposition of our state felt that the ruling party could not manage the situation well and hence called for a one-day bandh.'

There was a long pause.

I asked, 'Steve, are you there?'

'Yeah. I am here. Just thinking.'

'What?'

'I don't understand. Water sharing is the cause for closing office yesterday? But why can't you share?'

I replied, 'When the monsoon is bad, the river goes dry and there is insufficient water in the reservoir. So how can we share?'

'Huh? I still don't understand. ... What did you have for lunch today? Are you okay?'

I said, 'Chapati and daal, I mean bread and lentils. I am fine Steve.'

He grinned, 'I hope we will not have these kinds of incidents too often?'

I said, 'No. Not really. However, in the year 2000, we shut shop for almost three days when Veerappan kidnapped Rajkumar.'

Steve asked, 'Who are they?'

I said, 'Veerapaan was a bandit who lived in the jungles closeby and he kidnapped Rajkumar, a famous movie star.'

There was a long pause again.

'Steve?'

Steve said, 'I am here. Hey Venkat, why don't you take off today? You don't seem to be doing well. We can always catch up tomorrow.'

I said, 'I am fine Steve. Let us continue.'

He said, 'You have bandits kidnapping movie stars and all that going on there?'

I said, 'Steve, imagine Osama bin Laden kidnapping Tom Cruise, won't there be chaos in America?'

He burst out aloud. 'How in the world can that happen? And you guys still make quality software for us.'

Yes Steve, they are not related. I mean making software is not related to kidnapping.'

He said, 'And we are outsourcing our critical work to Bangalore.'

I said, 'No problem Steve ... we can manage.'

He said, 'God save America in the future.'

'Why Steve?'

'I don't mean to be rude, but you won't understand, so let us leave it at that.'

'Maybe.'

'Anyway, let us talk about work.'

I couldn't understand what Steve was thinking and he couldn't follow what I was saying. We lived in two different worlds, and though we didn't understand each other, we worked well together.

A few weeks later, I received a mail from Steve. Hitler and spineless Jayanthi were copied on the mail.

It read:

Dear Venkat

In my last one month of interaction with you, I found you resourceful, innovative and a solid team worker. I appreciate the work that you have done on functional documentation and thank you for your efforts.

Yours truly,
Steve

Hitler read the mail and sent him a reply at once:

Dear Steve

Thank you for the appreciative mail.
Venkat, thank you for doing such a wonderful job.

Regards,
Mani

Then he came over to my desk and said, 'VSAT, so the client is happy with you, huh?'

I said, 'Yes sir.'

He said, 'Did you ask him to send that mail or did he send it on his own?'

I stared at Mani and opened my third eye. It didn't work. It works only on peers and subordinates. Since, I didn't have too many peers, it worked only on Adi and Raj. Since I was the last in the chain of command and had no subordinates, it didn't matter.

Hitler said, 'You know how it works. You guys convince dumb American clients and they send mails of appreciation. I was making sure that this was not the case. I will forward Steve's mail to Amit and try getting you out of PIP.'

When it came to being mean, Hitler surpassed my expectations every time. This time he could be rated, 'Significantly above expectations' for his meanness. I thought of presenting him a spot award of a book titled *Seven Habits of Highly Effective Mean Managers.*

I said, 'Great sir. Thank you sir. What about Raj sir?'

Hitler asked, 'What about him?'

'Can you please get Raj also out of PIP sir?'

Hitler smiled, 'You think I am running a sales promotion? Get one out of PIP and the other comes free? For that, Pappu has to agree.'

I remained silent.

Hitler continued, 'He has the guts to tell Amit that his nickname is Pappu?'

I said, 'Sir, he was just kidding.'

'Kidding with an HR guy by giving him a nickname? You guys are out of your minds. Anyway let me talk to Amit and see what I can do.'

Though unwillingly, I thought for a fleeting moment that Hitler had mellowed down and was considering repealing our PIP. That is called 'being positive and optimistic'. Somehow Robin Sharma and his book *The Monk Who Sold his Ferrari* took over my mind briefly.

I pinged Raj on the chat board.

VSAT: Hitler willing to take us off PIP. Steve sent appreciation mail. Mail enclosed.

Raj: Cool dude. That is great. Does he know about the re-architecture project that we are doing secretly?

VSAT: No, I haven't discussed with Steve or Hitler.

Raj: Don't—we aren't ready yet. Chalo, catch you later. Let me know if you hear from Hitler or Pappu.

VSAT: Next time you bump into Pappu ... tell him that you are sorry ... it might soften things up ...

Raj: I will try. VSAT, by the way, your functionality document has been useful. I have done extensive test coverage. Anjali helped me with some programs. She is good, man! I hope you are taking care of her.

VSAT: ☺Give her a spot award.

Raj: ☺Very Funny. Is Hitler giving you a spot for the client appreciation mail you got?

VSAT: You must be kidding, we are on the coveted PIP scheme, mate!

Raj: Yeah, understood. Ok, bye.

I then forwarded Steve's mail to Anjali. She called on my extension and whispered, 'Honeybunch, congrats.' That is a great mail. So is Hitler taking you off PIP? What about Raj?'

I said, 'Hitler said he will speak with Pappu.'

Anjali said, 'That is great news, treat today?'

I laughed. 'Which one?'

She giggled, 'You can't think of anything else, can you?'

'What to do, we are like that only no!'

That evening all of us went out for dinner and had a great time. There was a new ray of hope. After all, we were not going to be pushed out of TCS.

Next day, Pappu called both of us to his cabin and said, 'Ok boys, so what is new?'

I said, 'Sir, Mani sir must have spoken to you. We got good client feedback and have done well. Will you consider repealing our PIPs?'

Pappu leaned back, smiled and said, 'People in this company have started calling me Pappu. What do you want me to do? Tell me if you have any other bad news immediately.'

I heard a scream in my head, *The Godfather*! *'Mr Corleone is a man who insists on hearing bad news immediately.'*

Raj shook his head and I said, 'Sir, we never talked about it.'

Pappu sarcastically said, 'Probably my room is bugged and directly connected to the company's PA system?'

Scream in my head again, *The Godfather! 'Never tell anybody outside the family what you're thinking again.' For all you know some nerdy software engineer might write a program to bug the room and actually connect it to the PA system!*

Both of us grinned, but didn't dare respond.

Pappu said, 'Anyway, that is fine, can't be reason enough to fire you. Next time you get into trouble, you know what Uncle Pappu will do. You can go now. I will send you letters saying your PIPs are repealed.'

Both of us thanked him profusely and stepped out. As we were leaving, his secretary looked up from her desk, smiled mischievously and asked, 'So, are you done with Pappu?'

We winked at her and scooted from the HR bay. We were in high spirits. February had turned out to be a great month. Thanks to Steve, we were out of the PIP zone. Sehwag had a good season and was back in the national team.

We headed directly to the canteen and asked Adi and Anjali to join us. In the canteen, I hugged Raj. He said, 'Fuck! Shameless fellow. You are now hugging me everywhere and anywhere. Leave me now, leave me.' I burst out laughing and let him go.

Adi and Anjali joined us and we updated them about our conversation with Uncle Pappu.

Adi said, 'Let us put his name on the anonymous bulletin board yaar. *Bada maza aayega.*'

Anjali said, 'Sure! *Bahut maza aayega*, when they trace the message to your PC.'

Raj said, 'We will send it from Hitler's room. That will be our sweet revenge for landing us in this mess.'

Anjali was peeved. She looked at me and said, 'I can't stop these jokers, but VSAT you do anything remotely as idiotic as these guys are suggesting, I will hang you upside down and whack you.'

Raj said, 'Ah! The pleasures of life.'

Adi said, 'Let's send it from Hitler's cabin yaar'

I said, 'Guys, we just came out of a mess and you are planning the next one? Count me out.'

Raj said, 'Why are you chickening out? Where's the man in you?'

Anjali said, 'Guys, can we stop this shit right here?'

Everybody was quiet. But I knew that these jokers were up to something.

The next day, there was an advertisement on the company bulletin board. It read: Three-year-old Maruti Wagon R, going cheap. Contact Pappu at extension # 4254. The extension number belonged to Amit Bagaria and within the first one hour, he got ten calls asking, 'I am interested in buying the Wagon R, can we speak to Pappu?'

Amit huffed and went to the IT administrator and got the advertisement removed. I knew trouble was brewing. I took Raj with me and went to Amit's cabin. He asked us to come in. Even before he could say anything, I said, 'Sir, before you charge us with anything, let me upfront clarify that we didn't put up the ad.'

Amit said, 'Then who did? It has come from Mani's room and I am sure Mani would never do such a stupid thing. Don't act so innocent.'

Another scream in my head, *The Godfather! 'Only don't tell me you're innocent, because it insults my intelligence and makes me very angry.'*

I said, 'We don't know sir and we are not interested in getting involved.'

Pappu dismissed us with a wave and said, 'If it leads to you, it will be my pleasure to send you boys home ... trust me to do that!'

We nodded and left his room.

While heading back, I asked Raj, 'Did you?'

Raj vehemently denied it. Both of us went to Adi and he said, 'Yes baby, *mazaa aaya*? Wrote a program, which can be traced to Hitler's machine. Now Hitler and Pappu can fight.'

A scorned software engineer is his own worst enemy. As a race, software engineers have the inane capability to self-destruct.

We both looked amazed. We had never known this side of Adi.

I asked, 'Adi, what if it leads to you?'

Adi said, 'It can't. There is a bug in the program, which I exploited to create the ad. It's fun man, and nothing else.'

Anjali got to know of this. She yelled, 'Adi, you lunatic, you will screw it up for all of us. Raj and VSAT, stay away from Adi, I mean it.' She stomped away. Anjali doesn't usually stomp, but when she does, it is great to see her cheeks turning pink. She looks more beautiful than usual.

Raj and I told Adi not to repeat such crazy stuff, though both of us secretly loved what he had done. Hitler asked Raj, 'Did you do that?'

Raj put on an innocent look which even the CIA and FBI couldn't fathom and said, 'Sir, we just got out of our PIP, why would we risk it sir?'

Then Hitler turned to me and said, 'I know you did it.'

I said, 'Mother promise sir, I didn't do it.'

In our country, Mother promise is the ultimate weapon when you have to swear innocence. Nobody lies after they promise on their mother, because the mother is the most revered and important figure in society. (Remember Amitabh Bachchan in *Deewar*, '*Mere paas ma hai?*')

Hitler laughed.

He said, 'Anyway, the fatso deserved it. Pappu—great name you guys gave him! He screwed all our increments last year. Whoever put that ad on the Net is a fucking genius.'

I didn't respond. I was not sure if this was his way to extract a name. I just smiled. Sometimes interrogators become extremely sweet to extract information. No way was I going to fall for that!

Hitler said, 'VSAT, this Saturday we are celebrating my son's fourth birthday. Why don't you and Raj join us at home for dinner?'

I said, 'Sure sir. We will come.'

On Saturday night, Raj and I went to Hitler's house. All our teammates were also there. Anjali had gift-wrapped Fischer toys for us to give to Bala's wife, which we dutifully did. My mom's laddoos for the DEO was equal to the Fischer toys. Objects and times change, but the intent is always the same. Please the boss, his wife and his sons (stay away from the boss's daughters, your boss will never trust you with his daughters).

Hitler and family lived in a nice three-bedroom flat in Indiranagar. The room was decorated with balloons and ribbons. Hitler introduced us with these lines, 'Ladies and gentleman, I want to introduce Venkat and Raj—the guys who nicknamed me Hitler. They are the youngest members of my team.'

Everybody laughed. We just shrugged our shoulders and smiled.

Mani's wife was holding the four-year-old birthday boy. She smiled and said, 'Apt name. He is a Hitler at home too.' Mani's parents squirmed and his in-laws laughed. He offered us orange squash, samosa, mixture and *gulab jamun*. Mani's wife, Vaishnavi, was a typical Tamil housewife. Mani's parents had got him married to Vaishnavi before he went on his first US assignment. Apparently, they were worried that Mani would bring back a white American bride. I thought it was the most ludicrous thought anybody could have! Anyway, by the time Mani got his H1 visa stamped, he was married and since he was going on a long-term assignment, his wife also tagged along. Mani stayed in the US for a couple of years and made enough money to buy a car and a flat.

Raj asked Mani, 'Own flat?'

Mani smiled, 'Yes Raj. Anything wrong with our house?' That was his sense of humour, downright wobbly, but he is the boss and you have to laugh and everybody did.

Raj smiled and said, 'No sir, I was just asking.'

Mani laughed and said, 'All my US dollars have been spent on the house and car. Nothing left now. Got to go once more to the US and save some money.'

His father said, 'I have been telling Mani to do that for some time now. It is better to be a software engineer than a project manager.' I could understand the old man's anguish. In an off shoring situation, project managers have to reside where large numbers of people are located. It is a cost-effective decision.

Mani got slightly irritated and said, 'Ok Pa, we will do something about it.'

Mani then turned towards his team and said, 'Guys, why don't you help yourselves to dinner?'

Mani and his South Indian Tamil family fed us curd rice, sambhar rice, yellow rice, lemon rice, tamarind rice, rasam rice, plain rice—every dish was rice-based. Everybody appreciated the rice varieties and Raj almost went hungry. Unless a roti and a raw onion go down his throat, dinner is incomplete for him. After the dinner, we thanked Mani and his family for inviting us.

While going back Raj said, 'VSAT if you ever celebrate your child's birthday party, make sure you have some paneer rice too, that will be a big solace for us, atleast we can pick on the paneer.'

Project ReA and Swamy Joins Us

SOMETIME AROUND THE END OF FEBRUARY 2007, JAYANTHI assigned me to work with Anjan. Anjan continued to speak in monosyllables and hardly shared information. He smoked a lot and looked spaced out most of the time. Once there was a problem in one of the programs and Matt, the director of planning at the client site, could not get some reports extracted. He screamed in the US and everybody in the Bangalore office panicked. All the engineers scampered to figure out where the problem was.

Jayanthi said, 'If only you had documented the tech specs properly, we wouldn't have had this problem.'

I got irritated and said, 'If only people had given me information, I would have documented.'

Eventually, it was diagnosed that Anjan's module had a problem and unfortunately Anjan was on sick leave that day. So Mani asked me to fix the bug. I tried hard, but without detailed technical specs, it would take a long time to decipher the code and solve the problem.

Meanwhile Jayanthi called Anjan at home and said, 'Hey Anjan, we are having a serious client issue, can you help?'

Anjan said yes and an office car was sent to pick him up.

(Indiana was busy teaching archaeology to students. Meanwhile, somebody from the Secret Service office says, 'Only Indiana Jones can fetch the relic from the Nazis.' Then the boss says, 'Send the chopper and ask Sliver to get him.' One of the Indiana Jones movies, and this situation was somewhat similar to it.)

Anjan came to office unshaven and with bloodshot eyes. I thought he had boozed the whole night and hence reported sick. Anjan came around 4 pm that day and worked until 2 am and solved the problem and the client was 'FUCKING DELIGHTED'.

Indiana Jones went into the jungles, fought with tribals, ducked the Nazis, met with Moses, swam through a piranha-infested river and emerged with the relic. The US Congressional Committee gave him a Medal of Honour and Harrison Ford took his heroine to bed.

Mani sent a mail to the team:

Dear Team,

I would like to appreciate the efforts of Anjan, who came to office even when he was sick. He stayed up late, solved the problem and the client is delighted. That is the kind of team spirit and performance one should display. Thank you Anjan.

Regards,
Mani

The next day, Mani came to our bay, called everybody and handed Anjan a spot award and a voucher for ₹1000. I thought it was ridiculous. Anjan doesn't document, doesn't share and he reports sick because of excessive boozing. He comes to office in the evening, stays late, solves a problem, which shouldn't have occurred in the first place and ends up getting appreciation and a spot award! This was a great way to surge ahead—horde information, don't share the code and the specs, talk less, solve problem in the last minute and become a hero. I was learning the tricks of the trade fast.

While Cathy Baker had agreed for the re-architecture project, it was moving at a very slow pace. It was too complex and very few people in the US and India understood functionality and architecture holistically. There were meetings galore but work dragged on. The working culture in the US is quite different. Almost everybody has to agree to a certain plan of action and then it gets communicated to all the key stakeholders. Accountabilities will be set, timelines will be fixed and work gets reviewed every week. However, people from the client site in the US were not very happy doing the re-architecting project because they felt that the project could lead to job losses in the US. So they started giving a rough time to all of us. Architecture and design was being tightly held in the US. Only specific modules and pieces of code were being sent offshore for review and testing.

Mani and Sankar were making their quarterly trips to the US, but there was hardly any progress. Mani said, 'People are worried about "redundancy." We have to use "Change Management Strategy".'

Mani called for a team meeting and said, 'Guys, if clients are not forthright with information, take it easy, don't push them too hard. Be diligent and flexible.'

We listened to his spiel and realised that things were not moving as well.

Raj called me aside and told me, 'Americans don't want to let go and TCS wants to offshore more. That is the conflict man. I was speaking to Jenny, my program manager in the US and she made it clear that she doesn't want to offshore more. Apparently, if they went ahead with the re-architecture project, they will have to close the Boston software development office and atleast 50 people will lose jobs. So the resistance is huge.'

I said, 'So, what will happen to the project?'

Raj said, 'It will go slowly. But the re-architecture project, which we are attempting secretly, will be useful in the next stage. So let us speed things up.'

That day, Adi, Raj and I had lunch together. Anjali joined us mid-way.

I asked Adi, 'Where are we on the re-arch project?'

Adi said, 'As per your functionality document, I have done the first level of design encompassing all the modules. Now, we will have to start making the components that will make the foundation. So, when do we start that?'

Anjali replied, 'Let us divide work. Each one of us can take a portion and submit it in the next few weeks. I have spoken to Srila and she agreed to be part of this project.'

Raj said, 'We should give a name to our secret project. Let us call it "Project ReA". How do you like it?'

Everybody liked the name and we divided the work among us. Adi said, 'Soon, we will need data to test out. How will we get that data?'

Raj said, '*Main hoon na*. I will download the simulated data and we can test it out.'

I asked, 'What happens if the client gets to know that you are downloading confidential data?'

Raj said, 'I am downloading simulated data mate, not the real one. You think I am stupid?' Surprisingly Raj was maturing.

Anjali said, 'Just be careful guys, somehow I am getting a nagging feeling that we are going to screw it up again.'

Adi said, 'You girls can never take risks or what? Imagine how much the company will benefit once we complete this project.'

I asked, 'What bug tracking and version control tools will we use?'

Adi said, 'There are so many freeware tools man. We can download and use them and I can manage that.'

Anjali had one license of Microsoft project and she agreed to use it for Project ReA. She said, 'The project scope is too big. We need to cut it down.'

Adi said, 'Let us just build the core platform where modules can be inserted based on need. Later we can decide the important ones to insert and integrate.' Everybody agreed. Srila called later in the day and we told her what she had to do.

All the important decisions were taken and Project ReA took off. The most ambitious and resource-constrained project was now taking shape. The project made us work every waking moment and seeped into our personal lives. We didn't have time to scratch our backs because we had to do our day job too.

One day while walking down the aisle, I saw a big poster on the notice board.

It read:*TCS Referral Program*

Don't you want to work with your friends on the floor?

BE/B.Tech with one-year experience preferable!

Decent proficiency in Java is a must.

I remembered the barber in Tirupati and dug out the old resume that he had given me. I called him that evening and his son Swamy sent me his updated CV. I submitted it to the staffing department. I spoke to Zafeer to call Swamy for an interview.

I said, 'Zafeer, Swamy is a barber's son. We need to give a chance to people who really need a job.'

Zafeer's father ran a car rental agency and he knew the hardships one had to face to get a decent job in the software industry. He said, 'Sure Venkat, let us call him. If he does well in the interviews, we will make an offer.'

Swamy was sent the invitation to attend the interview and he landed up at Bangalore. I picked him from the City Bus Stand and took him to our house.

Adi and Raj prepared him for the interview.

Raj said, 'If Manikantan interviews you, add a "sir" before and after each sentence. If Ashish Srivastav does, then get into technical aspects. He will love it. If it is Arun Gupta, just make a sincere plea.'

Raj was becoming a master at reading people. I wondered whether being street smart is a gift. I lunged forward and hugged him.

Raj said, 'VSAT, don't get senti now. Leave me, come on, leave me now.' All of us laughed and I let go of Raj.

Swamy asked, 'What is it with the hugging?'

Adi informed, 'Raj doesn't like VSAT's hugs and VSAT likes to irritate Raj.'

The next day, I gave Swamy my white shirt and tie, and took him to office with us.

Swamy went through a written test and cleared it. He then went through three rounds of interviews. Though his communication skills were rustic, technically he was sound. In the final round, Arun Gupta met him.

Swamy said, 'Sir, all my life I studied for this day. I don't want anything to go wrong today. I may not speak good English, but I am technically good and I can work hard. Give me a chance sir'. Arun's eyes welled up, he liked Swamy's plea and ticked his name for selection. Customising answers based on interviewers helps.

Zafeer made an offer and by that evening, Swamy had a job. He signed the offer letter and agreed to join the very next day.

That night, Swamy called his father and conveyed the news. His father said to me, 'Son, I have been handing over my son's resume to so many people and I don't even recollect your face. But I am happy that Lord Venkateswara sent you to get a job for my son.' He was crying. I didn't know how to react. I gave the phone back to Swamy. After he had spoken to his father, Swamy asked me, 'You have a house with two rooms. Adi is alone in his room. If all of you are okay, then I am willing to stay with him and share the rent.' Swamy had done his Electronics Engineering from Sri Venkateswara University and since not many companies had gone to the campus the previous year, he hadn't got a campus job. So, he picked up odd software programming jobs until he finally got an offer with TCS. He had a small build, (about five-and-a-half feet), weighed sixty kilos, was bespectacled and demure-looking. If Adi was a bull, which could make its presence felt by the sheer size of the frame, Swamy was like a cat that tiptoed around.

I later asked Raj and Adi about what Swamy had said. Both agreed. Adi said, 'Rent will reduce, it is a no-brainer. I can share the room with Swamy.'

It was settled that Swamy would stay with us. He joined TCS the next day and over the weekend he went home, got his luggage and settled down without a whimper. Our gang expanded to six people counting Raj, Adi, Swamy, Anjali, Srila and me.

Since Arun Gupta had interviewed him, Anish from resource management group assigned Swamy to Arun's project and Swamy ended up working with Anjali.

A few weeks after Swamy joined, Adi said, 'Guys, Swamy is great in Java programming. I would like him to join Project ReA. It will help reduce the load on us.'

We agreed. That night we asked Swamy to take an oath of secrecy and explained what we were doing. Swamy said, 'What will happen if they discover that we are doing this project secretly? Will they fire us and send us home?'

Raj joked, 'No, they may not fire us. They might ask us to leave nicely.'

I said, 'Jokes apart, once we are done, we will present the project to the innovation council and get it ratified. Subsequently, we will present it to clients and then implement. If people get to know, they might put up obstacles.'

Swamy asked, 'But why are we doing this in the first place?'

I said, 'It is our only chance to prove that we can also do something. We may be average people, but we are not losers. We can show that we can do something worthwhile.'

Swamy said, 'So, we are hitting back at the system for denying us an opportunity to do well? Is that right?'

I replied, 'It is not about system, revenge and all that crap. Here is an opportunity that will help us do better, help the client and make a difference to the company.' Sometimes it becomes difficult to explain the intent to simple-minded people and Swamy was one such person. If I told him, 'See, here is an ant,' he would politely ask me, 'What do you want me to do?' and if I told him, 'It is thirsty, give it some water,' he would go and fetch a jug of water. His brain did what it was told and it couldn't take too much of an emotional transaction overload.

Swamy said, 'Adi told me that you guys thought of this when you were put on PIP and this is very personal to all of you. I understand that. You guys helped me get a job. Let me help with whatever little I can.'

Adi said, 'Ok Swamy. Welcome to the team. We will assign work to you and review progress every week. Swamy was inducted into Project ReA. We almost had a half-full contingent now. We pooled in some money and purchased two second hand systems from e-bay and they were placed in Adi's and Swamy's room. Adi and Swamy started to work late at night.

Normal Distribution Curve

In April 2007, the official HR newsletter announced the launch of the year-end performance management appraisal process. People were appraised and depending on their performance, they were given one of the five ratings:

- Significantly Exceeded Expectations—To achieve this rating, the person had to walk on water all the time. These people are God's gift to mankind, atleast perceivably so. About 10% are assigned this rating. This is the VIP compartment on the train. These people get more than a 20% salary hike.
- Above Expectations—To achieve this rating, the person had to often walk on water. These people are God's gift to the companies they work for. About 20% are assigned this rating. This is like travelling in a two-tier AC coach. People get about 15-18% salary increase.
- Met Expectations—Almost 60% of the people were assigned this rating. People who get this rating do not walk on water. They are normal human beings, but they always like to believe that they walk on water. This is like travelling in the second-class compartment. These people get 7-12% salary increase.
- Below Expectations—About 7% are assigned this rating. People who get this rating are often victims of the HR

department's distribution curve and are put on Performance Improvement Plan (PIP). This is like travelling in the general compartment. Nobody gets a hike in compensation. Often these people leave with atleast a 20-30% increase. This is viewed as a blessing in disguise, though it is more of an afterthought.

- Inconsistent—About 2-3% make this rating and they are asked to leave. Euphemistically, they are called 'culture misfits' and often the competition picks them up as top performers. They end up getting 20-30% increase when they jump jobs. Somehow miraculously, most end up in nice positions at the new place.
- The HR department comes up with a quota system which decides how many people should be allocated what rating. These ratings form part of a normal distribution curve. For example, HR could say that 60% of all the people who get rated should have a Met Expectations rating. To achieve this, every project manager ranks people and appropriately adjusts the ratings, irrespective of their 'absolute' performance. The whole system is driven on 'relative' performance. Based on the ratings, salaries and promotions are decided. During the annual appraisal and compensation season, HR folks smoke pipe and come on horseback to the office and walk with a swagger like Clint Eastwood in the wild Westerns. Since Raj and I went through a PIP, we were apprehensive about the year-end appraisal.

Sometime around the end of May 2007, Mani summoned me to his room for an appraisal discussion.

Mani said, 'So, VSAT how was the last one year?'

I said, 'Roller coaster ride sir. Worked hard and delivered.'

He corrected, 'Worked hard and partially delivered.'

(Seven Habits of Highly Effective Mean Managers: The first habit is to correct your subordinates and put them down.)

I said, 'We got good client appreciation, sir.'

Mani said, 'But what about teamwork and office decorum?'

*(*The second habit was to keep reminding them where they had fucked up.*)*

I said, 'What about it sir? I work well with the team and we don't call you Hitler anymore.'

Mani said with a smile, 'How is it working with Anjan?'

(The third habit is to arm yourself with enough examples of where your subordinates have badly screwed up.)

I said, 'He is on the quieter side sir. He keeps to himself.' Obviously I couldn't say that he was an introverted ass, who just wouldn't talk.

Mani said, 'Ok, talk about three accomplishments of yours.' I said, 'I completed functional and technical documentation, got a good review from the client and helped complete all the coding work assigned to me by different team members.'

Mani said, 'Ok, what are the three things in which you didn't do well?'

I said, 'Sir, unfortunately we gave you a nickname and initially we didn't get along with some team members like Jayanthi. I can't remember anything else.'

'What about Amit's problem? Nickname, advertisment, etc.?'

'One thing led to another and it was perceived wrongly and I didn't have anything to do with the Ad on the bulletin board,' I replied.

*(*The fourth habit is to make your subordinate confess his fuck-ups.*)*

Mani said, 'See VSAT, I have about twelve people in the team and I have to go by a normal distribution curve. You know the directive from HR. I have no choice but to pick about one or two people for the bottom 10%. Since your performance has not been so consistent and you had team work issues, you might get a below expectations rating. I know you guys have done well recently, but that will be reflected in next year's appraisal.'

I said, 'Sir, that is unfair. We worked as hard as anybody else. We are new to the corporate world and you cannot penalise us. How can the normal distribution curve determine our performance sir? Does that mean you will put us on PIP again?'

Mani replied, 'No, since you have gone through PIP and crossed that hurdle, it won't be the case. I can speak to Amit about that.'

I replied, 'But that will be completely de-motivating us sir. That is the same as indirectly asking us to leave the company.'

Mani said, 'I know how you feel about this. But this is HR's decision and not mine.'

(The fifth habit is to drop a bomb on your subordinate and blame it on HR or for that matter, any other department that you can think of. For example, if Mani had a chance, he would have said, 'I am not saying this, house-keeping boys in the pantry decided this, can't help it buddy.')

I said, 'Sir, the HR department gives a framework, but they don't know what I did last year. How can they determine my performance? You—as my supervisor—should decide my performance sir. You know we did a good job.'

Mani said, 'I am not saying you will get a below expectation rating. I am just preparing you guys for the worst.'

I replied, 'Sir, we also wrote a white paper which helped secure the re-architecture project.'

Mani said, 'But you know that it has not made any headway.'

I said, 'Sir, we did our best, but at times things don't work out. Why blame us? In comparison to Joby, Josy, Srinivas or Guna, I believe I have done well.'

Mani said, 'Do not compare yourself with others, that is not right.'

(The sixth habit is to be righteous about all the wrong things so that all your subordinates perceive you as being fair.)

I said, 'But that is what normal distribution does. It compares, ranks and distributes people. I can't understand why we agree to such distribution curves.'

Mani didn't want to take the conversation forward.

He said, 'The discussion is over, do you have any questions?'

(The seventh habit is to have the ability to abruptly stop the discussion especially when subordinates ask logical questions. If you are effectively armed with these seven habits, then no subordinate can surpass you and you become indispensible because nobody can replace you. Succession planning done!)

I was seething with anger. I said, 'No sir.' I walked out and headed for Sankar's cabin and Sankar was Mani's boss.

Sankar was reading something and I knocked on his door. He asked me to come in.

I said, 'Sir, can I have 15 minutes of your time?'

He said, 'Yes sure.'

I explained the whole story to him. He laughed when he heard of the nickname episode.

He said, 'Let me speak to Mani and Amit. The distribution curve is a framework and there will always be exceptions to the norm. I will do my best. Now, you go back to work.'

I said, 'Thank you sir. Your help will be truly appreciated and we won't let you down.'

Sankar smiled. He said, 'In which case, present something interesting in the innovation council. Can you?'

'I will try sir.'

'Do that and let me know if you need any help. The council meets in a couple of weeks.'

I went to Raj's desk and informed him about the turn of events.

Raj said, 'I am sure Mani will do the same to me. What is the point VSAT? TCS doesn't deserve us, let us join competition. If we post our CV on the Internet, we will get calls in a week's time. A couple of quarters more and we will complete eighteen months with the company and that is a lot of time to be with one company. What do you say?'

I compared what Raj had said to my dad's argument about 'life long employment'. I wondered who was right, only time would tell!

I said, 'Raj, don't talk like a loser. How many companies will you leave? I believe we haven't done anything so drastically wrong and Project ReA is coming out reasonably well. Let us present it in the innovation council and see. We have never won all our lives, yaar. This is a great chance to win, let us not lose heart.'

Raj said, 'Ok, *tere liye*, I will give one last try.'

Then it was Raj's turn to meet with Mani. They spent about half an hour together and a similar fate awaited him. All seven habits were effectively conveyed and implemented. However, Raj was prepared for the meeting and knew what to expect, so he didn't step out of the room as dejected as I had been.

Since the time for presenting ReA in the innovation council was short, we started working late into the nights and were half asleep at our desks during daytime. One day Ashish caught Adi sleeping. Ashish said, 'Adi, fortunately the client is happy with your work, otherwise, I would have taken you off my project. Go wash your face and for God's sake, reduce some weight, otherwise you will stop fitting into these goddamn office chairs.' Adi went to the rest room, washed his face, and came back to work again on Project ReA. Anjali had begun to look exhausted because of the extra work. One evening, I took her out for dinner and said, 'Anju, I am sorry for making you slog so much.'

She said, 'No problem Teddy, anything for you. I want all of us to succeed. Only then will my dad allow us to get married.'

The thought of the conversation with the colonel frightened me.

I said, 'Anju, things will be fine. Just a couple of weeks and we will be done.'

Raj had dark circles under his eyes. Srila said, 'VSAT, you owe me a big favour for the amount of work you are making me do.'

Mani called me out of the blue and said, 'So, you spoke with Sankar?'

I said, 'Sir, I had no option. It was not a complaint against anybody sir. I just explained my perspective to him.'

Mani said, 'So, he asked you to present something in the innovation council? What are you going to do?'

I said, 'Not sure sir.' I didn't want to talk to him about Project ReA. I was worried that he might scrap it.

He said, 'What else can I expect from you guys. You have just a couple of weeks left and you still have no clue about what to present? Do something—else you will let him down too.'

Sankar was a part of the innovative council and was looking for fresh ideas to present to the management. If he was impressed, we had a decent chance at getting better ratings, salary increases and promotions.

Amit also called Raj and me. He wanted to know if he had spoken to Sankar.

The cardinal rule of working in the corporate world—your managers will never like it if you speak to their managers. Everybody says, 'We follow an open door policy', that is only for ventilation purposes, not for people to walk in.

Raj could have kept quiet. But he didn't. He said, 'We didn't want to get screwed anymore sir.'

Amit said, 'Look guys, it is not personal, there is a normal distribution curve and we have to follow the policy.'

Raj got irritated and asked, 'Who makes these policies? HR, right? Why can't they be changed to make them more employee friendly? How can we do relative comparison and fit people into a curve? It is so mechanical. When we deal with people, shouldn't we look at the human aspect?'

I hadn't realised that Raj could say such profound things. He had started talking like Peter Drucker (someone had told me that he was a management guru). I could never understand management anyway. All I knew was that they make simple things appear complex. My seniors had told me to stay away from the management guys, especially the ones from HR. Apparently, the HR guys had an uncanny knack of complicating things.

Amit said, 'Raj, the new HR guru in town, please teach me sir, I am all ears.' (A scream inside my head. *The Godfather. 'You sonofabitch, do you know who I am? I'm Moe Greene! I made my bones when you were going out with cheerleaders.'*)

We thought there was no point in talking to him. We said, 'Sorry, sir.'

He said, 'Sankar informed me that if you guys do well in the innovation council, then you stand a good chance.'

So, Sankar had spoken to Mani and Amit and all of them were expecting us to present something in the innovation council. We were not there yet, but we would be ready shortly.

We informed Adi, Anjali, Srila and Swamy about our conversation with Sankar.

Adi said, 'Don't worry buddy, we will be there. We will win and change their perspective.'

Swamy smiled.

Anjali said, 'When we present our project to the innovation council, they will surely like it. Then we get good ratings, a decent hike and we are done. I am glad all of this is coming to a nice end.'

Adi and Swamy

We had just a week to present project REA to the innovation council and all of us were working our butts off. One night Raj got up around 2.30 am to take a leak and he heard faint noises from Adi's room. He opened Adi's door and walked in.

As soon as Raj entered the room, he loudly exclaimed, 'Morons, what the hell are you guys up to?'

I rushed to Adi's room.

Adi and Swamy were semi-nude and it was obvious what they were up to.

My mind went numb.

Raj said, 'You are gay?' Adi started buttoning his shirt and said, 'Calm down Raj. Let me explain ...' Meanwhile Swamy got dressed. He was shivering.

Raj said, 'Aren't you guys ashamed of yourselves? Don't you come from good families?'

Adi said, 'Raj, listen that has nothing to do with being gay. You don't understand.'

Raj asked, 'Since how long have you been gay, Adi? Why didn't you tell us? I am so goddamn disappointed that I am your friend.'

Adi said, 'That is exactly why I couldn't tell you.'

I said, 'Guys, hold on a second.'

Raj said, 'These idiots are gay, VSAT. I caught them redhanded.'

Adi was staring blankly at me and tears were running down Swamy's cheeks.

Adi said, 'VSAT, I wanted to tell you both for a long time, but couldn't.'

I said, 'You are kidding, right?'

Adi shook his head and said, 'No, I am not kidding.'

I didn't know what to say.

Raj said, 'I am living with a freaking bunch of gays. I am so fucking disappointed.'

I saw that Raj was genuinely upset.

I said, 'Raj, just cool down a bit and let us talk quietly. We will be waking up the whole neighbourhood otherwise.'

Adi shouted, 'You fucking moron! You have no idea about our sexuality.'

Swamy said, 'I was never interested in girls. After coming here and meeting Adi, I realised that I was gay. I am sorry if I let you down.'

Raj said, 'You have not let me down. You have let your parents down, you idiot. Why can't you guys be normal like the rest of us?'

Adi said, 'We are normal, it is people like you who don't understand us.'

I said, 'Can we talk this over tomorrow?'

Adi was getting irritated and said, 'What is there to talk about somebody else's sexuality?'

Raj said, 'Yes, if they are normal!'

Adi retorted, 'So we are abnormal?'

Raj asked, 'Is there a doubt? Swamy, are you the male or the female?'

Adi said, 'Raj, get out of my room. Now! Get out!'

Raj kicked the table hard and the monitor almost fell. Swamy caught the monitor before it toppled over.

I caught Raj by his hand and pulled him out and took him to our room. Raj was visibly upset and said, 'VSAT, how could we live with these guys? I am ashamed that they are my friends.'

I said, 'I don't know what to say or how to react. Let us talk tomorrow.'

Raj lay down on his bed and continued to cuss. I went back to Adi's room. Both Adi and Swamy maintained a stoic silence.

As soon as I entered the room, Adi said, 'You are also like him, right? You hate gays and you have no idea what we go through.'

I said, 'Adi, forget what I think of gays and what I know. I don't want to make a scene, please go to sleep and let us talk tomorrow morning.'

Swamy said, 'I agree.' He switched off the lights. I saw Adi's silhouette in the dim light.

I looked at him for a few more seconds, went out and gently closed the door behind me.

Raj was still awake. He said to me, 'They must be screwing each other now. What a shame!'

I said, 'Raj, can you just take it easy?' Raj switched off the light in silence.

I picked up my cell phone and sent an SMS to Anjali, *'You are right, Adi is gay. Raj caught him in the act with Swamy ... bit messy ... don't talk to anybody till we discuss.'* I didn't expect a reply because it was 3.15 am.

By the time we woke up next day, Adi was gone. I think he must have taken the early morning shuttle to office. Swamy was also up early and was having breakfast. He was ready to leave for work.

Raj said, 'See, the rat has escaped. Swamy, what were you guys doing last night?'

Swamy didn't say anything. He just picked up his bag and left.

There was too much tension in the air.

I looked at Raj and said, 'Hey, what is your problem? Why are you so high strung?'

He didn't answer my question.

I asked, 'What is the problem? Is it that Adi didn't tell us or is it that he is gay?'

Raj said, 'Both.'

I said, 'But why should he tell us and how does it matter if he is gay?'

Raj said, 'It matters to me. I am not comfortable with them.'

I asked, 'But why?'

Raj angrily said, 'Do I have to answer all your questions? You are not asking Adi anything. Instead, you seem to be asking me all the questions.'

I said, 'Raj, what do you expect me to ask Adi?'

Raj said, 'I can't live with a bunch of gays. Either they move out or we are moving out. You decide.'

I said, 'Let us take it one step at a time. We are just less than a week away from the innovation council presentation.'

Raj didn't say anything and we both left for office.

I looked for Adi but I couldn't find him in the office. I called him on his cell phone but he didn't take my call. I called from the office number and he picked up the phone. I said, 'Adi ...' and he disconnected. I realised he didn't want to talk to me and I decided to give him time.

Meanwhile, Anjali came over to my desk and said, 'Can we talk?'

Both of us went downstairs.

She said, 'I saw your SMS and have been trying to reach you the whole morning. Why aren't you taking my calls?'

I told her what happened. She listened to the whole thing and slumped in her chair.

She said, 'It doesn't matter whether Adi is gay. Why did Raj over-react?'

'I don't know.'

She continued, 'Adi is an important part of Project ReA, and if he doesn't turn up, we won't have anything going ... Do you want me to speak to him?'

I said, 'Not right now. He may be very upset. You may want to speak to Swamy and make him feel comfortable.'

Anjali said, 'But Swamy hasn't turned up for work.'

I said, 'Maybe he has gone somewhere with Adi. I hope both of them are not doing anything stupid.'

I quickly took out my cell phone from my pocket and typed an SMS addressing Adi and Swamy, '*Guys ... take it easy ... no hang ups, let us talk ... VSAT*'

There was no response from either one of them and I hadn't expected one anyway.

The day passed in absolute drudgery. I couldn't concentrate on anything. Raj, Anjali and I went for lunch together but hardly spoke. Afterwards, we went for a stroll.

Anjali asked, 'Raj, what is the problem if somebody is gay?'

Raj said, 'I don't want to talk about it. I am uncomfortable. That's all I can say.'

Raj could be extremely hard headed at times.

When we went back home in the evening, we saw that Adi and Swamy's room was empty. There was a note on the table and two sets of keys next to it.

I quickly tore upon the envelope. Adi's note read:

Dear VSAT and Raj,

After all that has happened last night, it is impossible to stay together. We are moving out. Sorry for inconveniencing you.

Yours,

Adi

I read the note several times and passed it on to Raj. This was a big blow to our gang, our friendship and our project. Adi and Swamy must have taken the day off to hunt for a new place. I sent an SMS to Adi, *'Don't be stupid ... come back Adi ... VSAT.'*

There was no response.

The next day, I went to office and stood next to Adi's cubicle.

I said, 'Hi, Adi!'

He said, 'VSAT, I don't want to talk now.'

I said, 'Adi, it is okay ...'

Adi cut me short, 'VSAT, please ...'

I stood there for a few minutes and turned around and left.

I stopped by Anjali's desk. Swamy was sitting next to her cubicle. He appeared quite tense. I pulled a chair and sat down. I said, 'Swamy, it is okay. We aren't talking about it. We are sorry for what happened the other night. We are genuinely not interested in anybody's private life.'

Swamy said, 'My father is a barber in Tirupati temple sir. If he gets to know, he will be heart-broken. But I am like this and I don't have the confidence to speak up.'

I said, 'Who is telling your dad anyway? Eventually when the right time comes, you can tell him and hopefully he will understand.'

Swamy said, 'Educated guys like you can't understand. How will my father understand? Now, everybody in TCS will know about this and we will be ridiculed.'

Anjali said, 'Don't be stupid Swamy. Nobody will know. This is not a topic for national discussion. This is the private life of two individuals.' Swamy said, 'Thank you Anjali. That is nice of you.'

I wanted to change the topic. I asked, 'So, Swamy where have you guys moved to?'

He said, 'At the end of the street where you guys live. Not too far, we found a paying guest accomodation for two and we took it up.'

I asked, 'So, did you sign a long-term agreement or something?'

He said, 'No, we just paid an advance and moved in.'

I said, 'Ok. Your choice'

Anjali said, 'So, what do you guys want to do about Project ReA? Today is the last day to get the fifteen minutes slot for the presentation.'

Swamy said, 'I don't know. We have to speak to Adi.'

I said, 'Ok.'

The conversation ended and I went to my desk and pinged Adi on chat.

VSAT: Can we have lunch together?

Adi: Not sure I want to do that.

VSAT:☹ What about Project ReA?

Adi: What about it? What do you want me to do?

VSAT: I hope we are participating!

Adi: I will prepare the material, but will not be part of it.

VSAT: But why? ☹ We are sorry for what happened. You know how Raj is. We didn't expect it yaar.

Adi: Anyway, I will give the material. You guys go ahead. You have worked so hard for the last few months and I don't want to screw it up for you.

VSAT: As you wish. But if you want to join, you are most welcome.

Adi: Thanks

Innovation Council

I SENT A MAIL TO RAJ, ANJALI AND SRILA AND COPIED ADI AND Swamy on it. I informed them that we are going ahead with the presentation to the innovation council. It was agreed that Adi would make most of the architecture slides and Anjali would present them. She had the most blemish-free record amongst all of us.

I went to the TCS innovation council site and booked a fifteen-minute slot under the topic heading, 'Re-architecture'. The system automatically sent off mails to Sankar, Mani, Ashish, Arun Gupta, etc.

Sankar forwarded the mail to me and wrote, '*Good you are attempting something, and I look forward to your presentation. Hope it is a good one. Regards, Sankar.*'

Mani walked up to my desk and asked, 'So, what is this re-architecture stuff? Don't tell me it is the extension of the white paper which you guys put together earlier.'

I didn't reply. There was a pause.

Mani said, 'Ok. I got the hint. It is about re-architecture of our project, right? I can't stop you guys from presenting because it is already recorded in the innovation council site and Sankar knows about it. But let me tell you guys, don't screw the project and don't screw the team and me. This is your last chance to prove that you guys are capable of delivering. You screw up, you will hit "below expectations" and you won't get any salary increase. Probably thrown out too.'

I nodded and didn't say anything.

(*This was the eighth habit: Threaten your subordinate with dire consequences if he innovates or takes initiative.*)

The day of presentation arrived and our slot was at 5 pm.

Raj, Anjali and me waited outside the conference room. Srila agreed to join us via conference-call. There was no news of Adi and Swamy.

At 5.15 pm, Sankar peeped out of the conference room and said, 'Ok guys, it is your turn now. Get going and make it crisp. You have fifteen minutes and we are already running behind schedule.'

Raj said, 'Yes sir, we will do our best.'

Sankar, Mani, Ashish, Arun Gupta, Anish and Pappu were in the room. Pappu glared at us, which is the normal demeanour of most HR people. So, I didn't care much. We quickly set up the laptop, connected it to the overhead projector and sat down. I dialled Srila and put her on speakerphone. Anjali, Raj and me introduced ourselves.

We were about to start, when there was a knock on the door. Adi and Swamy peeped in.

Ashish and Adi looked at each other. Ashish said, 'What?'

Adi looked at me.

I said, 'Sir, Adi and Swamy are also part of this team.'

Sankar waved them in, saying, 'Shall we start?' I was thrilled that Adi and Swamy had joined the presentation because they had played a major role in developing the solution.

I started the presentation by saying, 'Sirs, thank you for this opportunity. In many software projects the biggest problem is "disjointed functionality," a lack of understanding of what we want to build holistically. Another is the creation of a scalable architecture—a platform where modules can be attached in plug and play fashion. In our experience with TCS and specifically for us in the NED project, we realised we could address these issues better. So, as you are aware, we presented the concept white paper and Cathy Baker accepted the re-architecture solution. But progress was limited due to various reasons. Meanwhile, with support from Mani and the team present in this room, we have worked diligently and redone the design and architecture. With this method, all modules can easily fit in and we can draw all kinds of reports and MIS out of it.'

Adi jumped up and started presenting the design, components and the way the new solution worked. Anjali and Srila explained the programming and quality standards that were adopted. Raj talked about how it was tested. Overall, we made a decent impression.

I could see that Mani was stunned. Sankar looked at the new solution and said, 'This is great. How did you guys manage such a big effort? You guys have done a parallel project.'

Adi gloated, 'Sir, we pooled some money, purchased some systems and worked a lot from home. Our system can easily scale and has the ability to dig out information from any remote application. The user wouldn't know that the data has been spooled. We can get concise reports and they can be displayed across any application.'

Pappu's eyebrows shot up. He kind of zeroed down on Adi. He was sure that Adi had planted the ad on the bulletin board. But he couldn't ask him outright. That would have been embarrassing to all.

Ashish listened intently and took notes.

Raj said, 'We downloaded the simulated test data and used it to test our new solution.'

I said, 'Sir, we worked very hard on this new solution. The solution is not fully complete and with some more effort, it can work well. We can present this new solution to the client. It will cut down the cycle time drastically and we can bill the client additionally for the IP (Intellectual Property).'

Sankar raised his eyebrows.

Ashish said, 'Wait a minute, guys. What software did you use and what about licenses?'

Adi said, 'We used freeware and we used the existing licenses that we had.'

Sankar turned to Mani and asked, 'So, were you in the loop on this project?'

Mani didn't know how to react. If he said, 'No, I was not in the loop,' he would lose out on the credit for encouraging us. If he said he had been in the loop, then he had a tough question to face.

Mani said, 'It is an interesting project and I think it is a workable solution.' The answer didn't corroborate anything, but it was an answer, nevertheless.

(The ninth habit: Mean managers answer all tough and direct questions posed by their managers tangentially.)

Pappu jumped in, 'So, you carried office IP home. How could you do that?'

(Scream in my head, *The Godfather! 'If anything in this life is certain, if history has taught us anything, it is that you can kill anyone.'*)

Srila said over the phone, 'No sir, we didn't take office IP home. We created IP at home and got it to office.

Everybody smiled.

Pappu said, 'But Raj, you downloaded confidential client data for testing.'

(Again the scream, *The Godfather! 'I don't feel I have to wipe everybody out, Tom. Just my enemies!'*)

Raj said, 'Sir, I downloaded the simulated data and not the real data.'

Arun Gupta said, 'What you guys have done, to say the least is audacious. What made you do this?'

I didn't want to say 'survival.' We were getting the hang of things. The industry makes you grow up very fast.

I said, 'Sir, we wanted to create something new and different and we all wanted to work on a project together.'

Sankar said, 'Nice, creative answer. You did this to improve your performance rating and self-esteem, right?'

Raj said, 'In a way sir ...'

Ashish asked, 'Since how long have you been working on this project?'

Adi said, 'About six months, sir. Since our mid-term review.'

Ashish smiled. 'No wonder, you were sleeping in the office.' Most software engineers have morning sickness, because they are always pregnant with work. They start work late in the morning and end late at night.

Sankar said, 'Other than the six of you, has anybody else worked on this project?'

Raj said, 'No sir.'

Sankar said, 'It is a great solution which we can pitch to the client. But this needs a lot more work. Mani, I think you should engage more team members to take it to fruition. Then, let us pitch it to the client.'

He looked at all of us and said, 'Great job guys, considering that you have done this in your spare time. However, I am not happy with the method you adopted—using home systems, downloading data, using freeware, etc. That is not how we work at TCS. We discuss things, seek permissions, budget time and ask for resources. What you have done is stupid, I can easily see through it. Though what you did is commendable, I don't think it is a great example to set. So we are not going to reward you.'

I said, 'Sir, we are only a year old in the corporate world. We have done the project like how we would have done it at the Insti. I don't think we have broken any rules. We just wanted to add value. It doesn't matter if we don't get any reward sir.'

Arun Gupta, the softhearted guy that he is, melted at my honest plea. He said, 'We understand that. Next time you want to do something, come to us.'

He turned to Anjali and said, 'You are in my project, you could have informed me. I could have helped you guys.'

Anjali said, 'Yes sir. We should have.'

Sankar turned to Mani and said, 'Mani, these are your boys, right? Take care of them.'

Mani said, 'Sure Sankar.'

Then Sankar said, 'Ok guys, all the best. Thank you for your efforts.'

We chanted, 'Thank you sir,' disconnected the laptop and left the conference room.

I wanted to go to the canteen and drink some tea. Raj and Anjali joined me, but Adi and Swamy excused themselves and headed for their desks.

I asked Raj and Anjali to go ahead and went to meet Adi. I congratulated him on his presentation.

Adi spoke very softly, 'Gay people also have decent presentation skills.'

I said, 'Ok Adi, I am sorry for what happened. You know it takes time for people to reconcile. Now, stop sulking and come over to the canteen.'

Candid Conversations

ADI AND SWAMY JOINED THE REST OF THE GANG IN THE CANTEEN. There was silence for a few minutes.

Anjali said, 'Today's presentation went off very well. Adi, you did great.'

Adi said, 'Thank you Anjali. I think everybody did well.'

I said, 'I thought Pappu was gunning for us, especially when he asked about the IP question. Srila answered well. Else, all of us would've been in trouble.'

Raj said, 'Let us hope we get great ratings and great hikes.'

I said, 'This is TCS man. So don't expect any miracles.'

I felt confident that Sankar would recommend us for decent ratings. Mani would have to give us atleast a 'Met Expectations' rating. I was in a good mood. I looked at Anjali and marvelled at her beauty. A naughty thought crossed my mind. I slid my hand under the table, put it on her thigh and slid it up. She almost opened her third eye and I had no option but to quietly retreat. But I loved that moment of mixed emotions: Arousal combined with instant anger.

She looked at me and said, 'Some people have guts. They think they can do anything in the office. I mean all of us had guts to pull this off. That is why Arun Gupta called it "audacious".' Swamy said, 'I want to thank you all for including me in the project. I learnt so much.'

Raj ignored him and said, 'Let us go guys, else we will miss the shuttle.'

We packed up and took the 6.30 pm bus. Got stuck in traffic and reached home by 8 pm. All of us got down at Koramangala.

I said, 'Guys, we worked so hard. Let us celebrate today.'

Anjali said, 'VSAT, it is drizzling and there is no power. The streetlights are also off, first drop me home and then you guys can do whatever you want.' Whenever it rains in Bangalore, there's no electrictiy.

Adi said, 'Nahi yaar, I feel exhausted. You guys go ahead.'

Raj said, 'I will get some beer.'

I asked Adi and Swamy to join us.

Adi and Swamy agreed to join us in fifteen minutes.

Raj proceeded to buy beer. Adi and Swamy headed to their new place and I walked Anjali to her place.

Anjali said, 'Honeybunch, what were you doing in the canteen?'

I said, 'Babe, it has been a long time. Why don't we do it today? At least a quickie.'

She gave me a mischievous smile and said, 'You know I live in a PG. If uncle and aunty see you, it won't look nice. So how will you come to my room?' All I wanted to know was her intent. Once the intent is clear, we can always find ways and means to have sex.

I said, 'Leave that to me, I will manage. Anyway, there is no power.'

Anjali agreed. Since she lived upstairs, I quickly raced up the stairs and stood under the lintel. She came upstairs slowly, opened the door and I went in along with her.

Once inside, we lunged at each other. It was weeks since we had made love and were in a tearing hurry. We stripped fast and started making love.

Anjali said, 'VSAT, I love you.'

It was a real quickie. There are different kinds of lovemaking. The symphony—you go in step with the conductor and live the motions slowly and gradually. The bungee jump—full of energy, you dive right in, reach the bottom and jive back. This is also termed as a quickie. The train—you are not in a hurry, the destination is far away and you keep crossing each station with a certain sense of accomplishment and contentment. What we did was the bungee jump. It had vigour and was thrilling.

Anjali bid me goodbye. She said, 'Go now, otherwise your dear friends will feel that we are up to something.'

I pecked her on the cheek and said, 'Love you babe … you are the best.'

She giggled, 'Yeah, in bed too.'

I said, 'You are a raunchy babe, good girls don't say such things.'

She said, 'Really!' After a moment, she added, 'Mom called to talk to me about some marriage proposals and I told them that I am not keen right now. The pressure is building up, so let us prepare to tell them quickly.'

I said, 'You are mine and can't belong to anybody else.' I couldn't get any more *filmi* than that, '*Tum meri ho, aur kisi ki ho nahi sakti.*' I thought girls love to hear such stuff; perhaps they like being prized possessions. That is why all gangsters in movies have great arm candy.

She smiled and hugged me tight. I kissed her and left.

But as I was leaving, the old man downstairs sensed my presence. He couldn't see me because it was dark. 'Who is that?' he asked.

'Sir, is this house 234?' I pretended I was lost. 'There's no power and I can't find my way.'

'House 234 is in the back lane. I think you missed the street,' the old man said.

I thanked him and scurried away.

I reached home and Raj was ready and waiting. He had placed the snacks and beer on the centre table of the room. Adi and Swamy were not to be seen.

I said, 'Let me take a quick shower and join you later.'

Raj said, 'Achcha, so you had a quickie!'

I said, 'Fuck off Raj Malhotra.'

He said, 'Instant denial means you had a quickie. Fucker, you are lucky to have sex on the tap.' Raj could sniff out sex. He had a sixth sense for that.

I took a long shower, changed into a fresh set of clothes and joined Raj. I was feeling very relaxed. I wanted to grab a few beers, have a good dinner and fall asleep peacefully.

I said, 'Raj, Adi and Swamy will come anytime now. Please don't create a scene. Take it easy.'

Raj didn't reply. Instead, he grabbed a bottle of beer and said, 'Cheers. To Project ReA.' He switched on the CD player. An old Hindi film song sung by Kishore Kumar started playing ... *Rim jhim gire sawan, sulag sulag ...*

Adi and Swamy walked in and looked uncomfortable. They picked up their beers and began to munch on the snacks quietly.

Suddenly, Adi asked Raj, 'So, what is your problem with me?'

Raj looked at me and then at Adi and Swamy. He said, 'No, I don't have a problem. You are what you are.'

I heaved a sigh of relief.

Adi said, 'I know why you have a problem with gay people.' Raj said, 'Oh, really?'

Adi said, 'Yes, I know. Tell us about your sister.'

Raj sounded wary. He said, 'What do you mean?'

Adi said, 'Your sister got married to a gay man. The marriage was not consummated and eventually ended in a divorce. Right, Raj?'

Raj said, 'You are spying on me. I will kill you Adi.' Adi said, 'Nobody has to spy on you Raj. A few extra beers and we all know you talk.'

Swamy and I were listening to the conversation intently.

Adi said, 'VSAT, you have no idea. Raj and I had a few beers together and he told me everything.'

I wondered what would happen if Mani and Raj had a drink together. Raj would spill everything and Mani would tie our nuts with a string and tug at it whenever he wanted to.

Raj's eyes started watering. He said, 'Yes, that son of a bitch screwed up my sister's life.'

He paused for a moment and continued, 'He just had to tell us that he was gay and we would have averted the marriage. The spineless idiot couldn't say anything to his parents and got married to my sister. A month into the marriage, my sister informed my mother of the state of affairs and all hell broke loose. My father didn't know what to do and took my brother-in-law for counselling, hoping he would change. The counsellor told my father that the wiring in the brain for gay people is different and that they are not attracted to women, and it cannot be changed. My sister had to get a divorce. Since then, my sister has been living by herself alone and she runs a beauty parlour for women. We have not got any offers of marriage for her.'

Adi said, 'Raj, not every gay man is like that.'

Raj asked, 'So, since when have you known you are gay?' I was curious to hear the answer to that question.

Adi said, 'I was in my twelfth. My elder sister's friend had a crush on me. One day, she came over to my room and started kissing me. I felt very uncomfortable when she asked me to make love to her, I couldn't. For about fifteen minutes, she did her best to get me going. But I was not interested. She said, "Adi, what a shame, you are gay." At that time, I didn't know what that meant. Then I came over to NIT. At NIT, I met Kundi Vijayan, you know that guy who lived at the end of our wing, third year Electrical?'

Raj nodded, 'That effeminate fellow?'

Adi continued, 'And we hit it off. Ours was a close bond and we moved on to physical intimacy. He made me realise that I was gay. But I haven't come out of the closet. My parents are not aware of this, probably someday, they will get to know. I dread the thought. I come from a lower middle-class, conservative family. I don't think my parents will ever undersand. But I promise never to get married and spoil any girl's life.'

Raj stood up and hugged Adi. Swamy's eyes were filled with tears.

I asked him, 'Hey, what is wrong Swamy. Are you okay?'

Swamy said, 'I have been thinking, sir. I was never interested in girls. Boys appealed to me. I have lived in fear of everyone including myself. My father is a barber in Tirupati temple, sir. How can I ever make him understand? Maybe one day with help from friends like you, all these people will understand what we go through.'

I said, 'Guys, please don't get into this self-pity trip. There is nothing wrong in being gay. It is not an ailment.'

Adi looked stunned and said, 'Why didn't you say this before? Anyway, thanks for understanding.'

I said, 'What do you want me to do? Declare it on a banner?'

Raj laughed. 'Moron,' he said. 'Understanding doesn't mean you screw around here in the flat.'

Adi said, 'No problem, we are living separately.'

I said, 'Adi, I suggest you live with us and let Swamy live in the new place, unless you want to be in a live-in relationship.'

Swamy said, 'That is okay with me.' Adi nodded.

Raj said, 'Yaar Adi, I am sorry for what happened the other day. I became too emotional.' When a Hindi film ends, everybody says sorry to everybody and poses for a happy group photo. The same scene was being replayed here.

Adi asked Raj, 'So, what is happening between you and Divya? Are you guys going steady? People are talking in the office.'

Raj said, 'Nothing much, we kind of ... well, have been enjoying each other's company.'

Adi said, 'VSAT ... he is not telling us everything. I am sure he is screwing around.'

I looked at Raj. There had been too many revelations in the last week. I suddenly felt like a saint for going to office, working hard and having a steady girl friend.

Raj said, 'Yup, that is true, we got close man. We made love a few times.'

Adi said, 'Made love? Not screwed around? You are in a serious relationship, man. She is older than you. Will your parents agree? Are you comfortable?'

Raj said, 'Old or young—how does it matter? I like her and she likes me too. Isn't Aishwarya older than Abhishek Bachchan? Look at what an excellent pair they make ... *Socho* ...'

I looked at Raj and said, 'Dude, when did all this start?'

Gossip time again, love it!

Raj gave a sheepish grin. He said, 'All things happen late at night.'

Adi said, 'Give me a break.' Raj grinned and continued, 'Couple of months back, one day we were working late in the office and she caught me looking at her cleavage. You know how the Malhotras relate to boobs, right? We just can't let go. Anyway, she smiled coyly and I knew we had something going. I kissed her and we left for her apartment. We've been going around since then.'

I said, 'How come I didn't know?'

Raj said, 'Where do you have the time for us mortals? Either it is Project ReA or Anjali!'

I said, 'Sorry guys, but I have been really busy of late.' I don't think guys in their twenties can stay away from sex for too long. They begin to feel as if they have been denied their birthright. They equate pre-marital conjugal rights with constitutional rights. I wish they viewed voting with similar fervour. I think if we strictly implement a law that says, 'sex is permitted only if you vote,' we will have 150% voting. Atleast 50% of the country would try to vote twice, just to be sure that they are on the safer side.

Anyway, the week had been filled with revelations. Adi and Swamy were gay, Raj was in love with Divya who is three-and-a-half years older to him and here I am, a small town guy, accepting everything that comes my way and moving along. I wondered what was liberating me—software or Bangalore? Whatever it was, we were headed for tons of problems.

Suddenly Swamy picked up his mobile and said, 'Let me call home. I will tell my family that I am gay, that I like guys and am perfectly normal. I want to tell my dad, "Dad, stop shaving heads. Come with me to Bangalore. Lead a better life." I will take my mother to Forum Mall and buy her a sari. She will be shocked, shocked man, shocked! She will not know what hit her. All she has seen is the air-conditioned grocery store in Tirupati and ... I will ...' He stopped suddenly, lay down flat on the bed and started snoring. One down and three to go.

I asked Raj about Divya.

'She's nice,' said Raj. That's how most men talk. This is the best description they can come up with. Anything more than that is a bonus.

Raj continued, 'She is good. I mean ... at times she dominates me. She comes from a decent family. Tells me stories about her father. He is in the police force.'

I said, 'Then you have a decent chance of getting screwed.'

Raj laughed, 'Punjabi car-dealer family and Kerala-police family, and Divya is three-and-a-half years older than me. What a combination man! It will be a quiet wedding. Nobody can relate to each other and nobody can talk to each other.'

All of us laughed.

Adi asked, 'You think it is going to work out?'

Raj said, 'I don't know. I mean I don't know where this will lead. Anyway, why break our heads now? *Chodo* yaar.'

Adi said, 'You are not sure about the relationship?'

Raj said, 'I am, but don't know about the future. We'll see.'

I asked, 'Aren't you committed to her?'

Raj said, 'I am.'

I said, 'Then?'

Raj said, 'Then what? That is how it is.'

I could never fathom such relationships.

Adi said, 'Guys, please keep this to yourselves. I don't want to talk about my sexuality to anyone.'

Raj laughed, 'No no, we are going to post it on the Internet with the head line – "If you like guys—talk to Adi".'

Adi stared blankly at Raj.

I said, 'Don't worry Adi, as I said, it doesn't matter. There might be many more people around, who knows?'

Raj mumbled, 'Yes mate, let's not talk about it. I am off guys. VSAT, wake me up tomorrow before you head to office.'

We sat there quietly for a while. I come from a lower middle-class family. My father is a teacher and so is my grandfather. My mom is conservative. I am in love with a Coorgi girl and I want to marry her. My Punjabi friend has a Malayali girlfriend, and they are sleeping together, but their future is undecided. One of my other friends is gay and his father runs a small tailoring outfit in Hyderabad. Swamy, the son of a barber in Tirupati Venkateswara temple, likes guys and wants to take his mother to Forum Mall. Everything is so complicated. The software industry seems to have changed people, towns and mindsets and the country.

Salary Hikes

THE NEXT MORNING, MANI CONGRATULATED US ON OUR EFFORTS. He called for a team meeting to explain the progress of the re-architecture project. He named each one of us and explained how hard we had worked. He didn't talk about any awards. The other team members looked stunned. Mani said that he was going to get fully involved and that Jayanthi was being moved to another project. I didn't know why he did that. Was it because he realised that she was not adding value? I was assigned to managing functionality and no longer had to work with Anjan. Harpreet and Adi were assigned to design and architecture. Savitha, Anjan and Srinivas were made the module leads. Divya and Raj continued on testing and Anjali was assigned to work with Savitha.There was no change in work allocations of Joby, Josy, Neil, Manoj and Guna. They continued with their existing reporting relationships. Srila refused to relocate to Bangalore, so she continued on her project.

Mani told us that Sankar and him had presented the new architecture and methodology to Cathy and she was extremely happy with the progress made. She wanted to modify some of the existing modules to fit the new model. Mani said, 'We have some challenges in the new model and I am hoping Harpreet and Adi will come out with solutions quickly. I would appreciate if VSAT nails the functionality for phase one of delivery and ensures implementation.'

The next weeks went in understanding timelines, preparing project plans and identifying key deliverables for each one of us. Mani started to talk to us about appraisal ratings and salary hikes.

Mani handed over my letter to me. It said, 'Met Expectations' and that from July 01, 2007 my salary would go up by 9%. My take-home pay would be ₹16350.

Mani said, 'You guys are lucky, you got a decent rating and a hike. You must thank Sankar for that.'

Mani could now write his own book titled, 'Managing the Mani Way.' Axiom one, give a measly salary increase to your subordinates and say, 'You are lucky.' No more questions are asked.

I asked, 'Why not "Above Expectations" sir? We worked so hard and brought the re-architecture project back on track.'

Mani said, 'We kind of averaged it out. First half of the year, it was more or less below expectations. Assuming the second half was above expectations, overall for the year it would be "Met Expectations," wouldn't it?' I wondered how one could apply Math and average out ratings. But Mani is capable of anything.

I asked, 'Sir, I don't understand the averaging. Can we ever get a better rating and compensation increase?'

Mani looked me straight in the eye and said, 'You don't know how tough it is to be a manager. I try to do my best, but HR always reduces the ratings and salary increases. Actually, I like you guys. I think you can make a difference to the project and the company. Next year, aim high, do well and you can get a better rating and compensation increase.'

This was a clever pact between HR and the managers. Ask HR and they say, 'We are just facilitators,' ask managers and they blame HR and the two never meet you in the same room. Their calendars will never coincide to have a joint meeting with the subordinate.

I said, 'Thank you sir.'

Mani said, 'Anything else?'

I said, 'No sir. We are very lucky to have you as our manager sir. We will work hard and do our best.'

He looked at me suspiciously and smiled.

As soon as I came out, the Kerala twins Josy and Joby went in. Both got 'Met Expectations' ratings and an average hike of 12%. Srinivas, Nagaraj, Manoj and Guna also got the same ratings. All of them got increments ranging from 14-16%. Divya and Anjan got 'Above Expectations' ratings and an increment of 16% and 19% respectively. Remember, Anjan had stayed up late at night and solved a customer problem, which shouldn't have occurred in the first place? That incident secured him 3% more increment. Harpreet and Savitha got 'Significantly Above Expectations' ratings and an increment of 21% each. Remember, Savitha had informed Mani that he was called Hitler? So she gets a better rating!

Raj was given 'Met Expectations' ratings and he got a 6% hike. I think the nickname 'Pappu' had gobbled up 3%. Else, Raj would also have got 9%. Adi was rated 'Above Expectations' and he got 18%. Though Ashish reprimanded Adi several times, I think Project ReA changed everything for Adi. He was a star in Ashish's eyes. Anjali, as expected, got a 'Significantly Above Expectations' ratings and an increase of 21%, more than double of what I had got. But that was okay. Together, we had got a 30% hike and that was good enough. Rationalising always helps. It gives you a sense of security.

Raj came to me and said, 'After all the hard work, I get 6%, what a shame!' Now I have to tell my dad that my first year increment is ₹800/month. He will chew me. He will ask me to join him in his business. He will ask me to sell used cars and not waste any more time on software.'

I said, 'Take it easy, Raj. Next year will be great.'

Raj said, 'I can't believe you can be content with this kind of increase.'

I smiled, 'I come from a lower middle-class family Raj. Any increase works for me. Chod yaar, next year will be better. Let us party.'

As we were speaking, Joby and Josy came with their letters and Joby asked in his Malayali-English, 'VSAT, *endo* ... how much did you get?'

I said, 'Nine and you?'

Both simultaneously said, 'We got 3% more and we worked so hard. But we got so little.' They are the Kerala twins, they think alike and say the same things. I think they will eventually get married to another set of Kerala twins who will be called 'Soma and Somi' and name their children 'Siby and Iby' and 'Sabu and Abu' respectively.

Then they looked at Raj. Raj was pissed with what he had got. He said, 'I will scan my letter and send it to you. You can then post it on the Net.'

Josy said, 'Don't be angry Raj. We know you didn't get any raise. Next year will be better.' I just laughed out aloud. Everybody expected Raj to just scrape through.

Then Savitha came to our desk and asked, 'So how much did you boys make?'

Before we could say anything, she said, 'I got "Significantly Above Expectations" and made 21%. See my letter!' She was being paid almost close to 4.55 lacs per annum. Raj and I showed her our letters. Savitha felt happy that she was faring much better than both of us and left contented. It looked as if Raj and I were the benchmark for salary revisions. Raj for being the lowest, and I was the benchmark of averages.

Raj said, 'Savitha bhabhi seems to be happy. Why are people happy if we get less yaar?'

As soon as Savitha left, Guna came in and he put his letter on our desk and said, 'Look, how little I got—14%. Damn! VSAT, how much did you get?'

By then Raj and I were tired of answering questions, so we pinned our increment letters on the desk pin-up board. Guna stopped talking for a while and compared his numbers with ours and quietly left. People felt triumphant after looking at our letters. We didn't realise we had such an innate capability to make people feel so happy.

Nagaraj was passing by our desk and Raj called him and asked, 'Want to look at our increments?'

Nagaraj smiled, leaned over our desk, felt elated and left.

Srinivas a.k.a Mahesh Babu, who was passing by, asked, 'Raj, *kitna mila*?'

Raj smiled and said, 'Six sir.'

Srinivas grinned and said, 'No problem brother. Next year you will make more than double. In the software industry, management fucks around for the first couple of years only. Once you gain experience, you can turn around and screw them. Don't worry.'

Raj suddenly stopped Srinivas and touched his feet and said, 'Guruji, take me under your wings and teach me all the management principles.'

Srinivas said, 'Fuck off Raj,' and went his way.

Adi came to the desk and leaned over to look at our numbers. He said, 'Morons ... you hit the bottom. We will do better next time.' We didn't want to ask how much Adi had made. Adi said, 'Ashish is happy with me, got 18%, which is not bad.'

I said, 'Great.'

Raj didn't say anything.

For the first time, the scatter graph didn't converge at the lower quartile. The graph was more like a line now going from the lower left quartile to the top right box.

Divya sauntered up to our desk and said, 'Hi guys. How are you today?'

I didn't answer.

Raj said, 'Not bad.' He pointed to the pin-up board and said, 'You can have a look too.'

Divya didn't bother to look at our letters. She just pinched Raj on the forearm and said, 'Don't worry Raj. Everything will be fine. I will treat you guys today, want to go out?'

I politely declined and Raj agreed to go with her. Divya left our desk.

Once she left, Raj said, 'At least I will have great sex today.'

I said, 'Hmm ... you are being gross. Just take it easy.'

By afternoon everybody knew everybody's ratings and increases. People made excel sheets, tabulated the details and calculated mean, median, mode and average.

By 3 pm, Mani came to our desk to discuss some functional requirement and he saw our increment letters on the pin-up boards. He said, 'What is wrong with you guys? Don't you know salary increase letters are confidential? If HR sees you pinning your letters on the pin-up boards, they will roast you alive.' I imagined Amit grinning and watching us as we were getting roasted on a horizontal pole and Raj saying, 'God, in my next life make me an HR manager and Amit a software engineer.'

I started removing the letters from the pin-up board and said, 'There is nothing much in these letters anyway. I am sure HR must have also felt bad about issuing them.' Mani looked at Raj's letter and asked, 'Where is the other moron?'

'He has gone for a smoke sir. Shall I call him?'

He said, 'Give me his letter and ask him to meet me once he is back. Okay?'

I didn't have much choice. Once Mani left, I asked Raj to come upstairs. I told him what had happened.

Raj said, 'Chalo yaar, come with me. Let's meet him.'

I refused. Raj said, 'Chal yaar, nothing will happen. Learn to stick with me, especially when things are screwed up.'

I reluctantly followed him to Mani's room.

Mani called both of us in and said, 'Please sit. Can I have the privilege of ordering coffee or tea for you guys?'

Raj said, 'No sir, instead if you can get my increment percentage increased, it will surely help. At least my dad will feel that I am working for a respectable company. If I tell him about my increment, he will ask me to leave TCS and sell used cars.'

Mani laughed aloud, 'Don't worry. If you guys leave, TCS stock price won't fall.'

(Managing the Mani Way: Axiom two—convert your subordinates' serious request into a joke.)

Raj said, 'Sir, atleast once do something for us. After working for twelve years in the company, don't tell us that you don't have the authority to increase a poor software engineer's salary by 3%.'

(Classic Bollywood cliché: *Mardangi ko lalkara*—Raj had challenged Mani's manhood!)

Mani was not sure how to react. I had never seen him googling for the right words before. He said, 'You know the budgets are stringent and I can't do much.'

Raj said, 'Sir, additional 3% increase is about ₹350 increase net of taxes.'

Mani said, 'It is not about the percentage Raj. It is about the prescribed method and available budget. If we open the door for one person, the rest will also ask. Where is the end to it?'

(Mani had finally found Axiom three—When cornered, knock down your subordinates with principles and methods.)

There was so much to learn from Mr Manikantan Doraisamy!

Raj was relentless, 'Sir, HR doesn't prescribe methods for innovation and high performance. They seem to prescribe methods only when it comes to paying increments?'

Mani smiled, 'Ok Raj, I will give it a shot with Amit, your favourite Pappu, let us see what he says.'

Raj said, '*Theek hai* sir.'

We were about to leave when Mani added, 'Guys, I am having a small get together at my home this weekend. Want to join us?'

Raj said, 'Sir, we have plans for this weekend. If you don't mind, we will join you the next time.'

I think Mani understood that we were not happy. He said, 'As you wish guys.'

After we left his room, Raj said, 'He will feed us the same old Frooti, gulab jamun, samosa, vanilla ice cream and all those rice items. Fuck it, I am not going.'

I nodded and we headed back to our desks. Raj hated formal get-togethers. He only enjoyed parties where booze flowed freely and one could happily gripe and gossip.

That evening, I called my mom and said, 'Lakshmi, I got an increment and please, no Tirupati this time.'

My mom said, 'Kanna, that is good *ra*. You must go to the temple and pray for your boss's health.'

I just smiled at mom's naiveté and said, 'Sure Mom, I'll pray.'

She asked, 'Kanna, when are you coming home? It's been a year since we saw you.'

I said, 'Soon Mom. Let me speak to dad.' Mom said, 'He is gone out and he is upset with you because you don't write letters.'

I said, 'Letters? You mean post box letters?'

She said, '*Avunu* ... yes.'

I said, 'Ma ... ok, I will write one and post it soon.'

She said, 'Ok. It is almost a year, so when are they sending you to the US *ra*?'

I said, 'Soon Ma, don't pester me. I will let you know when it happens. Ok bye, call you later.'

Raj was seated next to me. He asked, 'Family *khush*?'

I said, 'Yes, they want me to pray for Mani's health.'

Raj said, 'Why? What happened to his health?'

I said, 'I mean, for his well-being.'

Raj asked, 'But why?'

I said, 'Because, the belief is, if the boss does well, then we will also do well.'

Raj laughed so hard that he almost fell off his chair. He said, 'I have to meet your eighteenth century parents man. Do they have cars, cycles and bikes in your town or do all of them ride chariots?'

I said, 'Fuck off Raj.'

I decided to write a short letter to my dad. I had never written one before. I picked up an old letter he had sent. Using that as a guide, I wrote:

Dear Pa

Hope all of you are doing well. After the advent of email and mobiles, all of us have lost the habit of writing letters. But since you keep insisting, I am trying to pen one.

Before you ask, let me pre-empt a few things. TCS is a great company and the Tatas continue to take good care of all of us. I don't know when they will send me to the US, but I guess sometime soon ... The 'biscuit' is not far way. I continue to invest in the State Bank of India recurring deposit scheme. Right now, it is impossible for me to buy a house in Bangalore. But I can afford a bike and if I do, not to worry, I will wear a helmet. I am not getting tension headaches, but continue to store a bottle of Nuxomvica 30 at home, just in case.

I am not eating at roadside hotels because they put soda in all the dishes which could erode the stomach lining. Why end up with gastric problems? I am eating at the Tata canteen and they serve good meals, including fruits at times. My bowel movement is good, hence I could secure a 9% salary increment. I had called to share the good news with you.

Please tell mom that I am going to the temple and praying for my manager's well-being. Give my love to Swati. Tell her that I will get her some cotton salwars when I come home. Please convey my regards and love to grandpa, wish he could hear better, it is difficult to speak to him over the phone. Tell him, 'I'll change; I'll change. I've learned that I have the strength to change.' This is a line from The Godfather! He will like it.
Love you all!

Your affectionate son,
Venkata

I re-read the letter a couple of times. It had covered most of the points I wanted to make and I sent it home.

The next day, Amit was all smiles. He said, 'Back in trouble boys? You know that the salary increase letters are confidential. I hear you put them up on your desk pin-up board? Is that correct?'

(Scream in my head. *The Godfather: 'Do you still fear me Kay? I don't fear you Kay, I just dread you.'*)

Both of us didn't reply.

Amit said, 'You guys think you are studs?'

Raj grinned, 'You know that everybody knows everybody's salary. People compare ratings and hikes. We have not done anything new, sir. Instead of telling everybody, we just put it on the desk for people to see. In any case, we are paid the lowest, so people feel happy when they compare themselves to us. Imagine! We bring happiness to so many people.'

Amit was taken aback. He said, 'What? Is that your argument? Pinning increment letters to make others happy?''

I kicked Raj under the table and Amit let out a groan. I had kicked Amit instead.

Amit said, 'You guys need to get your brains tested. Who kicked me now?'

I said, 'Sorry sir. I wanted Raj to keep quiet and instead I kicked you.'

Amit said, 'You kicked me? The HR head for this office? I don't understand you guys sometimes.'

Raj said, 'Sir, we worked hard just like everybody else in the company and I got a 6% increment. I feel so bad.'

Amit tried his hand at counselling, 'Do well and hopefully you can get a better increment next year.'

I said, 'Sir, I am not asking for any increment. I am okay with 9%. Raj also worked equally hard sir. Can't he get atleast a 9% hike?'

Amit looked at me and said, 'Sorry guys, I can't promise. Let me see what I can do. You guys can leave now. But remember, salary increase letters are confidential and not to be put on pin-up boards. Be careful, I am being lenient this time. But don't insult our intelligence.'

(A voice screamed in my head. *The Godfather: 'Bonasera Bonasera, what have I ever done to make you treat me so disrespectfully?'*)

We left Amit's room. Raj said, 'Have you ever seen or heard an HR fellow committing to anything? Elephants can dance, whales can fly and Mani can change—may be—but HR will never commit to anything.'

I didn't say anything. After kicking Amit, though inadvertently, my quota for the year was over. I must have been the first guy in the software industry to kick an HR guy and walk out alive, that too, with a job in hand.

I prayed instantly, 'Lord Ganesha, I usually don't kick people, but just now I kicked, unfortunately the wrong guy, who turned out to be our HR manager. I know there is no redemption from such a heinous sin, but if there is a remedy, I would bend backwards to undo the deed. Let not any misfortune befall me or my family.'

A week passed. One day, Raj and I were having lunch in the cafeteria.

Mani walked in and said, 'Can I join you boys?'

Raj said, 'Sure Mani.'

Mani gave a sheepish grin. That was the first he had addressed Mani as plain Mani, without adding a 'sir.' A year had passed and things had changed. We kind of knew how things worked now.

Mani grinned and said, 'So, you boys are growing up. You have started kicking the HR people. That is amazing progress.' I said, 'Mani, you know it was not intentional.'

Mani said, 'Raj, Amit has agreed to give you 9%. So you are a lucky man. Now you don't have to sell used cars in Delhi.'

Raj got up, touched his heart with his right hand and said, 'Thank you Mani. I don't know what to say, I feel as if I just won an Oscar for our performance the other day. This three percent means so much to me, an additional ₹350/month in my bank balance. I am elated and would like to thank my mom, my dad, my sister and you and this fellow VSAT for being with me through thick and thin ...'

We laughed aloud.

Mani kept grinning. He said, 'You guys are funny. Now that you have got decent increments, can you guys start coming to office in some decent clothes? Bathroom slippers, torn jeans and weird T-shirts will only take you so far. Just straighten your T-shirt, let me read what is written on it?'

Raj straightened his shirt, it was written, 'With some bosses, you can only get so far'. Mani read it aloud and everybody laughed.

Raj said, 'With such increments, we can afford only torn clothes sir.'

Mani said, 'Oh, really. So if you don't get increments, you will come to office nude?'

Raj said, 'No sir, I will go back to selling used cars.'

Mani couldn't help laughing. He said, 'Come decently dressed guys.'

I said, 'Coming to office in formals is no fun. Our motivation levels dip.'

Mani said, 'So torn jeans and ragged T-shirts improve motivation?'

I said, 'Kind of sir, we feel a sense of freedom.'

Mani said, 'Come in lungis then. Undeniably, it gives the best freedom of movement.'

We laughed so hard that we had tears in our eyes.

Mani shrugged and said, 'Good luck guys, get some decent clothes. No Hawaii slippers, please.'

First Fight

RAJ GOT HIS 9% HIKE AND HE FELT THAT HE WAS NOT SCRAPING the bottom all by himself. The scatter graph put us back in the same league. A few weeks later, I saw Guna riding a new bike to the office. He looked cool. Nice helmet, a great shoulder bag and the new Honda ... I felt like buying a bike for the first time.

I went straight to Anjali's desk and said, 'Do you think I should buy a bike?'

She said, 'Wow. That would be great. Honeybunch, why didn't you think of it before?'

I said, 'Honey, I didn't have the money.'

She said, 'Don't talk so loudly, this is office.'

I grinned and said, 'Everybody knows we are an item.'

Anjali said, 'Ok great, let's make love here.'

I said, 'Great idea' and bent forward to kiss her.

She said, 'What's wrong with you, idiot?'

I smiled, 'So, what do you say?'

She said, 'No way.'

'I meant about buying the bike.'

She laughed, 'Sure. Let us go buy one over the weekend. I can pitch in with some money if you want. In any case, I have been saving up for the marriage.'

'Great. Since you are saving, I don't have to save for the marriage.'

She said, 'Are you kidding? Everything is fifty-fifty. So make sure you save up.'

'Yes, I must start doing that.'

She asked, 'So, you haven't saved anything so far?'

'Of course I have babe.'

'How much?'

'About 50,000?'

'Oh, great! So we'll get married with that amount?'

I asked, 'How much did you save?'

'80K.'

I said, 'Not bad, together we have 1.3 lacs.'

'Sounds big na?'

I said, 'But we need so much more to get married, to buy a house and a small car.'

'I think if we go abroad, probably we can save more?'

'I am from Andhra, won't the colonel pay me a fat dowry?'

She stared, opened her third eye and turned me to ashes.

She growled, 'You must be out of your mind, even to say that.'

I knew I had overstepped my boundaries. I meekly said, 'I was just kidding.'

She said, 'Don't ever kid with me or with my parents on this topic.'

She was just like Rani Jhansi, wielding a sword and galloping ahead on horseback. Unfortunately, there is no Coorgi equivalent of Rani Jhansi. May be Anjali is going to be remembered for generations to come as the rebel Queen of Coorg who successfully thwarted the Andhra scions.

I said, 'Sorry babe. But I won't joke about this ever again.'

She said, 'Leave now, I got work to do.'

I said, 'What about it then?'

She said, 'I said okay.'

I leaned forward to kiss her.

She said, 'What are you doing?'

I said, 'You agreed, right?'

She said, 'To buy a bike, you idiot.'

I asked, 'What about you? Want to buy something for yourself?'

She said, 'If you have a bike, you can pick me up and drop me. Why do I have to buy anything? Yeah, but you can always buy me a nice ring or a necklace. Shameless creature, you haven't bought me anything so far. Do you realise that?'

I said, 'That is not true. I got you so many gifts. Who gave you the bottle of Chanel 5?'

'Oh, so you keep count of what you give me? You seem to forget that I got you so many jeans and shirts.'

'Oh, so now you are keeping count?'

She said, 'Yes. You keep count, I keep count.'

I said, 'All you women are the same.'

She said, 'What about you guys? Sex, bikes, movies, boozing, smoking, screwed up performance and bad increments. How are you different?'

Ah! That hurt. I just blew her a flying kiss and walked back to my desk. She tried calling me from her extension, but I disconnected. She tried pinging me on my chat-line, but I didn't respond. I was angry; she should not have talked about my performance and increments. We had worked as hard; unfortunately, we didn't get a good rating and a decent increment.

This was our first tiff and I lost interest in work after it. I decided to surf the Net and started researching the topic of bikes. I spent almost half-a-day figuring out prices, models, colours, delivery, financials, etc. Anjali came over at lunch time and said, 'VSAT, I am sorry.'

I said, 'Never mind.'

She said, 'I mean, I am very very very sorry. I shouldn't have said what I said.'

Women think that if they use the word 'very' multiple times, men would melt. But what she had said had hurt me deeply and I was stubborn.

I said, 'Never mind.'

She said, 'Lunch?'

I said, 'You go ahead, I will eat later.'

She said, 'Oh, come on, now don't sulk like a child.'

I looked her in the eye and said, 'You go and I will eat later.'

She paused for a moment and said, 'As you wish.' And she was gone. I didn't feel like having lunch that day. I ate some cookies from the pantry and drank a large cup of coffee and surfed the internet till evening.

At about 4 pm, I sent a mail to Mani: *Have a bad headache, leaving a couple of hours early. Will make up for it over the weekend.*

Mani responded: *Ok. Take care, hope you are not attending any interview.*

I replied: *Not yet.*

I left early and went straight to Tanishq on Commercial Street and bought a ring worth ₹5,000 for Anjali. It had a beautiful stone and came with a wonderful velvet casing. On my way back, I stopped for dinner at Woodys. Then I hopped on a bus to go back home. There were many calls and messages from Anjali. I didn't respond to any of them. Thanks to the traffic, I reached Anjali's place around 9.30 pm.

I went up the stairs and gently knocked on the door.

Anjali asked, 'Who is it?'

I whispered, 'It's me.'

She held the door half open and looked at me with raised eyebrows.

I asked, 'Can I come in?'

She said, 'Why didn't you answer my calls?'

I said, 'We can discuss this here or inside. If I stand here, your PG uncle will think that you are going around with boys.'

She said, 'Ok, come in.' She was indifferent.

I stepped in. She closed the door behind me and stood in front of me with her hands on her hips. She was wearing a blue nightie and had wrapped a towel around her hair. She couldn't have looked any sexier. I was gaping at her.

She said, 'Stop staring and answer my question.'

I said, 'I was not staring. I was … well, admiring. You must be God's summer creation.'

She said, 'I know.'

I said, 'Ok, good.'

She said, 'So, why are you here?'

I said, 'Come, sit next to me and let me explain.'

She said, 'No. Just tell me.' I knew that her anger would melt with a little pacifying.

I caught her by her wrist, smiled and said, 'Sit down.'

She reluctantly sat next to me.

I said, 'Look, I never gave you anything and I never actually made you feel good. So, I got you something.'

'What?'

I dug out the velvet packet from my pocket and slid it into her hands.

'What is it?'

I said, 'Open it, babe.'

She quickly got rid of the wrapper and opened the velvet box.

'Wow, what a beautiful ring! You got it for me?'

I said, 'No, for your PG aunty downstairs. How is it?'

She said, 'This is beautiful. Must be expensive. How much did you spend on it?'

I took the ring from her, went down on one knee and asked, 'Ms Anjali Cariappa, will you marry me, even with my bad performance and lowly increments?'

She had tears in her eyes. She held my face in her hands, kissed me on the forehead and pulled me closer. I rested my head on her lap. She bent forward and said, 'Mr Venkata Subramaniam Adisankara Tanikaburla, I will marry you, even if your performance and increments are bad. You are my stupid idiot.'

She continued, 'Idiot, please take my calls when I try to reach you. I was so worried when you vanished earlier. Promise you will.'

I didn't allow her to speak any more and started kissing her. I tugged at her nightie and unwrapped the towel from her head. She looked beautiful. Her hair was wet and I could smell Chanel 5, her favourite perfume. She removed my shirt and I took off my trousers.

She touched my nipple and I stiffened. She ran her finger from my forehead to the base my neck, down my jaw line. The sensation was unbelievable. She bent down and bit my lip, which she always did. I couldn't take it any more. I flicked the light off and we made love the whole night. It was the 'train method' of making love, we were in no hurry, the destination was far away, and we kept exploring each other and crossed each station with a crescendo. We lay exhausted and there was a sense of contentment. I had a strong urge to smoke.

I woke up at about 4 am. I had to leave.

She was still sleepy and mumbled, 'Go quietly, Honeybunch, I love you ...'

I smiled. I knew the 'ring effect' was still working.

I kissed her gently on her lips and slid out of the room. Nobody saw me leave. I made it to my place and knocked on the door. Adi woke groggily and opened the door. He said, 'Fucker, is this the time to come home? Why don't you live with her or get married?'

I didn't say anything. Adi went back to sleep.

New Bikes

AT 7.30 AM ALL OF US GOT READY TO GO TO WORK, LOCKED OUR house and were on our way to the bus stop. Swamy joined us.

Raj said, 'Hi Swamy, *kaise ho*? Haven't seen you for quite some time?' Swamy said, 'I am doing Anjali's work, too much pressure from Arun Gupta. So all of us are working over the weekends too.' Raj asked, 'VSAT, where were you last night?'

I said, 'You guys know, why do you ask? Achcha, listen why don't we all buy bikes?'

Raj said, 'I have one in Delhi, I can ask my dad to send it across.'

Adi was excited, he said, 'Which one shall we buy?'

I said, 'I did some research, depends on the budget.'

Adi asked, 'What is the range like?'

I said, 'You want brands or the range?'

Adi scratched his head and said, 'Fucker, you think we are CEOs working for some multinational? We are with TCS and we just completed a year. Just give me some cheap options.'

I said, 'Most bikes are in the range of 30K to 60K. I think we can get a decent bike for less than 40K and I personally prefer Hero Honda. The mileage is good. So is the service.' Swamy said, 'Yes, most guys in our project have Hero Hondas. Adi, you may want to look at a Hero Honda.'

Raj grinned and said, 'Chalo Adi, you can also buy a Hero Honda.'

We reached the bus stop. Anjali was already there.

She said hello to us.

Raj turned to me and asked again, 'VSAT, where were you last night?'

Anjali smiled at Raj. I didn't bother to reply. Raj and Anjali sat next to each other on the bus.

Adi and I sat together and Swamy sat ahead of us.

Anjali asked Raj, 'So, how is it going with Divya?'

Raj said, 'Ok.'

Anjali asked, 'So, what next Raj?'

Raj said, 'We might take it forward. Maybe sometime soon, we will have to speak to our parents. What about you guys?'

Anjali said, 'Same here. I don't know when VSAT will muster the courage to do it.'

Raj said, 'Unless you push him, it won't happen. I guarantee that.'

I turned back and said, 'Anjali, don't listen to him, it will happen soon.'

Raj laughed out loud.

Adi asked, 'Achcha, when do we buy the bikes?'

I asked, 'Do you want to go for a loan or buy them outright?'

Adi said, 'Loan of course. What a question VSAT? You seem to be regressing.'

I said, 'Ok, this weekend, we will pick a Hero Honda, apply for a loan and buy it.'

Adi said, 'Done.'

Raj said, 'I will ask my dad to send mine and we will get it next week.'

Swamy said, 'Guys, once we get the bikes, we can all go to Shiva Samudram waterfalls the following weekend. What do you say?'

Anjali said, 'Great idea! Raj you must ask Divya to join us.'

Everybody agreed. Shiva Samudram waterfalls are in Mandya district, about 120 kilometres from Bangalore. They are the second biggest falls in India and the sixteenth largest in the world. I couldn't wait to buy the bike and ride away to Shiva Samudram falls.

Over the weekend, we went to the showroom and chose a Hero Honda CD 100 SS each. I liked the one in blue. Adi chose the black one. We filled up all the loan forms. I took a ₹24,000 loan and signed up to pay monthly EMI of ₹931 for thirty-six months. Not a bad deal. The dealer agreed to deliver our bikes on Wednesday, once the loan was disbursed and after the vehicle was registered in our names. Meanwhile, Raj's dad had dispatched his bike. It was expected to reach by Friday.

On Wednesday evening, we informed Mani and took off early from office to get our bikes. The new bikes were delivered on time. Adi went for a drive. I took the bike and went straight to Ganesha temple at Koramangala to do puja. Anjali joined me at the temple and both of us prayed, 'Thank you for the bike Lord Ganesha. This is our first possession in life, so please bless the bike with low maintenance and high mileage. I am sure this is a small request for you to fulfil.' Since childhood, mom had conditioned my prayers. I started off by thanking God and ended with asking for more. Fortunately, God listened to whatever we said, as long as our demands were within reasonable lower middle-class limits.

In the temple, we bought a ticket for ₹200 which included the cost of a two-wheeler puja. The flower basket with incense sticks, one coconut, vermillion and other accompaniments cost ₹100. In Bangalore, everything from CDs to flower baskets is packaged well.

I asked Anjali, 'What did you pray for?'

She said, 'You should not tell anyone what you prayed for.' I joked, 'So, how many children did you ask for?'

She said, 'Shut up VSAT, this is a temple.'

'So, we can't discuss children in a temple?'

She said, 'After children you will discuss sex, so I am nipping the conversation in the bud. Now shut up and let us go.'

I said, 'See, I didn't use the word "sex" in the temple, you did. Who is raunchy? You or me?'

She giggled, 'There is no point in arguing with you.'

After concluding the puja at the temple, Anjali and I drove through Koramangala on the bike. She sat at the back and held me tight. I liked it. It gave me a new high. Software job with TCS, a good-looking girl friend, a decent bike, not a bad appraisal and a just about okay increment—what else could one expect from life? I was grateful that the software industry was flourishing in India. Imagine, if India didn't have a growing software industry, what would have happened to millions of young graduates like me? The industry has changed the lives of many families, especially in small towns of India.

We had dinner at Shanti Sagar. Most South Indian fast food restaurants in Bangalore ended with the word 'Sagar'. You could prefix it with any nice South Indian name as long as it rhymed reasonably well. Some of the others were Krishna Sagar, Moti Sagar, Vishnu Sagar, Pawan Sagar, Sukh Sagar, etc., and the odd names were Adigas, SLV, etc. Anjali and I had masala dosa and Vanilla milk shake. After dinner, I dropped her home—actually, a hundred feet away from her gate—and I went back to my room.

Once I reached home, I called mom and told her that I had purchased a bike.

She said, 'Be careful Kanna, bikes are very dangerous. Don't drive without a helmet. Don't drive in the rain. Don't drive at night. Don't drive when it is too windy and never drive in the hot sun, you will faint. Don't drive in too much traffic.'

With so many precautions, I wondered when I could drive! I said, 'Ok Lakshmi, will do.'

Swati said, 'Why a bike? Have a girl friend or what?'

I said, 'How are you Swats? Studies going fine?'

She said, 'You haven't answered my question.'

I said, 'Some questions are best left unanswered.'

She giggled, 'That means you have one.' I said, 'Assume whatever you want.'

I wanted Swati to plant the seed in my parents' minds. I wanted them to be open to the idea of me having a steady girl friend.

Swati immediately said, 'Amma, Venkat has a girl friend.' Mom asked, 'Is that true?'

I said, 'Mom, she will say anything that comes to her mind and you'll believe it?'

My mom said, 'Your dad has gone out. I will tell him you purchased a bike. I am sure he will be happy. But I am worried *ra*. Call me daily in the evening. Even for a minute is good enough.'

I said, 'Fine Mom. I will catch you later.' The next day, all of us admired our new bikes. Raj was getting his bike on Friday and we decided to go to Shiva Samudram waterfalls on Saturday morning. Divya agreed to come along.

Shiva Samudram Falls

ON SATURDAY, EVERYBODY ASSEMBLED AT OUR HOUSE AT 6 AM and we started off to Shiva Samudram waterfalls on our new bikes. Divya sat behind Raj, Anjali rode with me and Swamy rode with Adi.

I whispered to Anjali, 'Hold me tight, all the way baby.'

She pinched me on the bum and said, 'Can't think of anything else? Get going now.'

It was a great ride. By about 7.45 am we had breakfast at MTR Shivalli after crossing Ram Nagaram. It was one of the best breakfasts of my life. We had hot idlis, upma, pongal, masala dosa, and steaming South Indian coffee. After breakfast, we headed straight to Shiva Samudram falls and reached there by noon.

The falls were fantastic. We climbed down the rocks and went downstream. The water level was high and the current was strong. We clicked a lot of pictures. Once we reached the base, all of us settled on a flat rock next to the river. It was such a beautiful and scenic place, probably one of the best picnic spots in the world.

Raj said, 'Let us have some beer.'

Adi and Swamy jumped up and said, 'Yes.'

Anjali said, 'Do you guys have some Sprite for us?'

Raj handed over a bottle of Sprite to Anjali and Divya.

Divya said, 'I don't mind having a glass of beer, but not more than that.'

I said, 'Guys, don't drink too much, we have to ride back in the evening.'

Raj said 'Drink, eat, sleep, feel refreshed and go back. What's the problem?'

Adi and Swamy opened the beer cans.

After a few glasses, Adi said, 'I want to test the waters.'

Raj asked, 'Know swimming? Ever swam in a river?'

Adi laughed and said, 'Of course.' He removed his jeans and shirt, and got into the water. He held on to a rock. Adi said, 'Bloody hell man, it is freezing. The water looks calm on the outside, but there is a strong current.' He stepped out of the water.

Raj laughed, 'Don't know swimming and making excuses!'

Adi said, 'See for yourself.'

Raj said, 'I will show you how it works.' He stripped to his shorts.

Divya said, 'Raj, you don't have to be a hero. Check the current out first.' Raj said, 'Don't worry babe, I've swum in tougher waters.'

Anjali said, 'VSAT, you don't know how to swim, so don't get in.'

I nodded.

Raj entered the water at the edge of the bank and waded closer to the rock. He swam a little bit, felt exhausted and stepped out. He said, 'Yes, the current is very strong.'

Meanwhile, Swamy had guzzled a bottle of beer and was feeling tipsy. He said, 'Guys, I am an expert swimmer and have swam in rough waters. I will show you how to do it.'

I said, 'Swamy, you had too much beer, I suggest you stay out of the water.'

Swamy said, 'You think I can't do it?'

'I am sure you can do it and that is why I don't want you to get in.'

'No VSAT, you don't believe me. I will show you.' He entered the water and waded to the rock. 'Yoo hoo, this is how it is done guys,' he shouted.

I shouted, 'Enough Swamy, come back.'

Swamy shouted back, 'Just a little more swimming and I will get back, don't worry.'

Adi shouted, 'Swamy, you are going a bit too fast, why don't you start coming back to the bank?'

Swamy shouted, 'Ok Adi.' He started swimming towards the bank. But the current was too strong. For every few feet he covered towards the bank, the current was pulling him several meters away. After a few minutes, he was clearly struggling.

Raj shouted, 'Fuck man, we have a problem.' He started running down the bank. Adi followed suit.

Anjali and Divya started shouting for help. Anjali ran around and found a a bamboo stick. Divya was too stunned and stood rooted to the spot with tears running down her cheeks.

Adi, who was running on the rocks, slipped, twisted his ankle and fell on his face. Blood oozed out of his nose and mouth. He must have cracked his jaw. He got up, sat down on the rock and held on to his jaw.

I called out, 'Divya, go to Adi, help him out.'

I grabbed the bamboo stick from Anjali and started running along the bank, trying to catch up with Raj.

Meanwhile, Raj was shouting, 'Swamy, hold on to the rocks. Hold on to any one of them. Don't try hard to swim, go towards a rock and hold on to it.'

Swamy didn't respond, he was trying his best to swim back to the bank.

I shouted, 'Swamy, hold on to any rock and I will throw the stick at you.'

Swamy was drunk. He stopped trying and shouted, 'Raj, help me.'

Raj shouted, 'Fucker, hold on to any rock that you get to and we will get the stick across to you … Hold on.'

Adi and Divya were watching. Anjali was running behind us. Raj was slightly ahead of me.

Swamy was now moving at a great speed. We saw a big, sharp rock ahead and I shouted, 'Swamy, be careful there is a sharp rock ahead, see if you can somehow hold on to it.'

I think Swamy was trying to do the same. He veered himself towards the rock and we thought that he was going to hold on to it.

Suddenly, Swamy's body twirled and landed on the sharp rock head on. Neither Swamy nor any one of us saw a small rock, just ahead of the big, sharp rock. Anjali spotted it and said, 'There is a rock in between, be careful.'

The damage was done, there was a thud and blood oozed out into the water and Swamy's body disappeared.

Raj started wailing, 'Swamy … Swamy … Swamy, where are you?' Anjali and I were stunned. We stopped in our tracks and tears rolled down our cheeks. Anjali started crying loudly and I was running aimlessly.

We didn't see Swamy's body for a few minutes and we kept running ahead. We reached the edge of the water. Raj climbed on to a big rock and desperately searched for Swamy.

In minutes, Swamy's body surfaced, hit a few more rocks and settled between two boulders.

It was very difficult to get to that spot. Raj and I clambered on to the rocks and managed to reach the place in a few minutes. Both of us lifted Swamy's body gently. There was a deep gash on his skull and blood was oozing out from it. Swamy's eyes were closed and his body lay motionless. There was no pulse or heartbeat.

Anjali shouted from the edge of the bank, 'Rub his chest, try and pump the water out from his stomach. He may wake up.' Raj pushed his stomach hard. I rubbed his chest hard and started kneading it in the hope of reviving him. But Swamy lay motionless.

Reality slowly started sinking in. Swamy was no more. I started throwing up. Raj held me. I started crying. Raj wept too.

People gathered around us. Residents of the area had spotted us huddled over Swamy' body. They too checked for the pulse. But Swamy was gone forever. We carried his body to the bank. Divya and Adi walked up to us. All of us sat down next to Swamy's body.

The police arrived in a couple of hours. Veeriah, the sub-inspector, took down our statements. He asked Adi, 'What happened to you?'

Adi said, 'I was trying to save Swamy and I fell on the rocks. I cracked my jaw.'

The inspector had to take the body for post mortem to Mandya Government Hospital. They wanted the contact details of Swamy's parents. Anjali decided that we must talk to Mani and Amit. She called Arun Gupta and informed him about what had happened. Arun said, 'Don't worry, stay where you are and I will be there in a few hours.'

Anjali called Mani and Amit also. Amit told us to proceed to Mandya Government Hospital. He would also get there as fast as he could.

Anjali disconnected the phone and started crying. Divya held her.

We followed the police van to Mandya.

On reaching the hospital, the body was taken to the morgue.

We sat on the benches outside the morgue and I called Amit. We had to inform Swamy's parents.

Amit said, 'Don't worry Venkat, we have taken care of that, Swamy's father and mother will be reaching Mandya by dawn. We should be there in an hour's time. So, hold on. Don't worry.'

It took them an hour-and-a-half. By then, the post mortem was done and the report said, 'Alcohol in the blood stream. Death due to gash on the head, resulting in drowning and leading to asphyxiation.'

The police inspector took us aside. He asked, 'Were you guys drinking before he jumped into the river?' We nodded. He said, 'Aren't you ashamed of yourselves? Don't you come from good families? Is this what they teach you at home?'

We were quiet. We were feeling guilty as hell. Who would have expected this tragic accident to happen? I felt miserable. Amit said, 'Ok guys, enough of all this, let us go grab a bite.'

We walked with him to the nearest hotel and he fed us some idlis. During dinner, he asked us about what had happened. We described the whole horrifying episode.

He listened to us carefully and said, 'It's sad that things turned out like this. But you guys don't have to blame yourselves.'

Swamy's parents arrived early next morning. Thanks to Amit's diligent handling, as soon as they came, the inspector took them to the morgue, got some signatures done and released the body. Swamy's father was stoic; his eyes were bloodshot and tears were streaming down his cheeks. Swamy's mother was wailing. The body was taken to a van and the doors were shut.

Just before leaving, Swamy's father came to me and said, 'I asked you to get my son a job and all of you got him a permanent job with the Lord.'

I broke down.

He put a hand on my shoulder and said, 'I know it is not your fault, it is my anguish which is speaking.'

From that day on I vowed never to drink again. Swamy's death had turned our world upside down. I felt a strange emptiness inside me.

We went home on Sunday. That day's *Times of India* carried a small column with the headline *'Another Software Engineer Drowns.'* Swamy's landlord read it and called up Adi. He asked us to come over.

Adi said, 'Come with me guys.'

Raj said, 'I am in no shape to go anywhere. You guys go ahead. Raj was very upset about not being able to save Swamy. He was so near, yet so far. I think Raj felt responsible for Swamy's death.

I went with Adi to meet Ramachandran, the landlord. He looked upset. His wife Shantamma offered us water and said, 'Don't despair; God calls back good people soon and Swamy was a nice boy. How are his parents?'

Adi said, 'Shattered, sir.'

Ramachandran said, 'So, what do you want to do with his belongings and the deposit money?'

I said, 'We will pick up the belongings and send it to his home, sir. You can write a cheque in his father's name and we will send it to him.'

Ramachandran agreed and took us to Swamy's room. Swamy had very few belongings. There was a *Bhagwad Gita* on his table, an old Philips cassette player, and a few technical books on Java. In a corner of the table stood a black and white family photo. We opened his cupboard and saw a few jeans and shirts. Underneath the shirts was a book. I realised it was porn, so I quickly wrapped it up in his clothes and put it in the suitcase. We packed his stuff and were ready to leave. Ramachandran gave us the cheque and said, 'Good luck boys. The paper said you boys were drunk and then went for a swim. I don't understand why boys from good families get into such things. You have no idea how much it hurts your parents.'

Both of us hung our heads in shame. We left quietly.

We reached home and slept through the day. Mani came home late in the evening to take us out for dinner. It was a quiet dinner and Mani tried to pep us up a bit.

He said, 'Don't take it to heart.'

Anjali also joined us. She was very upset. Swamy had worked with Anjali for the past few months and she had spent the maximum time coaching and teaching him.

She said, 'He was a nice person, really simple. I don't know why all this happened. Come to think of it, he proposed that we go to Shiva Samudram.' I put my hand on hers and said, 'Anju, take it easy.'

Everybody was quiet.

Mani said, 'Hope you guys are coming to work tomorrow.'

We nodded.

He said, 'There is so much to do.'

After dinner, we strolled back home and said good night to Mani.

On Monday morning, there was a mail from Amit to the entire Bangalore location. It read:

Dear Colleagues

It is with profound grief, I wish to inform all of you about the sad demise of our colleague Swamy. Swamy was a wonderful human being and an ace software engineer. He worked on Costco's retail analytics project and was one of the most insightful people.
We are holding a condolence meeting today at 4 pm in the main lobby and all are expected to attend. We will observe a two-minute silence. An obituary book is being placed in the lobby for you to write condolence messages.
We pray for the departed soul and hope that God provides strength and peace to his family.

Warm Regards,
Amit Bagaria,
Sr HR Manager

Most of our colleagues came to our desks and wanted to know what had gone wrong. At 4 pm, people assembled for the condolence meeting and observed a two-minute silence. Almost everybody who knew Swamy filled up condolence messages for the family.

After the meeting, Amit called Raj, Anjali, Adi and me to his cabin.

He asked, 'So, how are you guys?'

Raj said, 'We are okay, Amit.'

I said, 'We picked up Swamy's belongings from his home. We need to send them to his family.'

Amit said, 'No problem. We are also preparing the insurance, PF, gratuity and salary cheque to be sent to his parents. We will send the belongings too. I am asking Arun Gupta to go over and meet his parents. Any one wants to go with him?'

None of us had the courage to face his parents. We remained silent.

Amit said, 'Ok. That is fine. It is understandable. You know, we have an in-house professional counsellor if any of you need to talk.'

We looked at each other.

Amit said, 'Hey, it is okay to talk to counsellors. It makes people feel better.'

Anjali said, 'Maybe I should talk to a counsellor.'

Raj said, 'Yeah, me too.'

Adi was silent. So was I.

Amit asked, 'What about you guys?'

I said, 'I am okay.'

Adi said, 'Me too.'

Amit smiled and said, 'In case you guys need any help, don't hesitate to come and meet me. I am your neighbourhood Pappu anyway.'

We all smiled and he said, 'Ok guys, get going. Raj and Anjali, I will arrange for a meeting with Dr Chandy, the counsellor. He comes here every Wednesday, so both of you can speak to him.'

On Wednesday, Raj and Anjali met with Dr Chandy.

Afterwards, Raj said, 'It was good. He told me to take it easy.'

Anjali said, 'I cried a lot and he listened to me patiently. He said that it was good to cry and get it out of my system. He said that nobody should be blamed for such unfortunate incidents.'

Raj said, 'Yes, he told me the same thing.'

I asked, 'So, how many more sessions to go?'

Anjali said, 'Don't know, maybe a few, till we feel comfortable.'

I said, 'I worry about Adi.'

Raj said, 'Don't worry, he will be okay. If we get him involved in work, he will forget. How are you doing?'

I said, 'I feel bad, but I want to put things behind me.'

A Business Trip to the US

THE NEXT FEW WEEKS WERE HECTIC. CATHY BAKER MADE A conference call and said, 'Team, I want to increase the pace of work and ensure that Phase One with enhanced scope is delivered on time.' Mani increased work pressure and all of us were extremely busy. Adi was totally immersed in work and hardly had time for any of us. Savitha drove Anjali mad and she started working over most of the weekends. Raj spent time doing automation scripts and was busy as hell. Since I was playing the business analyst role, I was doing relatively better. I was free in the mornings and my work picked up speed by late afternoons. Almost every day, I had calls with the US clients and came home at about 10 pm. I was trying to define the functionality for each module and it affected the scope quite a bit.

Mani said,'VSAT, be careful on what you are adding in the scope. I am not comfortable adding any more for Phase One of the deliverables.'

I said, 'But the clients are pushing hard and I can't convince them on the phone.'

He said, 'Why don't you influence Steve?'

I said, 'I tried, but he is also under pressure from other module leads in the US.'

Mani said, 'In which case, why don't you go to the US for a couple of weeks and address this?'

Finally, I was getting my chance to go to the US.

I said, 'Sure, in which case, I suggest Adi and Raj also go with me.'

Mani said, 'We are not sending you to a circus, buddy. You don't want Anjali to go with you? Fucker, you are going on work, do you realise that?'

I said, 'Mani, I need Adi because he can finalise the architecture and Raj to conclude on the test coverage. That will give an idea of the scope.'

Mani said, 'Why not Harpreet?'

I said, 'Adi knows the new architecture better than Harpreet.'

Mani said, 'Ok, let me revert to you on this.'

I immediately pinged Anjali, Raj and Adi on the chat-line.

VSAT: Mani spoke to me, said he wants us to go to the US for a few weeks

Raj: Cool man.

VSAT: I said, I want Adi and Raj to also go along.

Anjali: What about me?

VSAT: Couldn't babe ☹

Adi: But how can I come? I have so many deliverables?

VSAT: Do it from the US?

Adi: Can't. My ass is on fire.

Raj: I am coming buddy. Make sure I am in.

VSAT: I told Mani, let us see what he says. Ok guys, got to go. Bye!

After a few days Mani came back and said, 'VSAT, I spoke to the client. We can send you and Raj for now. You guys have to go for atleast two to three months for business meetings. By the time you guys come back, you will be expected to nail the scope and test coverage across all modules.'

(Managing the Mani Way, Axiom Four—when things don't go your way, throw a biscuit at your subordinates and send them to the

US on the client's money and ensure they complete work as you want them to.)

I was excited. I said, 'Sure Mani.'

Mani said, 'I will speak to Raj also. Do you have a passport?'

I said, 'Yes, Mani.'

Mani said, 'Ok start the travel process, you can leave this weekend.'

'This weekend?'

He said, 'Yes. Why? Do you have to get married before you go?'

I laughed. 'No Mani, don't have to. My parents don't believe that I will return with a white American bride.'

Mani understood that I was referring to him when I talked about the white American bride. He smirked and said, 'Ok then, get moving.'

After Mani left, I called Anjali, Raj and Adi and gave them the information.

Raj jumped with joy and said, 'I am coming over to your desk. Hold on.'

Everybody crowded around my desk. Anjali asked, 'How long will you be gone?'

I said, 'Two to three months.'

'What? So long?'

I didn't say anything.

Adi smiled, put his arm around Anjali's shoulders and said, 'Don't worry Anjali, I will give you company and it will be much better.'

Guna who sat across my desk sarcastically said, 'One has to take a flight to go to the US. Before taking the flight, you have to get a visa.'

Raj replied, 'Oh, didn't know that. I thought people took boats.' Everybody laughed.

We filled up travel forms and applied for our visas. We went to a travel agent and booked our tickets. Then we had to attend a half-day orientation program before we left for the US. We reported for training and Pranati welcomed us warmly. There were about twelve of us in the room who were going to the US. She said, 'All of you are going on a business visa, so I will basically cover two modules today: Giving an interview at the US consulate and the cultural differences between India and the US.' The orientation lasted for almost three hours. We learnt the basics of life in USA.

Adi joined us for lunch. He wanted to know about the session.

Raj laughed and said, 'Moral of the training program is, you will be deported if you stare at or comment on anybody's body parts, including boobs.' I knew that the Malhotra khandaan's obsession for boobs would never subside. Not in this lifetime atleast.

I said, 'Even if you make any freaking personal comments on women,' then I looked at Adi, laughed and said, 'or men.' Adi laughed – by now, all of us were comfortable with his sexual orientation and he was ready to take our jokes sportingly.

I said, 'Guess what, you can't even ask about someone's family. You can't ask their age. You can't even ask if they are married or have children. Basically, you can't ask anything. You can talk about the weather and sports.'

Adi laughed and said, 'Hi, it is hot today. Gee, it is cold today. It may rain tonight. Did you watch basketball? Thank you. It is a pleasure to meet you. What kind of a country is it man?'

Raj said, 'You can't look at all those beautiful legs too. I am looking forward to meeting Jenny man, my counterpart in the US, she looks pretty good on Facebook.'

Divya walked in. She said, 'Yeah, yeah Raj, look out for Jenny.'

Raj said, 'Hi D, you know I am just kidding.'

Divya asked, 'So, how long are you gone?'

Raj said, 'About two to three months.'

Divya said, 'That's a long time Raj. When are you leaving?'

Raj said, 'As soon as we get a visa, probably next week.'

I said, 'We have to go to Chennai for a visa.'

Raj and I took the train and went to Chennai. We went to the US consulate early in the morning and stood in the queue outside the gate. At about 10 am, we made it to the interview room.

There were a lot of people in the room. The interview lasted less than five minutes.

A student was sitting next to me and was carrying all his certificates.

He said, 'My name is Gabbi Reddy. I am planning to study Computer Science in the US.'

I said, 'Great. Which university?'

He said, 'Alaska State University.'

I asked, 'Do you know where Alaska is?'

He said, 'Tip.'

I said, 'Yeah tip. You know the average temperature in Alaska?'

He said, 'America only, no sir? So, no problem. Actually Alaska is closer to erstwhile USSR than America. I am told it is only five miles apart.'

I said, 'The average temperature throughout the year is less than zero degrees Celsius?'

He said, 'No problem sir, we will wear sweaters and stay indoors.'

I said, 'Sweaters don't work there. You will need triple layered thermals. Special underwear to make sure that your nuts don't vanish.'

He laughed, 'So cold sir?'

I nodded. 'Did you read about the place when you filled up the forms?'

He said, 'No. What is the point in reading about the place? It is America only no!'

I was dumbstruck. I asked, 'But why Alaska?'

He chuckled and said, 'That is the only place I got admission. Maybe nobody else applied? I don't know.'

I said, 'Great, will you be coming back after that?'

He said, 'I am from Anantapur. My father is a farmer. He mortgaged his land to send me to the US. I will first make money, and then I will come to India get married. I will go back to the US with my wife. Then apply for a green card, and sponsor my parents too. Within fifteen to twenty years, our entire family will be American citizens, sir.'

This time I peered at him carefully. I thought his brain was about to explode. He had chalked out plans for the next twenty years. Either he was clairvoyant or plain stupid. Forrest Gump!

I said, 'Don't tell them that you are going to settle in the US. Tell them that you will finish your studies and come back to India or else your interview won't go well.'

'But why?'

'I don't have time to explain. Just do as I say and you will get your visa.'

He said, 'Tell me why.'

I said, 'They reject you if they feel that you are going to settle there. They don't like that.'

'Ok, but are you sure? Then why are they sending so many people from India to America? I am sure they want us to settle there. I hear all people in NASA and Microsoft are Indians?'

I said, 'Trust me, just do what I say. Tell them your family wants you to be back.'

He said, 'Ok, I will do that. But if …'

And then he was called for the interview.

He took about three to four minutes and then I was summoned. Gabbi Reddy was walking out as I was going in. He said, 'Thank you so very much. I got the visa. I told them that I am going to set up computers in Karupureddy Palle, near Anantapur district and hence going to Alaska to study.'

I said, 'And he bought that?'

He said, 'No, no, I didn't sell anything ...'

'He was convinced by what you said?'

He said, 'Yes, I am getting a visa. It is not a "he," it is a "she".'

I understood why he had got the visa. The visa officer must have been convinced that nobody in the US would give opportunities to such nitwits. But I wouldn't be surprised if nitwits like these became multi-millionaires in the US by starting companies in Silicon Valley.

I went in for my interview.

There was a lady sitting on a high chair with my papers in front of her.

She said, 'Morning. What is your first name, middle name and last name?'

I said, 'M'am, my full name is Venkata Subramaniam Adisankara Tanikaburla.' My first name is Venkata, my middle name is Subramaniam Adisankara and my last name is Tanikaburla.'

She said, 'Listen, tell me your middle name again.'

'Subramaniam Adisankara.'

She said, 'That is two names, give me one middle name.'

I said, 'M'am, mine is a long name, that is how it is in my state'

'Which state do you come from?'

I said, 'Andhra Pradesh.'

She said, 'Hyderabad, the software city?'

I said, 'I am from Kazipet, I mean Warangal.'

She said, 'Which one? Kazipet or Warangal'

I said, 'In India we have two names for the same place.'

She sighed and said, 'You have two middle names and you come from a place which has two names.'

I said, 'Yes madam. That is common here in India. We have Hyderabad, Secundrabad. We have Vizag, Visakhapatnam and Waltair; that's three names for one place.'

She kept my papers down and looked at me, 'That is damn confusing. My name is Lisa Ann Carpenter. Lisa is my first name, Ann is my middle name and Carpenter is my last name and I come from Bucks County, Philadelphia. Now, can you say something similar with respect to yourself?'

I said, 'Ok, m'am. My name is Venkata Subramaniam Adisankara Tanikaburla. Venkata is equal to Lisa. Subramaniam Adisankara is equal to Ann and Tanikaburla is equal to Carpenter and I come from Hanamkonda County, Warangal.'

She started laughing. That was the best I could do. How could I explain in three minutes, the genesis of three generations pertaining to my name and place?

She asked, 'What do you do? Wait a minute; you are from TCS, Tatas. Ok, so where are you going Mr Software Engineer?'

I said, 'New Jersey m'am. I am on NED, the North Eastern Drinks project.'

She looked up from a stack of papers and asked, 'Going on work?'

I said, 'No m'am, going for business meetings.'

'What meetings?'

I said, 'We are trying to understand the scope of the project and need to have lots of meetings for that.'

She said, 'Why?'

I wanted to say, because Americans don't get anything quickly unless they conduct ten meetings, secondly I haven't seen the US and peer pressure is building up, thirdly every idiot in my neighbourhood has gone to the US. Lastly, if you reject my visa, my mom will have a heart attack.

I said, 'The scope defines the extent of deliverables and that is what we are trying to determine.'

'Are you going to come back soon?'

'Yes m'am. My family is here and I am the only son to take care of them.'

She said, 'I heard that before, give me something new. Show more creativity.'

I smiled and said, 'Hmm ... ok m'am, I am sure you have not heard this before, because I want to contest elections and become a Member of Legislative Assembly.'

She started laughing.

I said, 'Because I have a girl friend here. She thinks I am going to marry a white American and settle there, but I won't make that mistake.'

She grinned and said, 'That is novel one, too. But what is wrong in marrying a white American girl?'

I said, 'Nothing wrong. Once the novelty wears off, we will get divorced.'

She said, 'What's the guarantee it won't happen here?'

I said, 'It doesn't m'am. That is why they say, marry an Indian girl, work for a French boss and drive a Japanese car.'

She grinned and asked, 'Why a French boss?'

I said, 'Two reasons. The French take the maximum holidays and secondly, neither of us can understand each other, so work stress is low.'

She laughed and asked, 'Got any relatives in the US?'

I said, 'No m'am, I am the first from my family to even try going to the US. Our house, three cows and four goats and everything else we own, is here.'

She was surely amused hearing about cows and goats. She took a big rubber stamp and stamped my papers. 'Venkata, you are really funny. I enjoyed talking to you. Have fun in the US. By the way, what do people call you?'

I said, 'VSAT.' She shook her head and smiled.

I walked out, relieved. I went to the water cooler and drank a glass of water.

Raj went in next and came back within a minute.

I said, 'So fast?'

He started laughing. She asked me my name. I said, 'Raj Malhotra, first name, last name and no middle name. My father owns a Maruti showroom and I am going to the US because I am compelled to attend business meetings. She didn't ask me any questions, she just stamped my papers and said, 'Ok Mr Raj, have a nice trip to the US.'

I hugged Raj tightly.

He said, 'VSAT, fuck man. I thought you were out of the habit of hugging me. Leave me now, this is the fucking US consulate man.'

I laughed, loosened my grip around him and said, 'All the more reason.'

Raj came closer and said, 'But did you notice the cleavage? What boobs man!'

I looked at him and said, 'I didn't notice anything. She was grilling me man.'

Raj said, 'Fuck, my eyes popped, nice babe she is. I wish every babe in the US is like this man.'

I asked Raj, 'I have a question yaar. We guys talk about sex so freely, is it a guy thing or do girls also talk about it?'

He said, '*Puttar*, girls talk about it more than all of us put together. It is just that they don't come out in the open. What do you think, 100 crore people were born just like that? Fucker, it is a national pastime. People come home in the evening; have dinner, watch stupid tv serials on Star Plus and screw each other. The serials provide an anti-climax and the screw provides the climax, it balances out. Why do you think Ekta Kapoor is so popular?'

I said, 'You mean its because she makes anti-climax serials? Bullshit!'

Raj grinned and said, 'No, because she is partially responsible for all the screwing in the country. God has given you brains, *socho na*?'

Anyway, I was overwhelmed by the 'tv serials and sex theory.' Surely Raj and his family were intellectuals in this field and I had a lot to learn from them!

I said, 'Fuck off, Raj. You are ridiculous. The whole world swears by her as the serial queen.'

We started the same day from Chennai and came back to Bangalore. We were expecting the passports to reach us in a day. We had the tickets, now we had to pack and leave.

That night, I called my mom and said, 'Mom, I am going to America the day after tomorrow.'

My mom said, 'Praise Lord Venkateswara. Finally he listened to our pleas. Why didn't you tell us the good news before?'

I said, 'It happened suddenly Lakshmi. I came to know about it a few days back. Yesterday we went to Chennai for our visa. We will be leaving on Saturday night, I mean Sunday early hours Ma.'

She said, 'But how can you go so soon? How many years are you going for?'

I said, 'Lakshmi, this is my first trip and I am going for only a few weeks. I will come back in a couple of months.'

Mom said, 'Why such a short trip? Everybody goes for a couple of years or so. Why are you going for such a short trip?'

I said, 'Ma, going to the US is work-dependent. I am going to attend some meetings and come back.'

She said, 'Why don't you tell your boss, two years or nothing.'

My mom has an innate capacity to brush everything aside, and focus on the crux of what she wants. I thought about Mani's plight if my mom was a software engineer and reported to him. She would have probably assigned him tasks daily from the US.

I said, 'It doesn't work like that Ma.'

She said, 'Ok, are you catching a flight from Bangalore? Which one?'

I said, 'Lufthansa flight. Bangalore to Frankfurt and Frankfurt to Newark, New Jersey.'

She said, 'We will come to see you off.' I said, 'No need Mom, I will come back from the US and then come home. It is just a couple of months.' She said, 'Kanna, I haven't seen you in a year. I don't know how you are doing *ra*. Shall I ask your father to come and see you?'

I said, 'No Ma. There is so much work to do.'

She said, 'Will you call us regularly from America?'

I said, 'Of course. Don't worry.'

Mom said, 'Kanna, Swati is teaching me Microsoft and email. I will soon send you emails.'

I said, 'Wow Lakshmi, that will be cool.'

Mom surprised me by asking, 'Are you on "Sipe"? Raghuveer's mom talks to him on that, free of cost.'

I laughed aloud and said, 'Lakshmi, it is called "Skype". I am impressed! Now you are truly a software engineer's mother.'

Swati said, 'Mom is learning how to send emails. Can you believe that?'

I said, 'Amma, learn Java also. You can also join TCS and we can go to the US together.'

Mom said, 'Enough of all your jokes. I am trying my best to be in touch with you and you don't make any effort from your side. You didn't even come home for a year.'

I said, 'Lakshmi, don't be so senti. I will call you regularly.'

Swati shouted, 'Get me some perfumes.'

I said, 'Ma, tell Swati that I will get her perfumes. I will call you again, tell me what you want.'

Mom said, 'I understand America has nice crockery sets. Can you get one full set for home?'

I said, 'Ok Mom, will do. Tell dad about my America trip and ask him what he wants. I will call again tomorrow. Give my love to grandpa. How is his health?'

Mom said, 'Grandpa is missing you Venkat. Come home as soon as you can.'

I said, 'Sure Ma, as soon as I am back from the US, around Christmas time.'

The next day, I collected my tickets, visa and foreign currency.

Anjali said, 'Come, let us go to Commercial Street and buy some winter clothing.'

I went along with Anjali.

Raj told me that he was going to spend the night at Divya's place. Adi said he was going out on Friday evening visiting some cousins and he couldn't join us. Anjali and I shopped for a nice jacket, bought some Arrow shirts and a couple of Allen Solly trousers.

She said, 'You should present yourself well when you are visiting clients.'

I said, 'Yes babe, I am usually well dressed, that is why you fell for me.'

She coyly replied, 'I didn't. You fell for me and then trapped me.'

I said, 'Let us have dinner at my place. I will make Maggi for both of us.'

She said, 'Great idea, let's go.'

We rode back home and picked up a few noodle packs on the way. She said, 'Chicken for me.'

I said, 'Dear Anjuji, we are vegetarians.'

She said, 'Ok, what to do! I am getting married to one.'

We went home and Anjali sat on the kitchen ledge and I made Maggi. Once the noodles were ready, I served it in one plate and found two spoons for us. We ate from the same plate and fed each other a bit. She forked a long noodle strand and slowly dropped it into my mouth. She said, 'My dad used to do this when we were kids.'

I promise, 'Once I am back, I will speak to your dad.'

She nodded.

We washed up and moved to the living room. We sat down on the mattress in front of the tv, held hands and surfed channels.

After some time, I leaned over and kissed her on the neck. She let out a small groan and I continued to kiss her as I moved up from the base of the neck to her pink lips. I kissed her on her lips and she responded by putting her arms around me. She said, 'Teddy, I love you. I will miss you for the next two months.'

I said, 'Same here.' I moved my hands under her shirt, unhooked her bra and felt her soft breasts. I caressed them and her nipples stiffened. She removed her shirt and said, 'Do you want to make love here?'

I said, 'No baby.' I carried her into my room and locked the door. Then I slowly unzipped her jeans and pulled them off gently. She was wearing pink panties. She asked, 'Do you want to remove your clothes or not?' and helped me remove my shirt and jeans. Then she flicked the light off and we started making love in the dark. After a few minutes, the power went off and we started sweating profusely, but we didn't stop. We lost count of the hours and lay exhausted in each other's arms. It was a symphony—the motions were slow, gradual, and rhythmical. I said, 'That was great baby.'

She said, 'Yeah, I felt good too.'

I said, 'I will miss you.' She said, 'You will miss me or miss making love to me?'

I laughed and said, 'Both.'

She giggled. She said, 'Don't screw around in the US. I heard sex is easy there.'

I said, 'Give me a break. I am not that kind of guy.'

She said, 'I am not saying you are that kind of guy. I know it is difficult for men to stay without sex for a long time.'

I said, 'Why, can women live without it for a long time?'

She said, 'No, but we can manage, you guys can't. That is why I am saying, keep your snake caged.' She started laughing.

I said, 'Now you are being gross. Let me drop you home. Adi may come anytime now.'

Both of us washed, dressed and we were just about to leave when Adi stepped in. He said, 'Hi guys, where are you going?'

I said, 'I am dropping Anjali at her place.'

Adi said, 'Chalo, I will also come, if you love birds don't mind.'

Anjali said, 'Come.' We walked Anjali to her house and then walked back home.

Adi said, 'Don't worry VSAT, as I said, I will be good company for Anjali when you are gone.'

I thanked Adi. Compared to Raj, Adi was sober, sensitive and most importantly—sane.

Dial 911

WE REACHED NEWARK ON SUNDAY EVENING. IT WAS QUITE COLD. Ramana, the Human Resource coordinator from the TCS east coast office, came to receive us. Ramana was in his mid- thirties, about five feet ten, weighed probably seventy kilos and had an athletic build. He welcomed us with a smile and said, 'Hi, my name is Ramana, welcome to the US.'

I said, 'Thanks for coming to the airport.'

Raj said, 'Do we have to go to office tomorrow, or can we take off a couple of days to adjust to the new place?'

Ramana grinned and said, 'Amit spoke to me about you guys. Tomorrow 7 am, I pick you up and drop you at the client's place.' Our reputation preceded us.

(Scream in my head: *The Godfather! 'Tom, you should have told me that you work for Don Corleone.'*)

I was dismayed at TCS's amazing capability to pick the same kind of HR DNA across the globe. All the HR people in TCS talked the same language. I think HR has a different orientation program than the rest of the folks. Probably, they are hypnotised and brainwashed on the first day!

Raj looked at Ramana and said, 'So, how long have you been here?'

Ramana said, 'Couple of years.'

'Enjoying yourself?' asked Raj.

Ramana grinned and said, 'So far. Now that you guys have come, things might change.'

I just grinned and shook my head. Raj smiled.

I said, 'Can we have some decent coffee before we head to the apartment?'

Ramana said, 'Sure, let us go to Starbucks.'

Raj asked, 'Can we smoke?'

Ramana said, 'Smoke what?'

Raj sarcastically said, 'Marijuana! Obviously cigarettes,'

Ramana said, 'No, can't smoke in public places. You will be viewed as a social outcast if you smoke in public. It is just a suggestion you may want to consider. At least don't smoke in front of your clients.' Raj said, 'So, nobody smokes in the US?'

Ramana looked at Raj with a faint smile. Ramana mumbled, 'Amit was right.'

Raj raised his eyebrows and asked, 'I heard that ... what do you mean?'

'I mean, he said, you kind of ask a lot of questions.'

Raj persisted, 'What else did he say?'

Ramana shrugged.

Raj continued, 'So people don't smoke around here? But they do dope!'

Ramana said, 'Don't want to talk about dope. Healthcare premiums go up if you smoke cigarettes. Remember, in this country, everything has a repercussion.'

We nodded and Ramana changed the topic.

He said, 'You guys will share a corporate apartment with Parvinder. Each one gets a room with attached bath.'

I asked, 'Many TCS people keep coming?'

Ramana said, 'Yup, people come and go. If they stay for a month or more, we allot corporate apartments, for short trips, they stay in hotels.'

Ramana paid at the counter and we took our café lattes.

Raj said, 'Three dollars, hundred and fifty rupees. Wow, that is expensive!'

Ramana said, 'If you translate everything into Indian rupees, you cannot eat and live in this country. Don't compare. Live economically, stay within the per-diems you get and life will be okay.'

We headed to the car park. It was quite cold outside and the jacket Anjali had given me was very useful.

Raj asked, 'Ramana, is it usually this cold out here?'

Ramana said, 'I hope you guys have decent winter clothing. It is really going to get cold here. Temperatures will be less than 5 degrees centigrade shortly.'

Raj came close to my ears, grinned and whispered, 'VSAT, balls will freeze. I can then rub yours and you mine.'

Raj was in a playful mood and Ramana in an awful mood. I decided not to say anything. It was worse than being an umpire for India-Pakistan matches.

Ramana started his car and we were on our way. The roads were unbelievable. I said, 'India will take ages to develop like this.'

Ramana smirked, 'Ages? It never will.'

Raj said, 'Got US citizenship?'

Ramana stared at Raj. Raj said, 'Hey, I am just kidding. Wanted to see how you look when you smile.'

Ramana ignored the jibe. He said, 'This country has 300 million people and utilises almost 50% of the world's resources. India has a billion people. If we use resources like the way these people do, planet earth will have nothing left.'

Raj said, 'But we can have good roads.'

Ramana said, 'Yes we can, if we want to. Where is the will to do it?'

We got into a debate on India vs. US. I guess this was a common debate for most *desis* to get into on the day of their arrival. How could we not compare the two countries? Ramana drove for an hour and we reached the apartment. It was carpeted, had a fully equipped kitchen with a fridge, microwave, hob, chimney and dishwasher. I asked, 'Hey where is the washing machine?'

Ramana said, 'It is in the basement. Whenever you want to wash, go downstairs and put forty cents in the slot, it takes care of one load. There is a dryer next to it. No dhobis here. The Laundromat is way too expensive. There is an iron box and board in the cupboard. By the way, you wash your utensils and you keep the place clean. Once a week, we will have the apartment cleaned by a cleaner. Remember, no noises, no fights and no blaring music.'

I said, 'I want to call home. How do I do that?'

Ramana showed us the phone and said, 'I am sure you have calling cards. So use the instructions and dial. India code is +91. Then dial the STD code and the number. If you are calling a cell phone in India, after the country code, dial the cell number.'

Ramana continued, 'Guys, no damages to the apartment. Don't screw it up. It is on corporate lease and any damages will be deducted from your salary.'

Raj asked, 'How does one get around here?'

Ramana said, 'Car, the vehicle which has four wheels.' He had tried being humourous with Raj. Big mistake.

Raj quickly fired back, 'No six, you forgot the steering wheel and the spare wheel in the boot.'

Ramana said, 'Oh, I was counting the ones that touched the road.'

Raj smirked, 'I was counting the ones that kept you on the road too.'

Ramana shrugged. The conversation wasn't going anywhere.

Ramana continued, 'I am sure you guys have taken international license in India. Do you know how to drive a car?'

Raj said, 'I do.'

I said, 'I can't. What about bikes?'

Ramana laughed and said, 'Here, the rich drive bikes, the rest drive cars.'

I smiled and said, 'Really.' Ramana said, 'I mean it. You will get to know. Also, it will be freezing cold, nobody drives bikes.'

I said, 'Ok, we will take a car. It will be chauffer-driven by Raj. Hopefully, I will also take some driving lessons.'

Ramana said, 'Ok, do that, I guess about five lessons should be okay. TCS has a reimbursement policy for that.'

We nodded our heads. It was a long time since I heard the word 'policy'. I felt at home.

Ramana added, 'Tomorrow, I will take you guys to the client's place, be ready by 7 am. By afternoon, we will get you a rental car. After that, you guys are on your own.'

I asked, 'What about dinner?'

Ramana once again tried his hand at humour. He said, 'I don't cook.'

We smiled out of courtesy. He opened the fridge and said, 'Lots of stuff in here, you can cook?'

We said, 'Ok.'

He said, 'I think Parvinder has gone out, he will let you know everything once he is back.'

I asked, 'Can we have your phone number, just in case?'

He said, 'Yeah, sure. Here is my card. Call me anytime between 7 am to 4 pm and on weekdays only. Call me in an emergency, no problems. Here are some basic rules for you. Don't do free walking on the roads, it is an offense. Don't talk loudly, don't whistle. Don't get into political, racial, sexist or any kind of confrontational discussions. Steer clear of them.' Raj said, 'Any dos?'

Ramana smiled and said, 'Be nice to HR, because when in trouble, they are the only people you can turn to. Work hard. Client is God.'

We nodded.

Ramana said, 'Yeah, one more thing. Americans don't understand when you wobble your head at forty-five degrees. That is uncertainity for them. If you agree, nod your head forward and backward. If you don't, move your head from left to right and back again.' Then he gave a quick demo and asked, 'Understood?'

We bobbed our heads again at forty-five degrees.

He shook his head in exasperation and said, 'Ok guys. Got to go. Any questions?'

I said, 'Thanks for your help Ramana. We will see you tomorrow at 7 am.'

Raj asked, 'Do we have to go so early? I mean, how far is the client's place from here? Can't we start at 8.30 am or so?'

Ramana said, '7 am is late in this country. People go to work by 6 am and wind up by afternoon. The NED office is not too far from here; it is in Parsippany and is a fifteen-minute drive. So, we can be there by 7.15 am. We can introduce you to everyone and by 7.30 am you can start work.'

Raj said, 'Oh, ok.'

Ramana waved goodbye and left.

After Ramana left, Raj said, 'Too many rules. Don't do this, don't do that, don't piss, don't breathe, I hope they don't say, don't fuck!'

I said, 'How can they? Didn't you notice that most porn videos are from this country?'

Raj said, 'I never focused on sub-titles man.'

I said, 'Yeah, like I collect trivia on porn.'

Raj laughed and said, 'Who knows?'

I said, 'Ok you take a shower. I will call my parents.'

He headed for the bathroom.

I called home. My dad picked up.

He said, 'Venkat, reached safely son?'

I said, 'Yes Dad.'

'How are you?' 'It is fine Dad. Ramana, our HR person came to receive us and we are now at the TCS corporate guest house.'

'Is it cold there?'

I said, 'Not too much Pa. I am fine. Can I speak to mom?'

Then mom came on the line and said, 'Kanna, did you reach safely? How is America?'

I said, 'Fine Lakshmi.'

She said, 'I consulted the astrologer today. He said you are going to have a good time in the distant land (America), but warned to be careful about your closest friends—they could create trouble for you. Don't eat non-vegetarian food. Swati told me you are smoking. Please stop.'

I said, 'Mom, I just reached, please don't give me a lecture.'

She said, 'Remember what the astrologer told you.'

I said, 'Ok Ma. I am going now and will talk to you later. Say Hi to grandpa.'

She said, 'Ok call me tomorrow. You must be tired. Srimangala's mother visited us today. She likes you so much.'

I said, 'Ok Mom, I will talk to you later. Bye.'

Srimangala was the latest entrant in my life and was creating a mess. I realised that the proposal was picking up steam back home. I had to act fast.

Meanwhile, Raj came out of the bathroom and said, 'So stud, spoke to your parents? This time do we pray for the health and well-being of Steve or Jenny?'

I said, 'Shut up. You want to call your parents? Do that. I am going for a shower.'

He asked, 'Not calling Anjali?'

I said, 'I will call her later dude.'

I went for a shower.

After 10 minutes, Raj knocked on the bathroom door and in a stoic voice said, 'VSAT, the police are here.'

I said, 'Fuck off, don't joke. Give me ten minutes and I'll be out.'

He said, 'No, I am serious.'

I said, 'Raj, go jump.'

But this time, there was a louder knock and an American voice came from the other side, 'Sir, would you mind coming out? My name is Joe and this is the county police.'

I said, 'Yes, yes, sir. I am coming.'

Then Joe said, 'Come out slowly and gently, don't surprise us sir. I mean open the door slowly and steadily. Please put your hands forward, make sure you show your hands to us sir.'

There was a mumble from outside and Raj said, 'VSAT, do it very slowly. These guys are serious and have guns and all that.'

I was fucking scared. I had no idea what had happened or what we had done. Fuck, what the astrologer said was right. Raj was the problem child.

I unlocked the bathroom door from the inside, slowly and steadily, opened it. I was just wearing a towel around my waist and had applied oil to my hair. I looked like a mafia don.

There were two cops wearing blue uniforms. One was African American and well built. Probably six-and-a-half feet and weighed more than a hundred kilos. The other was a white policeman, almost six feet tall. He was the more athletic of the two.

Joe, the white cop said, 'Easy, easy. Keep your hands in front and slowly walk out sir.'

I did exactly what I was told. I walked to the drawing room and the bigger cop asked, 'So, who dialed 911? You? Or was that you?'

I was shitting in my towel. I didn't know what was going on. Raj looked equally scared. I said, 'No, I didn't dial any number.'

Raj said, 'I was dialling my home in Gurgaon.'

The black cop asked, 'Which place?'

Raj said, 'Gurgaon.'

The black cop asked, 'Hey Joe, is that in Afghanistan?'

The white cop shook his head.

'Pakistan?'

The white cop said, 'Not sure.'

I added meekly, 'India sir.'

Black cop said, 'You from India?'

Raj said, 'Yes sir.'

'So, why did you dial 911?'

Raj said, 'No sir, we didn't dial 911, I was dialing +91 India code and then I dialed 124 for the area code, but the phone was disconnected after the 1. So, it must have dialed 911. I am not sure what happened sir.'

The white cop said, 'So, when did you come to the United States?'

I replied, 'An hour back sir'

The black cop said, 'FOB.'

The white cop nodded and said, 'Mind if we look around?'

I said, 'No sir, please go ahead.'

Then the cops searched the house. They entered Parvinder's room. There was a big poster of Guru Gobind Singhji on the wall. He was riding a horse and wielding a sword. Both the cops looked at the poster and started to feel nervous.

The black cop asked, 'Who lives here?'

Raj said, 'Parvinder sir.'

'Is he also from India?'

We nodded our heads.

I said, 'We haven't met him yet sir.'

The black cop asked the white cop, 'Are you sure about this place "Googoon" or whatever it is, is in India?'

The white cop said, 'Don't know. Call and figure out.'

The black cop picked his radio and called. 'Hi Syl, this is Mace. You know of a place called googoon? No, I don't know how to spell that. Hey, can you help spell it for me?'

Raj said, 'GURGAON.'

Mace repeated that on the radio and said, 'Ok. Ok. Gotcha. Yup. ... India ... all right. That is fine. No ... routine stuff, talk to you later.'

He then turned towards us and said, 'Ok, so you boys are from India, huh?'

We said, 'Yes sir.'

The white cop asked, 'If you never met the other guy, how did you get in the apartment?'

I said, 'This is the company's corporate apartment, has three keys and our HR coordinator dropped us here and left.'

Joe asked, 'Ok, do you have your HR coordinator's number?'

I said, 'Yes sir. His card is on the table over there.'

Mace picked up the card and read, 'Tata Consultancy Services.' He picked up his phone and called Ramana.

Mace said, 'Hi, this is the county police, am I speaking to Mr Neeemagada?'

Ramana's surname was Nimmagada, somehow that had become Neeemagada with a twirl and a twist.

Mace then said, 'Mr Neeemagada, we are at your corporate apartment and there are two people here who claim that you have dropped them here an hour back. Is that right?'

Mace said, 'Ok, so you did ... No, somebody dialed 911, so we are here ... you want to come, ok. Good! We will wait here. How long are you going to take? Ok, fifteen minutes ... ok.'

Then Mace turned to us and said, 'He will be here in fifteen. What are your names?'

Raj said, 'I am Raj and he is VSAT.'

Joe said, 'VSAT. Is that your name?'

I said, 'That is the shortened version sir.'

Mace said, 'Ok, what is your full name?'

I said, 'Venkata Subramaniam Adisankara Tanikaburla.'

Mace said, 'Don't read me some alien text book. I want your name.'

I said, 'Yes sir, my name is Venkata—Subramaniam—Adisankara—Tanikaburla.'

Mace got irritated, 'Is that your name?'

I said, 'Yes sir.'

He shook his head.

Joe turned to me and said, 'Can I see your passports?'

Raj said, 'Sure.' He started opening his travel kit.

Mace said, 'Easy, go easy on that. Do it slowly.'

I said, 'Would you mind if I wore my shirt and jeans?'

Joe said, 'Sure, after we are done with the passports.'

I slowly picked up my passport from the travel kit and showed it to them.

Mace said, 'You got a long name my friend.'

I said, 'Yes sir, that is why we take the first alphabet of each letter and use it as my name.'

He said, 'What does your name mean?'

I said, 'The names of four gods.'

'How many gods do you have?'

I said, 'I think three million sir.'

They looked at each other and grinned.

Joe said, 'You got three million gods?'

Raj said, 'Yes sir, something like that.'

I said, 'Sir, can I wear my clothes?'

Mace said, 'Yup, do it here, slow and steady.'

I picked up my jeans and T-shirt and slowly put them on. I had never taken so long in my life to wear a pair of jeans and a T-shirt.

Meanwhile Joe went towards the kitchen. There was a pressure cooker on the stove.

He looked at that and said, 'What is this?'

Raj said, 'Pressure cooker sir.'

Mace said, 'Why do you need a pressure device at home?'

I said, 'Sir, we cook daal in that.'

Joe said, 'Daal? What is that?'

I thought for a while. Fuck, what is daal called in English? I studied in Telugu medium till my tenth grade and then shifted to English medium and I think in the vernacular.

I suddenly remembered. I said, 'Yes ... lentils sir.'

Mace said, 'You cook lentils in a pressure device? Why?'

I said, 'It cooks faster and tastes better sir.'

Joe shook his head.

He then took us to Parvinder's room and showed us the photo of Guru Gobind Singhji and asked, 'Who is that?'

Raj said, 'He is a spiritual leader of the Sikhs.'

Mace asked, 'Spiritual leader of who ... sorry?'

I said, 'Sikhs. They are a religious community in India.'

Mace asked, 'Are they from Afghanistan, Iraq, Iran, Pakistan—any of these countries?'

I said, 'No sir, they are from Punjab, a state in India.'

Raj added, 'Bordering Pakistan.'

I looked at Raj in complete disbelief. Nincompoop ... he was displaying his talent in geography and world affairs at the wrong time.

I said, 'Part of the Indian union, but borders Pakistan.'

Mace immediately said, 'Joe, tell you what, radio for some force man.'

If looks could kill, I would have instantly choked Raj. He was so fucking dumb.

Joe said, 'Sure.' He reached for his radio and said, 'Hi Sergeant, yeah, this is Joe. Could you send another patrol, yeah we are at, yeah, you got it, that's right. No, things are fine, we are waiting for another one.'

Within minutes, a patrol car siren rang out and two more cops came up to our apartment. Both were white. Mace said, 'Why don't you guys stay below and let us know when somebody turns up. We are waiting for Mr Neeemagada, HR coordinator from TCS and the other is, what did you say his name was?'

Raj slowly pronounced his name, 'PARVINDER.'

Mace said, 'Yeah, that is his name.'

One of them took a notepad and pencil and quickly scribbled something and both went downstairs.

Meanwhile, Parvinder arrived and the cops who were waiting downstairs got him to the apartment. To him, all of us were strangers. But he had been briefed that we would be coming.

He looked at us and said, 'You must be Raj and Venkat, what's happening here?'

Parvinder was a senior software engineer. He had three years of experience with TCS and this was probably his third trip. He was a Sardarji and wore a turban. Looking at his turban, the cops were visibly concerned.

Joe said, 'Somebody from this apartment dialled 911 and we came. Want to know that everything is fine out here. We checked their passports. Can you show us yours.?'

Parvinder looked at us and said, 'Why did you dial 911?'

Raj said, 'I was dialling Gurgoan. I dialled 91 and then I wanted to dial 124, but the number somehow got disconnected after the digit 1 and these guys landed up.'

Parvinder then tried to explain, but Mace said, 'Can we see your passport sir?'

Parvinder said, 'It is inside. Can I fetch it for you?'

Joe said, 'I will come with you, do it slowly and steadily please.'

Parvinder went in with him.

Within a minute both of them came outside and Joe said, 'Passport looks clean. He is from CHANDIGARH, India. Has a letter from TCS that is here on a business visit. Been to the US three times before and hasn't visited any other country so far.'

Mace said, 'Ok. That is fine.' He asked, 'Whose poster have you put on the wall?'

Parvinder said, 'Our Guruji, revered Guru Gobind Singhji.'

Mace said, 'Guruji?'

Parvinder said, 'I mean our religious leader.'

Mace said, 'Then why is he on horseback and wielding a sword?'

Parvinder said, 'He motivated his people to drive out the enemy and led from the front. That was in the late sixteen hundred sir.'

Parvinder added, 'Sir, all of us are working at TCS, one of the most renowned software companies in the world. We are here on work. This is a genuine mistake. I hope you understand.'

Mace looked at Parvinder's turban.

Parvinder understood his doubt. He said, 'I come from the Sikh community in India and all of us wear turbans. Our prime minister Dr Manmohan Singh is also a Sikh and he wears a turban. Not all people who wear turbans are terrorists sir.'

I liked Parvinder. His communication, confidence and diction were excellent. He knew how to speak to Americans in the most convincing way.

Mace looked at Joe and said, 'Ok gentleman. I hope this is a mistake. Please make sure you don't ever do this again. You call 911 only when it is an emergency. Do you get it?' Raj said, 'Yes sir.'

Joe said, 'Any questions before we leave?'

Just then Ramana popped up at the door. He asked, 'What happened?'

Mace explained, 'Your boys dialled 911 by mistake, so we turned up. Ask them to be careful next time.'

Ramana said, 'Sure sir. Thank you for your understanding.'

Raj said, 'Sir, one question. When we said we arrived an hour before, you said FOB. What does that mean?'

Mace chuckled and said, 'Fresh off the boat, son. Be careful next time. Call 911, only ...'

Raj completed the sentence, '... When in trouble.'

Joe nodded and said, 'Take care, stay out of trouble.'

Mace and Joe left. One of the cars drove away and the other stayed back.

Parvinder said, 'Stupid morons!'

Raj said, 'It was a mistake. I didn't even know that we had to dial 911 in an emergency. Do you think we like calling the cops?'

Ramana said, 'It has been two years since I came to US and this is the first time I have spoken to a cop. You arrived an hour ago and have already met with the cops. Guys, this is exactly what I told you. Stay out of trouble.'

I said, 'It is a mistake. So please let it go. We will be careful next time onwards.'

Ramana peeped out of the window. The patrol car was still there. Ramana said, 'Now you guys will be watched for sometime. So, be extremely careful. Do you get me?'

We said in unison, 'Yes sir.'

Ramana left in a few minutes.

Parvinder laughed and said, 'Ok mates, welcome to the United States, the country of doubt, fear and uncertainty.'

Raj said, 'Looks like they have everything, except peace of mind. We don't have anything, but seem to be happy.'

This, I thought, was the most profound statement made by Raj in the last two years. I patted him on his back and said, 'Very perceptive son. Call 911 and tell them this.' All of us laughed.

After all, my mother and that damn astrologer were right! Be careful about your close friend. I wondered what else Raj would do while we were there!

Divya Dumps Raj

RAMANA CAME SHARP AT 7 AM TO PICK US UP. RAJ WAS READY and I wasn't. He came up to the apartment and said, 'Come, let us go, we are getting late.' I couldn't understand the urgency and said, 'Give me a few minutes, let me grab a sandwich and we will go.'

He said, 'I don't think you guys understand the importance of time in this country.' His tone indicated that he was not happy and I didn't want to start my day with another HR sermon.

I grabbed the sandwich and said, 'Let us go.'

Ramana sarcastically said, 'I don't know why TCS recruits kids and sends them here.'

Raj said, 'Because kids work hard, deliver, are smart and because kids are willing to go to the US at short notice. Also, kids are paid low in Indian rupees and billed high in US dollars!'

Ramana calmed down and gave a smile. He said, 'Guys, take it easy. Just understand that things work like clockwork out here.'

We reached the NED office in fifteen minutes and took the elevator to the third floor. There was a small reception at the entrance and a really fat receptionist was busy taking calls. She waved and we approached her. Not all Americans had great cleavage. A ton of them were mazingly obese. Ramana said, 'We are here to meet Matt Ralston.'

She called Matt and he came over to the reception. He looked at Ramana and said, 'Hi, I am Matt.'

Ramana said, 'We are from TCS.'

Matt said, 'Yes, great. Yeah, we have two people to work with us starting today.' That's right. He opened his iphone, read something and said, 'Raj and Venkata, welcome to NED.'

Ramana said, 'Hi my name is Ramana and I am the human resource coordinator. I came to introduce you to these guys.'

Matt said, 'Good. They are in safe hands.'

I said, 'Hi Matt, I am Venkat, I mean VSAT. We talked on conference calls and this is Raj. He is in automation testing.'

Matt said, 'Oh yes, of course VSAT. Nice to meet you Raj.'

Ramana added, 'Matt, they just landed last evening and they have to rent a car and finish some formalities, so today they will be leaving early. I will pick them up at 3 pm, if that is fine with you?'

Matt said, 'Sure. No problems. Actually, you guys could have taken the day off and started from tomorrow. You will be jet-lagged anyway.'

Ramana said, 'That is fine Matt.'

Raj looked at Ramana and almost growled.

Ramana said, 'Ok, I will see you at 3 pm then. Bye.'

Matt got us the 'contractor badges' and took us in.

He said, 'These are your cubicles. Your machines are all set. Your login ID and password are stuck on the keyboard. File saving details and IT rules will pop up once you log in. Rest is as usual. That is the telephone. You can call international, no problem. Dial zero and you will get the external line. We have fifteen minutes to go for the team meeting. The meeting room is right over there. You may want to pick up some coffee. Call me on extension # 3202 if you need anything. Feel at ease, we have so much work to do together and welcome to the United States.'

Raj said, 'Thanks Matt.'

Matt said, 'See you in fifteen.'

I badly wanted to talk to Anjali. After last night's debacle, I didn't have the heart to call her. I logged in and opened the chatting tool. It was evening; about 5.30 pm in India. I pinged Anjali and she came online.

Anjali: Hi Teddy bear. How are you?

VSAT: Good you are in the office. I will call you on your IP phone in a minute, hold on.

Anjali: Sure ☺

I dialled Anjali's extension via IP phone.

Anjali picked up and said, 'Hi my Sweety bear, how are you?'

I said, 'Very good. I have already started missing you.'

Anjali asked, 'How is the US?'

I said, 'Very cold. Good you got me the jacket.'

She said, 'See, I told you.'

I said, 'Baby, what is new?'

She said, 'Nothing much. Things are as usual. Adi picked me up today. I think I will go back with him.'

I asked, 'How is he doing?'

She said, 'Cool. He is very busy. He is into architecture. Says he has too much work to do.'

I asked her how was Mani doing. 'He is as usual. Listen, you just left and there is nothing much to tell. You tell me.'

I said, 'We landed last evening and Raj dialed 911, the local emergency number by mistake, and the police landed up at home. They thought we were terrorists. Got even more scared when they met with Parvinder, a surd with whom we share the apartment. He is on the CostCo project.'

She said, 'Yes, I know Parvi. He is a cool guy. He is from Chandigarh or something like that. He is in the US now?'

I asked, 'How do you know?'

She said, 'He was in my project before, forgot?'

I said, 'Ok. Got it. Achcha listen, I got to go now. Have a meeting in five.'

Anjali said, 'Five what?'

I said, 'Minutes. Everybody here says only the number, that is cool.'

She said, 'Remember what I told you ...'

I said, 'It is freezing out here. Snake will be inside, don't worry.' Both of us laughed.

I didn't notice that Raj was standing behind me.

He said, 'Fucker, what are you saying about the snake and all that?'

I said, 'Shameless fellow. Eavesdropping.'

He said, 'Ok ok. I spoke with D, she is fine.'

I said, 'D, who?'

He said, 'Divya, man. Everything in the US is short.'

I laughed and we went into the conference room.

It was a beautiful conference room with every possible gadget one could think of – IP phones, sockets, overhead projectors, charts, boards, electronic scroll screens, etc. I mean, infrastructure-wise, it had everything.

Exactly at 7.30 am, almost everybody turned up. There were ten of them. Stacy Chapel, Mike Blotiff, Matt Ralston, Joseph Steimburger, Tim Scott, Lucy Albiem, Jenny Herkins, Lucy Turnbill, Jane White and Kate Millerman. Matt was the on-site coordinator and reported to Cathy Baker.

He started the meeting with, 'Morning ladies and gentlemen, I want to introduce you all to the TCS personnel VSAT and Raj. They have come from Bangalore. VSAT will be working on defining the overall scope and functionality, as part of the re-arch project. Raj will work on automation testing. Raj will be anchored to Jenny and they have been in touch over the last few months. VSAT will work with Steve. Unfortunately Steve isn't here today, he will meet you guys tomorrow.'

Everybody welcomed us warmly and introduced themselves. They explained which area they worked on and what their responsibilities were. Matt said, 'Do you guys want to introduce yourselves?'

Raj said, 'Yes, sure. My name is Raj. I know Java coding and I work on automation testing.'

I said, 'Yes, I have a long name, my colleagues call me VSAT. I am also into Java, and now I am working on functionality and scope. More like a business analyst.'

All of them gave us a weird look. Jenny came to our aid and said, 'Ok guys that is a nice and short introduction. Do you want to talk about what you intend doing here in the next few weeks?'

Raj said, 'Yes Jenny. Thank you. My father owns a Maruti dealership in Gurgaon. I have a sister who runs a beauty parlour. I graduated from NIT Calicut, one of the most prestigious engineering colleges in the country and joined TCS. For the last year-and-a-half, I have been on testing.'

I smiled and said, 'Ok. Here I go. My name is Venkata Subramaniam Adisankara Tanikaburla. That is a long name. You can call me Venkat or VSAT, whatever is convenient for you. Raj and I are classmates, my father is a schoolteacher, mom is a housewife. I have a younger sister who is studying. I will work with most of you on functional scoping.'

There was a pause for some time and then Stacy asked Matt, 'Hey Matt, are we going to offshore more work?'

Even before Matt could answer, Kate laughed sarcastically and said, 'Well, that is the whole idea. Bangalored!'

There was more conversation around the offshoring topic and some heated debates on the methodology to be adopted. I thought there was a strong undercurrent against offshoring. I thought people were uncomfortable doing the re-arch project, because their jobs were at stake. After that meeting, we went back to our desks and started clearing pending emails.

I sent an email to Mani:

Hi Mani,

Hope you are well. Reached the US safely. As discussed earlier, I am assigned to work with Steve and Raj with Jenny. We had our first intro meeting today. It was nice and cordial. I think there is a strong undercurrent against offshoring. Wonder if this will slow our progress. Talk to you tomorrow.

Regards,

VSAT

Mani replied instantly: *I am aware, let us talk tomorrow. Have you met with Cathy?*

I replied: *No, not yet. Possibly tomorrow.*

Mani replied: *Take care, don't push too hard, focus on nailing scope and functionality.*

I said: *Yes Mani, good night.*

At 3 pm, Ramana came to pick us up and took us to the car rental place. Raj filled the requisite forms and said, 'Let us take the red Cadillac. It will be fun.'

Ramana said, 'Insurance is higher for red. Because it is flashy, sporty and people zoom in them. Take a simple car.'

Raj said, 'Fuck. This country is amazing.' He added, 'Guess what, I am breathing with only one nostril, because if I breathe with both, they might charge me extra.'

I said, 'PJ (poor joke). Let us take this Honda Accord, it looks cool and I like the silver colour also.'

Raj said, 'Ok brother. Whatever you say.'

Ramana said, 'Ok guys, also pick up the county route maps and I will help you with a couple of rounds and then you are on your own.'

Raj drove, Ramana navigated and I sat at the back enjoying the drive. We drove around for an hour and then Ramana said, 'There is a South Indian restaurant in Edison, if you guys want to eat.'

I said yes. I was already missing home food. We headed for Edison, a place with a huge denomination of Indian settlers. As soon as we entered the shopping area, I realised that the place had to be Indian. We could smell spices, and the carry trolleys were strewn all over the place. There were red marks on the walls, it looked like people had spit paan all over the place. Needless to say, we felt at home. We went to the South Indian place and ordered masala dosa and coffee. We felt alive. After dinner we went back home.

Next day, Steve was at the office and I had my first meeting with him.

Steve said, 'Hi VSAT! Welcome to the United States. Hope you are enjoying your stay.'

I said, 'Steve, it is great to see you. We've talked on the phone and now I finally get to meet you.'

Steve was many years senior to me and his tone was patronising.

He took me to the pantry and we made hot cappuccino. We chatted for a while. He said, 'We got tons of work to do. Let us draw up a schedule and see how much we can accomplish. How long are you here?'

I said, 'My visa is for three months.'

He said, 'Good, that is a long time. I will also show you a little bit of the US.'

I was delighted.

A couple of weeks passed uneventfully. Parvinder finished his engagement and left. We dropped him off at the airport. I took driving classes and learnt to drive a bit. Raj and I had the whole apartment to ourselves. We had a routine now: We left early and came back late in the afternoon. We watched TV, made dinner, washed the vessels and went to sleep. Life became monotonous. I called Anjali and home regularly. Raj called his dad and Divya from time to time. Jenny kept Raj busy and I was caught up in meeting all the module leads.

I learnt a lot in the initial weeks. Americans fiercely protected their privacy, weekends were sacrosanct for them and they loved to eat, drink and have loads of sex. On Monday mornings, most people talked about what they had done over the weekend. By Tuesday, depression set in. Wednesdays were a big chore. Thursday passed in anticipation. Friday mornings were spent on figuring out what to do during the weekend. By noon there was irrational exuberance and by late afternoon, the desks were empty. During weekends, we drove to malls and converted everything from US dollars to Indian rupees. Raj was on a liquid diet—beer, almost on all the weekends. His complaint was, 'Weekends are a bore, there is nothing to do.'

One day Raj came over to my desk and said, 'Man, did you see Jane today? She is fantastic. Her boobs are world-class. I wonder if she wears a bra.'

I wondered what 'world-class boobs' meant.

I said, 'Steer clear buddy. You will get screwed.'

He said, 'Have you seen them or not?'

I said, 'I haven't noticed them yet.'

'What do you see in the office man?'

I said, 'How do you get the time to do this shit?'

Raj said, 'That is the Malhotra clan's speciality man. We can spot a nice pair of boobs even in a crowd.'

I grinned and he continued, 'My uncle once told me that great boobs come in three packs: Deep cleavage, uptight and assertive, and the big ones which are slightly apart. Jane falls in the first category. Great cleavage man.'

I laughed and said, 'I didn't realise that your family has a PhD in boobs.'

He said, 'Malhotra khandaan's speciality.'

He continued, 'You can spot them when she comes to the pantry. Come as soon as I call you. Ok?'

I said, 'Ok fine. But fucker, don't make it too obvious. Both of us will be screwed.'

Raj said, '*Chad yaar*. Just see, that's all!'

After a few hours Raj called and both of us went to the pantry. She was beautiful and her assets were of global standards. We grinned at each other and didn't say anything.

Jane said, 'Hi guys, what's up?'

Raj said, 'Nothing Jane'

Jane said, 'Something funny? You guys are grinning.'

I didn't know what to say. So I said, 'No Jane. Nothing funny. Just an Indian joke.'

'What is it?'

Raj said, 'Nothing, don't bother.'

Within the next hour, we got a call from Stacy Cooper of NED's HR department.

Raj came to my desk and said, 'I think we are fucked.'

I said, 'What will we do now?'

'Nothing. Let's meet her.'

We went to Stacy. She was in her mid-thirties. Auburn hair, slightly chubby. She looked like a warm, motherly person.

She said, 'Jane talked to me.'

I said, 'About what?'

She said, 'Gentlemen, do you know it is inappropriate to pass comments and grin?'

Raj said, 'But we didn't pass a single comment.'

Stacy said, 'You guys were grinning because of some Indian thing?'

I said, 'Yeah. We grinned, but that had nothing to do with Jane.'

Stacy said, 'Yeah, you don't do these things in this country.'

Raj asked, 'Grinning?'

Stacy said, 'No, I mean …'

Then she paused for a moment and said, 'Ok boys, let me make it easy on you. Jane hasn't pressed any charges, but she made a passing remark. I called to give you two a piece of advice. Don't screw around here; you won't even know what hit you.'

She then turned to Raj and said, 'Would you mind not staring at my breasts and controlling your libido a bit? Eh?'

Raj stammered, 'No m'am, I mean sorry m'am, yes m'am.'

I thought of explaining to Stacy that the entire Malhotra khandaan had a mania for breasts and it was a medical condition. I didn't know the technical terminology to explain this syndrome. But on second thoughts, I let it be. What if she didn't believe me?

Stacy added, 'Listen, there are some decent folks in this country. Most of you might have ill-conceived notions about sex in the US. America is not what you see in Hollywood movies. Do you get it?'

We both blurted out in unison, 'Yes. m'am.'

She said, 'Take it easy and have fun while you are here, but be careful, let this not get out of hand. I suggest you keep the "Indian thing" out of the office. No Hind here.'

Raj corrected her, 'Hindi m'am.'

Stacy said, 'Ok, Hindi or whatever it is.'

We left Stacy's office. As we were heading back, Steve called us.

He said, 'What are you guys up to? Did you comment on Jane?'

I turned pale. I said, 'Of course not. Why do you ask?'

He said, 'She told me that you guys were grinning. Some Indian joke.'

Raj said, 'Nothing like that Steve. We grinned at each other. I think she misunderstood. We are fine with apologising for it.'

Steve said, 'Nothing to worry about, but be careful. You don't want to make people uncomfortable out here, right?'

I said, 'Sure Steve.'

He said, 'Ok boys. Now tell Steve uncle, what is this Indian joke? This is off the record.'

Raj said, 'It is not an Indian joke Steve. I told VSAT that Jane was well-endowed.'

Steve smiled and said, 'Oh!'

I opened up a little more and said, 'Well, Raj said that her assets were world-class and that is why I grinned.'

Steve laughed aloud and said, 'Well, those drive the largest internet traffic in the office anyway. That is not new.'

We felt a little relieved.

Steve laughed again and the conversation ended there.

A few weeks later, Srila came on the chat line. She asked:

Srila: Hi buddy. How are you?

VSAT: Ah, what a surprise lady.

Srila: VSAT, I'm coming to the US in a couple of weeks. Pick me up?

VSAT: Cool. Coming to Newark? Send me your travel plans. How long are you here?

Srila: I will be there for a couple of months. What about acco?

VSAT: Great, we will have company. We have an empty room in our corporate apartment, which you can use.

Srila: Good, my pop will shoot me for sharing a house with you guys.

VSAT: Who is asking you to tell him?

Srila: ☺ We will see. How is Raj?

VSAT: Good.

Srila: Anjali and Adi?

VSAT: Missing them.

Srila: Ok chalo then, I will ping you again shortly.

VSAT: Ok, bye. Catch you soon.

Srila: Don't visit too many places before i come. All of us can go see them together ☺

VSAT: Ok, c u soon. ☺

After the quick chat, I told Raj the news. He gave a stoic reply, 'Ok, we will go and pick her up next week. Is she staying with us?' Of late, he had become pensive and was not in his element. There were no comments on boobs, legs and booze. He spoke very little to me. I thought Jenny was driving him hard and left it at that.

The next morning I called Anjali.

She said, 'Honeybunch, I have bad news for you. Divya has dumped Raj!'

I said, 'Don't tell me!'

Anjali said, 'Yes. She is going around with Unni Krishnan.'

'That idiot?'

'Yes, that idiot. Apparently they are getting married in ten days or so.'

'Wow, things are moving that fast?' She said, 'Yes, I think she told Raj a week back.'

I said, 'But how do you know?'

She said, 'They are going around and people are talking about it.'

I said, 'How can Divya do that? Wasn't she going steady with Raj?'

She said, 'Some girls are like that VSAT. India is changing.'

I said, 'Hmm ... No wonder he's been so moody. But he didn't tell me.'

Anjali said, 'I can understand, what will he tell you anyway? I am sure he must be feeling bruised.'

I said, 'Yeah. Maybe. Srila is coming to the US and we are picking her up and she may stay with us. Any objections?'

She said, 'Of course not, stupid. Why do you ask? I trust you guys.'

I said, 'No, I mean it is good to tell, right?'

Anjali said, 'Yeah, that's fine. So, when are you coming back?'

I said, 'Another month maybe.' She said, 'I am missing you badly Teddy.'

I said, 'Same here.'

That evening, Raj and I were driving home and there was hardly any conversation between us. I asked, 'So, is it all over?'

Raj nodded.

I said, 'Don't worry. Maybe she doesn't deserve you.'

He nodded again.

I asked, 'Want to talk?'

He shook his head. I kept quiet.

We reached home and were preparing dinner when Raj said, 'That bitch dumped me.' I could clearly see the tears in his eyes.

I said, 'Don't bother yaar. *Hota hai.*'

He said, 'She called me and casually told me that her parents have chosen Unni Krishnan and she is getting married to him shortly.'

I asked, 'Didn't you say anything?'

He said, 'She said that's her decision too.'

I said, 'Don't bother.'

He said, 'It all started with a great fuck and ended with a fucked-up feeling.'

I said, 'I am not sure you guys were emotionally involved anyway.'

Raj said, 'Maybe it was more physical? I don't know. Can't say. But I enjoyed being with her. Now, how do I go back and work with her?'

I said, 'Yes, that will be tricky.'

He said, 'Saala, all office relationships are tricky man.'

I said, 'I am sure she will move out of the project. It won't work. You want to speak to Mani about it on your return?'

Raj grabbed a beer from the refrigerator and said, 'Want one?'

I shook my head.

He opened the can, and said, 'Yes, may be I will speak to Mani, once this settles down.'

I said, 'Raj, take it easy. You must be happy that all this happened before you got married. Imagine if something like this had happened after marriage?'

Raj said, 'I know. Fucking software girls are like this only man.'

I stared at him. He quickly realised his folly. Anjali was a software girl too.

He said, 'Yeah, I know there are exceptions, but most are like that.'

I said, 'You are feeling betrayed, that's why you are saying that. Most of them are not like that. They come from good families Raj. Some get screwed up when they come to the city. Maybe too much freedom goes to their heads.'

He opened the second can and said, 'Anyway, screw it. I hate her. I am through with her and all the girls in the world.' I said, 'Well ...'

He said, 'Well what? Adi is smart. I should just join his gang.'

'Don't be stupid. You are fucked up in the head right now.'

'How could she just dump me like that?'

'May be compulsions. Who knows? Just leave it man. Move on.'

'Yeah, I guess so. What option do I have anyway? But why did she get into it in the first place?'

I said, 'Probably for the sex?'

He said, 'Yeah. May be. We did it the first time, then the second, then the fascination overtook us and we thought we were close emotionally too.'

I didn't want to interrupt him. I think the guy who said—'That the thing that takes up least amount of time and maximum amount of trouble is sex' is a genius. He continued, 'But I must say VSAT, she was great. I feel bad she dumped me man.'

I said, 'Just let it go Raj.'

He said, 'Yeah ...' Tears trickled down his cheeks. I couldn't believe Raj could get so emotional. I wondered for a moment whether he missed Divya or he missed having sex with her. Anyway, I didn't want to analyse any deeper. I am a software guy, not a philosopher.

I hugged him and he didn't say anything. I said, 'Easy Raj. Don't feel bad. I am sure you will find somebody better.'

He opened the third, fourth and fifth cans of beer, got thoroughly sloshed, piled up on the sofa and started snoring. I knew he was done with Divya. Five beers and a few tears is all it takes for a guy to get over it, especially if the girl has dumped him. I thought Raj should send flowers to Vijay Mallya for keeping people like him going. I was sure he would move on in a few days.

The following week, I called Adi and Anjali and told them that Raj was coming to terms with the breakup. Adi said, 'Divya has applied for a transfer to TCS Mumbai. Apparently Unni is relocating and Mani has agreed. He might speak to Raj today.'

I felt relieved and said, 'That is fantastic. So, who is Raj going to work with?'

Adi said, 'I think Srinivas a.k.a. Mahesh Babu.'

We laughed. Srinivas was bit of a simpleton and adored Telugu film hero Mahesh Babu. Apparently during his last vacation, Srinivas had stood at the gate of Mahesh Babu's house for days to get a glimpse of his favourite actor. He sported Babu's hairstyle in his passport-sized photograph. I don't blame him; in Andhra, hero worshipping can go to any heights. When I was a kid, we had got tickets for first day morning shows from the Chiranjeevi Fans Association. Before the movie started, the president and secretary of the association performed puja before the big Chiranjeevi cut-out, which stood in front of the theatre. They would garland his picture, a ceremonial lamp would be lit, and finally *prasadam* (holy offering) was distributed to all the fans. Chiranjeevi was a mass hero and most of his movies were blockbusters. They ran in more than 100 theatres in Andhra for more than 100 days. He was a cult figure.

The following day, Mani called for a team meeting and announced that Divya was getting married and relocating to Mumbai in a few weeks. Everybody congratulated her and Raj was quiet. Mani informed us that Srinivas would take over the additional responsibility of testing and that Raj would be anchored with Srinivas.

Subsequently, Mani asked Raj how he was doing. Raj said, 'I am fine Mani.'

Mani said, 'Fuckers, that is why I keep telling you not to fuck around with office babes. Office relationships, they don't work. But when do you guys listen?'

(Managing the Mani Way, Axiom five—Over-sympathise with your subordinate at the wrong time. Make the subordinate feel indebted.)

Raj said, 'I don't regret it, Mani. I enjoyed spending time with her and it is over now and I have no complaints.'

Mani asked me, 'How is it going with Anjali? Or do I have to relocate her also to Mumbai?'

(Managing the Mani Way, Axiom six—Use the existing screwed up situation and check what is happening with other subordinates. Subordinates will feel compelled to answer.)

I said, 'Mani, thankfully it is going fine. No worries.'

Mani asked Raj, 'Can you manage the workload without her?'

Raj grinned and said, 'Don't worry Mani. Actually, in any case, I was doing most of the work while you gave her the increments.'

Mani heaved a sigh of relief and said, 'Ok morons. Do your work well and this year, hopefully you will get great hikes. When are you guys back?'

(Managing the Mani Way, Axiom seven—Promise something way into the future, which can easily be forgotten or denied subsequently. Subordinates feel a sense of loyalty for the time being.)

We replied that it was going to take anywhere from four to six weeks. He discussed the project for some more time and said goodbye to us. I guess Divya's story ended here. Raj cannot feel 'depressed' for too long. Raj is like Bill Clinton, like a ping-pong ball, the harder you hit him, the higher he bounces back. Good for him, he will do well in life.

Bill did well, didn't he?

Atlantic City and the Return

THE FOLLOWING FRIDAY, STEVE CAME OVER TO MY DESK, WHICH was adjacent to Raj's cubicle and said, 'Hi boys. Let me give your libido a wake-up call. Want to go over to Atlantic City today?'

I asked, 'What's in Atlantic City?'

Steve said, 'Play the slot machine, watch strippers, have beer and get laid, may be?'

I thought Steve was living it up.

Raj said, 'Steve, count me in.'

Steve raised his eyebrows. I said, 'Yeah, let's go.'

We left for Atlantic City in the evening. The place was fantastic. I had never seen so many casinos and strip clubs in one place.

Steve asked, 'Ok boys. Where do we start?'

Raj said, 'Babes' club?'

Steve laughed aloud. 'Ok buddy, lets go.'

We went into Babes' Club. The place was semi-lit and in the centre, almost nude pole dancers were gyrating to blaring music and the audience was in raptures. Drinks were being served on the double and dancers were all over the place.

This was our first experience in a strip joint and I had a lump in my throat. I couldn't believe what was happening around me. Truly, sex and drinks were on the tap.

Raj looked around in utter amazement. He said, 'Wow, what a place!'

Steve asked, 'Never been to a strip club before?'

We just shook our heads, the American way, left to right and back.

He said, 'Ok, let us sit at the table over there and order some drinks.'

We sat down. Steve ordered Vodka on the rocks and Raj ordered a Bloody Mary. I asked for Sprite. Steve looked perplexed. He asked, 'You don't drink?'

I said, 'No.'

He asked, 'Why?'

I said, 'Long story, not now.'

Raj said, 'You don't want to get into it now Steve.'

Steve nodded and said, 'As you wish, don't want to intrude.' That is the best part about Americans, they just don't want to interfere with anything which is private.

As we were talking, a nude girl came by and sat on Raj's lap. Raj couldn't control his excitement and he fell off the chair and the girl fell on him. Everybody laughed and as he stood up, Raj said, 'Didn't expect that.'

Steve said, 'I understand. No sweat.'

Another one sauntered around and put her hands around Steve and asked, 'Are you staying around honey?'

Steve, 'Not sure, let you know.'

Raj asked, 'Aren't we staying for sometime?'

Steve said, 'Don't you guys want to explore the place, play the slot, eat good food? We can always come back here.'

Raj reluctantly said, 'Yes, but we can come back quickly, right?'

Steve said, 'That babe is asking whether we guys want to spend the night here? I mean, get laid.'

I said, 'Not me.'

Raj was a little sceptical.

Steve looked at me asked, 'Anjali?'

I said, 'Yes, can't do this.'

He looked at Raj. Raj smiled and said, 'I just broke up with someone.' He was basically implying that he had a license to do whatever he wanted.

Steve laughed and said, 'Ok, let's decide later. Don't want to spoil good Indian boys anymore.'

We stayed there for another hour and headed for Caesars, a casino joint. The place was full. People were playing on the slot machines. The place looked like a big honeycomb. People were like bees, glued to the machines. There was intense excitement all around. Raj and I occupied one slot machine each. For every eight times we played, we almost got our money back, but we were not able to make a decent amount. We played for an hour and Raj made ten dollars. I lost about fifteen. I quickly rationalised—between us, we had lost five. That was okay. I had never won a lottery in my life. Steve played and won USD 80 and got out immediately. He smiled and said, 'When you win, you should get up and go.'

After playing slots we went for dinner. Post-dinner, Raj suggested that we go back to the strip joint. Steve said, 'Raj, I think this is enough. Enjoy the experience. If you get deep into it, you can never escape.'

Raj reluctantly agreed. We drove back to the office. We picked up our car from the basement and Steve left for his place. We thanked Steve for showing us around. Most Americans don't spare time over weekends. Weekends are way too precious for them to spend on visitors unless the visitors are really close friends and family.

While driving back, Raj said, 'What an evening, never had such a wonderful experience!'

I laughed and said, 'Stud, you fell off your chair.'

Raj said, 'I didn't expect that man. She came way too fast.'

I asked, 'So, what is the Malhotra motto for this situation?'

Raj grinned and said, 'If a nude babe sits on you, hold the fucking chair, not her.

I laughed heartily.

The following weekend, Raj and I went to Newark airport to pick up Srila. She had not told her parents that she was sharing an apartment with us. If they knew, they would have had a heart attack.

As soon as she saw us, she gave us a warm hug. I thought she had put on a little weight, but hadn't changed much.

Raj mockingly said, 'Srila, you look really cool.'

She smiled and said, 'Raj, you too look like a real stud.'

We then went to Starbucks and got her a 'latte'. It had become a norm to drink 'latte', every time we passed a Starbucks joint. The taste was addictive.

After that we drove back to our apartment and Srila settled down in Parvinder's room.

That evening Ramana dropped by for dinner. He gave the same set of instructions to Srila. He looked at the three of us and said, 'Guys, behave. Neither I, nor the company is responsible for any untoward incidents.' That was a super-euphemism for 'we are not responsible if any one of you get pregnant.'

We smiled.

He said, 'Thank God you are from Chennai and not from Gurgaon.'

Srila asked Ramana, 'What did he do?'

Ramana said, 'What don't these guys do!'

He then gave us a mean look and said, 'They got the cops to the apartment on the day of their arrival. and then they were summoned by the client's HR department too.'

I looked at Ramana, completely bewildered.

Ramana rolled his eyes and flexed the muscles of his forearm. He said, 'I know everything.'

(Oh, my God, another *Godfather* in the making. A scream in my head, *'Woltz awakens in a pool of blood, and finds Khartoum's severed head in his bed and SCREAMS.'*

Raj whispered to me, 'He is from HR, has his testicles spread everywhere, no, I mean tentacles. They are like the FBI of TCS.'

I whispered, 'Who is the CIA then?'

Ramana said, 'I hear ya boys. Our overseas counterparts.'

Srila was clueless. She said, 'Guys, I have no idea what you are talking about.'

Raj said, 'It is a big conspiracy theory, will tell you sometime.'

Then Raj explained the police episode.

Srila asked, 'What happened with the client's HR department?'

I said, 'We will leave that for the time being.' Obviously I couldn't tell her that we were hauled up for grinning at 'world-class' boobs.

Ramana had dinner with us. Before leaving, he said, 'Srila, you have given a declaration that you are okay staying with these two lunatics and that your parents are aware of it. I hope you have 'truly' informed your parents.' Srila bobbed her head at forty five degree, the Indian way. In the sovereign US territory, it meant nothing.

We looked at her. She just stared at us.

Raj said, 'Ok sir. Good night.'

The next day, Ramana came to pick up Srila. She had to go to Pathmark a retail chain, on system enhancement work. Ramana wanted to introduce her to the client. I wondered what Ramana did other than picking up and dropping off people. Was he handling cops, pushing dope and running a spy network? Fuck, anything is possible with HR guys and that too in the US.

The following week went smoothly. Cathy Baker appreciated my work and said, 'Venkat, I am happy to see you working hard, managing the scope. It is remarkable that all of you have come up with the new re-arch solution. I know Adi and Harpreet are also doing a great job. Do you think you can deliver Phase One by next October?'

I said, 'It is possible, if we limit the scope of functionality coverage for each module.'

She said, 'I understand. So, how long is your stay going to be?'

I said, 'A few weeks, m'am. We should be leaving before Christmas vacation.'

Cathy said, 'So, will you be coming back after that?'

I said, 'I am on a business visa now and don't have any plans to come back. Also, Mani has not informed me about anything.'

Cathy said, 'Ok then. Wish you the best and let us hope we work this out well.'

I thanked her and walked out of the room.

That evening, Srila cooked authentic South Indian food in the apartment. She made sambhar, rice, avial, and papad. We enjoyed the meal. She gave our apartment a feminine touch. Nude posters of women came off Raj's walls. A small idol of Ganesha adorned a corner in the kitchen. There were flowers in the hall. Clothes and shoes, which were otherwise strewn all over the place, now had their corners. We woke up to *suprabhatam* everyday.

After the meal, Srila was fishing for compliments and asked, 'How was it guys?'

Raj burped and said, 'That was good.' I said, 'Super. I wish Anjali cooks as well.'

Raj joked, 'The way to a man's heart is through his stomach. You have pleased me, if you promise to cook like this, I am willing to marry you.'

Srila said, '*Chal chal*, go marry a cook.'

The following weekend the three of us decided to go and see Niagara Falls. It was a few hours away. Raj drove and I navigated.

Srila sat at the back. We reached there around mid-morning. The view was fantastic. The cascade was gigantic and the foam rose high and we could feel the chill.

We wandered around till late afternoon and decided to head back. Srila said, 'Can I sit in the front seat atleast while going back?'

I said, 'Sure, be my guest. I will get some sleep.'

So, Srila sat in the front and Raj drove. I had finished my driving classes and was comfortable with my skills. But with Raj around, I didn't feel like driving. He loved it anyway.

We drove for a few minutes and Srila asked Raj, 'Heard you split with Divya.'

Raj nodded.

Divya continued a little cautiously, 'How have you taken it?'

Raj said, 'Cool.' His answers were in monosyllables. I guess he didn't want to talk about it. I kept quiet and let the conversation go on.

Srila said, 'You don't want to talk about it?'

Raj nodded.

Srila said, 'That means you still are feeling bad about it.'

Raj looked at me from the rear view mirror and then looked at Srila.

I said, 'Raj is obviously over with that episode. How is it going at Pathmark Srila?'

She said, 'I have a *khadoos* client manager.'

Raj said, 'Tell me something new. Why are managers always like that?'

I said, 'That is unfair Raj. Jenny is nice to you.'

Srila asked, 'Who is Jenny?'

Raj said, 'My client manager. Yeah, she is good. Nice babe actually.'

Srila said, 'Don't tell me you are hitting on her?'

I grinned and said, 'Don't you know, Raj hits on anybody who is remotely female.'

Srila said, 'I never felt it.'

Raj smiled and said, 'Because I am subtle with you or may be you are too thick-skinned.'

I think something happens to people when they go on long drives. They just open up. I guess one cannot jump out of the window, so you keep talking.

Srila said, 'I think you are too subtle. I am not that thick-skinned.'

I was listening to the conversation intently now. There was a new chemistry that was building up and I was concerned. Srila comes from a pure South Indian Brahmin family—lungi, Hindu newspaper, filter coffee variety. Raj comes from the Punjabi-Maruti dealership family—milk, jalebi, aloo parantha variety. It was an unviable proposition. And besides Raj had just come out of a broken relationship.

Raj said, 'I asked you to marry me. But you told me to marry a cook.'

Srila giggled and said, 'You need a cook, not a wife.'

Raj asked, 'So what about you Srila? Did your dad find you somebody? Sons of bureaucrats?'

Srila said, 'Yup, I met a few. But haven't settled on one yet.'

For the first time, I looked at Srila carefully. She was about five-and-a-half-feet tall, dusky, decent curves, exuded a certain class. She had a very homely face. Her movements were graceful and she smiled easily. Perfect 'wife material'! I looked at Raj and tried to visualise them together. Raj was a simpleton at heart who could get quite emotional and he needed somebody who could hold him together. Srila would just fit the bill. Actually they were made for each other. On second thoughts, I said to myself, 'Fuck it VSAT, don't go that far.'

Raj asked, 'Why?'

Srila said, 'Because I didn't find the right guy.'

Raj said, 'And what does this right guy look like?'

Srila said, 'Not "looks" like, "sound" like!'

Raj said, 'Ok, who is the right guy according to you?'

Srila said, 'Somebody who is sincere, has a sense of humour, who could be sensitive and emotional. Importantly, somebody who loves me.'

Raj smiled. He said, 'You want to marry five men?'

Srila sneered, 'What do you mean?'

Raj said, 'You are looking for somebody who is sincere, witty, sensitive, emotional and who loves you. That makes five guys because, one guy can't be all that.'

She laughed aloud and said, 'What kind of girl do you prefer?'

Raj came straight to the point. 'Somebody like you.'

She said, 'Tell me what kind of girl you like.'

'See, you are thick-skinned. I told you, I prefer somebody like you. Simple and nice, no frills attached.' Srila giggled again and there was long pause.

I decided not to interfere and took a nap. When I woke up, we decided to stop at McDonald's for burgers and coke. We chatted for a while and started driving back home.

We only had a few weeks left before Christmas and had to complete a ton of deliverables. Meanwhile, most of the American clients were busy with their vacation plans. Steve wanted to spend Christmas with his daughter in Boston. Cathy wanted to take off from 15 December to 3 January. She was off to Barbados with her family. But she said she was available for critical calls. I was working hard, putting the finishing touches on my work. I kept the last weekend for shopping.

One day Steve and I stayed back late in the evening and he dropped me home after dinner. I reached home to find that Raj and Srila were watching tv. Srila's head rested on Raj's shoulder and they were comfortable in each other's company. They didn't squirm when I entered the apartment.

Srila asked, 'Hi VSAT. Working late, had dinner?'

I said, 'Yes Srila. What's happening?'

Raj said, 'What?'

I looked at both of them quizzically.

Raj said, 'You are asking the obvious buddy.'

I said, 'I don't understand'

Raj said, 'What is there to understand?'

Srila said, 'VSAT. Come on. Don't tell me you didn't realise until now.'

I said, 'Ok guys. So both of you are going steady?'

Both nodded in the American way. Affirmative!

I said, 'Congrats. Good for you.'

I wanted to ask a lot of questions, but considering my own situation with Anjali, I decided not to. I was not sure if their families would ever agree, because there was too much of a cultural gap between them. But I did feel happy for both of them. They were nice people and I wondered why they had waited to go full circle before settling for each other.

Somebody said that soulmates eventually find their partners. Maybe that was the case here. I said, 'Raj and Srila ... nice pair. So when did this happen?'

Raj said, 'Post-Niagara.'

I said, 'I felt that when I heard your conversaation on the way back.'

Srila said, 'Smart boy.'

I smiled.

I asked, 'So Srila, you will relocate to Bangalore?'

Srila said, 'No, pa may not allow that. We have to figure out the next step.'

Raj said, 'Initially I will spend my weekends in Chennai, let us see.'

I was never comfortable with those three words—'Let us see'. They pre-empted the impending FUD (fear-uncertainty-disorder) factor.

I said, 'Yeah. Wish you the best guys.'

We talked for some more time about our respective futures. We had big dreams and plans. But how were we going to make them come true?

That night, I called Anjali and said, 'Hi sweetie! A few weeks more and I am back.'

She said, 'I am waiting, baby.'

I said, 'Do you know Srila and Raj are hooked?'

Anjali said, 'Yeah Srila told me about it.'

I said, 'Why didn't you tell me before?'

She said, 'I wanted to, but Srila was kind of not sure, or something like that. You know how girls are.' I remembered what Raj had told me during the NIT days. 'Girls confide in their best friend and if they get the green signal, then the relationship is on, else it is the redlight for the poor bloke.' How true!

I smiled and said, 'Oh, she was asking for your opinion, like the way you asked for hers?'

She giggled, 'Yeah, something like that.'

'So what did you tell her?'

She said, 'Well I told her that she has to nurture Raj because he could be quite sensitive and emotional.'

'Hmm ... sensible.' I asked, 'Ok baby, what do you want me to get you from here?'

She said, 'I want you Teddy. You have no idea how much I am missing you.'

I said, 'Same here baby.'

In the last two weeks, we submitted our preliminary work reports and bid goodbye to all the team mates and wished them 'Merry Christmas and a Happy New Year.' We had farewell lunches with the clients. On the last weekend before we left for India, we shopped a lot. I purchased a Fossil watch for grandpa, it had an elegant dial and I thought he would like it. I got an electronic shaving kit for dad, a nice crockery set for mom, super expensive Chanel 5 perfume for Swati and Anjali. Since I had made up my mind to talk to Anjali's parents, I purchased a Citizen watch set for them and a make-up kit for her sister, Ameya. I purchased assorted chocolates for office mates. For myself, I brought a pair of Nike shoes, Ray Ban glasses and a couple of Levis jeans and T-shirts. Raj and Srila also shopped for themselves and their parents. The damn shopping bills burnt a big hole in my pocket. I blew whatever little I had saved in two-and-a-half months, but I guess it was worth it because I was spending on my own (current and future) family. Rationalisation once again made me feel good.

Raj and I went to Steve and thanked him profusely for all his help. He said, 'I intend coming to India shortly. Will catch up with you boys.'

He looked at Raj and asked, 'Are there strip joints in Bangalore?'

Raj laughed. He said, 'Yes Steve. We own one and have two strippers—VSAT and me. Ha, ha. Bars close at 11 pm in Bangalore.'

Steve asked, 'What about night life?'

Raj said, 'Indian night life is about watching soaps on a TV channel called Star Plus. Let me translate the name of a popular soap for you, "Mother-in-law was once upon a time daughter-in-law too." Raj looked at me and said, '*Saas bhi kabhi bahu thi*!'

Steve said, 'Wow, you make serials on mothers-in-laws too? It is unheard of in this country.'

Raj said, 'You have no idea how powerful mothers-in-laws are in our country.'

Steve said, 'They are here too, but I am not aware of any soaps on mothers-in-law.'

I said, 'Actually Steve, it is more complicated than that. It will take a life time to explain.'

Steve laughed aloud and said, 'I can understand. I hope atleast we will get time to have Kingfisher beer together.'

We nodded.

On the day we were leaving, we had lunch with Ramana. We thanked him for his help and handed over the apartment and car keys. He dropped us at the airport. As usual, we had a latte at Starbucks. Subsequently, we checked in our baggage, cleared immigration and took the flight home. I think the best part of travel is going back home. While I slept like a log, Raj and Srila talked throughout the journey from Newark to Frankfurt. At Frankfurt, Srila boarded the flight to Chennai, while Raj and I boarded the Bangalore flight. En route from Frankfurt to Bangalore, Raj slept like a log and I was wide awake, filled with the anticipation of meeting Anjali.

The Oracle Offer

THE FLIGHT LANDED AT 12.30 AM ON DECEMBER 17, 2007. WE WERE back to standing in long queues again. Four counters were trying to deal with about 300 people. It took us almost an hour-and-a-half to clear immigration. Then we waited at the baggage carousels for our luggage for another half hour. Once the baggage arrived, I started walking through the green channel. A custom's executive caught me and said, 'I have to inspect your baggage.'

I said, 'Sir, I have nothing to declare other than a few perfumes, a shaving kit and a couple of watches.'

He said, 'Please open your bags.'

I hesitated for a moment and the officer said, 'Open up.'

I reluctantly started to unzip my bags. One of the baggage boys came to me and whispered, 'Give him fifty dollars and you can go.'

I declared loudly, 'I have nothing to declare and I am not paying.'

Seeing my adamant stance, the officer understood that I wouldn't budge.

He said, 'You can go now.'

Raj said, 'No sir, now that we have opened our bags, please go through them and clear your doubts.'

The officer said, 'No need. You can leave now.' But we continued to insist.

He stared at us and moved on.

Everybody wants to fleece software engineers. They think we make a lot of money and have a good life. They don't know the truth that we slog our butts off for almost twelve to fourteen hours every day. We are under intense stress through the year. We don't get adequate vacations. Even our salary increments were screwed up this year. We could hardly afford a decent home in Bangalore. But who cares?

I walked out of the airport and atleast twenty cabbies mobbed us. The realisation that we were back sunk in fully. We felt at home and waded our way through the mob. I heaved a sigh of relief when I saw Anjali and Adi. As soon as Anjali saw me, she ran up to me and hugged me hard. I held her for a long time in my arms. I saw the tears in her eyes. I felt truly happy to be back, to be in her arms. I had missed her so much.

We didn't speak for a few minutes. We just looked at each other. Then, Adi came forward and gave a warm hug to both of us.

Raj said, 'How are you Anjali?'

She smiled.

I asked Adi, '*Kaisa hai re*?'

Adi said, 'Great. Chalo, we booked a taxi. Let me take your trolley.'

Raj and Adi took the trolleys and started walking.

I held Anjali's hand and we tagged along. She said, 'Idiot, next time if you go without me, I am going to kill you.'

I squeezed her hand and smiled.

We sat in the cab. Adi and Raj started chatting about movies in town, who was screwing who and Mani's latest idiosyncrasies.

Adi said, 'Mani has gone mad, the fucker is behaving like a slave driver.'

Raj said, 'Don't worry Adi. Now that Jai and Veeru have come, we will put the English jailor in his place.'

We grinned.

Adi asked Raj, 'So, you are going steady with Srila?'

Raj said, 'Yes. Let me clarify before you hit me with your questions. It is for real this time, we want to get married and we are going to talk to our parents.'

Adi patted Raj on the back and said, 'Good Raj. You have attained puberty now.'

Everybody laughed.

Anjali asked, 'VSAT, what about us?'

I repeated, 'What about us?'

'When do we tell our parents?'

'Next week, all of us will go to Coorg and break the news.'

Anjali said, 'Yeah, we better do that. Dad is trying to fix an alliance. His name is Pratap Karumbiah and is an IIT, IIM graduate, works with Goldman Sachs, makes tons of money and is a high flier. So, you have big competition.'

I said, 'What did you say?'

'Of course, I agreed. Who will decline such a wonderful alliance?'

I said, 'I see.'

Anjali said, 'Don't see idiot, atleast act now.'

Adi and Raj were enjoying our conversation.

I said, 'These bloody IIT, IIM guys are such an over-hyped minority in this country, but they turn up at the right moment.' Anjali giggled. Obviously, she was the object of attention now.

Raj said, 'Then why didn't you try for IIT?'

He sounded like my dad and I felt like choking him.

I said, 'If they had increased the quota intake, I would have tried. With so few seats and so many idiots cramming for years, I didn't want to interfere and disappoint others. Anyway, look at my face, do I look like an IIT product?'

Raj said, 'Not really.'

Adi asked, 'So how do they look'

I said, 'They have a different kind of face. Can't explain, will show you sometime.'

Adi said, 'Ok, in which case, why don't you try for IIM now?'

I said, 'With my aptitude, general knowledge and speaking skills, I don't think I am cut out for IIMs.'

Anjali said, 'That is the problem Venkat. That would be my dad's grouse. He will look for a person with a good understanding of trivia and general affairs.'

I said, 'Then let him get you married to Siddharth Basu or Derek O' Brien. I am a technical guy yaar and technical guys are good at what they do. Why should I go to IIM because your dad wants it? That is stupid. Let him assess me on Java. I will answer all his questions.'

She said, 'So technical people need not have a good profile? Is that what you are saying?'

I said, 'I come from a small town and am the son of a school teacher. I am happy that I came so far. I am happy that India leaped ahead in software and fortunately all of us have decent jobs. Almost 80% of engineering graduates in this country are like me. So, are you saying that if we don't know trivia, we can't get married to good-looking chicks like you? That is bullshit. This whole IIT and IIM thing is blown out of proportion. Let me tell you something, we understand technology and we give the edge to software industry. Not some IIM types who market the products. If we don't make world-class products, what will they market anyway?'

Raj and Anjali were stunned at my outburst.

Adi said, 'Bravo my friend! Now you can stand on a pedestal and say, "Friends, Romans and Software Engineers."'

I was anxious and asked Anjali, 'Is the colonel serious about this Pratap guy?'

Anjali said, 'Yes VSAT. I told my mom that I have somebody in mind. She must have said that to my dad by now.'

'How did she react?'

Anjali said, 'My mom said, "Andhra? How will you manage? They don't speak Coorgi."'

'What did you say?'

'I tried convincing her and told her about you, your family and how long we have known each other, etc.'

'Was she convinced?'

Anjali said, 'What do you expect? Obviously, she didn't jump with joy.'

'No, obviously not.'

Anjali said, 'Let us see what happens.'

The cab dropped us at home. We paid the driver and he didn't return the change, Bangalore-style. We rationalised it as his tip and let it go. We didn't want to get into an argument with the cab guy at 3.30 am.

Adi said, 'Anjali, you can stay back if you want to. I will sleep in Raj's room.'

Raj stared at Adi for a moment, smiled and said, 'Yeah, stay back. Go tomorrow.'

Anjali said, 'Ok'

Raj and Adi slept in one room. Anjali and I were in the other room. We wanted to make love, but I thought it was inappropriate. So I kept the bedroom door open and we chatted for an hour. I started feeling hungry. I was still on US time. Anjali agreed to make Maggi for both of us. It was wonderful to be back. I sat on the kitchen ledge and pulled Anjali closer. She looked beautiful. I took her face in both my hands and looked at her intently. She said, 'What?'

I said, 'Nothing Anju. I don't want to lose you.' I pulled her closer and hugged her.

She said, 'I love you baby.'

I kissed her on the forehead. Then I kissed her eyelids.

She raised her forefinger and pointed it to her left cheek and I kissed her there. Then she pointed at her right cheek and I kissed her dimpled cheek. She pointed at her chin and I kissed her there. When she pointed at her neck, I kissed her neck.

I gently kissed her lips. She put her hands around my neck and bit my lower lip.

I said, 'Ouch, that hurts.' There was a love bite on my lower lip and she giggled.

I said, 'Easy baby.'

She pulled me close to her and kissed me hard on the base of my neck and left another love bite.

I smiled and said, 'You want to advertise in office that we made love?'

She said, 'Doesn't matter Teddy. Come, I can't wait.'

She calls me 'Teddy' only when she is really, deeply, madly in love with me. Otherwise it is VSAT or Venkat.

I said, 'Raj and ...'

She put her finger on my lips, pulled me off the kitchen ledge and we went into Adi's room. She quickly latched the door, took my hand and put it under her shirt and I could feel the soft flesh. Her nipple stiffened. She softly groaned and said, 'I like it when you have stubble.'

I couldn't wait any longer, I took off her top and unhooked her bra. I quickly removed my shirt, and embraced her. I could feel her soft flesh against my hot skin. It was an unbelievable feeling. She flicked the light switch and we made love. I was jetlagged and she was really exhausted, so we woke up quite late in the morning.

We took a quick shower and walked into the drawing room. There was a small post-it slip on our door. Anjali picked it up, read it and started laughing. It read, '*We are off to office, once you are done with all the acrobatics, you can come too ... Raj and Adi.*'

We grabbed lunch at one of the Sagars and headed for office. I went to meet Mani.

Mani looked the same. He said, 'So hero, back after a successful trip?'

I said, 'Yes Mani. Couldn't come in the morning, was jetlagged.'

He said, 'Even Anjali was jetlagged, right?'

(Managing the Mani Way, Axiom eight—make your subordinate feel that you know everything that is happening in his personal life. It instills a sense of uncertainty!)

I smiled.

He said, 'No worries. So, what is your plan?'

I said, 'Mani, you know I haven't gone on vacation the whole of last year. I need a vacation now. Anjali is getting marriage offers and we can't wait any longer. I need ten days off to talk to my parents and hers.'

He said, 'I can understand. You think it is going to work out?'

I said, 'I don't know, but it *has* to work out.'

He said, 'Ok, take off from next week.'

(Managing the Mani Way, Axiom nine—never give in to requests, put a rider. Show subordinates who the boss is.)

After finishing my discussion with Mani, Raj and I distributed chocolates to the team. It was like a tradition. Any one who returned from the US had to get chocolates for the rest of the team. We talked for an hour about the US experience and after that I got busy with emails. My phone rang. It was from a placement consultant, an external recruiter.

She said, 'Mr Venkat?'

I said, 'Yes. This is Venkat.'

She said, 'My name is Mala and I am calling from A1 Recruiters. Is this a good time to talk to you?' I chuckled at the name of the recruitment agency. There was an 'A1 Drycleaners' at the end of our street in Hanamkonda.

This was the first call I had got from an external recruiter and it felt good. I lowered my voice and said, 'Yes, this is a good time.'

She said, 'Our Bangalore-based client is looking for people with Java skills. The pay and the position are good, would you be interested?' Pay and Position are the two P's that move software engineers from one company to the other.

I said, 'Could you tell me who your client is?'

She said, 'You know Oracle? It is an MNC. They are looking for senior software engineers with eighteen to thirty six months experience. They are willing to pay almost 3-3.5 lacs/year.' Suddenly the 2.2 lacs/annum which I was drawing and was content with, appeared measly. The temptress made an irresistible offer and I had no option but to take it forward.

She said, 'So, would you like to send me your resume?'

I said, 'Could I know more details? Where is their office? What projects do they work on?'

She said, 'Their swanky office is on Bannerghatta Road and they are looking for people in their CRM practice. They offer great benefits like hospitalisation insurance for self and family, bike loan, HRA, etc.' Again, the temptress was baiting me. The rat was in the trap; the cheese was too inviting to let go of.

I said, 'What is the selection process like?'

She said, 'Two rounds of technical interviews and one round of HR interview. Send your cv to mala@a1recruitment.com.'

I immediately called Anjali and informed her about my chat with the headhunter.

Anjali said, 'So, what do you want to do? Tempting, isn't it?'

I said, 'Yes. Shall we take it forward?'

Anjali asked, 'If you make it, will you leave?'

I said, 'Let's first make it and then we will decide what to do.' Most software engineers start job hunting this way and end up moving on, whether they want to or not.

Anjali said, 'Mani will be disappointed if he gets to know.'

I said, 'Anju, let us see.' To me Mani was the least of the problems.

That night I discussed it with Raj and Adi. They said, 'That is great. How did the headhunter know your number?''

I said, 'I don't know yaar.'

Raj said, 'If you make it, then we can also apply. That salary is great, man.' Adi nodded.

I asked, 'What about the project? It is in a critical stage.'

Adi said, 'Do you know that Joel and Nagaraj resigned last month? They got terrific offers. Almost 40-50% more than what they are getting now. I think they are joining Google. So, if we get a chance, why not?'

Anjali said, 'I didn't know. How did you know about that?'

Adi said, 'That's the gossip on the floor.'

Raj got excited and said, 'VSAT, take it forward. We are with you.'

That night, all three of us sat down and compiled our respective resumes and I shot mine off to Mala.

The following morning, Mala called me and said, 'Can we meet in the evening at our office in Barton Centre?' I promptly went and met Mala. She was in her mid-twenties, wore braces and was a warm person. She looked at my resume and asked me a lot of questions. She asked me about my education, my project, my US experience and my current salary. After taking notes diligently, she said, 'There is a recruitment drive over the weekend. Please make yourself available on Saturday.'

I asked, 'Recession and Christmas, are you sure they are serious about this whole thing?'

She said, 'No recession for MNCs in India. Vacation time is best suited to conduct interviews, because candidates are available.'

The Oracle office on Bannerghatta Road was quite impressive. Multiple panels were conducting interviews and the place was filled with expectant candidates. I saw a few TCS faces, but decided not to talk to any of them. I ducked behind newspapers and they also did the same. I was told that the technical panels had their hands full and was first called for the HR round.

There were two interviewers and one of them spoke first.

He said, 'My name is Anand and this is my colleague Kasi. We appreciate you for making it to the discussion today.' They looked the same to me, like gangsters, though the long overcoats were missing. I wondered why all HR people looked the same to me. I have to get my eyes and probably my brain tested.

I said with a smile, 'No problem sir.'

The HR folks at Oracle were slightly different from the ones at TCS. They looked like hoodlums all right, but more polished, and used more American slang.

Kasi asked, 'So, you have been with TCS for almost a year-and-a-half. Why do you want to move jobs?' Every HR guy knows the answer to this question, but he still asks in anticipation of a novel answer. The obvious answer was, 'a better salary.' Or should I have come up with, 'My astrologer said, join a company whose name starts with the letter O?' But Anjali had coached me to give the right answers, the ones that every panel would love to hear.

I said, 'I was not looking for a change. When the headhunter said it was Oracle, I was compelled to explore the opportunity.'

Kasi said, 'What do you want to work on?

I said, 'Java?'

He said, 'I mean, specialise in.'

I said, 'Java.'

He said, 'Functionally, I mean the domain.'

I thought, 'Idiot, any domain as long as it is development work, the pay is world-class and the work minimal.'

I said, 'I understand that you are looking for developers in the CRM space and that is a good starting point.'

Kasi continued, 'Ok tell me something about yourself.'

I said, 'I work with TCS, have one-and-a-half years of experience. I am a graduate of NIT and I work in Java.'

Kasi asked, 'That's it? Give me more.'

I thought for a while. How about, 'I am Nelson Mandela; I helped free South Africa. I was in jail most of my life, I am a dignitary and I rub shoulders with the who is who of the world. It is incidental that I am attending an interview to be a Java programmer. What do you expect me to say? I am a regular software engineer who codes in Java? I am just back from the US; I can't talk about my family anymore, that is an invasion of privacy. So, what do I talk about? I use a pink toothbrush, which Anjali gave me and I clean my tongue with a steel tongue-cleaner, which broke in half this morning. I don't like wearing underwear when I go to sleep.'

I said, 'My hobbies are watching movies and visiting new places. At TCS, I worked on the NED project and have been in the US for the last three months. I can code in Java and also scope and document functionality. I have been involved on testing a bit.'

Kasi asked, 'What kind of boss do you prefer working for?'

First, I thought of Mani and he reminded me about the kind of boss I didn't want to work for. I wanted to say, 'I don't want to work for somebody who is a micro-manager, is egoistic, bossy, idiotic, a task master, slave driver, rulemaker-cum-breaker, buck-passer, decision procrastinator, boss sucker, leech, etc.' But the question was 'kind of boss I wanted to work for,' so I thought of Steve.

I said, 'Somebody who is mature, understanding, sensitive and jovial. Who can relate to me and give me my independence.'

Anand said, 'That is asking a lot from one individual.'

I said, 'It is possible. There are excellent people to work with.'

Kasi said, 'Is that your current boss?'

You don't refute such questions; instead you duck and let the bouncer pass.

I said, 'My client manager.'

Kasi said, 'Do you know that people leave managers, not companies. What is your view on it?'

The HR jargon didn't matter to me because people leave companies which have bad managers anyway. But I decided to play along.

I said, 'Yes sir. May be.'

Anand asked, 'What was your last appraisal rating?'

'Met Expectations, sir. Borderline Above Expectations is what my manager said.'

Anand said, 'What is that?' I wanted to tell him that because of HR guys who had come up with the stupid normal distribution curve, I had to be rated Met Expectations. But I said, 'It is a euphemism for high performance sir.'

Both of them laughed and said, 'Your manager was probably trying to convince you. So, your rating is Met Expectations.'

I nodded.

Kasi said, 'Ok, give me some of your strengths.' I can lift a 100 kg weight bar with my little finger, punch Mike Tyson to death. Why did they ask the same stupid questions? I was just a regular software engineer! What are our strengths? Obey orders. Work like a dog and code. What else?

I said, 'I am hard working, a good team worker and good at coding, sir.'

Anand asked the next question, 'What about some of the challenges you have had to overcome?' Here comes the booby trap. No discussion with HR can ever go smoothly.

I said, 'Sir, I work so hard that at times if I don't take a vacation, I feel stressed.'

They looked at each other. Was this the most professional answer they had ever heard?

'Another one?' asked Kasi.

'Sir, when I work hard, I lose track of time and sometimes, I need to manage my time better.'

'Another one?' he persisted.

'Sir, I want to complete whatever is assigned to me as quickly as possible. So I tend to work hard and wrap it up quickly and once I'm done, I end up relaxing.'

Kasi said, 'All you software guys have learnt to bullshit the nice way.'

I wanted to say, 'We are behind you HR guys anyway.'

I hesitated for a moment and said, 'Its difficult to admit one's own weaknesses, sir.'

Anand asked, 'If we call your manager and ask him to give us the truth, what will he say?'

Idiots, did they think I was going to give Mani as my reference? Over my dead body! I imagined Mani standing in court taking the oath on the *Bhagwad Gita* and these two lunatics waiting to pounce on him and ask questions. Even after taking the oath, Mani would lie. Obviously he wouldn't let me go at this stage since I hadn't documented most of the scope yet and probably wouldn't. How would I be indispensable otherwise? He would probably say that I was the world's worst software engineer and that they could take me. He might even waive off my notice period. And then these two lunatics would believe him and not touch me with a barge pole.

So, I decided to play it safe by talking technical stuff. HR guys didn't have a clue about it. 'Sir, my manager's feedback the last time was similar, he asked me to pay attention to the functionality, code coverage and syntax, specifically when we were using classes. Even the component nomenclature ...'

Kasi stopped me and said, 'Oh. So he said that technically you need to do better?'

I replied, 'Sir, technically everyone learns daily.'

Both Anand and Kasi exchanged looks. Kasi summarised my challenges as, 'You can't manage time and stress, besides you need to be better technically.'

I was amazed at his ability to cut through the chaff. When you ask them for a salary hike, they will present thirty power point slides and tell you that you are already over-paid. When they have to cut you down to size, they succinctly put in a few words.

I smiled and said, 'Something like that, sir.'

Anand then asked, 'So, if we made an offer how long will you take to join?'

I said, 'We have a two-month notice period.'

Kasi said, 'Suppose we buy the notice period?'

I said, 'Don't know, sir. May be it could be reduced by a week or two but not more than that.' I didn't want to give them the feeling that I was totally dispensable and could be let off in a couple of weeks, if need be.

Anand asked, 'What is your salary expectation?'

I said, 'The placement consultant informed me that it is in the range of 3.5 lacs/annum.'

Kasi said, 'That is a range. But you are at about 2.20 lacs; you are expecting more than a 50% hike? Isn't that a lot?'

I hesitated for a moment.

Anand said, 'Let us see about that later. Do you have any questions?'

I said, 'When will I know about the selection?'

Kasi said, 'In a couple of days after you are done with the technical rounds.'

I thanked him and left.

I was summoned for the technical round. The first one was short. They asked me to write code and checked the syntax. Miraculously, it was right. I qualified and I was called for the second round. In the second technical round, they asked me about my project and I explained the Re-Arch project and how we were trying to work out the Phase One deliverables. The technical panel seemed impressed. At least, that is the impression I got. One of them asked whether I would join if an offer were to be extended. I didn't want to blurt out that, for the kind of salary they were proposing, I would join the next day. Instead I said, 'I am inclined to consider it, sir.' The interview ended on a positive note and I went to pick up Anjali.

She asked me, 'So, how did it go at Oracle?'

'I think it went well. I might get an offer.'

Anjali said, 'That'll be great VSAT, it will be another feather in your cap and will help when we speak to my dad.'

I asked, 'Did your mom inform your dad about us?'

She said, 'I think so.'

'What do you mean I think so?'

'You know VSAT, not everything is black and white. Mom said she kind of alluded to me having a boyfriend.'

'What did your dad say?'

'Apparently he didn't react,' said Anjali.

I said, 'But we are going home today. Are we welcome?'

'If you didn't know young man, the Coorgis are famous for their hospitality.'

'I hope so.'

Meeting the Colonel

ON DECEMBER 22, 2007, RAJ, ADI, ANJALI AND I TOOK THE OVERNIGHT Volvo bus and headed to Madikeri, the capital of Coorg district. Raj and Adi had taken a few days off and we were looking forward to having some fun. We also had a plan in place to gently break the news and convince the colonel and Kaveri aunty. Ameya was manageable. Raj would be the bad cop, I was the good cop and Adi would be neutral. We were all in great spirits and wanted to make the plan a success.

I said, 'Jai paaji, you will speak to the colonel and convince him na?'

Raj said, 'Veeru paaji, I will do that.' Anjali said, 'Remember, though my dad loves *Sholay*, but he is not the Bollywood variety. He is more the *Gone with the Wind* kind.'

Raj asked, 'What is that?'

Anjali said, 'You don't know *Gone with the Wind*?'

Raj shook his head vigorously, the Indian way—at forty-five degrees.

Adi said, 'What? Some new kind of software bug?'

Anjali looked horrified.

I said, 'Ok baby, don't mock, tell us.'

Anjali said, 'It is an American classic written by Margaret Mitchell and the movie was released in 1940 and won eight Oscars.'

Adi added, 'All that happened before we were born. So, we don't have to bother about it now'

Anjali said, 'I give up guys. I am not sure we will be married in this birth. I live in the company of three idiots.'

The bus reached Madikeri at 3.30 am. It was freezing. We pulled our jacket zippers. right up to our necks and dug our hands into our pockets. Raj said, 'Hey, can we have tea and cigarettes before we head home?'

We agreed and went to the tea-stall at the bus stand. The tea tasted fantastic. Though I was not a regular smoker, I took a drag from Raj's cigarette.

Anjali asked, 'Started again?'

I said, 'You know it is an on and off thing. I just had a drag, nothing else. It feels nice.'

Anjali said, 'Now you will stink.'

I said, 'No, we have gum.'

Adi doesn't smoke. He quietly sipped his tea. He can stay up all night but if he has to get up early in the morning he becomes very quiet.

Anjali irritably said, 'If we are done, can we get going?'

We started walking down the main road towards Mangala Devi Nagar. There were hills all around us. The church on the main street was decorated with stars and twinkling lights. It was beautiful.

We came closer to the house and I spit out the gum. Anjali opened the gate and Pluto jumped on her. She said, 'Pluto boy, how are you?' Pluto was their black Labrador, a beautiful creature.

Raj asked, 'Does it bite?'

Anjali said, 'He is sweet.'

Adi said, 'Sweet, fine. But does he bite?'

Anjali said, 'No. He doesn't bite. Want to pet him?'

Adi said, 'Later, later.' He quickly walked past Pluto.

I walked up to the main door.

Kaveri aunty opened the door and Anjali hugged her.

Aunty said, 'Did you pet Pluto?'

Anjali smiled. She said, 'Yes, Mother Kaveri.'

Her mother said, 'Go wash your hands.' Then she smiled at all of us and said, 'Welcome to Coorg. Please come in.'

Raj said, 'Coorg is cold Aunty.'

She said, 'Yes, it is cold in winters. Want some tea?'

Adi said, 'I wouldn't mind Aunty.'

Aunty showed us our rooms and went into the kitchen. We dumped our bags in our rooms.

Raj said, 'Where is the commander yaar?'

Adi said, 'No, the captain.'

I said, 'Fuckers, you will screw it up even before we start. He is a colonel and Anjali told me that he was particular about his rank.'

Both looked at me and Adi asked, 'Any more instructions for nitwits like us?'

I said, 'No more for now.'

Raj looked at the large bed and said, 'Do the three of us have to share this bed?'

I said, 'May be.'

Anjali came in carrying three cups of tea and said, 'No need to share. There is a mattress underneath, you can sleep on it.'

Both of us looked at Adi and he said, 'That will be me.'

Meanwhile, aunty came in and said, 'Anjali you want to show them the washroom?'

Anjali introduced the three of us to her.

She said, 'Mom, this is Adi, the technical genius, that is Raj and he is a "character," and then there was a momentary pause, and she added, 'That is Venkat, who I talked to you about.'

Kaveri aunty gave me a quick glance and sized me up. We all smiled and nodded.

Raj asked, 'Aunty, where is uncle?'

Kaveri aunty said, 'He must be getting ready to meet you. Let me go now and switch on the geysers so you can take a shower.'

Anjali said, 'Dad is properly attired for all occasions.'

I asked, 'So, should we also wear suits?'

Raj added, 'May be our military uniforms?'

Anjali said, 'Stop making fun of my dad.'

Adi asked, 'Hey, where is Ameya?'

Anjali said, 'She is sleeping guys. It is 4 am. Let me see if I can wake her up.' And she left the room.

Raj said, 'Two cups of tea in the morning. Let me quickly go to the loo. Will be back in a minute.'

Adi said, 'Let me lie down for a minute.'

I sat on the bed and started to think.

Fifteen minutes passed by and Anjali came into the room looking refreshed. She had taken a quick shower, and was wearing a blue salwar suit. She looked ravishing. She had a towel wrapped around her hair. She looked as homely as I imagined my wife to be. I wanted to take her in my arms.

I said, 'Baby, you look beautiful. Give me a kiss.'

She said, 'Why only a kiss? Let us get into the act.'

'Really!'

'Idiot. My mom is in the kitchen across the dining room. My dad is waiting for you guys in the hall and you want to kiss me now? Listen, the first meeting is the best meeting, so give it your best shot.'

I nodded. Raj, Adi and I went into the hall. The colonel was pacing there. I was now damn sure that he was a tad shorter than Kaveri aunty. It was probably a sore point, which was not to be discussed, ever!

The colonel looked as fresh as a cucumber at 4 am in the morning and wore crisp olive cotton trousers and a white, full-sleeved shirt.

The olive trouser was held in position by a thick, black belt with a steel buckle. In the centre of the buckle, three alphabets 'CKC' (Colonel Krishna Cariappa?) were etched prominently. I was reminded of Ajit, the famous villain in Bollywood movies.

The colonel looked very much like Anjali, a very old version of her. Actually, Anjali looked like a fresher version of him. Anjali had inherited his sharp features and her mom's complexion and personality. I guess that is how it works with Coorgis.

All three of us said, 'Good morning, sir.'

Raj muttered, 'Do we have to salute?'

I stared at Raj. If Raj had saluted, even inadvertently, we would have been probably fired at.

The colonel who was pacing in the room stopped in his tracks, looked at us and asked, 'So, what is the most popular song in the whole world?'

I thought: Interesting introduction, another nutcase in my life.

I blurted out, '*Crazy Kiya Re*, from *Dhoom 2*?' I could be quite innovative at times. The movie was the highest grosser in 2006 and I thought atleast 300 million Indians, roughly the population of the US, would have seen it. Besides, that was one of the few Hindi movies, which ran in Sridevi Talkies for more than a hundred days and the song was played in every Irani tea and paan shop in the entire state of Andhra Pradesh. Also, Andhra has the unique distinction of tilting the popularity charts for most blockbusters, including the Bollywood ones. The state runs on movies and mass hysteria.

Raj looked at me as if I was some kind of a suicide bomber who was ready to blow up any moment.

Adi intelligently added, 'Uncle, I am sure Venkat is kidding. Let me guess the answer—Rasputin, Boney M?' Probably that was the only English song he heard in his entire life and his effort bombed.

He laughed aloud and said, 'What did you say? Wrong answer.'

Adi meekly asked, 'What is the right answer sir?' and the colonel jovially replied, 'You cannot question a colonel, only colonels have the right to question you'. Krishna is a retired colonel from the Indian army, medium built, thick mush, sharp eyes and wholesomely gregarious, sometimes bordering on being invasive.

I was meeting Anjali's family for the first time and wanted to make a good impression. I put my best foot forward and respectfully asked, 'Sir, that is a very interesting question, what is the answer?'

He laughed aloud, his whole body shook and he started singing, 'Happy birthday to you, happy birthday dear Anjali, "Happy birthday to you" is the answer to my quiz question.'

He then added, 'Let me remind you, just in case you forgot, today is my Anjali's birthday. She was a pre-Christmas baby, the joy of our lives.'

I looked at Anjali and it was too late, in my anxiety to meet her parents, I forgot that it was her birthday. Even before I could wish her, Anjali hugged her dad and said, 'Papa, you are so sweet'.

Raj, Adi and I were again made aware, that we were morons. Nothing unusual about it, it was just that the timing was not right. I realised that to get married, I might have to go through a buzzer round with negative marks for wrong answers. The things people do to get married! Thank God, the colonel was not fond of equestrianism, else he would have asked me to learn horse riding, my nuts would have split even before I got married.

Adi said, 'Sir, this time ask a simpler question and we will crack it.'

I looked at Adi in sheer disbelief. I wanted to choke him. Going to Anjali's house was like entering the lion's den and encouraging the colonel to ask quiz questions was like putting your head right in the lion's mouth. Adi avoided me; he could have been turned to ashes by the intensity of my third eye. '*Bhasmam*' as they say in Telugu.

Krishna said, 'All right, here goes the next one and an easy one boys. Who said, "I'm the President of the United States and I'm not going to eat any more broccoli?"'

I thought, 'The only idiot who could say such a thing could be Bush Junior.' I said, 'Uncle, is it Bush Junior?'

Krishna Cariappa gleamed and said, 'Good. At least you guys seem to know the idiots.'

Raj and Adi laughed. I laughed too, thinking that these were the perks of having a potential father-in-law who was a quizzing nutcase.

Since Raj hadn't spoken for the last five minutes, the colonel looked at Raj and asked, 'English problem?'

Raj quickly blurted out, 'No sir. I can talk English, I can walk English and I can laugh English because English is a very phunny language. Bhairo becomes Byron because their minds are very narrow.'

The colonel laughed and asked, 'What was that?'

Raj said, 'Courtesy Amitabh Bachchan in *Namak Halal*, uncle.'

The colonel gave a sarcastic grin and shook his head.

He said, 'Ok, how about some introductions? My name is Krishna Cariappa and I was a colonel in the Indian army. I served for more than thirty years before I retired. I believe that a person with a good personality has a deep interest in trivia and general affairs. Do you agree?'

We nodded our heads. Was there a choice? Put the knife on a chicken's throat and ask, 'Do you want me to?'

Raj said, 'My name is Raj and ...'

The colonel interrupted him and said, 'Full name, please.' Raj started all over again, 'Sir, my name is Raj Malhotra.'

Aunty felt exhilarated hearing the name. She said, 'That is Shah Rukh Khan's name in *DDLJ*.'

Raj smiled and said, 'Yes Aunty, didn't know you were a Shah Rukh fan.'

Ameya who had just entered the room said, 'Not just a fan, but a huge fan. She subscribes to *Filmfare*, reads everything about him and the last time we were in Mumbai, we stood in front of Mannat, his bungalow, for a few hours just to catch a glimpse of her favourite super star.' Ameya was studying engineering (second year) at NIT Suratkkal and was home for Christmas vacations. I thought Anjali must have asked Ameya to be home. Uncle said, 'Ok Raj, continue ...'

Raj said, 'I am from Gurgaon sir and my father owns a Maruti showroom. My mother is a housewife and I have one sister who runs a beauty parlour. Anjali and I are batchmates.'

Uncle looked at Adi. Adi said, 'My name is Adithya Dikkipati. My father runs a tailoring shop in Hyderabad. Mom is a housewife and I have an elder sister.' I was surprised that coming from Andhra, Adi had only two words to his name. I wondered what his full name was.

I came last. I said, 'My name is Venkata Subramaniam Adisankara Tanikaburla, you can call me Venkat or VSAT. My father's name is Subramaniam Garu and he is a primary school teacher in Warangal, Andhra Pradesh. My mother, Lakshmi is a housewife and my sister Swati is studying BSc., computer science.'

I thought the colonel was nonchalant about the introductions. He just heard us and said, 'Ok boys. Welcome to Coorg. Feel at home and be comfortable. I will go for a walk now, meanwhile, all of you wash up, get ready and we will have breakfast at 6 am. We leave at 6.45 am for the coffee estate. It will be fun.'

We went back to our room.

Raj said, 'Not a bad guy, man!'

Adi said, 'Maybe eccentric?'

I didn't know what to say. I just nodded. This was my first interaction with Anjali's parents and I had hardly scored any points.

Ameya came into our room. She was wearing jeans and a tight top. 'Hi everybody, I am Ameya, Anjali's sister.'

Adi said, 'Good to meet you Ameya. I am famished, can you help with some breakfast please?' Intros are passé, food comes first.

Raj said, 'Didn't you hear? Breakfast at 6 am.'

Ameya said, 'That is ok Raj. If you are hungry, come over to the kitchen and mom will feed you hot rice rotis and bamboo shoot curry.' Raj and Adi jumped at the offer and followed Ameya to the kitchen.

Anjali and I were in the room. I said, 'I am sorry, I forgot about your birthday.'

She said, 'You forgot my birthday even before we got married. You will forget me after marriage.'

I planted a kiss on her lips and said, 'Happy Birthday sweetheart.'

She pecked me on the cheek and said, 'That will do honeybunch.'

Adi and Raj finished their breakfast sitting on the kitchen ledge.

Meanwhile, the colonel came back from his walk. I wanted to have breakfast with him, Aunty, Anjali and Ameya.

Sharp at 6 am, we sat down at the table. Adi and Raj excused themselves on the pretext of taking a quick shower.

During breakfast, Uncle said, 'So, you want to get married to Anjali?'

I said, 'Yes sir.'

'What do you know about marriage?'

I said, 'I know how to take orders, Uncle.'

And everybody laughed. Even the colonel grinned.

He asked, 'I heard you've known each other since your college days?'

I said, 'Yes Uncle.'

'Do your parents know about it?'

'Not yet. I wanted to seek your consent and then talk to them next week.'

'Do you think they will agree?'

'I will try convincing them.'

'There are too many differences, Venkat.'

'I understand, but we love each other,' I said.

The colonel became serious and said, 'We don't speak the same language, our cultures are very different and our food habits are also not similar. It will be nice now. But later, it will be tough to adjust. Besides, we are looking for a boy who has a good personality, with a good understanding of trivia and general affairs. Don't get me wrong son, but you may not be the right person for her.'

I said, 'So, will I be the right match if I pick up trivia and general affairs?'

He said, 'It takes years to build a good personality. It is not about cramming for exams. It is about a lifestyle, Venkat.'

I said, 'If that is what you are looking for, I will work on that Uncle.'

Aunty interrupted, 'Both of you are not eating. Please eat Venkat, don't hesitate.'

Anjali said, 'I love him Dad. Please give him a chance. Besides, he just gave an interview at Oracle and he might get an offer for almost 3.5 lacs per annum. Together, we can live a comfortable life.'

The colonel said, 'You know how much Pratap earns? 15 lacs per annum. You know his qualifications? IIT and IIM. Do you know what he does? Investment analytics for Goldman Sachs.'

I hated the IIT, IIM varities at that very instant. I thought they survived on branding, we made the technology for them to do analytics. We get paid less and they get more—it was so unfortunate.

Anjali said, 'I am sure he does all that Pa ... but I love Venkat.'

Kaveri aunty didn't say anything. She was listening to the conversation intently and so was Ameya.

The colonel said, 'Look Venkat, I am from the army and we are trained to be straightforward in our dealings. So let me make it clear, I am not convinced. You are a friend of Anjali, you have studied together, you are a nice boy and we respect you. You have come as our guest, accept our hospitality, have a nice time and leave. Let us not spoil this whole vacation. Ok?'

Momentarily Mani and the HR folks paled in comparison to the villainous colonel.

I didn't know what to say. I said, 'What will convince you Uncle?'

The colonel said, 'Too many differences and too many unmet expectations. I don't think I can be convinced. Pratap and his family are visiting tomorrow. You can meet them and know the difference.'

I felt a lump in my throat and could not speak. Anjali had tears in her eyes. The colonel looked at her and said, 'Anjali, trust me. I am your father and I try to do what is best for you. So, don't spoil your birthday and be cheerful.'

I didn't feel like eating breakfast anymore.

I excused myself from the table. Aunty tried saying something, but stopped midway.

Raj and Adi looked at my face and knew that a disaster had happened. I told them about our conversation.

Raj said, 'We have three days here and if they are okay, we can extend it by a couple of days and do our best. I am sure we can convince the old man. Don't lose heart, buddy.'

Anjali came into my room and her eyes were wet with tears. She said, 'Now what?'

I said, 'Give me time to think. Your mother was quiet throughout. Do you think she can help influence your dad?'

Anjali said, 'Difficult.'

'But there is a chance. Right?'

She nodded.

'So how do we handle Goldman Sachs tomorrow?'

Anjali said, 'Leave that to me. When I meet him one on one, I will let him know. Listen, when you go to the estate, be at your best.'

We nodded dutifully. We didn't have any other option.

Raj said, 'Anjali, why don't you stay back and try to convince mom?'

Anjali said, 'Not a bad idea.'

Adi said, 'Your mom is a fan of Shah Rukh Khan. You should have told us. We would have got all his DVDs for her.'

Anjali said, 'It never occurred to me.' I shook my head.

Raj said, 'Can we get some SRK DVDs here?'

Anjali said, 'That would be great. The day after is her birthday. It coincides with Christmas.'

Adi said, 'You are kidding me.'

Raj said, 'Why don't we try asking Shah Rukh to wish her on her birthday?'

Adi said, 'Brilliant idea. Actually why shouldn't we try that?'

I was exasperated. I said, 'Guys, give me a break. You will call Shah Rukh and ask him to call Kaveri aunty in Coorg and wish her on her birthday. Let us also ask him to send some flowers.'

Ameya said, 'But if you can pull that off, you have no idea what you can achieve. It is like moving heaven for mom. She will do whatever it takes to help you guys.'

I said, 'Ok, I will call Shah Rukh Khan, he is my langotiya yaar! Forget it.'

Adi said, 'We are the software people, man. We can get his email ID or we can go on Twitter and request?'

I said, 'And he will call? Come on guys, please think of something more sensible.'

Ameya said, 'Dad loves Single Malt. If I arrange for an evening get together, probably you guys can talk?'

I hugged Ameya. *Saalis* can be so useful with vital information.

Raj said, 'I have an unopened bottle of Glenfiddich in my bag. Got it from the US. Thought it will be great in Coorg weather. Didn't know it will come of use. Great. So, that is a done deal.'

I said, 'I got a Citizen watch set from the US for your parents. I will offer that on your mom's birthday.'

Anjali said, 'Didn't realise that you guys could be so resourceful. But do you think offering Single Malt and watches will swing the deal?'

Raj said, 'It will soften the deal a bit.'

I said, 'Ok, let us understand the issues. I have to improve my personality. Obviously picking up trivia and general affairs is going to take time. Secondly, understanding Coorg culture—that is easier, it is an emotional requirement and can be managed with positive vibes. Lastly, probably I don't make as much as the Prataps of the world make. Damn these IIM guys! But if I move up the ladder with a few job changes, it is definitely possible.'

Everyone in the room nodded.

Meanwhile the colonel called out to us, 'Ok everybody, get moving, I will show you the estate and we will be back home by late afternoon.'

We quickly got into the colonel's jeep and started off for the estate. It was about twenty kilometres away at a place called Cherambane. At Cherambane, he took a detour and drove a few kilometres before he stopped at an old rusted gate. He parked the jeep adjacent to it and said, 'Ok boys, get down. This is our estate.'

We got down. It was a steep climb and on both sides of the trail coffee plants were growing in profusion. We started climbing up the trail and all of us were panting, especially Adi. He was gasping for breath.

He said, 'Uncle, all of you go ahead, I will follow slowly.' I wanted to keep up with the colonel and make sure I was a step ahead. Raj was just behind me.

The colonel said, 'We grow Robusta.'

Raj and I looked at the colonel blankly. He said, 'Coffee is of two kinds—Arabica and Robusta. In Coorg, mostly Robusta is grown.'

I asked, 'An acre would yield how much coffee?'

'Depends on several factors like crop, rainfall, etc. You can roughly take it as thirty to forty bags or so and each bag is about 50 kgs.'

Raj asked, 'Uncle, where do you sell the coffee?'

'Coffee Board,' the colonel said.

Then there was a pause and the colonel smiled. I expected a quiz question and it came all right. The colonel asked, 'Ok, answer this question. Which is the largest coffee producing country in the world?'

I quickly said, 'Brazil.'

The colonel said, 'Not bad.' I knew the answer because I had read somewhere that Brazil is the largest coffee producer in the world. I was saved and my day was partially made.

Adi gave me a blank look. Probably he never heard of a country called 'Brazil'. I don't blame him, not knowing names of counties has never bothered him, since he focused all his life on two things—architecture and booze.

Raj changed the topic quickly. He said, 'Uncle, we have a surprise for you. We are hosting a small birthday party this evening.'

The colonel smiled warmly. He said, 'That would be great. I look forward to it. Maybe I will ask Chaatu to send some wood for the fireplace. We can sit up late and play cards. We used to do that in the army. How I miss it!'

I said, 'Excellent idea, uncle. Let us do that.'

We climbed up the trail and saw a beautiful sight. The clouds were touching the treetops and the silver oaks and coconut trees glistened in the warm sunlight. Every inch of the estate was covered with greenery. Chaatu, the head worker, waved at us. Uncle waved back.

We went towards Chaatu's house and he invited us to sit on the verandah. He was a big-built man. He was wearing a loose shirt and super loose shorts. There was a pinkish-red cloth on his shoulder. He was in his late forties. He said something to us in Coorgi, which we didn't understand. Uncle had a short conversation with him.

Then, he looked at us and pointed at a coconut tree.

Raj joked, 'No, I don't know how to climb. Adi knows how to climb.'

Uncle laughed and said, 'You have a good sense of humour, Raj.' The bad cop had turned good cop. I looked at Raj and he shrugged.

Raj smiled and said, 'Thank you uncle, Venkat taught me how to be humorous.' I marvelled at his ingenuity. He could really be creative at the most inopportune of times.

Uncle looked at me and I looked back at him blankly.

Adi pointed at the coconut and said to Chaatu, 'Coconut, eat ... ok, drink also.'

Chaatu fished out a big knife and picked up a coconut. He quickly shredded the outer husk, chopped the head and made a hole in it with the knife. Adi took a swig and said, 'It's sweet.'

Raj came close to me and whispered, 'Did you see how Chaatu chopped the coconut? If the colonel gets to know that you are screwing his daughter, your head will meet the same fate as the coconut's.'

I looked him in the eye and said, 'Nice positive thoughts Raj. Keep encouraging me like this.'

The colonel asked, 'What's up with you two?'

Raj said, 'Nothing uncle, we were thinking of taking some coconuts for the evening. We could mix coconut water with Vodka and Glenfiddich.'

The colonel stopped in his tracks. His face turned cherubic. He said, 'You have Glenfiddich?' Remember Archimedes' enthusiasm when he shrieked 'Eureka'? Both the expressions sounded similar.

Raj said, 'Venkat bought a fifteen-year-old for you.'

I stared at Raj. He was obviously overdoing it. Raj ducked my stare and grinned sheepishly.

The colonel said, 'That is very nice of you boys. I can't wait to get back. But before that, let us go down to the other side of this hill. We have a stream flowing through our estate. We can go for a quick swim if you boys are upto it.'

Adi said, 'Great idea Uncle. I am only worried about climbing all the way up again.'

The colonel laughed and said, 'Don't worry beta, we will go together.'

I think the word 'Glenfiddich' changed the whole equation and softened up the colonel because the word 'boys' changed to 'beta'.

We started going downhill. The trail was rugged, but we enjoyed it. Uncle pointed to a big bunch of yellow leaves extending outwards and said, 'That is cardamom.' He showed us a creeper and said, 'That is pepper. We also grow betel leaf. Chaatu has packed some for us.'

The colonel stopped us and said, 'Did you know that if you eat more than 30 grams of betel nut in one go, you will have a cardiac arrest?'

The three of us shook our heads in disbelief as if our fates hung on betel nut and cardiac arrest. I thought, 'In what way will betel nut ever change my life, unnecessary information overdose!'

As we were climbing down, Raj asked, 'So what do you say about the SRK idea?'

I said, 'Raj, it is impossible. How can you expect to reach him and also think that he will call?'

Raj said, 'At least let us try, yaar. What is wrong in asking?'

I sniggered, 'You have his cell number? Call him!'

Raj said, 'I have been surfing the net for the last one hour. Apparently his secretary's name is Sushama and her cell phone is listed. You want to call her?'

I was stumped. I hugged Raj. He said, 'For god's sake don't hug me here, man. Not in front of your future father-in-law. Senti fellow.'

I said, 'SRK's secretary's mobile number is listed on the internet and you think it is the correct one? You are nuts. Ok, let us assume the secretary's number is right and imagine she picks up the phone. What will I say? My name is Venkat, we have a bit of a problem, and we would appreciate it if Mr Shah Rukh Khan calls my future mother-in-law and wishes her happy birthday on Christmas day. Why don't you take down the number so that he can call?'

Raj was staring blankly at me.

I said, 'She will say, "Oh, how sweet, I will definitely make sure he calls. Give me the address too. We will have some flowers sent across!" Raj, wake up. Where are you?'

Raj thought for a moment and said, 'Let's send him an email and follow it up on Twitter.' I was amazed at Raj's persistence. This was highly improbable, almost impossible. It was like trying to identify the sex of a mosquito with the naked eye and confidently saying, 'I confirm, it is a female.' Only Rajnikanth can do that, not mere mortals like us.

I shrugged and asked, 'Are you fucking serious Raj? I mean, you want us to send an email to Shah Rukh Khan?'

Raj said, 'What is wrong in sending an email man? If he feels good, he will call, otherwise, he will junk it. In any case, most of his movies are about love, romance, family and all that crap. If he does this good deed, we will write about it on TCS Intranet. That will give him even more publicity.'

I shook my head in complete disbelief. I thought Raj had lost his mind. I said, 'We will get you examined when we get back, until then take some rest, Raj. I know you are under intense pressure at work. You will tell SRK that the call will give him publicity? You are out of your mind!'

Raj continued, 'You have no clue about the power of blogs and social networking. Imagine writing about this on TCS Intranet, hundred and fifty thousand people will know about it in less than ten seconds. Now, imagine the software industry. That's atleast ten million people ... VSAT, no, don't come near me, don't hug me.' I smiled and did not hug Raj.

I was tempted by the idea. I said, 'But you think it is possible?'

Raj said, 'I read in the papers that sometimes actors do things like that.'

I said, 'Ok, in which case, there is no harm in trying. But how do we get his email ID?'

Raj said, 'Let us use the TCS network. Let us talk to Mani and a few of our software guys. I am sure they can figure out the email ID.'

Meanwhile the colonel asked, 'What are you two doing? Walk quickly.'

I said to Raj, 'Ok let us give it a shot. But let's be discreet. What will Mani think?'

Raj said, 'Don't worry. Let me handle this.'

I said, 'Ok.'

Raj picked up his phone and called Mani.

He said, 'Hi Mani, need your help with a crazy idea that we have.'

Mani said, 'Can't expect anything normal from you guys anyway. What is it?'

Raj explained to him what had happened.

Mani said, 'I can understand what VSAT must be going through to agree to such a ridiculous idea. But let me see what I can do.'

Raj said, 'Why don't we put a request on the Intranet asking for the right address? The person who gets the right address will get two free movie tickets? Who knows?'

At critical times like these, Raj can come up with innovative ideas.

Mani said, 'Yes, we could do that too. Anyway, I will get back shortly, take care guys. I am glad I am able to help in whatever little way I can.'

I was surprised at Mani's response. He was turning into a good samaritan. That meant he would surely demand something in return. A pound of flesh, in all probability!

Raj and I joined Adi and the colonel, and we trekked down the hill towards the stream. The water was crystal clear.

The colonel said, 'This is Mother Cauvery, it comes from Talakaveri. It is the purest form of water.' He stepped into the stream as he was speaking. We followed him. The water was very cold. We washed our hands, legs and faces. We felt extremely refreshed. After spending an hour at the stream, all of us proceeded to the Bhagamandala Temple.

I prayed hard. '*Lord, I am back. Need help on two counts. First, my nitwit friend Raj wants me to send an email to the actor Shah Rukh Khan asking him to call Kaveri aunty on her birthday, the day after tomorrow. It is fine even if SRK doesn't call, but just make sure that this thing doesn't blow up in my face, because most of Raj's theories backfire on me. The colonel fellow who is standing next to me now, is not agreeing to let me marry his lovely daughter, Anjali. Please change his mind. Brainwash him so that he forgets the past and sees me as a knight in shining armour. Help this hapless devotee of yours ... Once the marriage happens, I will break a hundred coconuts for you, fifty for the first request and fifty for the second one. Nowadays, we don't get good increments, so a software engineer can afford only so many coconuts, what to do?'*

After the visit to the temple, we had lunch at a small shack nearby, named 'Hotel Santosh'. The sambhar was wonderful and we ate to our hearts' content. After lunch, we started on the journey back. Raj wanted to drive the jeep. The colonel agreed and sat next to him. We sat in silence for some time. The colonel fell asleep and started snoring. Such are the perks of old age; you can snore and keep others awake. It took almost an hour for us to reach home. We dropped off the colonel and Adi and went to Madikeri town to buy condiments for the evening's party. Raj wanted to smoke and I wanted a break from the colonel. I would have choked the colonel, but for Anjali. I was probably the first idiot in the universe who was going through a quiz round to get married.

Glenfiddich and SRK

ON THE WAY TO MADIKERI TOWN, RAJ GLOATED, 'MANI SENT ME SRK's email ID. We will go the internet café and send him a mail. What do you say?'

I thought, since we had come so far, we may as well try it out. I said, 'Ok Raj. Let us do that and pray for the best.' It is difficult to type a complicated letter of this nature on a mobile, so we decided to go to an internet café. It had to be crisp, carry the right message and sound genuine. We got the final draft ready. It read:

Dear Mr Shah Rukh Khan (please don't trash the mail after reading the subject line)

Subject: *Can you please call my future mother-in-law, Mrs Kaveri on Christmas (day after) and wish her a happy birthday? Her number is 08272 ...*

Sounds like an insane request, but circumstances so prevail, sir. No, I am not writing from any mental asylum, I am a sane software engineer (probably an oxymoron) working at Tata Consultancy Services (TCS), Bangalore. Hope that adds some credibility. Anjali (Kajol) is from Coorg and we were batchmates in Engineering, now workmates at TCS and want to become lifemates, but Amrish Puri (Colonel Cariappa), her father is not allowing it. Much to my discomfort, he has identified a high earning, ISI brand certified IIM product, who works for Goldman Sachs. Can't understand how one can compare technical people with IIM fellows! Can we compare Viswanathan Anand with Sachin Tendulkar? One is a gotibaaz *and the other is* ballebaaz, *and both are doing well. Career-wise, I too can grow as fast as any Goldman fellow; I just have to hop jobs every 1.5 years. The real problem though is Amrish Puri, and Farida Jalal (Kaveri aunty) could be the key influencer.*

Amrish Puri loves Glenfiddich (Single Malt), which is happening tonight and hopefully should level him. Else the performance will be repeated, till such time he levels with us. Farida Jalal is a super fanatical fan of yours (apparently she saw DDLJ *fifty times) and her birthday is the day after (Christmas day). My friends and I were of the opinion that a call from you will help seal the deal for us. Besides, your movies are mostly about love, family and relationships. (Barring of course* Swades *[great movie],* Chak De *[yet another greater movie].)*

Lastly, this mail has to overcome two obstacles. I doubt if this email ID is for real, because my manager has sent it to me and you very well know that any information given by one's managers is mostly invalid. Secondly, your secretary could trash this email, thinking that this is sheer stupidity. If this mail reaches you, give her a salary raise, sir. She is good at heart. If it doesn't, fire her, she doesn't have sensitivity towards your fans (so much for our software logic).

But I guess it is worth a try, you could read this mail, empathise with us and call. Who knows? We wait in anticipation sir and regret the inconvenience caused (if any) for giving such short

notice, but as you know, we do our best only during slog overs. I am sure 'dada' will vouch for it!
Thank you sir,

Yours truly,
Venkat, Software Engineer, TCS, +91 98450 ...

PS: Please call na!

Raj said, 'Brilliant email Venkat, let us send it.' Whenever Raj says something is brilliant, I am always scared. I prayed for a second, 'Lord Ganesha save me,' hesitated for a moment and finally pressed the 'send' button. The deed was done. The rest was in the hands of SRK, his secretary, my manager and Lord Ganesha.

We walked out of the café and picked up some snacks for that night's party and went home. By 7 pm, thanks to the beautiful winter, the place was pitch dark and it was freezing. We lit a fire and all of us settled down on the mattresses piled up close to the fireplace.

We placed the cake on the centretable and all of us sang 'Happy Birthday.' The colonel, Kaveri aunty and Ameya hugged Anjali and fed her cake. I wanted to join them, but I held back. We were all served cake. Anjali looked at me and said, 'Thank you guys for the wonderful cake. Immediately after that, colonel said, 'Ok boys, what are we waiting for? Serve the Single Malt and let us regale ourselves with some wonderful trivia.' Hearing the word, 'trivia,' my heart sank. But I still managed a smile.

Raj made three drinks. The colonel asked, 'What about Venkat?'

I said, 'I stopped drinking, Uncle.'

He said, 'You don't have to please me. I am okay if you want to grab a drink.'

Raj said, 'VSAT, have a little bit. Come on man.'

I nodded and asked him to give me a small one. I didn't want to displease the colonel and in any case, we software engineers don't have a strong resolve in booze-related matters. What would happen to Vijay Mallya, if all of us turned teetotallers? I rationalised that I was contributing to Mallya's business and the country's GDP, and decided to drink in moderation. I felt as if I was doing a good deed – it felt nice.

The colonel drowned the first one pretty fast and cleared his throat. He said, 'That is fantastic. Now we will all go slow. Ok boys, let us get into some common sense trivia which I picked up from the Net. According to Anderson Consulting, 90% of professionals couldn't answer these four questions. But let me try with you boys as well. Remember, it is absolutely simple and you can answer all the questions or atleast three of them with common sense.' The colonel had a knack to build suspense.

We became very attentive.

The colonel said, 'Ok. Here is the first question. How do you put a giraffe in the fridge?'

I was stumped, 'A giraffe in a fridge?' What a stupid question! I wanted to say, 'Ask the African poachers, they can stuff anything anywhere.'

Adi quickly said, 'Make a big fridge.'

Raj and I didn't say anything. We thought this was a trick question. For our pea brains, anything out of whack or anything we didn't know was always a trick question.

The colonel said, 'Ok, let me tell you the answer to the first question, which will help create the context for you. The answer is—you open the door and push the giraffe in. Ha, ha!'

I thought if this was the level of trivia, I could marry Anjali that day, go for our honeymoon the next, and have twins by day after. I grinned to myself; I thought only Raj, Adi and I were morons. But here was the fourth one, an experienced one at that. Suddenly you feel nice when the other person also falls in the same bracket. My confidence began to pick up steam.

The colonel said, 'Ok the next one. How do you put the elephant inside the fridge?'

Raj said, 'Simple, open the door and push the elephant inside.'

The colonel said, 'Wrong. Think, think, think.'

We came up with all kinds of answers. We will buy a bigger one, we will remove the trays, we will have a single door fridge, etc. He said, 'Wrong, wrong, wrong. Let me tell you the answer. We pull out the giraffe and push the elephant in.'

Raj looked at me and winked. His expression conveyed everything. He thought that the colonel was a complete nincompoop. I looked at Adi—he was lost in translation.

Ameya said, 'Papa, that is very stupid.'

The colonel said, 'What is stupid about it? It is commonsense, isn't it?'

I thought, commonsense or weird sense? Fuck, what an answer—'Pull the giraffe out and push the elephant in!'

I smiled and nodded my head vigorously. I said, 'Uncle, you are right, it is sheer common sense.'

I badly wanted to be on the colonel's side. Raj grinned and I felt like a moron. He transferred the title of world's best moron to me and I gladly accepted it from that moment on.

The colonel said, 'Ok boys. Shall we continue?'

We said in unison, 'Yes sir.' I was waiting for the next one from the nitwit.

The colonel smiled and said, 'Here is the third question. A lion called a meeting of all the animals, but only one was missing. Which animal was it?'

I thought, 'It could be dinosaurs, they are anyway extinct', but the mad colonel might say, 'well we are not discussing pre-historic times anyway', and I would be pooped.

Meanwhile Adi said excitedly, 'Birds?' I just realised that in Adi's head birds were animals too. I have intelligent friends.

The colonel said, 'Think guys, think.'

Raj was busy slurping his Single Malt and eating masala chips. He chose a better vocation than answering trivia.

I thought hard. I had to crack this one. I said, 'Is it the elephant? It is still in the fridge?'

The colonel said, 'That is commonsense. Fantastic! Yes, that is the right answer.'

I felt great. On top of the world. I winked at Anjali. Scored a major point. My chances were now enhanced by 0.0000002%, and any miniscule progress was substantial. Apparently that much percentage deviation is sufficient for a meteorite to avoid colliding with planet earth. See what I mean?

The colonel said, 'Ok here is the last question. Crocodiles use a river which you have to cross. How do you cross it?'

Adi said, 'Tie a rope to the trees on either side of the river and cross it.'

The colonel said, 'Good idea. But how can you cross to the other side?'

We said, 'We give up.'

The colonel said, 'Ok, here is the answer. Since the lion was holding a meeting, all the animals went to attend that. So, the crocodiles are not there and you can easily swim and cross the river.'

We laughed. Ameya asked, 'Dad, were you able to answer any of the four?'

Colonel said, 'No beta. Like Venkat, I answered the third one.'

Finally, I had something in common with the colonel. I felt great, at times even morons think alike.

Raj joked, 'But Uncle, one crocodile could take leave and stay back na?'

The colonel grinned, 'We send people like you first to check out. That is how the phrase test the waters came into being.'

Raj was flummoxed, the old fox had him by his balls.

The colonel asked his wife, 'Kaveri, please get us some *garam* pakoras.'

Kaveri aunty said, 'These boys are not answering most of the questions. So, why don't you play cards instead?'

We wanted to sneer at aunty, but we smiled dutifully instead. She was currently a goddess to all of us. Temporarily we changed our brain circuitry to do only nice things and smile, irrespective of what was being said about us. Unusual, but circumstances do change people.

The colonel said, 'Sounds reasonable. Ameya beta, get us the cards too. Let us play some rummy.'

I liked this idea better.

Adi could have kept quiet, but he said, 'We are okay with trivia, Uncle.'

The colonel said, 'We can go on, if you are interested.'

I said, 'Sure Uncle. Let us.' I didn't want to be the last one to nod. The colonel said, 'Ok let us continue. We will ask simple questions, so that all of you are comfortable. Which was the first company in the world to manufacture computers for commercial use?'

Raj asked, 'IBM?'

The colonel shook his head.

I said, 'HP?'

The colonel smiled and shook his head again.

He smirked and said, 'I thought you boys from the IT industry will know this, but seems like none of you have a clue. It was Remington Rand.' I bet I can prepare atleast a hundred questions on the defence services, which the colonel wouldn't know. But what was the point in proving him wrong?

Anyway, honestly I hadn't even heard the name before. So the question of answering it was not a possibility. If it was a multiple-choice question, I would have atleast flipped a coin.

Adi said, 'Give us something simple Uncle.'

The colonel said, 'Ok, here is the simplest one. I am sure all of you have heard about SAP? Can you give me the full form?'

Raj said, 'Systems Algorithms and Programs.' The colonel shook his head.

Ameya said, 'Software Application Provider?'

The colonel said, 'Wrong beta.'

I said, 'Systems, Applications, Programs.'

The colonel said, 'Only the last word is wrong.'

Adi said, 'Products?'

The colonel said, 'Right.'

I felt good. At least I had two-thirds right. 66.66666666%, an awesome lot!

The colonel said, 'Ok, here is another simple one. I am sure you know Google.'

We nodded. 'What does Google call its offices?'

Anjali jumped up and said, 'Googleplex.' The colonel gave a proud smile and said, 'My daughter!'

I thought, 'My love!'

By now the colonel had finished his third round of Glenfiddich and was feeling mellow and warm towards everyone. He turned towards Kaveri aunty and said, 'I think that much trivia is enough for today. Let us play cards now, why don't you also sit?'

She sat next to him dutifully. Raj piled up some more wood in the fireplace and all of us started playing cards. We played for a couple of hours and then aunty served us dinner, but we continued to focus on the Single Malt and hardly ate.

Around midnight, when most of us were high, Raj asked, 'Uncle tell us, was yours an arranged or a love marriage?' I was reminded of an old Salman Khan movie—*Hum Aapke Hain Kaun*—where a similar conversation had taken place.

The colonel smiled and answered in typical Bollywood style, 'In those days, you fell in love after you got married, son. I fell in love with her as soon as I saw her and it continues even today.'

I found the courage to say, 'Same here Uncle. I fell in love the first time I saw Anjali.'

Aunty looked at me and almost sneered. Uncle said, 'She is my daughter, I am not surprised. But remember what I told you this morning.'

I said, 'You are not even giving me a chance?'

Anjali's eyes were wet. With so much Glenfiddich inside him, the colonel could not bear to see his daughter crying and he said, 'Come here my baby. Do you really love this boy?'

She sat next to the colonel and he took her in his arms. She looked at him and nodded.

He said, 'Ok, Venkat. I can't bear to see my daughter sad. Let me re-think. But you have to improve your personality and if you could do better on the career front, it would be a plus point. Besides, I would appreciate it if you learnt our customs.'

I smiled and said, 'Done. Will do Uncle.' I had my foot in the door. Now I had to get in.

Anjali hugged her dad. Her big eyes were filled with tears.

Kaveri aunty asked, 'What about Pratap? Their family is coming tomorrow.'

I said, 'Uncle, how can she meet prospective grooms? That is not fair.' As if I was deciding the rules of the game. But nevertheless, it was a good try.

The colonel shook his head and said, 'Since we have invited them already, I want Anjali to meet him and take an informed decision.'

An informed decision meant, look at Pratap, the hero and look at Venkat, the side-hero. Who do you want? I didn't like it one bit, but beggars can't be choosers. Can they?

We continued playing cards for some more time, finished the Glenfiddich and went to our respective rooms. As soon as we were in the room, Raj said, 'Old man has agreed VSAT, the Glenfiddich worked.'

Adi said, 'Keep quiet. He is from the army. He could have bugged this room.'

I said, 'Wish he had bugged this room, then he will know how much I love his daughter. Anyway, tomorrow we have to contend with Goldman Sachs.'

Anjali and Ameya came into our room and said, 'Ok guys, good night. Tomorrow is another day.'

I looked at Anjali and said, 'Did you get to speak with mom?'

Anjali said, 'I did my best, but it is not working. She is sympathetic, but not convinced.'

I was slightly irritated. I said, 'You can't convince your mom?'

She had tears in her eyes. I wondered how women could invoke them so fast!

I looked at her and said, 'Ok, I am sorry. I hope you had a good birthday.'

She smiled through her tears and said, 'Thank you all for making it so beautiful and memorable.'

Ameya said, 'Come Anjali, let's go. Good night guys.' She turned to us and said, 'I thought you were studs and could easily convince my parents, but it has turned out to be otherwise.'

Raj said, 'Venkat, saalis are usually dumb, she is proving the theory right.'

Ameya said, 'Oh really, we'll see tomorrow.'

I said, '*Meri* ma, it is already screwed up badly, please don't add any more complications to it.'

She smiled and said, 'Jeeju, don't worry, I am on your side.'

I hugged Ameya and kissed her on her forehead and she hugged me hard. I felt that sisters-in-law are naturally affectionate. Everybody should have one.

Raj grinned at me and said, 'Senti fellow, please don't hug me.'

Sharp at 5 pm, Goldman walked in with his parents. He was tall, slim and looked very handsome. He was wearing a designer suit. His parents had an army background and displayed amazing finesse. My heart sank. I knew I could never be like him. Then I thought—do I want to be like him or do I want to be myself, or should I be both? Damn, why was my head spinning? As usual I was confused.

The colonel introduced us to Goldman and family as Anjali's classmates. He shook hands with us and we smiled too. Then Anjali, Ameya and Kaveri aunty joined. Anjali was wearing a red saree with a green border – Coorgi style. She had tied her hair into a neat pony. She looked beautiful. Goldman couldn't take his eyes off her. Who would anyway? The colonel stared at me. The message was clear—stay out of this.

Raj said, 'Following the tradition of the house, let me ask you a quiz question.' And he took out his cell phone where he had stored the questions that he had picked up from the Net.

The colonel looked at him quizzically, but he liked the idea. Raj said, 'Since Pratap is an IIM product and works in investment banking, let me ask a question related to banking.'

Pratap took it easy, smiled and said, 'Not all bankers will know everything about banking'. I thought that was the smartest thing he could have said.

Raj continued, 'The word "bank" came from the Italian word "banco". What does it mean?'

Pratap looked at us and said, 'Can I sit on the "bench" here?' He stressed on the word 'bench.' Raj looked dismayed and said,

'Perfect. The word banco stands for benches which Lombard Jews used in market places to transact business deals. The people became banco people and the area banco. Banco became bank.'

The colonel was overjoyed and he patted Pratap on the back. Pratap said, 'Guys that was a fluke. You can ask me another one.'

Raj said, 'Ok, here is a simple one. Which Swiss watch has a brand name that means always in motion?' Pratap smiled and said, 'That is a tough one. Give me a choice and I will try.'

Raj said, 'Longines, Antima, Movado?'

Pratap said, 'Guess it's Movado.'

Raj said, 'Absolutely right.'

Pratap said, 'I used to be an avid quizzer in IIM-A and I participated in the corporate brand equity quiz too. Since we are at it, let me ask a few questions, which I remember. Ok, here is the first one to the IT whizzes. Who are steel collar workers?'

I cursed Raj for picking a quiz fight with Derek O'Brien's first cousin! Leave it now, drop it, and choose another topic. Let us talk about how coffee is made. Coorgis talk, we listen. Problem solved.

Adi said, 'Robots.'

The colonel said, 'Bravo boys. I love this. Let me pitch in and ask the next one. Who are called summer soldiers?'

Pratap's dad Karumbiah grinned and said, 'Colonel, are they soldiers who fight in the summer only?'

Everybody laughed, but nobody answered.

The colonel said, 'The management of a company which puts up a token fight before a hostile takeover. Huh! See, nobody answered my question.'

Pratap said, 'Let me ask the next one. Name the world's renowned management guru who said that we have moved from knowledge to knowledge.'

The only management guru I knew of, was Peter Drucker. So I said, 'Peter Drucker.'

Pratap said, 'Perfect!'

The colonel said, 'Not bad boys. Not bad at all.'

Adi said, 'Since I have not asked any question, it's my turn now.' Name the famous painter who lived in the mid-fourteen hundreds and was gay.' He winked at us and we grinned.

The colonel said, 'Let me guess, Leonardo?'

Adi said, 'Yes. You are right, Uncle.'

Colonel said, 'Good question Adi. Anyway, I was just guessing. I think quizzing is mostly about guessing, right?'

Kaveri aunty jovially added, 'Will you keep quizzing or will you let Pratap and Anjali talk?'

Colonel said, 'Of course. Beta, you want to step outside and talk as we continue to quiz?'

Pratap nodded. Anjali followed him out of the room. I felt miserable. I couldn't take it.

Raj understood my anxiety and said, 'Let us continue Uncle.'

The colonel said, 'Ok, boys. Here is the next one. What is the meaning of Kludge?'

I said, 'Separating two love birds?' The colonel stared at me.

Adi said, 'This question relates to our field Uncle. Assembling hardware and software, usually in haste.'

The colonel said, 'Pleased, very pleased.'

I said, 'Let me ask a question. Who coined the name Coca Cola?'

The colonel said, 'That is simple, my dear. It is Frank Robinson. Ask a tough one.'

For me, that had been a tough question. I had memorised it from the Net. I decided not to get into asking any more questions.

Raj said, 'Let me ask the next one. All of us have heard of Accenture. What does it mean?'

There was silence for a minute and Ameya answered, 'They came to our campus for a placement talk. Accenture means "Accent on the future." Apparently a Danish employee from the Norway office coined it for an office competition.'

I said, 'Ameya, that is really cool.'

The colonel said, 'Quizzing is in our blood. Come here Ameya, give me a hug ... Ha, ha.'

We continued quizzing for another fifteen minutes, but I couldn't concentrate. I was thinking about Pratap and Anjali. After a while, Pratap and Anjali came back. Anjali looked pleased and Pratap shot me a quick glance as soon as he entered the room. That was good enough for me, the message had been conveyed. There was some more chit chat before Goldman and family decided to leave. The colonel and aunty walked with them to the gate.

I sneaked away to my room with Anjali. I said, 'You look fantastic.' I planted a kiss on her lips. She put her hands around my neck and kissed me hard. I put my hands around her waist and kissed her on the base of her neck and said, 'Sweety, I love you. She groaned softly and said, 'Enough, not here. Stop, please ...'

I let her go. I asked, 'So, beautiful, what did you tell Goldman?'

Anjali said, 'I told him that we are in love and that we want to get married.'

'What did he say?'

'He asked me whether I was sure. I said I was. He smiled and shook hands with me and wished me the best.'

I said, 'That is sweet of him.'

Anjali said, 'That is Coorgis for you. Dignity personified!'

I said, 'That is why I am marrying one.'

She planted a kiss on my lips and left the room.

I was glad that the disaster was averted.

The colonel returned and said, 'See guys, that is Pratap. Isn't he a polished young man?'

I said, 'Yes Uncle, he is a wonderful person.'

The colonel was surprised to hear that.

'Each one of us is a wonderful person. It's a matter of perspective,' I added.

The colonel smiled. He said, 'Ok, I have a Glenlivet. Who is game?'

Raj said, 'What a question! You shouldn't even ask.'

He said, 'Ok team. Set the fireplace. Ameya beta, get the cards and let us start our session.'

Kaveri aunty said, 'You had way too many drinks yesterday. Please make sure you guys don't go over the limit today.'

All of us chorused, 'Yes Aunty.'

But once you opened a bottle with the colonel, where was the question of limiting it? And anyway, it was at times like these that software engineers agree to change and expand scope without a whimper.

The session that started at 7 pm went on till 12 pm and all of us were totally sloshed. We crashed without having dinner.

We were woken up the next day at 7 am by Kaveri aunty. She served us fresh, steaming coffee. Beautiful Coorgi aunties definitely know how to make their coffee. All traces of my hangover vanished. We quickly washed, changed and sat down at the breakfast table. Aunty made rotis and served it with pumpkin curry, homemade butter and honey. I loved it. Ameya also joined us. Anjali was getting ready. The colonel was at the table. He said, 'We had a great time last night, thanks to you boys. I was reminded of my army days in Jammu.'

Meanwhile the phone rang and Ameya picked it up. She said, 'Mom, somebody is asking for you.'

Kaveri aunty picked up the phone and said, 'Yes ... what?' Then she laughed and muttered, 'And I am Katrina Kaif,' and banged the phone down.

Raj asked, 'Who was that, Aunty?'

Even before Aunty could answer, the phone rang again and she picked it up.

She said, 'Yes, this is Kaveri ... Yes, Venkat is here ... Who did you say you are? Shah Rukh? What a joke?...Yes, it is my birthday today. Oh, thank you ... are you really Mr Shah Rukh Khan? But how do I know you are Mr Khan?'

Raj lunged forward and switched on the speakerphone.

It was distinctly Shah Rukh's voice.

Shah Rukh said, 'Kaveriji, how do I convince you that I am Shah Rukh?'

Kaveri aunty said, 'Ok. Say the best line of dialogue that you liked from *DDLJ*.'

Shah Rukh said, 'Hmmm ... ok, ... *It's all right Senorita, bade bade deshon mein, aisi choti choti baatein hoti rahti hain.* ... In the current context, it is best for me to say, *chote chote sheheron me aisi badi badi baatein bhi hoti hai* Kaveriji.' He was laughing.

Kaveri aunty looked at us in complete disbelief.

We whispered, 'That is Shah Rukh, your favourite actor. Trust us.'

Kaveri aunty said, 'Oh my God. That is Shah Rukh Khan ... oh my God.'

Shah Rukh said, 'I got a mail from Venkat, who works at TCS asking me to wish you on your birthday. I liked the mail. It is neat and humorous. So, I decided to call and surprise you. So, happy birthday Auntyji.'

Kaveri aunty said, 'Shah Rukh ji, I don't know what to say. I am ... I am so happy you called. I can't even believe you called. Please, please speak to my husband too.'

The colonel came forward and said, 'Mr Khan, I am touched that you called.'

Shah Rukh said, 'Sir, I was impressed by Venkat's mail and so I called. I hope all of you have a great time. Looks like your daughter and Venkat are in love with each other. Though it may not be right for me to give advice, I thought it would be nice if you could consider it.'

The colonel didn't say anything.

I said, 'Sir, this is Venkat. I have my friends Raj and Adi with me here. I am deeply indebted to you for calling, sir. Honestly, I didn't expect it sir.'

Shah Rukh said, 'Your letter was very nice.' He laughed and added, 'You might want to consider an alternate career in movie script writing.'

I asked, 'Sir, do you read all your mails? I mean ... I can't believe that you read our mail and called.'

Shah Rukh said, 'My secretary is good at heart and if I hadn't seen your mail, I would have fired her.' Laughter again.

I said, 'Sometimes, that is how software engineers think sir.'

Anjali and Ameya jointly said, 'Sir, we are Anjali and Ameya, the colonel's daughters. We will remember this warm gesture for the rest of our lives, sir.'

Ameya added, 'Sir, I am Ameya. Can I ask you one question sir?'

Shah Rukh said, 'Sure, go ahead Ameya.'

Ameya asked, 'Sir, where are you calling us from? Which movie are you shooting for?'

Shah Rukh said, 'I am calling from Goa. We are not shooting anything today. I came here for some other work.'

Adi said, 'Sir, make more movies like *Swades* and *Chak De*. They are fantastic, sir.'

Shah Rukh said, 'Thank you.'

I said, 'Sir, please repeat your best dialogue.'

Shah Rukh said, 'I like most of my dialogues, but I guess this is apt for you. It's from *Kuch Kuch Hota Hai … Hum ek baar jeete hein, ek baar marte hein, shaadi bhi ek baar hoti hai, aur pyar….ek hi baar hota hai.*'

We were all moved by his intensity. We stood there in silence.

He added, 'Ok, then. Thank you for taking the call. I hope I have not intruded. Wish you the best. I hope your story ends well.'

Raj asked, 'Sir, can we keep in touch with you?'

Shah Rukh said, 'Sure, I am on twitter too. See you then everybody. Happy birthday to you once again Kaveri aunty ji.'

Kaveri aunty said, 'Thank you Shah Rukh ji.'

He disconnected the call.

After the call, aunty slumped down in a chair. She had fainted. We rushed her to the nearby clinic and the doctor put her on IV fluids. In the hospital, the colonel said, 'You guys are nut cases, see what you did to my wife?'

Dr Thimmiah interrupted and asked, 'How did she faint?'

Adi said, 'Shah Rukh Khan called her to wish her on her birthday.'

Dr Thimmiah removed his spectacles, placed a hand on Adi's shoulder and said, 'Son, we don't take physchiatry cases here, for that Mysore is the closest.'

Raj said, 'Sir, it is true, we didn't expect that SRK would call and that she would faint!'

Dr Thimmiah looked at the colonel. The colonel initially nodded and then shook his head in exasperation. Dr Thimmiah raised his eyebrows and gave a sheepish grin.

Adi said, 'Uncle, we will write an email to SRK and tell him not to call any of his fans on their birthdays anymore. It leads to disastrous results.'

Uncle came close to Adi, held his head in his hands and closely examined it for defects. Adi gave him a blank stare. The usual one, which no FBI or CIA agent can read.

I thought, 'Fucked if you do, fucked if you don't!'

Aunty regained consciousness after an hour, looked at the colonel and said, 'Shah Rukh.' Then she fell asleep. We ducked for cover and avoided the colonel's gaze.

Anjali and Ameya didn't know how to react.

I said, 'Sorry Uncle, we didn't realise it would be this bad.'

By afternoon, much to the colonel's relief, Kaveri aunty regained both consciousness and her senses. We took her home.

Kaveri aunty hugged me and said, 'You have no idea what you have done. I am deeply indebted to you. Imagine Shah Rukh Khanji calling me on my birthday. You boys are ingenious.'

Usually in all mythological movies, after performing infinite penance, goddesses appear before you wearing shimmering saris and big golden crowns over long tresses. They usually ask '*Bhakta*, I am pleased with your devotion, ask for one boon and it will be yours.'

I was waiting for something like that to happen. Instead, aunty said, 'I will reciprocate with a great dinner for you all today. The best you have eaten.' She was trying to please our stomachs, but we wanted something else.

I looked her in the eye and begged, 'Aunty, please....'

Kaveri aunty understood my anguish and said, 'I am not against it. I will talk to the colonel about it.'

I hugged her and said, 'Aunty, I will do whatever it takes.'

Then I handed over the gift case to aunty and said, 'Happy birthday Aunty.'

She said, 'What is this?'

I said, 'Please open it.'

She carefully unwrapped the gift and saw the watch set.

Her eyes were filled with tears and she said, 'This is beautiful. Is it expensive?'

I said, 'No Aunty. Anything for you and uncle.'

She unhooked the ladies' watch from the case and started to wear it. Precisely at that moment, the colonel entered the room. He asked, 'What is happening here?'

Aunty said, 'I was thanking these boys. Krishna, they are good boys. You must give them a chance.' She handed over the bigger watch to him and said, 'This is for you from Venkat. And look, this is for me.'

I think, when aunty used his first name, the colonel melted, I could see the puddle. The colonel smiled warmly and his moustache quivered. I was reminded of Donald Duck. He rubbed his hands on his bald patch and said, 'Thank you for this watch Venkat. I was thinking about you. You seem to be pulling off the impossible. Also, I had a good time with you for the last three days. It reminded me of my younger days. I don't have sons and want to relive my life with my sons-in-law. We would like to meet your parents.'

Tears started rolling down my cheeks and I looked at Raj. He came forward and hugged me. I said, 'Don't, don't hug me. I hate it.'

All of us laughed.

That night, aunty cooked a great dinner and the colonel opened a very expensive bottle of Chateau d'Yquem wine. He put his arm around my shoulders and said, 'I said to myself that when I find my first son-in-law, I will open this wine and today is the day.' Anjali and I hugged the colonel. Adi took a picture with his cell phone and time stood still. Mission accomplished.

The following morning before we left, the colonel asked, 'So, how do you want to take it forward?'

I said, 'Uncle, I will speak with my parents and arrange a meeting.'

He asked, 'Will they be convinced?'

I said, 'We will convince them.'

Aunty asked, 'So, this time which actor is going to call your parents?' All of us laughed and bid her goodbye.

On the way to Bangalore, Raj called up Mani and informed him about what had happened. Mani wrote a blog and posted it on the TCS intranet. The tagline was '*Shah Rukh Calls Anjali's Mother and Settles Marriage*'. He had written a full-length article under the able guidance of real time reporter called Raj Malhotra. The blog became an instant hit and flooded the Net. I sent a copy of the blog to Shah Rukh with a thank you note.

He sent a one-liner, '*Hi Venkat, didn't expect this. Hope things have worked out for you. Best, Shah Rukh.*' Subsequently, most national and regional newspapers carried the article called *Shah Rukh: The Tie-Maker*.

My father called me after reading it. He asked me, 'The papers quoted someone called Venkat from TCS, Bangalore. Hope it is not you.'

I was silent and he stoically said, 'Oh! Come home.'

Oracle vs TCS

ON REACHING BANGALORE, I GOT A CALL FROM MALA OF A1 recruiters informing me that Oracle was willing to extend an offer. I was overjoyed, but didn't express it.

I said, 'Great, I am on vacation now. When do I pick up the offer letter?'

She said, 'Today evening at 4 pm, if you are free?'

I said, 'Make it 4.30 pm.' I wanted to show that I was a busy guy.

She said, 'Should be ok.'

At Oracle, I met with Anand. He congratulated me and said, 'We are happy to extend an offer to you. How soon can you join? Next week?' The demeanour during the interview is very different from the time of making the offer.

I said, 'No Anand, I can't join in a week.' If I had said that a week was fine, then the figure in the offer letter would diminish.

He said, 'But we are planning to start the program next week. How soon can you make it?'

I said, 'Eight weeks.' I thought, 'Be confident, make it sound as if it is a big deal.'

He exclaimed, 'Eight weeks? No way.' HR people can comfortably dramatise. It is one of their core competencies. I thought, 'Don't give up VSAT, more the eccentricity, higher the pay.'

I said, 'No option Anand. My notice period is two months and my manager will not relieve me.'

'What if we pick up the cost of the notice period?'

'Even then, it is not possible.'

'But why?'

'Because I have deliverables to complete. It will take a minimum of four weeks.'

'Ok, in which case, why don't you speak to your manager for four weeks and see if he can reduce it?'

HR guys never give up.

I said, 'I could try, but can't promise.' I thought that Anand was putting unnecessary pressure on me. Their performance was measured on offer to joining ratio, and the best way to improve that ratio is to make the candidates join as soon as possible.

He then paused for a minute and said, 'Venkat, I have a question for you. Are you the same Venkat from the SRK story?'

I had become a celebrity overnight. I said, 'Yes Anand.'

He asked, 'So, you spoke with Shah Rukh?'

I said, 'Yes.'

He asked, 'How was it?'

I said, 'Nice.'

He repeated what I said, 'Nice?'

I said, 'He is such a wonderful person.'

Anand asked, 'How did you guys get this idea in the first place?'

I said, 'My roomies got the idea, they are crazy.'

Anand said, 'Wow, that is wonderful! You must refer them to join Oracle.' I realised that Oracle also preferred morons.

I smiled.

He said, 'So when do you plan to get married?'

I said, 'Only when the other half of the story is done. I still have to convince my parents.'

He said, 'Oh, they are not convinced as yet?'

I shook my head.

He said, 'With all this, that should be a cakewalk, right?'

I said, 'I don't know. I hope so.'

'What will you do if they don't agree?'

I said, 'I will make them agree.'

He said, 'I like your confidence.'

Next, he asked me about my salary expectations.

... This was the question I had been waiting for.

I said, 'Before the interviews, I was told that it was 3.5 lacs per annum. Anything more than that?'

Anand laughed. He said, 'What we tell recruitment agencies is a range and you guys always assume the higher end of it.'

I said, 'Anybody would do that, sir.' I added a 'sir' at the end of the sentence. As I said earlier, the damn thing works big time. I was sure he had done the same thing when he was joining Oracle.

He said, 'Ok, we will make it a perfect 3.5 lacs per annum. That is more than a 50% jump. I hope with this salary, you will surely join.' I said, 'Yes Anand. But I have to consult my family once.' I was damn sure I would join. The jump in the salary was unbelievable.

He said, 'I understand that. So when will you let us know?'

I said, 'In a couple of days.'

He agreed and issued me the offer letter. I shook hands with him and left the place.

First, I called Anjali. She was still in Coorg. I said, 'Anjali, Oracle made an offer today.'

'Great. How much is it?'

'3.5 lacs'

'Wow! That calls for a party.'

'When are you coming back?'

'Day after,' said Anjali.

'Tell your parents, they will be happy to hear about it.'

She said, 'I will honeybunch. Miss you. Did you speak to your parents?'

'I still have to. I am leaving tomorrow night for Warangal.'

She said, 'Please convince them, do your best.'

I showed Raj and Adi the offer letter. Irrespective of confidentiality agreements and NDA (non disclosure agreements) which Americans make us sign, no information is left unshared between roomies. The bond is eternal.

Adi said, 'Did you tell him that you have two VIPs to refer to Oracle?'

I said, 'Yes. Told them that sending the mail to SRK was your idea.'

Raj asked, 'Did they like our creativity?'

I said, 'They wanted me to refer your CV. Once I join, I will refer and we will get the referral money. Then all of us can go for a holiday, what do you say?'

Adi said, 'You are turning into a genius VSAT.'

I asked, 'What do you mean?'

Adi said, 'You can kiss your moronship goodbye now.'

We laughed.

Raj asked, 'So, when are you going to tell Mani about it?'

I said, 'I will speak to my parents today and tell Mani tomorrow.'

Raj said, 'We will look forward to the fireworks. *Kal* office *mein maza aayega*.'

I called mom. She said, 'Why are you calling us? I thought home was Coorg for you now.'

I said, 'Lakshmi, what are you saying?'

She said, 'You don't come home for one-and-a-half years, but have time to go to Coorg to convince your girlfriend's parents?'

I said, 'Lakshmi, I am starting tomorrow night and will be home the day after. You want me to come or not?'

She melted. 'Kanna, are you sure or are you saying it to please me?'

I said, 'No Ma, I am coming home for a full week. How do you like that?'

She said, 'That is wonderful. I will go and buy brinjal tomorrow. You like brinjal curry so much.'

I said, 'Lakshmi, I have some good news for you.'

'What is it?'

'I have a job offer from Oracle for 3.5 lacs per annum.'

She said, 'You mean "Vercle" company? Rupees 30,000 a month?' For mom, Oracle was "Vercle" and that was fine as long as she understood the concept.

I said, 'Yes Ma.'

'Did you thank Lord Ganesha?'

'No Ma, I wanted to thank you first.'

She said, 'What ra? Why are you buttering me up?'

I said, 'Where is pa? I want to tell him too.'

My dad came on the line. He said, 'So Mr Anjali, what can we do for you? You finally have time for us?'

I felt good because he had registered Anjali's name. That meant he must have read and re-read the news article multiple times.

I didn't say anything. Mom told him about the job offer. He asked, 'Is that right?'

I said, 'Yes Pa.'

He said, 'So what do you want to do?'

I said, 'I want to seek your advice.'

He anxiously said, 'You want to leave Tatas? They did so much for you and this country. You want to leave them?'

I thought for a second and said, 'What do you want me to do Pa? I will not get 3.5 lacs per annum in TCS in the next two to three years because increments are very slow and so are the promotions.'

He asked, 'Then how come thousands have been working at TCS for a long time? Don't they get good offers?' I said, 'Maybe inertia.'

He said, 'Maybe job security and job satisfaction.'

'I don't know Pa. But the offer is tempting.'

'Listen, MNCs have a hire and fire culture. How safe is Oracle?'

'It is expanding rapidly Pa. They don't fire people in India.'

'How come they are giving you such a high salary?'

'Competence, Pa!'

He said, 'Every other software engineer is also competent.'

'I don't know why they give such high salaries, Pa.'

He said, 'I read somewhere that companies which pay high salaries do not give good job satisfaction. So, you may want to think about it. I think the choice is yours. By the way, will they send you abroad?'

I said, 'It is a global company and they have rotation program.'

He said, 'Check for job satisfaction and good work culture. If you are comfortable, then decide to move. But if you ask me, I would be happy with TCS.'

I said, 'Pa, I am inclined to move. The job content and salary are irresistible.'

He said, 'Ok Venkat, all the very best son. Pray to Lord Ganesha and then inform TCS.'

I agreed.

Next morning, before leaving for office, I prayed to the Lord, *'Lord, though of late, Mani is changing a bit, but he is still a pain and you know that. I am going to inform him that I am leaving, please make sure it works out smoothly.'*

I went to the office and met Mani.

He said, 'What are you doing here? Aren't you supposed to be on vacation?'

I said, 'I am leaving for home tonight Mani. Thanks for the help with SRK's email ID.'

He said, 'That was simple, I pinged on the Net and I had atleast ten email IDs in less than a minute. Luckily, one of our software guys verified it for us. Apparently he got a mail from SRK about six months back.'

I said, 'I didn't know it was so simple to get the contact details of celebrities.'

He laughed. He knew something was up.

I was nervous too. I started fidgeting a little bit and Mani noticed my body language and said, 'Oh my God, you are resigning?'

I nodded.

He said, 'Obviously I can't let you go. I have already lost Divya, Noel, Nagaraj in succession and if I lose you, Steve and Cathy will eat me alive. I am not even listening to you. Complete this project and we will talk next year. Until then, don't discuss anything else with me. You can leave me alone now.'

This was the first time I had seen Mani so vulnerable! He had no axioms to quote! I felt a little bad for him. He was visibly upset.

He asked, 'Raj, Adi, Anjali are also leaving?'

I shook my head and said, 'Why do you ask Mani?'

He said, 'You guys are one gang and software engineers move in gangs. Enjoy your time at home and come back. There is a lot of work to be done.'

I said, 'I have an offer from Oracle at 60% more than what I am getting here. How can I refuse Mani? I am being assigned to work on CRM development platform and I think it is a good opportunity.'

Mani said, 'Go now. I don't want to talk to you now. I will talk to you later.'

I left his room and Mani called Amit and informed him about our conversation.

Meanwhile, I went to my desk and sent an email to Mani with a copy to Amit. I wrote,

Dear Mani

As discussed, I would like to resign from the services of the company with immediate effect. Please don't misunderstand me, and I would appreciate if you can understand me and relieve me with great understanding. You will understand my predicament and as per our understanding, I am willing to pay in lieu of notice period if I am relieved earlier.

Thanks and Regards,
Venkat (VSAT)

Mani replied:

Dear VSAT,

As discussed, I am very disappointed with your decision. As I said, we will discuss once you are back from your vacation next week and I am not considering your resignation at this point.
Enjoy your vacation.

Regards,
Mani

I called Mani and said that I was willing to reschedule my vacation if need be, since I need to sort this out first. I was running against time and had to commit to Oracle.

Mani said, 'Let's talk tomorrow morning.'

I informed mom that I would be starting a couple of days later. She was hung up on making my favourite brinjal curry on the day of my arrival. She was upset with my decision. But I explained to her that I had to sort out a lot of things and asked her to have a little more patience. She understood my predicament.

The next day, I went to office as usual and Mani called me to his room. He said, 'I spoke with Steve and Cathy last night. They are very disappointed on hearing that you intend to leave us.'

I said, 'The work here is good Mani and I have no complaints. I like the people too. But I am not sure of my career and compensation increase at TCS. Oracle has made an irresistible offer which my parents are also okay with.'

Mani said, 'How about if we relocate you to the US for a year or two? Steve and Cathy are happy to do that.' I suddenly felt super-important. I had not expected such a swift reaction.

I didn't react to what he said. This was even better than what Oracle was offering.

Mani asked, 'So? What do you want to do?'

I said, 'I have to think about this. What would the salary be?'

Mani said, 'I don't know the exact figure, but roughly 60K USD.' I calculated that at forty-five to a dollar, it was about twenty seven lacs. Minus expenses and taxes, I could save about eight to ten lacs per annum, if I was careful. That was much more than what Goldman was making. Besides, I could continue working with friends who I knew from my college days.

Mani was grinning. He raised his eyebrows and asked, 'Isn't that better?'

(Managing the Mani Way, Axiom ten—When you know that the game is over, throw an irresistible carrot at the subordinate amd make sure he drools. You are back in control.)

I said, 'Yeah certainly. Let me think about this and get back.'

Mani said, 'This is not a big algorithm to crack VSAT. It is simple math, you make better money here, the project is exciting and you continue working with your gang. So, just call up Oracle and tell them that you are not keen to join them.'

I nodded. It was simple. But I didn't want to call Oracle till I got the deputation letter from TCS. What if Mani and Amit decided not to send me abroad after I said 'no' to Oracle? I lose both the opportunities.

I asked, 'When do I get the letter?'

Mani said, 'Go and meet Pappu, he will probably have the letter issued.' By now Amit was completely rechristened as Pappu.

I said, 'That fast?' Just last year, they cried for weeks to give an increment of ₹350 per month, now they are working double time to send me abroad. Srinivas was right, managements cannot screw around after you gain experience.

Mani grinned and I left his cabin and went straight to Pappu's room.

Pappu called me in and said, 'You are a valuable asset to the company, and you don't have to leave.' I smiled. The same Pappu had been screwing our happiness a year back. HR guys, I tell you, are amazing. We have to take their DNA samples and identify the HR gene to conduct research on how it evolved.

I said, 'Thanks Amit.'

Pappu continued, 'We got your deputation letter ready and you can leave once the visa is issued. Your salary in the US is 60K dollars and relocation terms and details are given in the letter.'

I asked, 'Amit, can you do better than that?'

He smirked and said, 'You are stretching it!'

I felt totally and absolutely indispensable.

Pappu issued the letter and I went back to Mani. He asked, 'Done?'

I said, 'Yes Mani.'

He said, 'This evening at 7, there is a video conference with Steve and Cathy. They would like to talk to you.'

I agreed to stay back late.

I said, 'Mani, I would like to take the next week off, I have to talk to my parents about Anjali.'

Mani said, 'Oh, Part-2 is pending. I understand. This time which actor's email ID do you want? Aamir? Salman? Akshay? Hrithik? May be the Telugu actor—Nagarjuna?'

I laughed and said, 'None Mani. I have to convince my parents, no other option.'

Mani said, 'Ok, go ahead. I hope you won't change your mind on the Oracle thing!'

I said, 'No, I am staying back.'

'Good. Make sure you inform Oracle accordingly.'

I went back to my desk and thought about the best way to inform Oracle that I was not keen to join them. Did I really need to tell them? If and when they called, I could tell them that my grandmom had measles and hence I could not join. They would understand. Nah, probably it was better to call and be upfront. In any case, I had not accepted the offer yet, so what was the problem in declining it?

I called Mala of A1 recruiters and said, 'Hi Mala, this is Venkat from TCS. Want to tell you that I may not be taking up the offer with Oracle.'

She said, 'But I thought you were interested. What happened?'

I said, 'Nothing, I spoke to my parents. They want me to stick to TCS.'

'Oh, come on. I am sure TCS must have made a counter-offer. Are they sending you to the US?'

I said, 'Ok, yes, that is the truth.'

'Even Oracle will send you to the US and at a much better salary,' Mala said.

I said, 'Look, I have made up my mind.'

Mala said, 'Ok, let us do this. Let us have one call with Anand of Oracle and after that you decide.'

I said, 'I have already made my decision and I don't want to pursue Oracle.'

Mala said, 'I understand. At least for courtesy's sake you must make a call to Oracle and inform them, right?'

I said, 'But you are the recruitment agency. Why don't you do that?'

Mala said, 'Venkat they made an offer to you and it would be nice if you called them and declined. At least talk to them once.'

I relented. Recruitment agencies do a great job of enticing people to jump jobs. They know what buttons to push. She could have conveyed the message that I was not keen to join, but she convinced me to take the call so that the HR of the other company could throw some more baits. Everybody tries to confuse the innocent software engineer. All for getting the code going!

Mala set up a call with Anand and I dialled the bridge number.

Anand said, 'What is this Venkat? I heard you are declining the offer. TCS is sending you to the US? We could do that too. Spend a little time in the India office and you will get opportunities to go abroad. If compensation is an issue, then I am willing to increase it. Is four lacs per annum a decent figure for you to consider?' The same Anand was whining to give me ₹3.5 lacs per annum, now he was willing to go up to ₹4.0 lacs per annum. That means the compensation range must be huge. Nobody had given so many boosts to my self-worth. Every conversation in the last couple of days had given me a new high.

I said, 'It is not about money, sir. I have committed to my manager to stay back.'

Anand said, 'There is nothing like a commitment Venkat. If you make up your mind, you could always move. Tell me two things that will make you move from TCS and let me work on them.'

I was amazed at the desperation for talent in this industry—high demand and lack of skilled manpower. For the first time in my life, I felt super-proud to be a software engineer.

I said, 'Right now I don't want to move, sir.'

Anand's parting line was, 'I am disappointed you are not considering Oracle, a global MNC, as your career choice. Please do not hesitate to come back to us in case you have a change of heart.'

I then called Anjali and informed her about the latest happenings. She said, 'Oh my my, you are in big demand Mr Venkat.'

She then quickly shouted, 'Pa, Venkat is being sent to the US. Want to talk to him?'

Colonel took the phone from Anjali and said, 'Ah Venkat, you are being deputed to the US, that is excellent news.'

I said, 'Yes Uncle.'

He asked, 'So when are you speaking to your parents?'

I said, 'I am leaving for home tomorrow and will talk to them as soon as I reach home.'

He said, 'Good, I hope everything goes smoothly. Give our regards to them. And before I give the phone to your aunty, here is a quick quiz question for you. Are you game?'

I thought the colonel would never change. I said, 'Sure Uncle.'

He asked, 'Since you are going to the US, let me ask you a question related to that country. Where was JFK shot?'

I said, 'This one I know Uncle, it is Dallas. Ask me a tougher one.'

He said, 'Aha, that's my boy! Ok, which newspaper won the Pulitzer for Watergate coverage?'

I said, 'I watched the Robert Redford movie, *All the President's Men*. The answer is *Washington Times.*'

Colonel said, 'No beta. It is the *Washington Post.*'

I said, 'Oops, almost there.'

Kaveri aunty came on the line and I asked, 'So, what is the latest from your friend Aunty?'

She said, 'Friend … who?'

I said, 'Shah Rukh Khan.'

She coyly said, 'Oh, Shah Rukh. Come on Venkat, thanks to you boys, he called and that is good enough for me. I think he will never call again. By the way congrats, you are being sent to the US?'

I said, 'Thank you Aunty.'

Aunty said, 'Are Raj and Adi also going?'

I said, 'They aren't going now. But there is a good chance for them to join me later. They could also try the same stunt with Oracle and coerce Mani to send them to the US. Who knows it may work? Elephants may fly and Jahapanah may come alive?'

She said, 'Give our best wishes to them too and listen, please come to Coorg again before you leave.'

I promised I would.

I pinged Raj and Adi on chat.

VSAT: *Resigned from TCS and Mani made a counter offer, and is sending me to the US.*

Adi: *Great news buddy.*

Raj: *Kya baat hai. So when do you have to go?*

VSAT: *Going to the consulate next week again and have to leave within 30 days.*

Adi: *Told the colonel?*

VSAT: *Yes, they are happy.*

Raj: *Cool. Now, we will also put pressure on Mani to send us* ☺

VSAT: *Yes, you must do that. Start talking to Oracle. Get an Offer, screw Mani, get US offer, decline Oracle and then you can join me* ☺

Adi: *Ok. But what a lengthy process na? Oracle has to help us for TCS to send us abroad* ☺ *Got work to do. Catch you later.*

Raj: *When are you going home? Want us to join?*

VSAT: *Nope, can manage it.*

Raj: *Ok, enjoy. Catch you later* ☺

VSAT: ☺

At 7 pm, we dialled via the video conferencing equipment. Steve and Cathy were seated in the conference room in New Jersey.

Steve started the conversation. He said, 'Hi VSAT and Mani. How are you?'

Mani said, 'Great. And you?'

Both said, 'Great.'

Cathy said, 'Mani, I am back from vacation today to attend this call because I am deeply concerned with attrition in India. But I am glad that VSAT is staying back. We have so much work to do.'

Mani said, 'I am trying to retain Nagaraj and Joel too. Let us see.'

I knew Mani was lying. Joel and Nagaraj were working out their relieving formalities.

(Managing the Mani Way, Axiom eleven—Coin your sentences in such a way that you inform work in progress. You don't have to tell the truth or lie. The client feels confident.)

Cathy turned to Steve and said, 'Steve, let us review the budgets. I want Venkat and Adi here atleast for a year.'

Mani rephrased and said, 'Venkat you can relocate atleast for a year, right?'

I said, 'Yes Mani.' And then I looked at the camera and said, 'Steve and Cathy, I thank you for giving me this opportunity.'

Steve said, 'It will be great to work with you. Look forward to seeing you here.'

I asked, 'Steve, what about Raj?' Steve replied, 'He can keep coming based on requirement. With Divya moving out of the project, I want Raj to divide his time between Bangalore and the US.'

Cathy nodded.

Steve said, 'But we would like to have Adi here atleast for a year.' I thought Cathy and Steve wanted to make sure that they retained Adi. As an architect, he was too critical for the project.

I said, 'I might need thirty to forty five-days to get my visa, wind up things and relocate.'

Steve said, 'That sounds reasonable.'

We talked for a few more minutes about the project and the meeting concluded. After the meeting, Mani thanked me for handling it well and said, 'Don't inform Adi yet. I will talk to him tomorrow.' I dutifully agreed, which I had to obviously.

Immediately after Mani left, I talked to Raj and Adi.

I said, 'Steve wants Adi in the US as well. Mani will talk to you tomorrow. Don't tell him that I spoke to you.' Asking software engineers to keep things confidential, that too with close friends and roomies, is like telling an alcoholic to abstain. It doesn't work.

Adi said, 'Wow! That is the best news I've heard in ages.'

I said, 'Good yaar, we could work together in the US.'

Raj asked, 'Did Mani say anything about me?'

I said, 'I asked, but Steve said he wants you to do up and down to the US as needed.'

Raj said, 'Fuck! Adi and you will be in the US and what about Anjali?'

I said, 'I don't know. If my parents agree, then we can get married and I can take her with me.'

Raj said, 'If none of you are here, I will take a transfer to Chennai to be with Srila.'

I asked, 'How is she doing? Has she talked to her parents?'

Raj said, 'She is going to. I haven't met her parents yet. May be soon.'

Then I called my parents and told them about the US offer. My mom was overjoyed. Her dream was coming true. She said, 'I am waiting for you Kanna.' Dad said, 'See, I told you, Tatas take care of their people. You were so hasty. Next time, listen to your old dad. I think for your good only. Srimangala is a nice girl ...'

Before he could complete that thought, I said, 'I am coming the day after Pa. Let us discuss everything then.'

Mom and Dad

Grandpa, mom and dad, and Swati were overjoyed to see me.

Swati's first question was, 'You spoke to Shah Rukh Khan? How was it? Tell me … tell me …'

I said, 'Yes, it was hardly for a minute. But it was good to talk to him.'

My parents were indifferent to this topic. I went to bed early because I was tired after the long journey. When I woke up, mom offered me coffee.

I started unpacking my bags and distributing gifts. I started with my grandfather. I opened the wrapper and slid the Fossil watch on to his left wrist.

He twirled his wrist a couple of times. Then he put on his reading glasses and read the brand name inscribed on it. He laughed, looked at my father and said, 'My son never gave me such a beautiful watch. I never expected you would bring me anything.'

I touched his feet and quoted from *The Godfather*, '*Some day, and that day may never come, I'll call upon you to do a service for me. But uh, until that day—accept this gift …*'

Grandpa laughed aloud, placed his hand on my head and said, '*Godfather*, you remember so much! May Lord Ganesha bless you.

Why is your head so hot? Lakshmi, put some Navratna oil on his head.'

Swati said, 'I will.' She went to fetch the bottle of oil. Meanwhile, I handed over a sari and crockery set to my mom and a shaving set to my dad. Swati came back with the oil bottle and I said, 'Your perfumes and salwar suits are over there.'

She said, 'Ok, I will look at them once I am done massaging your head.'

I sat down on the ground and Swati sat on the sofa behind me. She parted my hair and poured the Navratna oil on my scalp. I felt the oil seeping in. The heat started dissipating and I relaxed.

My father chose this opportune moment to start the duel and he entered the combat zone without losing any time. F-16 launched the first torpedo.

'So who is this Anjali?'

I said, 'She is my batch mate from NIT and also my colleague at TCS. She is from Coorg and her father is a retired colonel, and manages coffee estates.'

The second torpedo came in quick succession, 'She is not from Andhra, she is from a different culture, and doesn't even speak our language. How will it work? What if we don't agree?'

The city started reeling under the effect of the torpedoes. Citizens were running helterskelter.

I turned around and said, 'Swati, why did you stop? Continue.'

From the corner of the room, a scud missile was thrown. Mom said, 'Does she know how to cook? Can she take care of us?'

The citizens of the city didn't put up any defence.

Then a scatter bomb was dispersed by dad, 'Son, at your age it is common to get infatuated. Love is very temporal – once you get married to Srimangala, you will start loving her. From my experience, I am telling you, these inter-regional, inter-caste marriages don't work. They look good from afar, but are actually no good.'

The citizens of the city decided to go underground for the time being. There were too many F-16s and the ground force was not sufficient and this was not the time for an aerial attack.

Mom launched a cruise missile. She said, 'Are they vegetarians? You are saying her father is from the army. Then they must be drinking and smoking too. I have seen army people do that in most movies.'

Citizens could not take it anymore and decided to launch an ICBM (Inter Continental Ballistic Missile). I said, 'I love her and I want to marry her.' I looked at my father and fired a few rounds from an AK-47.

I said, 'Pa, what do you look for in a life partner? Somebody who you can be happy with. Somebody who you are compatible with. I believe Anjali is the right choice for me. She knows how to cook, she is respectful towards elders and she is willing to give up non-veg. I can't stop her parents from eating or drinking, or whatever other habits they have.'

Then mom dropped the ultimate bomb—tear gas. Tears started flowing down her cheeks and she said, 'What about us?'

I asked, 'Lakshmi, please stop crying. Let us have a meaningful discussion. What do you mean?'

She said, 'She doesn't speak Telugu. How can we converse with her? Tomorrow you will have kids, what language will they speak? What names will they have? I am so distraught. Oh Lord Ganesha, save us from this calamity.'

If you have read Phantom comics in your childhood, you will remember an old jungle saying—'A hysterical mom is more potent than the growl of ten lions (maybe more).'

I said, 'Mom, please stop this. She has promised to learn Telugu and I am sure she will take care of all of you. You must meet her and then you will know.'

The enemy started firing from the flanks. Pa said, 'Where is the question of meeting anybody when we are not inclined?'

I thought, 'Hysterical mom, stupid son, rational father, immature sister, an unusually quiet grandpa—non-standard situation. The terrain was unchartered. Marines were inadequately trained to handle war in desert conditions.'

Suddenly, the UN peacekeeping force came to the rescue and grandpa said, 'Venkata, I need to pee, can you take me to the loo?' He is diabetic and has to visit the loo often. He often takes my help whenever I am in town. We also want to be careful because we don't want him to slip and fall in the bathroom.

I said, 'Sure Grandpa.' I held his arm and went along with him. While we were walking to the bathroom, he asked me, 'Are you serious about this girl?'

I said, 'Yes. You must meet her and I am sure you will like her.'

He said, 'When you were born, I showed your horoscope to a renowned astrologer. He told me that you would get married to a person from a distant land. Looks like it is coming true.'

I grinned.

He asked, 'I heard you went to their parents' place to convince them?'

I said, 'Yes Grandpa.'

He said, 'Let me ask you a direct question. Are you marrying her under any pressure? Is she pregnant, etc?'

I said, 'No Grandpa. I have known her for three years and I like her a lot.'

He grinned and said, 'Remember Venkata, for the rest of your life, when you wake up in the morning, she will be the first face you will see. Will you be happy with that?'

I nodded my head vigorously. American way, super-affirmative.

He said, 'Don't say much now. Listen to them. Then talk to them individually and let us see how this works out.'

I agreed with him. By the time I went back the scenario had changed. Swati was looking at her clothes and perfumes and my mom was admiring the cutlery. She asked, 'How much did you pay for this? Can we use this in the microwave?'

I said, 'Yes Mom. I didn't know we had a microwave.'

She said, 'Yes, your dad finally purchased one.'

I looked at my dad. The F-16 was still hovering, but didn't release more torpedos. He said, 'Thanks for the electric shaving set. Is it safe?'

What a question! He was asking as if I had given him a grenade without the pin.

I said, 'Absolutely Pa. It is very safe and you can finish shaving in minutes. Let me show you how it is done.' I switched on the shaving set and gave a quick demo. He said, 'Yes, this looks nice. I like it.'

The war was averted for the time being. I went out to meet my friends and came back late in the night. After dinner I started an SMS conversation with Anjali.

She: Hi HB, how is it going?

Me: We talked today.

She: Agreeing?

Me: Not yet.

She: Try harder.

Me: Yes, I am doing that.

She: When r u back?

Me: Starting after three days.

She: Ok.

Me: Pick up some Telugu. It will be useful.

She: But u r not learning Coorgi.

Me: Don't be stupid

She: What do you mean?

Me: I mean, don't compare...

She: One rule for you and another for me?

Me: Good night, talk 2 u later. U r not getting it.

She: See, u r avoiding the hard topics.

Me: Let's talk 2morrow.

I wondered why she couldn't learn a little Telugu. It would please everybody and things would work out. I was angry with her. I felt squeezed from both sides.

The next day, I woke up early and went into the kitchen to speak to mom. She asked, 'Want to eat a dosa?'

'Yes Lakshmi.'

'Ok, sit down on the kitchen ledge there and I will give you hot ones.'

I sat down on the ledge and held a plate in my hands.

She served me coconut chutney and gunpowder. She served a hot dosa straight from the pan.

I took a bite and said, 'Hm ... Lakshmi, you make the best dosas. Love you.'

A scud landed, 'Can your girlfriend, what is her name, make such nice dosas?'

Actually, Anjali could hardly make decent Maggi. This was another skill she had to pick up.

I said, 'No Ma.'

'Then why do you want to marry her?'

I said, 'Ma, you don't marry girls because they make good dosas.'

She said, 'Ultimately it boils down to making good food.'

I nodded—the forty-five degree nod.

I said, 'Ma, atleast meet her. Then you can decide.'

She looked at me and said, 'Ok, you meet Srimangala first.'

I said, 'Even if I meet her, I will say no and it won't look nice.'

Ma said, 'I will do the same thing with your girl. Even if I meet her, I will say no.'

I thought my mom would make the world's best negotiator. She should be sent to Pakistan to negotiate the J&K deal.

I said, 'Ok, I will meet her if you promise to meet Anjali and parents.'

She hesitated. Cold dosa dough was poured on the hot pan. It sizzled. She nodded.

That evening, we went to Srimangala's house on a courtesy visit. They are our neighbours and we had known them for years. Aunty made chilibajji, onion pakoras and Hyderabadi mini samosas. It was a long time since I had eaten some 'real' snacks, the deep-fried, junk kinds. Coke was served as a side dish. A combination of mini samosas and coke could give you the ultimate high. The conversation was about software, the US, education and current affairs. Then out of nowhere, uncle launched a missile. He said, 'If the boy and girl are okay with each other, then we can have the engagement now and they can get married when Venkat is back from the US. What do you say?'

I took a larg swig of the coke and coughed. Didn't expect the missile to land so fast.

My father looked at me and said, 'Do you want to talk to Sri?'

He had cut out the 'Mangala' in her name and made it sound as if I was about to talk to Sridevi, the real one from *Himmatwala*. I thought, 'What a *Chaalbaaz* he is.' We are the Bollywood generation. What to do, we are like that only no!

He probably wanted me to say, like any dutiful son, 'No need Dad. Your wish is my command.'

But I had tasted the software industry and that too in Bangalore, where 'I' comes before most products—ipod, itunes, etc.

I said, 'Sure Pa, will talk to her.'

My father raised his eyebrow, grinned and said, 'Today's generation wants to talk before marriage itself and in our time, I didn't talk to Lakshmi even after Venkat was born.'

Everybody laughed.

Srimangala was summoned and a chair was arranged for her to sit in front of me. She was decked from head to toe. I had never thought things would be so formal. She wore a lovely red sari, red blouse, a ring with a red stone, red slippers and had a red dot on her forehead. She looked like an approaching fire engine, a warning of impending doom. Copious amounts of Parachute coconut hair oil was applied to her braided hair. It looked like a well-laid out fibre optic cable. She looked like ideal wife material. I was sure she could make dosas the way mom did. But she couldn't make Maggi like Anjali did.

Aunty smiled at me. She said, 'Here she is, talk to her.'

Everybody was sitting there but she expected us to have a private conversation. This was great.

I asked, 'How are you Srimangala?'

Her head was bowed and she said, 'Ok.'

My mother said, 'She is so sweet.'

I looked at my mom and pleaded silently. What kind of torture was this?

I asked, 'Do you want to ask me anything?'

She shook her head.

I asked, 'How are your studies?'

She looked at her mom for help and Srimangala's mom said, 'She has finished her graduation and is staying at home now.'

I said, 'Hm ...'

My dad said, 'Now that they have talked, you can take her inside.'

I smiled at my dad. Our talk felt like the first day of ragging at NIT.

Uncle said, 'No, no. Ask her if you have any more questions.' I shook my head and felt a burp coming on. Pakoras, samosas and Coke were a lethal combination. Everybody laughed. Aunty said, 'See how satisfied he looks!'

I asked, 'Can I use the bathroom please?'

I sat in the loo for a good ten minutes and came out. Instead of going to the drawing room, I found my way to Srimangala's room. She was sitting on the bed and staring at the ceiling fan.

She was startled by my sudden entry. I said, 'Please don't scream. I am not here to do anything.'

She said, 'I don't want do anything wrong before the wedding.'

I was confused. I said, 'Sri, I have known you since we were children. So, let me keep this simple. I am in love with somebody in Bangalore and intend to marry her. I am sorry if this is overtly candid.'

She said, 'Then why did you come today to meet us?'

'I was told that it was a courtesy visit and I didn't expect such a freaking formal event.'

She had tears in her eyes.

I said, 'If I knew that I was going to see you so formally, I would have flatly refused. I am very, very sorry. I don't want to hurt your feelings.'

She said, 'I understand. You may go now.'

I said, 'Can you tell your mom that you are not keen to marry me?'

She said, 'Is that other girl more beautiful than me?'

I thought, 'How does it matter?'

But I said, 'No.'

Raj had taught me the golden rule, 'The girl who asks that specific question is more beautiful than any other girl in the world.'

I asked, 'So would you tell your parents that you are not interested?'

She nodded. Raj Shastra worked atleast this one time.

I said, 'I am sure you will find somebody better than me.' This was typical Bollywood style.

She said, 'You don't have to tell me that.'

I said, 'I am sorry.'

She said, 'You may go now. I don't want anybody to find out that you are here with me.'

I agreed and quickly made my way back to the drawing hall. My dad sneered at me for using the bathroom for so long. My mom asked, 'Are you ok Venkat?'

I said, 'Samosa and Coke Ma.'

Everybody laughed.

We left their house in a few minutes.

The next day, I reminded mom that I had agreed to meet Sri according to her wish. So when was she coming to Bangalore to meet Anjali and her parents?'

She didn't respond. I asked her again.

She said, 'I don't know what you did yesterday. They don't seem interested to take it forward.'

I thanked Srimangala in my thoughts. She had done her job.

I asked, 'Did they give any reason?'

'No. Apparently, Srimangala wanted to study further and they didn't want to push for the marriage.'

I said, 'Ok that settles it. Can we all go together?'

There was silence. I said, 'Ok, that means yes. Can I book tickets for all of us?'

She nodded. One down, one more to go!

In the afternoon, my dad took me to the library, which I had helped repair with my first month's salary. It was a small library, and had about 1000 books for primary school children. There were three benches in the room. A teacher was using one bench. One was broken and was not in use, and two children sat on the third one. There were about ten children seated on the cement floor.

I asked, 'Pa, is this the library we helped repair?'

He said, 'Yes, see we have new books, the ceiling is not leaking anymore, we have two benches and the children are using it. See, there is a table fan too.'

I thought, 'And we keep complaining that we don't get subsidised food in the TCS canteen.' This was an eye-opener. My dad was obviously feeling proud and was thoroughly enjoying the moment.

We sat down on the floor, pa started reading from the *Panchatantra*, the story of a sage and his daughter, to the children. The story went like this: Once when a sage was praying, an eagle dropped a she-mouse in his hands. Since the sage and his wife didn't have any children, the sage turned the she-mouse into a lovely girl and they decided to adopt the she-mouse as their daughter. When the daughter became marriageable, the sage asked his daughter whether she was interested in marrying the Sun God. The daughter replied, that he was too intense. Then the Sun God suggested the Cloud God, but the daughter refused saying that he was too dark. Then the Cloud God suggested the Mountain God, but the daughter refused saying that he was too cold. The Mountain God suggested a he-mouse who could burrow holes through the mountain. The daughter agreed to marry the he-mouse and the sage turned her back into a she-mouse and married her off to him. Then the sage said, 'Look at what destiny has to offer. People always end up choosing someone of their own kind.'

The moral of the story: One's destiny cannot be changed.

As soon as he finished the story, I looked at him and pleaded, 'Pa, I am the he-software-mouse.'

He paused for a long moment. Then he smiled and said, 'Make reservations, let us go and meet the she-software-mouse and her parents.'

The Bangalore Summit

I CALLED ANJALI AND SAID, 'ALL OF US ARE COMING BY SATURDAY evening to Bangalore.'

She asked, 'Have they agreed?'

I said, 'They have agreed to meet you all. Anjali, the rest depends on you.'

'What do you mean it depends on me?'

I said, 'Depends on how you manage them.'

She said, 'Don't worry, I will.'

I said, 'I will coach you before you meet them.'

She said, 'But I didn't coach you before you met my parents.'

'That is because I am smart.'

She smirked, 'Ah, you are implying I am not.'

I said, 'I didn't say that. Make sure you pick up some Telugu phrases. Buy a book. Something like *Learn Telugu in Thirty Days*.'

She agreed.

I said, 'You may want to learn how to make tea, coffee, etc.'

She said, 'Ok.'

I asked, 'What's up?'

She said, 'Too many conditions, Venkat. My parents never put any conditions on you.'

I said, 'Oh really? I didn't know that.'

She said, 'Enough of your sarcasm.'

I said, 'Improve your profile, have a better career, learn our customs—what are these?'

She said, 'Requests for your own good.'

I said, 'Learning Telugu, learning cooking is better for "our" good.'

She said, 'No, it is good for your parents. Are they expecting me to cook? Do they know I am working and I will not be able to cook?'

I said, 'They know you are working and they don't expect you to cook. But they expect you to know cooking.'

She was caustic now. 'Do you know how to cook?'

I said, 'I can.'

She smirked, 'Besides Maggi?'

I said, 'Yes, I can make tea, coffee, biryani, daal, rice. I mean the basics. But why are you comparing?'

She said, 'It can't be one rule for you and one for me.'

I said, 'Ok. I will learn Coorgi. Will you learn Telugu?'

She said, 'You don't have to learn Coorgi and I don't have to learn Telugu.'

I said, 'Why are you making it difficult?'

She said, 'Oh, now I am making it difficult? Aren't your parents making it really difficult?'

I asked, 'But why are you fighting now?'

She said, 'Who is fighting?'

I said, 'Ok Anjali, leave it now. Can we all meet on Sunday morning for lunch?'

She asked, 'Where will your parents stay?'

I said, 'I will ask Raj and Adi to adjust with our other friends for a few nights'

She said, 'Ok. I will tell pa and mama to come along for Sunday lunch.'

We said goodbye. I wondered why equations change the moment parents enter the discussion. The colonel had almost gobbled me up. But according to Anjali, he was 'sweet'. Now, my parents were reconciled to the idea but they were being perceived as difficult.

Fuck man! Women make relationships so complicated.

Our family reached Bangalore. Raj and Adi agreed to sleep over at Srinivas' place. Bachelors have simple requirements in life—a bottle of beer, an ipod and a mattress to crash on. I was going to say goodbye to my simple needs and my freedom and get married. Many conflicting thoughts were churning in my mind.

Anjali came over on Saturday evening to meet my parents. She wore a nice blue sari and a matching blouse. There was a small bindi on her forehead. Her lipstick was hardly noticeable. She applied transparent nail polish on her nails. She smelt of Chanel 5 perfume which I had gifted her. She had tied her hair into a pony. She looked like a Greek goddess. I wanted to make love to her then and there.

As soon as she came in, she whispered, 'How am I looking? Ok?'

I said, 'Honey, you are looking great. I mean, fantastic.'

She whispered, 'Don't stare at me like that. Your intentions are obvious.'

I grinned. My parents joined us. Swati gravitated towards Anjali.

Anjali folded her hands and said, '*Namaskaram* Uncle, *namaskaram* Aunty ... *Bagunnara,* Bangalore *ki swagatam* (Hope you are well ... Welcome to Bangalore).' I knew she had picked up *Learn Telugu in Thirty Days*. That first sentence worked very well. My mom and dad melted like ice creams in mid-summer.

My mother said, 'Come here Anjali.' And all the ladies went in.

When she came out, Anjali was wearing a brilliant golden necklace with a sparkling white stone on it. Mom had gifted it to her. I hadn't expected things to work out so well. Anjali was beaming.

My mom said, 'My mother-in-law gave it to me when she met me the first time. I thought I would give it to you when I met you the first time.'

I hugged my mom. She said, 'Enough, enough, you hug me only now. Huh?' Anjali said, 'Thank you Aunty, this looks beautiful. My parents are looking forward to meeting you for lunch tomorrow.'

My dad said, 'Sure, we are looking forward to it too.'

There were no missiles, scuds, scatter bombs and rifle firing so far. It was going very smoothly.

Mom asked, 'So Anjali, Venkat tells me that you are learning Telugu and cooking. His favourite is brinjal curry. I hope you are learning how to cook that.'

Anjali didn't say anything. She nodded. Obviously the softener (necklace) was still working on her.

Mom went on, 'Tell me what items you can cook.'

Anjali said, 'Hm ... I can make idlis.'

Mom said, 'That is nice.'

Anjali added, 'But mom usually makes the batter.'

We laughed.

'I can make rice,' she said.

Swati said, 'But mom usually washes it and puts it in the cooker.'

Anjali smiled and pinched Swati.

Grandpa said, 'Anjali, come closer to me. Let me have a good look at you.'

Anjali went forward and stood in front of grandpa. He said, 'Sit down, sit down.'

She kneeled in front of him. He held her face in his hands and said, 'You are very very pretty my dear girl. Fair skin and brown eyes. You know, there is British blood in the Coorgis. I read somewhere that the British couldn't take the heat in India and headed for the hills. Apparently, the locals and British inter-mingled and that is why Coorgis have such features.'

Anjali said, 'Yes, Grandpa, that is what they say. We are the coffee people anyway.'

My dad asked, 'What kind of coffee do you grow?'

'Robusta, Uncle.'

'How many acres do you have?'

'I don't know Uncle. Maybe fifty? I think if you speak to my Dad, he will be able to tell you more details.'

My dad nodded.

My mom said, 'Learn Telugu quickly beta, so that I can converse with you easily. I find it hard to speak in English.'

Anjali replied, 'Yes Aunty. I will also teach you English.'

Ma said, 'I am too old for all that.'

Anjali said, 'There is no age bar to learn, Aunty.'

My mom smiled and didn't say anything.

My dad suggested I drop Anjali home because it was getting late.

We agreed and I went to drop Anjali. While walking her back, I held her hand and said, 'Give me a kiss. You were fantastic today.'

She said, 'So was your mom. Nice of her to give me the gift.'

I asked, 'What about the kiss?'

She said, 'Shameless! On the road?'

I said, 'Yes.'

She coyly said, 'Stupid idiot. Can you ever think of anything other than that?'

I laughed and asked, 'Where are your parents staying?'

She said, 'With me.'

'All of them in one room?'

She joked, 'I don't have many parents, just two of them and Ameya. My parents are staying with the PG uncle and aunty downstairs. Ameya is with me.'

When we reached Anjali's place, she asked me to come in and meet her parents.

I went in. The PG uncle—Narendra immediately recognised me. He said, 'Ah, you have come to the wrong house. House # 234 is in the backlane.'

I grinned. He said, 'I recognised you the first day itself, but didn't want to embarrass you and Anjali.'

The colonel asked, 'So was he a regular visitor here?'

Narendra laughed, 'What do you expect two young love birds to do? Stay away from each other? Get them married Krishna.'

The colonel said, 'I understand what you are saying.'

The colonel asked me, 'So when do you plan to go to the US?'

I said, 'Next week, I have to go for my visa interview. I'll leave a few weeks after that.'

The colonel said, 'What is your plan? Want to get engaged before you go? Want to get married and go together?'

I said, 'I don't know, we can discuss tomorrow. Though I prefer we get married and leave together.'

The colonel nodded and said, 'Ok Venkat. Let us see about that. So, what is the trivia question of the day?'

I said, 'Let me ask. Which country lost almost 17% of its population in World War II?'

He said, 'Poland. Give me something better.'

'Which country was the first to allow voting via the internet?

He said, 'Well, that is a good one. I have no idea.'

I laughed and said, 'Thanks to you, I am picking up all this stuff from the Net. It is Estonia. The Net was first used in 2005 in the local elections and then in 2007 for parliamentary elections.'

He said, 'My turn now. What is the longest station name in the country? Let me also give you a clue. It belongs to your state and perhaps is as big as your name.'

I said, 'What could it be? Visakhapatnam? Hyderabad, Secunderabad ... I don't know.'

Colonel said, 'Venkatanarasimharajuvaripeta. At times "Sri" is prefixed to it, making it even longer.'

I said, 'Do you know its meaning?'

He said, 'No.'

I said, 'It is a full sentence. It means, the place belongs to (Sri) Venkata Narasimha Raju ji.'

He said, 'Wow, that is interesting.'

I said, 'Last one before I get going.'

Uncle said, 'What last one? Have a drink with us and then go.'

I said, 'No Uncle, my parents wouldn't like that.'

He said, 'It is ok, have one on me, I say.'

I was tempted.

The colonel quickly poured three large Single Malts and said, 'Cheers to Venkat and Anjali. To your happiness.'

The one glass became three glasses. Since I was in a hurry, I gulped them down quickly and felt tipsy.

Anjali said, 'Papa, you are making him drink too often!'

Kaveri aunty joined in, 'And of late, you are also having too much.'

The colonel said, 'My dear sweet Kaveri and even sweeter Anjali. These are the best days of our life and let me relish it with my son-in-law.'

Narendra uncle said, 'It is okay Kaveri. Once in a while, some amount of indulgence is ok.'

Both the ladies were quiet.

I ended up spending a good two hours there and reached home by almost 10 pm.

My mom opened the door and immediately smelt the booze. She said, 'Shameless fellow. You had a drink?'

I said, 'Sometimes I drink Mom. I just felt good and had one extra.'

My dad joined her and said, 'You are spoilt after coming to Bangalore. No one in our family drinks. Now you are marrying that Coorgi girl and I am sure you will drink daily. You went to drop her and why didn't you come back home immediately after that?'

I said, 'I wanted to ...'

He said, 'Oh, her military dad made you drink? Don't tell me you had drinks with him.'

I kept quiet. For a primary school teacher, his son having drinks with his would-be father-in-law was unfathomable.

He said, 'Go sleep now, we will speak tomorrow.'

My mom said, 'Eat something and then go to sleep.' I quickly grabbed a roti and hit the sack. I was sure my mom and dad spoke about me through the night.

I woke up late, had breakfast and got ready to go for lunch. I had organised the lunch at Taj Gateway, Karavali Restaurant. It was my favourite place. They served the best southwestern coastal seafood in town. We reached there at about 1 pm. The colonel and his family were already there.

As soon as we entered, the colonel and Kaveri aunty stood up and warmly welcomed us. The colonel said, 'Venkat, we have been here since 12.30 pm, you should have brought your parents on time. Anyway, we made good use of the time. Kingfisher tastes fantastic. Ha, ha!'

My heart sank and I looked at Anjali. I had instructed her to tell her dad not to drink or eat non-vegetarian food. Anjali shrugged and didn't say anything.

Dad said, 'Looks like this is an expensive restaurant, Venkat. We could have gone to some inexpensive place.'

I said, 'It is okay Pa, this is our first meeting with Anjali's parents and I wanted it to be special.'

Mom said, 'Still. I believe this is too expensive.'

The colonel said, 'Subramaniamji, don't worry about money, come join us and let us have a good time. We will pay for it. Shall I order a bottle of beer for you too?'

Dad's face turned red, and I almost fell at his feet. Dad said, 'Don't worry, we can afford to pay and no, I don't drink.'

Uncle said, 'What a shame that you can't enjoy a good beer on a sunny morning like this.'

Dad said, 'Drinking is not everything, Mr Krishna.'

The colonel corrected, 'Colonel Krishna.'

Dad said, 'Whatever!'

The colonel sniggered, 'It is not whatever. I have earned the rank with my sheer hard work and diligence.'

Dad said, 'Everybody works hard. I do too.'

Colonel said, 'You are a primary school teacher Subramanyam Garu, a few classes in the morning, a few classes in the evening and you are done. We have the arduous task of protecting the country.'

I counted the number of empty beer bottles on the table—one, two, three and half of fourth. I thought that this meeting was a fucking disaster.

Dad said, 'True, true. Walk in the ground in the morning, left-right-left, swim in the evening and drink at night.'

I said, 'Pa and Uncle, can we please stop this.'

Uncle said, 'Your dad has no respect for me or the army. How can I…'

I pleaded, 'Uncle, please stop it, you are going overboard now.'

Kaveri aunty said, 'He is going overboard? It is you who came and pleaded for Anjali and you have called for this meeting. We didn't.'

I said, 'Aunty, enough is enough. I can't tolerate anymore. What did my parents say for you to get so angry? All they said was that this was an expensive restaurant … right?'

Anjali said, 'VSAT. You can't talk to my parents like that.'

I said, 'Anjali, can you please keep out of this? I am trying to resolve things here?'

Anjali replied, 'Why should I? I think you and your parents should stay out of this. We haven't put any conditions on you like your parents have on me.'

Mom joined the fray. She asked, 'Tell us dear, what conditions have we put on you? Did we ask for dowry or something like that?'

Anjali said, 'So now you want dowry? Haven't you asked me to learn Telugu, cooking, etc?'

I lost my cool and said, 'Hasn't your dad kept conditions too? Learn trivia, have a better career and make more money and all that shit?'

My parents stared at me quizzically. They said, 'What are we hearing Venkat? What is this quiz thing?'

I explained that the colonel wanted me to learn trivia to improve my personality.

My dad got up and started laughing. He looked at the colonel and said, 'You make my son drink, you put conditions on him and expect us to say yes to this alliance. Never!'

The colonel said, 'My dear primary school teacher, we are not begging. Our beautiful daughter will get a thousand better alliances.'

Grandpa intervened and said, 'Ladies and gentlemen, I am an old man and I have a request to make. Can we stop this meeting now and have it some other time?'

The colonel looked at me and said, 'We will continue to have our lunch because we have already started it, you may leave, if you wish to.'

Grandpa got up and started walking out. All of us followed suit. Mom and dad didn't talk for sometime. I could see that pa was seething with rage.

Grandpa said, 'Culturally they are way too different Venkata.'

I kept quiet. I had tears in my eyes. I had never expected the meeting to turn out to be such a big farce. I was angry with Anjali. I took out my cell phone and sent an SMS, 'Thanks for screwing it up.'

I got a response, 'Stop contacting me.'

I sent an SMS back, 'Fuck you.'

And I didn't get any answer.

My parents wanted to stay back for one more week before they left. I called Mani and asked for an additional one-week vacation.

Mani said, 'Too many days VSAT. I will manage this week, but I want you in the office next week.' I realised the vulnerability of his situation too. I promised to go to office as soon as I could.

I called Raj and Adi and explained what had happened. They were stunned. Raj said, 'We are better than these elders yaar. We fight, but we get back together quickly.'

I said, 'Fuckers, tell me the solution.'

Adi said, 'Even Anjali has not come to office today.'

I said, 'Where is she?'

Raj said, 'Maybe home?'

I asked, 'What do we do now?'

Raj said, 'Let me speak with Anjali.'

He dialled her number and she picked up the phone. He put her on the speaker phone. Raj said, 'Hi Anju, VSAT informed me about what happened. Sorry to hear about it.'

She said, 'I know VSAT is with you now and I want to come over and give the necklace back to his mother. Otherwise, they will say that we stole the necklace.'

I said, 'Anjali, I am here and stop being stupid.'

She replied, 'Raj, I am not talking to VSAT. My parents have asked me to go over and give the necklace back to his mother.

She gave it to me and I must give it back to her. This relationship is over.'

I said, 'She can come anytime and hand it over, if that is what she wishes.'

She said, 'Ok, I will come by 3 pm today.'

At 3 pm sharp, Anjali came home. We were all seated in the hall. She said, 'Aunty, thank you for giving me the necklace, but after what happened yesterday, I don't think it is right on our part to keep the necklace,' saying this, she handed over the necklace to my mom.

As she was walking back, Anjali had tears in her eyes.

She had almost reached the door, when grandpa called her, 'Hey, my dear lovely Coorgi girl. Come here to grandpa.'

She stopped and looked at him. He almost stood up. He said, 'Come here beta. Come.'

She walked straight into his arms. He sat down in his chair and she sat down on the floor next to him. She rested her head on his lap and sobbed uncontrollably.

She said, 'Grandpa, I love your stupid grandson, but nothing seems to work out. He had never scolded me in the last three years. But yesterday he scolded me and my parents.'

Grandpa placed his hands on her head and said, 'Venkata, come here now and apologise to her.'

I was slightly reluctant. He waved his walking stick at me and said, 'Come here now and apologise to her.'

I came forward and stood next to her and said, 'I am sorry.'

He said, 'Not like that. Sit next to her and pacify her. Tell her you are sorry. Remember Venkata, whenever you both fight, the boy should be the first to say sorry. Do you understand me? Forgot *The Godfather*? Wife and family come first. Come now, pacify her.'

I said, 'Yes Grandpa.' Then tears started trickling down my cheeks and I held Anjali's hand. I said, 'I am sorry Honeybunch.' She hugged me in front of everybody.

Grandpa said, 'Now take me to your parents.'

Anjali and I walked him to her home.

The colonel, Kaveri aunty, Narendra uncle and his wife Palu stood up when they saw the old man.

Grandpa looked at them and said, 'I hope you won't ask me to go.'

The colonel said, 'No sir. We are Coorgis sir, we are known for our hospitality. Please come in.'

Grandpa said, 'Before we talk, may I use your bathroom please? I am a diabetic and I have to go to bathroom quite often.'

Narendra uncle said, 'Sure sir.'

I walked grandpa to the bathroom. As he was relieving himself, he said, 'When you use somebody's bathroom, you get close to them emotionally. You enter their private space. That helps.' I smiled. I realised he was the true Don Vito Corleone. My *Godfather!*

He said, 'Don't say anything Venkata. Just tell them you are sorry for what happened yesterday. Nothing else. Do you understand?'

I said, 'Yes Grandpa.'

When we came back, grandpa said, 'Gentlemen, with folded hands I want to say that I am very sorry for what happened yesterday. We don't spoil the lives of our children because of our egos or cultural differences. Cultures have to bring people together and not separate them.'

He looked at Anjali and said, 'Beta, when was the last time you fought?'

Anjali said, 'Yesterday Grandpa.'

Grandpa asked, 'Did you ever fight before that?'

Anjali replied, 'Never before Grandpa.'

'So, you started fighting only when your parents started entering into your relationship?' We nodded.

Grandpa lowered his voice and said, 'Young people build their small homes around love and affection. We have to make a nest for them and not break their little homes.'

Kaveri aunty started crying. The colonel had a lump in his throat.

Grandpa continued, 'No culture or profession is bigger or better. Cultures and professions are a way of life. Let us not kill the affections of our children on the pretext of customs and expectations. Let them lead their lives, Colonel.'

The colonel became very emotional. He came forward and shook hands with grandpa and said, 'Thank you sir. We are willing to talk to Venkat's parents and settle this alliance.'

Narendra uncle said, 'I was telling them the same thing since yesterday. It is very easy to break an alliance and difficult to make one. If you hadn't come today, we were thinking of coming to your place to settle this.'

After that emotional pitch, all of them landed up at my home. My parents were surprised to see them.

We were falling short of chairs at home. We are bachelors, why do we need chairs anyway. The colonel said, 'Subramanyam ji, you are a teacher. That is the noblest of professions. Please sit on the chair and let me sit on the mattress.'

My father said, 'No, no, you are the army man. We respect the military. You take the chair.'

Grandpa said, 'Let all the ladies sit on the chairs. Things will work better. They know how to make homes.'

Everybody laughed. Everybody apologised to each other. Anjali and I sat in a corner. Raj and Adi were waiting outside.

The colonel asked my father, 'Sir, do we get them engaged and married, right away?'

My father said, 'As you wish Colonel.'

Anjali pinched me and whispered, 'Say you want to get married before you leave.'

I said, 'Given a choice we want to get married before leaving for the US.'

Everybody laughed.

It was agreed that the marriage ceremony would be held in Madikeri and the reception in Warangal. The engagement was on the weekend and the wedding was in a couple of weeks.

I called Mani and asked him for one more week's leave.

He smirked and said, 'Fuck off, go join Oracle.'

I said, 'Mani come for the engagement tomorrow. The wedding is in two weeks from now.'

He was perplexed, 'What? All settled?'

I said, 'Yes, Anjali will also go with me.'

He said, 'How can husband and wife work on the same project?'

I said, 'Mani, they can work on the same project, but the wife can't report to the husband. The husband can report to the wife. Then there is no problem.'

He laughed and said, 'Ok, let me speak with Steve and work this out.'

The next day Mani called me. He said, 'Fortunately Steve has agreed. But since he has a budget for only nine months, Anjali can join you after three months. What do you say?'

I said, 'Sounds okay. Meanwhile, I can set up a place and settle down and then she can come over. But you are screwing my honeymoon.'

He said, 'Don't worry. I will send her on business visa for a couple of months.'

I asked, 'Mani, are you going on a long vacation or something?'

He said, 'How did you guess?'

I said, 'You are being so nice, I am sure you want us to cover up for you.'

He laughed and said, 'Fuckers, you are amazing.'

(Managing the Mani Way, Axiom twelve—when intending to take a long vacation, ensure that you walk the extra-mile in taking care of your subordinates. Subordinates will feel incredibly obliged to perform in your absence.)

Later, I sent an email to Shah Rukh.

'Dear Shah Rukh Khanji,

Thanks to your efforts, Amrish Puri, Farida Jalal, Anupam Kher and Kirron Kher—all finally agreed and our marriage is fixed for Feb 12th2008 at 10.21 hours in Madikeri, Coorg (Choultry, next to the bus stand). Request you to kindly grace the occasion with your wife (Gowri) and children (Aryan and Suhana). I know you can't make it, but who knows, life is full of surprises, for all you know, you may turn up and we'll be delighted.

Yours truly,
Venkat, Software Engineer, TCS, +91 98450 ...'

There was a quick response from him by mail, *'Great news. Obviously I can't make it and our best wishes are with you all. Remember, henpecked husbands make the best families.* ☺

Best, Shah Rukh

I smiled at his response. No wonder he has women from the age of five to seventy-five in his pocket.

Anjali and I went back to office immediately. The colonel and aunty took mom, dad, grandpa and Swati to Mysore and from there to Coorg with them. Raj and Adi returned to live at home. Srinivas gave them an overdose of actor Mahesh Babu and Raj started mouthing Telugu movie dialogues. I understood their plight.

That evening, all of us were having dinner at home and Raj said, 'Guys, I have an important announcement.'

We waited.

He said, 'Srila is pregnant and I am responsible for the good deed. She has spoken to her parents and I have spoken to mine. No issues at all. Complete smooth sailing. We are having a registered marriage in Chennai this weekend. All of you are welcome.'

I looked at Raj intently and he said, 'Yes, you can hug me.'

I hugged him hard and asked, 'When?'

He said, 'In the US.'

I said, 'Fuck fuck fuck ...' Sometimes, saying it three times conveys a lot more than saying it once.

He said, 'That is what I did. Real men don't shoot blanks.'

All of us laughed.

I asked, 'Both sets of parents agreed? Was it so cool?'

Raj said, 'When you get pregnant buddy, everything works at break-neck speed.'

He then looked at Anjali and me and said, 'Try it.'

She giggled and I laughed.

Raj left for Chennai the following day and Mani was facing a nightmare.

Joel and Nagaraj were leaving. New replacements were on their way.

Anjali and I were getting married and were hardly working. The internet was being extensively used to invite people for the wedding, booking air tickets, ordering wedding cards, etc.

Raj had taken a couple of weeks off for his wedding.

Divya was gone anyway.

Anjan, as usual was working from home.

Srinivas had taken a couple of days off to see Mahesh Babu's film shoot somewhere near Mysore.

Savitha bhabhi, Josy and Joby were preparing for the annual day social event.

Developing software came to a full stop and social events were the order of the day!

Mani was the only person trying to take all the client calls.

(Managing the Mani Way, Axiom thirteen—when the deck is empty, start swabbing the floors yourself, you give the perception of working hard and subordinates will feel dispensable.)

On Saturday, January 12, 2008, we got engaged. We exchanged rings in a simple engagement ceremony. I missed Raj. He was getting married the same day.

In the evening, I took Anjali aside and said, 'I want to make love to you. But there are people everywhere.'

She said, 'Can't think of anywhere? Can you?'

I said, 'Why don't we do it in the office?'

She said, 'Are you mad?'

I said, 'It will be fun. After 6 pm on Saturday, the third floor conference room is empty and there is no camera too.'

She said, 'You have gone mad. Forget it.'

I said, 'Let's us go there. If you don't feel comfortable, we will come back.'

We went to the office in the evening, crept into the video conference room, switched off all the lights and sat on the sofa. We hadn't made love for a long time and we lunged at each other. We kissed. As usual, she bit my lower lip like a female version of Count Dracula. It was difficult to make love on a two-seater sofa, but the excitement of doing it far outweighed everything else. This was a 'bungee jump,' a twenty-minute affair, full of energy, and a dive into the abyss of unimaginable pleasure. The whole experience was amazing and I wondered if making love in such places added to the thrill.

While riding back, Anjali sat crossed-legged on the bike and hugged me hard. I could feel her soft bosom touch my back. I was getting excited again. She said, 'Don't stiffen now. Take it easy. I am not going back in there again.'

We laughed.

The following week, the TCS travel desk sent me to the US consulate in Chennai for my H1 interview.

I met with Lisa Ann Carpenter, the consulate officer. She immediately recognised me.

She said, 'Mr Venkata, what brings you back?'

I said, 'This time I am going to the US on work. Maybe for a year or two.'

She chuckled, 'I remember you. You have a girlfriend and wanted to get married to her. Indian wife, French boss, Japanese car, right? See, I haven't forgotten.' I smiled and said, 'We are getting married, M'am.'

She said, 'Great, congratulations. So, is she going with you?'

I said, 'She will join me after a few weeks. As of now, I am going.'

She asked, 'Will you guys come back?'

I said, 'Yes M'am.'

'What is the guarantee?'

'My assignment is for less than two years M'am.'

'That is the usual answer. Give me something new.'

I said, 'I just got engaged and I am kind of running short of fresh ideas.'

She started laughing and said, 'I can believe that.'

With a loud thud she stamped my visa and said, 'Good. Enjoy your stay in the United States.'

•

A Promotion

ON FEBRUARY 12, 2008, EXACTLY A MONTH FROM OUR ENGAGEMENT date, we got married in Madikeri, in Coorg style. Coorgi guests wore their saris the reverse way. The women from Andhra wore it the regular way. Men who had a drink and danced were Coorgis. Men who wore half shirts, had a great meal and traded commodities on their cell phones were from Andhra.

On the wedding day, in the morning, I wore Coorgi clothes, wielded a sword and chopped banana plants in one swish. For all the bananas I was force-fed in NIT, this was my revenge. Anjali changed clothes every half hour. Wedding days turn ordinary girls into models!

People showered gifts and blessings on us. Both our mothers cried. Swati and Ameya flirted with boys. My father talked to the guests, grandpa kept smiling and the colonel had his occasional swigs of Single Malt. The happiness quotient was high everywhere and finally in the evening, the priest declared us married. We had dinner at home and Anjali's cousins arranged our first night at Hotel Raj Darshini—a decent hotel by Coorg standards.

We were pushed into our room at 9 pm. All the cousins said, 'Enjoy your first night.' Preetam, my first cousin, gave me a pack of condoms and said, 'All yours, bro.' The worst part about the first night is that everybody encourages you to have sex. Incidentally, that is the one night when you are at your worst. You are totally exhausted from all the smoke you inhaled from the sacred fire. Your spinal chord gives up with the excessive bending, because you touched the feet of atleast 300 people in return for their blessings. Lastly, you feel overwhelmed by the fact that everybody assumes that you are going to have sex on the first night.

As soon as we went in, Anjali locked the door and sat on the bed. Every nook of the room was covered with flowers.

Anjali looked around and said, 'Teddy, don't you have pollen allergy?'

I smiled at the anti-climax. My sneezing started in full flow. I quickly took my handkerchief and tied it around my nose. Anjali called the bell boy. and he knocked at the room and I opened it.

I said, 'Please come quickly and remove all the flowers and clean the room.'

He was reluctant to enter the 'honeymoon special suite', probably because he had been instructed not to enter or disturb.

In between multiple sneezes and watery eyes, I said, 'We are not doing anything, you can come in.'

He slowly walked in. I offered to pay him for cleaning up.

I walked down to the nearest medical store to get anti-histamines.

By the time I came back, the room was clean and I was feeling drowsy. Anjali looked at me said, 'I am tired, Honeybunch.'

I said, 'Same here.'

She said, 'Seems like you don't have any naughty ideas anyway?'

I said, 'My mind has so many ideas, but my body is not cooperating.'

She said, 'I have an idea.'

She slowly undressed me and I looked at her.

She said, 'Birthday boy. Do you want to undress me?'

I stated undressing her fast. She asked, 'What's the hurry? Catching a flight?'

I smiled and we both got naked. I stared at her.

She said, 'Now come with me.' She led me to the bathroom. The bathtub was filled with hot water. She stepped in and asked, 'Want to join me?'

That was brilliant. We stepped into the bathtub, hugged each other and sat in the hot water for a long time. We almost fell asleep caressing each other and she woke me up. We got under the covers, hugged each other and fell asleep. No, we didn't make love.

Wait a minute, is that really true? We did make love early the next morning. We had a first morning, not a first night! As soon as I woke up, I saw an SMS from the colonel, sent at 2 am. It said, 'Did you know that the sperm of a mouse is longer than the sperm of an elephant? Ha ha ha!'

I shook my head in disbelief. The colonel must have been completely sloshed the previous night!

After our marriage, we went back to Bangalore. The colonel and his family stayed back at Coorg. My parents spent a few days in Bangalore and went back to Warangal. I moved to Anjali's room. Since Adi was also leaving for the US, Raj retained the house and Srila joined him after their marriage. Meanwhile, I put an advertisement on the TCS intranet to sell my bike. The same day, Ankit paid the token advance and promised to pay the balance to Anjali subsequently. Things moved at lightning speed.

My flight was after two weeks. Mom, dad, the colonel, aunty, Swati, Ameya and Anjali—all of them came to Bangalore airport to see me off. Mom had tears in her eyes. I promised to visit her as soon as I could. The colonel said, 'Venkat, remember to call regularly, don't forget trivia and stay healthy.'

I hugged all of them.

I turned to Raj to hug him and hesitated for a second, I was not sure how he would react. He said, 'Aaja yaar,' and I gave him a warm hug. Adi was taking the flight from Hyderabad, so he didn't come to the airport.

Anjali said, 'I will miss you Teddy. I will join you next month. Put pressure on Mani.'

I nodded and hugged her hard.

I told her, 'At the US consulate, if you meet Lisa Ann Carpenter, tell her you are VSAT's wife. She will be happy to see you.'

I checked my baggage, cleared immigration and boarded the flight.

Fast forward >>Fifteen months later>> May 2009

We spent fifteen months in the US and went back to Bangalore. While in the US, I picked up quite a bit of trivia, and a bit of American accent. Between Anjali and me, we had saved a decent amount of money. We came back as coveted NRIs. We had NRE accounts with ICICI bank.

A few days later, all of us went to Raj's house for dinner. Raj and Srila had a daughter named Shweta Malhotra Iyer Iyengar.

She was beautiful. Anjali took her in her arms and said, 'What a beautiful baby!'

Srila asked, 'Anju, when are you due?'

Anjali said, 'November. Another five months.' Our parents wanted us to have a baby in the US. US citizenship helps in securing admissions in premier colleges in India under foreign quota. But the due date was too far away and our respective assignments came to an end.

We had implemented phase two of the project successfully and Cathy was delighted. However, due to the recession, budgets were slashed and onsite resources were being sent back to India. We came back and the project was in maintenance mode.

Adi decided to stay back in the US for a longer time. He became a top-notch architect and Cathy was happy to extend his tenure there. Besides, Adi had good reason to stay back in the US. He was under tremendous pressure from his parents to get married and he didn't want to. He had found an American partner named Dave Milroy.

I asked, 'Raj what is this yaar? You have also served Frooti, samosa, and gulab jamun? You have also become like Mani now.'

Raj scratched his head and said, 'Recession yaar.' I realised some things in life just don't change.

Srila said, 'This fellow was lazy to order something better.'

I asked, 'How is the recession in India?'

Srila said, 'What recession? India employees are getting promotions and salary increases.'

I said, 'But we didn't get one in the US.'

Raj said, 'Probably there's a freeze in the US. Ask Pappu tomorrow and hopefully he will work out something.'

I nodded.

Next day Anjali and I went and met Pappu. He said, 'Welcome back my dear NRIs.'

I said, 'Amit, you know that we haven't been promoted in a long time? Is there something on the cards?'

He said, 'The recession must have hit your promotions too.'

I said, 'But Oracle is making offers. Why do you say there is a recession?'

Pappu got the message. He smiled and said, 'For the last couple of quarters we have been selective on promotions and hikes. Let me check your records and see what can be done.'

Srinivas was damn right, management screws around in the initial years. But once you have experience, they can't afford to.

I said, 'But Joby, Josy, Srinivas, Manoj ... everybody is promoted.'

Amit said, 'Let me check your records and get back. Give me some time.'

I realised that in the software industry things work only when you make demands.

Pappu called after a couple of days. He said, 'I think both of you deserve promotions. Mani and Sankar have cleared them. Effective July 01, you are promoted to Senior Software Engineers.'

We were relieved.

My dad congratulated me. He said, 'If you continue with TCS, one day Tatas will make you the vice president.'

My mom said, 'Remember Venkat, once Anjali delivers a healthy baby, you will have to give your hair to the Lord Venkateswara at Tirupati.'

More than the tonsure, I dreaded meeting Swamy's dad. But I had no option. Mothers will always dictate terms to you, even when you cross fifty. Wives too. Actually both of them.

I called the colonel next. He said, 'Son, congrats. When are you coming to Coorg? Did you get the Single Malts from duty free or not?'

I said, 'Yes, I did. Next weekend, once we buy a small car, we will drive down.'

The colonel laughed and said, 'I have a trivia question for you.'
I said, 'Shoot.'

He asked, 'Name the world famous musician and composer, who was so particular about his coffee that he counted sixty beans a cup when he prepared his brew.'

I said, 'Bach?'

He said, 'No.'

'Cavelli?'

'No.'

'Mason?'

'No.'

The colonel said, 'Son, I am happy you know these names. But keep guessing.'

'Dvorak?'

'No.'

I said, 'No? It must be Mozart then.'

He said, 'No!'

I said, 'I give up.'

He said, 'Ok, give it one last shot.'

I said, 'Ok, let me think. Who did I miss? Beethoven?'

The colonel excitedly said, 'Yes. Yes. You got it right this time. I am impressed with you. You know the names of so many composers.'

I said, 'Thanks to your encouragement.'

He asked, 'How about a last one before I disconnect?'

I said, 'Sure.'

'Who is called a cork-tease?'

I said, 'Huh. That is tough. Don't know.'

He said, 'Think think, expand on the question itself.'

'Somebody who teases with a cork,' I said.

'Yes, that is right. A cork-tease is someone who talks about wine, he or she intends opening, but never does it ... I am not going to be a cork-tease. When you come, I will open a 2003 Chateau Martinat Epicurea Cotes du Bourg for you. So come soon.'

The very next day, we went and booked an Alto car. Anjali chose a beige coloured one. We paid 100% by cheque. We had just come back from the US, I say!

The following weekend we drove down to Madikeri. The colonel and Kaveri aunty hugged us as soon as they saw us. The colonel said, 'You seem to have put on some weight, Venkat. Looks like American cheese has worked on you.'

Anjali said, 'Lazy bum he is Pa. Loves pizzas, but doesn't exercise a bit.'

At dinner, we opened one of the colonel's precious bottles of wine.

We spent a couple of days in Madikeri and went back to Bangalore. The following weekend, we booked an apartment in Whitefield. Fortunately, it was a readymade two-and-a-half bedroom apartment and the all-inclusive deal worked out to ₹45 lacs. I paid eighteen lakhs and took a bank loan for the rest. We chose an auspicious day for *Griha Pravesham*, the house warming ceremony. Everybody turned up. Sukh Sagar catered South Indian meals. The Sagars were active and Bangalore was thriving.

A few months later we threw a baby shower for Anjali. She was growing fatter by the day. By the time she was in her seventh month, she was like a teddy bear. I could barely hug her. Every evening, I put my head on her stomach and felt the movements of the little one. I was about to be a father—soon, very soon.

Anjali asked me, 'You will be with me in the delivery room, right?'

I confidently said, 'Yes baby.' Deep inside, I was not very sure. I was afraid that I would faint.

The last time I had seen blood was on the cricket ground when a ball hit the batsman on his face. He had blood gushing from his mouth and since I was fielding on forward short-leg, I rushed forward to help him. But as I got closer, I fainted. He recovered quickly and I was taken to the hospital. I can't stand the sight of blood.

Rahul

ANJALI WOKE ME UP IN THE MIDDLE OF THE NIGHT AND SAID, 'I think it is time.'

I was still groggy and I said, 'For what?'

'Idiot, the baby is coming.'

I froze. I said, 'Wait, I will take you to the hospital. But isn't the due date still a week away?'

She got irritated, 'Ok, go back to sleep, we will go next week. Baby can wait! Idiot, get up, let's rush.'

I didn't say anything. I woke up the colonel, Kaveri aunty and Ameya. We changed quickly and I drove her to the hospital. She was admitted in the pre-delivery room.

The duty nurse said, 'It is not time yet. Be with her.'

We waited for a couple of hours more and Anjali screamed from the pre-delivery room, 'Idiot, go call the doctor now.'

I ran out of the room, grabbed the nearest available nurse and said, 'She is calling. Urgent.'

The nurse said, 'Ok. I am going in, stay out of the way.' She pushed me aside and went straight into the delivery room. Women in power can be tough, especially when they know that you are at their mercy.

I sat down in the plastic chair outside the delivery room meant for expectant fathers. As I sat, my sister-in-law Ameya, all of twenty one years, paced up and down the corridor. I looked at her and wondered why everyone in my wife's family paced.

She said, 'Don't worry Venkat, all will be well.'

I nodded.

The colonel came and sat next to me. He said, 'It takes time, so hold on. Nothing to get tense about.'

I said, 'How long do you think it takes?'

Colonel said, 'Sometimes a few hours. And sometimes, it happens fast. Let us pray for the best. Do you want to go out and have tea?'

I stared at him.

He said, 'There is nothing we can do now. It is better to relax and things will be okay.'

I smiled.

He said, 'Ok, if you don't want to go for tea let's ask each other interesting trivia questions.'

I said, 'It is 3.30 am, Anjali is in labour and you want to play trivia?'

He said, 'What is wrong with that? It is the best way to pass time. Otherwise, I will look at your face and you at mine. How long do you want to do that?'

I relented. He said, 'Ok. Here goes the first one. What is the largest number of children born to a woman?'

I said, 'In the *Mahabharata*, Gandhari had a hundred children. I don't know in real life. But let me guess. About twenty three?'

He said, 'Way off.'

I increased it by ten.

He said, 'Still way off.'

I shook my head in disbelief.

He smiled and said, 'Sometime in the 1700s, a Russian peasant lady gave birth to sixty-nine children. So, don't worry. Anjali is delivering only one now.'

I laughed weakly.

He said, 'Ok, here is the next one. What can a baby do in the first seven months which an adult cannot?'

I said, 'Pee anytime, anywhere it wants.'

He laughed.

I asked, 'What?'

He said, 'Babies can swallow and breathe at the same time. If adults do that, food will get into your windpipe and you will choke.'

He proceeded to the next question, 'How long does it take for a disposable diaper to decompose?'

I said, 'No idea? Twenty years?'

He said, 'Way, way, way off.'

I said, 'A hundred?'

He said, 'No Venkat, it is five times that. 500 years. That is why in India, our ancestors used old clothes. Old clothes reduce skin rash and are biodegradable.'

I was dismayed at the colonel's knowledge. He reads trivia for almost four to six hours a day.

A nurse walked out of the room and I looked at her. She said, 'She is in labour, wait.'

She talked to me as if I was the culprit. What to do? Isn't it a man's destiny to inseminate and a woman's to get pregnant? Once Arnold Schwarzenegger tried reversing it in one of his movies and the movie bombed. Never take such chances!

The colonel looked at me and said, 'Don't worry, she will be okay. She is my daughter.'

There were several expectant fathers who were waiting around us. Almost all of them were tense. We were the only ones who were atleast making an effort to laugh. The doctor on duty arrived after a while. She said, 'My name is Dr Renu Gupta. She is in labour and is doing fine. She may take some more time. Have patience, things will be fine.'

She asked me if I wanted to meet Anjali.

I looked at the colonel and he said yes. Dr Renu took me with her. Anjali was lying on the delivery table and a nurse was holding her hand. The nurse said, 'Take a deep breath and push slowly and push hard. Keep doing that.'

Dr Renu said, 'Anjali, your husband is here. Don't worry, he will take care of you.'

Anjali shot me a quick glance and said, 'Doctor, let him wait outside. He will faint.'

Dr Renu gave me a look and led me out of the room. That one look conveyed everything. It said: 'You guys can screw, but can't do anything to help?'

I didn't feel like making love ever again in my life. But I thought that was one resolution one shouldn't make in haste.

When I went back, the colonel asked me to relax. I wasn't sure I could handle any more trivia though. We all waited for half an hour in complete silence. My stress levels were going up.

Colonel said, 'Come on beta, let us play trivia. We can pass time without stressing ourselves out.'

I agreed and asked him a question, 'The four kings in a deck of playing cards represent four kings from history. Who are they?'

Colonel said, 'I know this. Spades is David, Clubs is Alexander, Diamond is Caesar and Hearts is Charlemagne.'

I said, 'Correct. Let me ask you an army question. How was the word "jeep" derived?'

The colonel said, 'Hey, that is simple. It came from general-purpose-vehicle. G.P. and that became jeep.'

I said, 'Correct. What is the original name of Mickey Mouse?'

A nurse walked out of the room and I stood up at once. She said, 'Sit down.' I sat down.

The colonel said, 'I don't know.'

I looked at him blankly. He repeated, 'I don't know the answer to your question.'

I said, 'Mortimer Mouse.'

The colonel said, 'Let me ask you an easy one. Which mammal produces the biggest babies?' I said, 'Let me guess. Whale?'

He said, 'Wow!' He asked, 'Which is the world's oldest airline?'

'KLM,' I said.

The colonel said, 'Perfect. That was neat. Here is the next one, how many hearts does an octopus have?'

I said, 'Two?'

He said, 'No, three.'

He was about to ask the next question when Dr Renu emerged from the room carrying a baby in her arms and I stood up. She gently placed the baby in my arms and said, 'Your son, born on November 17, 2009, at 4.05 am. Have you decided the name yet?

I spoke through my tears, 'Rahul.' He was awake and very quiet. Maybe he was unsure of me, not unsure like me. There was a twitch and I thought he was smiling. I felt truly contented. This was my child.

I asked, 'How is Anjali?'

Dr Renu said, 'She is fine. Resting. Do you want to see her?'

I said, 'Yes.'

She led us all in. Anjali looked weak and was almost asleep. I placed my hand on her head and whispered in her ear, 'Rahul is beautiful. He looks like you. Love you babe.'

She smiled and whispered back, 'Idiot, I love you too.'

Kaveri aunty took Rahul in her arms. Ameya and the colonel were looking at the baby.

I held Anjali's hands and said, 'Rest now. I am here.'

She held my hand tightly and went to sleep.

I sent an SMS to Raj and to all my other friends. It read: Rahul was born at 4.05 am. The baby and Anjali are doing fine. I started getting congratulatory SMSes soon after.

Mani sent a nice SMS: You can take five days of paternity vacation.

Raj replied in his own style: Fucker, u r now a baap like me. How do u feel? Adi sent a quick email: Very happy to know. Dave and I give our best.

I sent an email to SRK. It read:

Dear Shah Rukh Khanji,

Hope you are doing well. A couple of years back, you helped us get married by calling Kaveri aunty on her birthday. Today we are blessed with a baby boy. My friends say he should be named Rahul Rukh Khan! We have named him Rahul Tanikaburla. Two-word name—first name and last name, otherwise there is too much confusion, sir.

Yours truly,
Venkat, Senior Software Engineer, TCS, +91 98450 …

Pat came an email: Congrats! Rahul Rukh Khan is not a bad name But retain Rahul, it is a nice name. Love to the baby and all the best to your family. Shah Rukh.

Meanwhile the colonel called my parents. They were overjoyed.

Dad said, 'Congratulations son. We will be reaching over the weekend. Come to the station to pick us up.'

My mother asked, 'So, when are you going to Tirupati?'

I said, 'Soon Lakshmi.'

She said, 'Pray to Lord Ganesha. Make sure you pray for the well-being of your boss.'

I thought of Mani and grinned.

Within a year of Rahul's birth, all of us drove down to NIT. It was one of the best journeys of our lives. We had lunch at Pappacchan's, watched a movie at Dhanya Theatre in Kattangal, drove to Mukkam and Mavoor, had banana milkshake at Vijayan's fruit stall and watched a movie at Crown Theatre. We also met our professors. They were happy to see us. We took many digital pictures for posterity.

One afternoon, we went and sat at Nair's canteen and ordered lime soda. Nair recognised us and said, 'Andhra boy and Coorgi girl! Is that your little one?' I got up and hugged Nair. Raj shook his head and grinned.

Nair smiled warmly and asked, 'Boy or girl? What's the name?'

Raj laughed and said, 'We wanted to name him Shah Rukh. His name is Rahul.'

Nair asked, 'Where is your third friend, that fat boy?'

I said, 'He is in the US now.'

Nair asked, 'Software?'

I nodded.

On our way back, we stopped at the Krishna temple at eighth mile near IIM, Kozhikode and prayed, '*Lord, the last few years have been really eventful. I got married to Anjali, became a father, went to the US, got promoted, and purchased a car and an apartment. I learnt about Coorgi culture, picked up trivia and improved my personality. I even had an opportunity to talk to Shah Rukh Khan. I am happy being a software engineer. Otherwise this journey wouldn't have been possible. Thank you for being there for us, along the way.*'

References

The Ultimate Business Quiz Book—Volume 1 by Derek O'Brien. Penguin Books India, 2002.

The Mega Business Quiz Book by Bijay Bhujabal. Vision Books, 2nd Edition (2008, 2009). Enlarged and updated.

The Marketing Quiz Book by Bijay Bhujabal & Rashmi Ranjan Tarenia. Vision Books Reprinted (2009).

The Computer and IT Quiz Book by Bijay Bhujabal & Saranga Mahatwo. Vision Books Reprinted (2008).

The World's Best Book by Jan Payne, Mike Phillips and Sally Pilkington. Buster Books, London, Reprinted (2009).

Quick Wit by Des Mac Hale—Prion, an imprint of Carlton Publishing group, London, Reprinted (2009).

E-Tales Two—Cassell Compiltion, part of Orion Books, London. Reprinted (2004).

The Godfather—by Mario Puzo—G.P. Putnam & Sons. Published in 1969.

The transcript of the movie *The Godfather* from www.thegodfathertrilogy.com

www.gkpedia.com

www.imdb.com, www.wikipedia.com for all general information and references.

(1)

9-9-11
07